CHRONICLES OF TARC

545–1

STALLION AND STEWARD

Jiryü Räsen

3RD EDITION EXPANDED AND REVISED

PUBLISHED BY J. KASSEBAUM

February 18, 2022 3rd Edition Expanded and Revised
Second Printing September 10, 2023.
Paperback ISBN 978-1-949359-02-2
eBook ISBN 978-1-949359-03-9
© **Jiryü Räsen**. All rights reserved.
Published by J. Kassebaum, Indianapolis.
Cover background ©Sumners Graphics via Canva.com.
#NaNoParticipant2016
#CampNaNoWinner2018

Contents

Prologue

The cries of the carriage driver alerted the passengers of impending danger. The sound of crumbling rock was quickly crescendoing into the thunderous roar of a rock slide. The carriage jerked away from the path of the rocks, but here the road narrowly led right along the rocky cliffs climbing steeply up and away into the barren northern reaches of Suiran in the northernmost part of the kingdom of Ryokudo, while on the other side was a downward slope of rock and scrub.

They were heading back to the Lady's home, the Earldom of Tokumade. Her husband had ordered her to return from her winter self–pity trip at the outlying village of Osterly. It was justifiable, whispered the servants. He'd again had his fun while she was away and had only called for her after having sent his rough and rowdy friends and their women home. Likely as not he was ready now for her to come and clean up the messes.

That had always been the job of the Earl's steward before he'd married the Lady but, peculiarly, this time the steward had gone along with the Lady on her trip. The Earl himself had ordered it, claiming that he wanted to ensure that his Lady wife wasn't going off to have a tryst just to make him jealous — as if it were *her* fault that she wanted to keep running way.

While the Lady was justifiably outraged, she was just a bit relieved. Her own jealousy would be somewhat mollified by the arrangement. The Earl was just a little too close to his steward for her comfort. The years–old rumors that they — the Earl and his steward — had been lovers long before she came into the picture still regularly haunted her. At least the steward had been solicitous on the journey and hadn't been much of a bother at all, but then that was often the case at the Earldom proper as well. She really found the steward unfathomable.

What really rankled the most, though, was that the Earl had not deigned to raise her to the rank of Countess after the marriage. He'd promised many things before the wedding that hadn't been fulfilled, but that promise she still held over his head in the few moments of time she had opportunity to open her mouth in his presence. What could have been a marriage of convenience quickly became hell.

As the Lady looked out her window, watching in horrified fascination her rapidly approaching death, she felt a draft come from the downhill side of the carriage. She turned to see that self–same steward glance at her, then leap from the carriage to go tumbling down the southern slope. The first rocks hit the carriage, sending it and her with her two ladies–in–waiting careening forward, then it fell on its side, crashing to the ground to be buried by the landslide.

Her last thought was to wonder at the look in the steward's eyes. It was the same look of tender pity that she'd caught being thrown her way before and wondered at. At least someone would regret her death, even if only slightly. But, ...why would it be the steward?

it yet. If she was a part of Earl Shicchi's household, and she'd recognized him, who was she?

His thoughts went to one person, all unbidden. It couldn't be, could it? She was the right age. She shouldn't recognize him, should she? She was younger than he was, after all. He wasn't sure she would still be alive regardless, although who was he to say. *He* shouldn't still be alive. And the look had said, *what are you doing here?* not *why are you alive?*

Ore took a shuddering breath at that. Not only had she recognized him, she knew where he was, or where he was supposed to be. If she knew him and his movements, did the Earl as well? Or was it the third party again? Ore struggled to calm his heart. For now, she wasn't talking. He'd stick close, though, and make sure he was the one who heard what words she had to say.

-o-o-o-

The Osterly garrison field surgeon, Bonner, a greying man in his fifties, stepped out of the small room he'd been using as a surgery. He was feeling today like he really should have retired and settled down with a sweet plump woman somewhere warmer and quieter.

Wiping his rinsed hands on a clean rag, he looked around the open area of the lodge that served the village of Osterly as town hall and celebration center, and in the long cold winters of the north as the market place. Currently this corner of it was an infirmary, coroner's office, and mortuary.

Mizi and the village midwife, each followed by a young lady assistant, were going through the few bodies, straightening them, washing them as best they could, and generally preparing them for delivery to Earl Shicchi. It was a little surprising to see that the young court healer was keeping calm and working efficiently. While watching the young miss from the foreign country of Yamanzar who'd caught the eye of the Ryokudo royals, he could hear Leeds wrapping up his report to the garrison captain.

"...Lady Shicchi, her two ladies–in–waiting, the two mounted guards, and the driver all dead by the time we found them. The horses as well. Miss Ilena was thrown from the carriage and is the only survivor. But a huge boulder has crushed her hip and the surgeon —"

"— Thinks she'll survive." Bonner had moved over to join the conversation. Both other officers nodded acknowledgment of his arrival as he continued. "I've cleaned the wound and set the bones as best I can at this time. There's quite a bit of swelling of course and many of the pieces of the bone are no more than fragments. I expect some amount of infection and will likely need to perform more surgery later."

"But you think she'll survive?" The young female voice at his elbow told him the court healer had also come to hear his report. He nodded once. "That's good. Will she be able to walk again?" Mizi looked genuinely concerned for the long term welfare of the survivor.

"Lady Mizi, it's fortunate that this accident happened so close to this garrison," Leeds told her somewhat proudly. "Our field surgeon here is the best in Suiran. He's set and repaired the bones of many a soldier that otherwise

Prologue

The cries of the carriage driver alerted the passengers of impending danger. The sound of crumbling rock was quickly crescendoing into the thunderous roar of a rock slide. The carriage jerked away from the path of the rocks, but here the road narrowly led right along the rocky cliffs climbing steeply up and away into the barren northern reaches of Suiran in the northernmost part of the kingdom of Ryokudo, while on the other side was a downward slope of rock and scrub.

They were heading back to the Lady's home, the Earldom of Tokumade. Her husband had ordered her to return from her winter self–pity trip at the outlying village of Osterly. It was justifiable, whispered the servants. He'd again had his fun while she was away and had only called for her after having sent his rough and rowdy friends and their women home. Likely as not he was ready now for her to come and clean up the messes.

That had always been the job of the Earl's steward before he'd married the Lady but, peculiarly, this time the steward had gone along with the Lady on her trip. The Earl himself had ordered it, claiming that he wanted to ensure that his Lady wife wasn't going off to have a tryst just to make him jealous — as if it were *her* fault that she wanted to keep running way.

While the Lady was justifiably outraged, she was just a bit relieved. Her own jealousy would be somewhat mollified by the arrangement. The Earl was just a little too close to his steward for her comfort. The years–old rumors that they — the Earl and his steward — had been lovers long before she came into the picture still regularly haunted her. At least the steward had been solicitous on the journey and hadn't been much of a bother at all, but then that was often the case at the Earldom proper as well. She really found the steward unfathomable.

What really rankled the most, though, was that the Earl had not deigned to raise her to the rank of Countess after the marriage. He'd promised many things before the wedding that hadn't been fulfilled, but that promise she still held over his head in the few moments of time she had opportunity to open her mouth in his presence. What could have been a marriage of convenience quickly became hell.

As the Lady looked out her window, watching in horrified fascination her rapidly approaching death, she felt a draft come from the downhill side of the carriage. She turned to see that self–same steward glance at her, then leap from the carriage to go tumbling down the southern slope. The first rocks hit the carriage, sending it and her with her two ladies–in–waiting careening forward, then it fell on its side, crashing to the ground to be buried by the landslide.

Her last thought was to wonder at the look in the steward's eyes. It was the same look of tender pity that she'd caught being thrown her way before and wondered at. At least someone would regret her death, even if only slightly. But, ...why would it be the steward?

CHAPTER 1 Finding a New Patient

"There's quite a bit of commotion all of a sudden." Mizi turned towards the sounds of soldiers and men milling about near the stables where she and her lithe companion had just left his horse.

Ore shaded his golden eyes with his hand resting just at the edge of his black hair that was so short as to be standing nearly on end, peering in the same direction. "Shall we go see if we can learn something, Mistress?" He looked at her with that expression that was teasing and obliging at the same time.

Mizi nodded after pausing for a bit, "Mmn." They'd just arrived in Osterly, but Ore's business at the garrison there would be brief he'd already informed her, so they had some time.

Ore guided her, taking his usual care to ensure she was placed where she would be safe from the chaos itself, then snagged a passing man and began to question him. *As usual*, Mizi smiled as she watched him, *Ore finds it so natural to talk to perfect strangers as if they'd always been next door neighbors.*

She was watching the stable hand check his work when the familiar warmth of her guardian and friend appeared at her side again. She looked up at Ore questioningly. *I forget until we're standing this close that he's taller than me by a whole head. When all of us are together, I'm the smallest, but when it's just the two of us he works so hard to make me feel comfortable that I forget.*

Ore's expression was somber, although his voice was carefully neutral. "Mistress, they're saying that there was a landslide back up the road we just came in on. Apparently a passing carriage was caught in it. They're putting together a joint town and garrison search and rescue party."

"Oh! Is it the one we passed on the way here then?" Mizi remembered that the carriage had been a private one, rather than one of the public ones that even she'd rented a seat on in the past. It had been guarded by two guards on horseback and been marked with the arms of a noble house.

"It seems likely," Ore nodded. "What do you wish to do, Mistress?"

Ore always seemed to know when Mizi was about to go into action, but then he'd been watching over her closely as her guard for over four years now. "Do you know who's in charge, Ore?" and, as he pointed to one of the garrison soldiers, "I'd like to speak with him."

Ore deftly steered them through the concerned chaos until they reached the officer in charge. "Lieutenant Leeds, may we have a word with you for a moment?"

The lieutenant looked across his shoulder at Ore and Mizi, then respectfully turned to face them, "Certainly, Sir Ore." Ore was a knight in the direct employ of Rei Touka, First Prince of Ryokudo and Regent of Suiran (since seven months ago), and was well known by the garrison since he was also Rei's Messenger — all of that in addition to being assigned directly by Rei to watch over Mizi.

Mizi tucked away a wisp of her sunset–red hair back under her traveling hood. It had caught her attention when the sunlight glinted goldly off of it. "Lieutenant Leeds, we've heard about the accident involving the carriage we passed on our way here. I'm a court healer and would like to offer my services."

"Of course, Lady Mizi, your skills I'm sure would be of great use," Leeds paused and Mizi's eyes widened slightly at not needing to be introduced. "But you are, I'm sure, on important castle business. We're only waiting on the arrival of the garrison field surgeon at this time."

Mizi looked at Ore quizzically. He raised his hands indicating that she could choose. Mizi turned back to the lieutenant, resolute. "We'll come with you. Our business isn't so urgent that we must leave behind us injured nobility and their retainers."

Leeds bowed in acquiescence and Ore took the opening to ask, "Whose carriage was it?"

"Earl Shicchi of Tokumade's," Leeds answered. "His Lady wife and her escort and ladies were on their way to return to the Earldom seat from this place."

Mizi, intent on her mental inventory of medicinal supplies she had on hand with her, asked distractedly, "Will you please retrieve your horse again, Ore? ...Ore?" she repeated and looked up when he didn't answer. The look of shock on his face disappeared in an instant, leaving Mizi to wonder if anything had been there.

"Yes, Mistress," he said, bowing to her. He quickly turned away and headed towards one of the stable hands, leaving her temporarily in the care of the lieutenant.

Mizi pulled her castle–issue black wool cloak around her knees to keep them a little warmer as a spring wind tried to blow up her cream colored knee–length tunic. The tunic's short length and the blue leggings under them helped her when she needed to get close to the ground to harvest herbs or take care of her plantings, but they weren't as warm as she would have liked. Still, it was nice that winter was finally over and the snows were melting from these foothills of the mountains that rose just to the north of them.

When Ore arrived again, he and Mizi mounted his brown quarter horse, Fenrier, in their usual way: Ore in the saddle holding the reins and Mizi balanced comfortably behind him. They joined the group of people gathering to head back up the road. Mizi rested one hand on Ore's back to keep steady, noting his firm muscles were slightly more tense than normal, but he did normally pay more attention to their surroundings when in crowds.

-o-o-o-

Ore was the first to go scrambling up the rockfall. He was nimble and the rocks under his feet didn't move like they did for many of the other rescue workers. He found the driver first, still partially lying out of the rocks, his head wounded. Ore called to him, then looked closely at the wound.

He looked back at the other workers and shook his head, indicating the driver wasn't alive. Looking around the rock–buried carriage, he could see that it wasn't likely anyone inside had survived. There certainly weren't any noises to indicate the possibility. He would leave the unburying of them to the others.

Looking up above, he could see where the rocks had scratched the cliff face as they rolled and bounced down it. At the top of the scrape was a ledge. If it was an assassination, that would be where the assassin would have stood waiting to start the slide. He'd get up there and make sure. Ore looked down at the driver at his feet again. That wound was inflicted by a staff, not a rock.

He looked closely at the ground around him. There it was. A spot of blood. He followed after it, looking for the trail. There, and there, and there...and here a smear of blood. Had the staff been set down? He looked a little farther on. Another smear, this one perpendicular to the lower hill rather than mostly parallel to it. And the rocks here looked shifted.

Lieutenant Leeds came up to him, looking at the place Ore was looking. Ore pointed to the blood. Leeds nodded, then looked farther down the hill. "Look!" he exclaimed, pointing down the hill. He quickly called for more men to come help them.

Ore looked down the hill and froze. Below him he could see a woman with long black hair and a slightly dark complexion similar to his own, lying not quite perpendicular to the hill and half buried by the rocks. A trickle of blood darkly stained her cheek. Farther below her at the base of the hill and then some was a large boulder. It didn't look like it had hit her upper body, so it likely had hit her where the rocks were covering her, smashing them into her — if it hadn't bounced past her.

He was down the hill and next to her before he was aware he'd moved. He reached out and touched her neck, finding the artery with two fingers. Her pulse was present, her skin warm. "She's alive!" Ore called back up.

That got everyone at the top of the slope scrambling around. Smaller rocks bounced past them as people began to set up belay lines attached to a stretcher and he could hear the field surgeon and Lieutenant Leeds issuing orders.

Ore carefully shifted so he was below the injured woman to catch her if she should slip, then began to lift rocks off of her and throw them to the side. Soon others joined him, helping to remove rocks and prevent more rocks from coming down on them both, until she was uncovered.

"Her hip looks pretty crushed," one of the other rescuers called up to Doctor Bonner, the field surgeon from the garrison. "Still losing some blood now that we've removed the pressure of the rocks."

Ore glanced that way, then paused at the anomaly his brain focused on. He only knew one other woman who wore pants rather than skirts. It took a strong woman to do that in Ryokudo.

"Try to support that hip as much as possible as you move her to the stretcher," Doctor Bonner called back down.

Ore helped to carefully lift the young woman onto the stretcher, holding her head and shoulders. When she was secured to it, he followed the stretcher up the slope, helping to keep it away from the rocks and to protect her from further damage. Once they were all back at the top, he stepped away, allowing space for the field surgeon and others to lift her stretcher and carry her to the wagon.

He watched until the stretcher, Doctor Bonner, and Mizi were in the wagon. Then he looked up at the ledge above. Grabbing a passing soldier, he pointed up to it. "I'm going up there to look around," he said. The soldier nodded and Ore was off.

He found the little trail and climbed quickly. Once he was on the ledge, he looked carefully at the ground. Eventually he found the place where it looked like the assassin had hid out of sight of the carriage. He looked out over the road and the valley below. It was a good vantage point. He would have seen the carriage coming but they wouldn't have seen him.

Turning, Ore could see the rescue efforts below. He tried to see what would have happened in his mind's eye. The carriage coming; setting off the slide. He could see the instinctive reaction of the driver pulling the horse's head to turn the carriage away from the slide just moments before the rocks hit.

He looked to where they'd found the young woman. It was before the area where the carriage lay broken. He frowned. If she'd been in the carriage, she would have had to jump out of it at the early signs of the slide to have been that far back of it. Most of the villagers were removing the rocks from the road and throwing them down the hill now, and they'd already almost cleared the road above where she'd been.

He could picture her opening the carriage door and jumping out just as the driver was turning the horse, then rolling and tumbling down the hill, rocks following after her. It was a pretty daring thing, to trust that she wouldn't die just from that, but she'd certainly had a better chance of life, and it had (so far) played out that way.

From where he stood, the assassin had surely seen the door open and someone jump out. He would definitely have gone to investigate. Ore traced with his eyes the path the assassin took after the rocks had come to a standstill. Climbing down the hill; walking past the driver, who may have moved, trying to unbury himself; making sure he wouldn't ever again; then over to look down at the person who'd jumped.

Ore wasn't sure where the assassin would have rolled the boulder from, but he could see how it was placed, then levered over the edge of the road. Had he been trying to kill the woman, too? Or was severe injury sufficient? He hadn't bothered to climb down the hill and kill her off. Was it laziness, or was she somehow implicit? Had she been meant to live? Ore shook his head. They were questions with answers that might come later if she did live.

For now, he looked around the scene again. Where would the assassin have gone next? Away from the village for sure since rescue would come from that direction. Wait. How had the village learned of the accident? Would he have actually gone *to* the village to make the report so that the woman could live? It didn't seem like it had happened all that long ago.

Ore shuddered suddenly. He and Mizi had passed below this location while the assassin was sitting here. He had watched them pass, and let them go unharmed. They hadn't been his target, but it was still unsettling. Had he noticed anything at the time?

He remembered. He had. He'd seen the rocks above, felt eyes on his back, and his worry had made his horse sidestep briefly. He'd picked up the pace so as to remove them from the danger zone quickly. They'd passed the carriage much closer to Osterly and he'd forgotten by then so hadn't done any more than raise his hand in greeting to the carriage driver and guards.

He frowned. There was something else. He'd seen the woman in the carriage, very briefly through the window. Her dark hair and eyes. Eyes that had seen his and widened ever so slightly, following him until they were past each other. He hadn't given it much thought at the time. It wasn't uncommon for passing strangers to watch each other with casual curiosity. But now that he thought on it again, did she somehow recognize him?

It would be very bad for someone from the House of Shicchi to recognize him. It was a place he had no intention of ever returning to. If the Earl found out that he was still alive.... Ore didn't take that thought any further. He headed back down the slope to the rescue scene and Lieutenant Leeds. He had questions that needed answers.

-o-o-o-

The field surgeon decided he needed to work on the woman right away, and not in a wagon. Mizi volunteered to stay in case another living victim was found. Ore would normally have suggested she go back with the field surgeon, but he wasn't sure where the assassin was — except not here. So here was safer.

He cast about in both directions along the road, looking to see if he could find evidence of which way the assassin had gone when he left. Ore was sure he could catch up with him. It looked like he'd gone towards the village. A small scrape of blood from the staff, a thread here.

He'd heard from the Lieutenant how word had come. Surely the villager that had gone to him had heard from the assassin himself. Ore's sharp eyes missed nothing as he swept along the road. The assassin had held to the edge of the road, moving quickly but close to cover if it was needed.

All of a sudden Ore stopped. There: a break in the foliage at the side of the road. Had the assassin gone into hiding? He ran to get a closer look. Taking care to not disturb the evidence he was looking for, he moved into the tall scrub that grew here farther down the mountain from where the trail had been up in the rocks before.

He followed the trail carefully, then stopped short and hid behind a stubby tree. He closed his eyes and used his ears, listening carefully for the sound of breathing. Nothing. No movement other than the air and wildlife. He waited for the requisite time, plus some. Then he carefully turned and peeked around the tree, crouching as he did so to make himself a smaller target.

He really couldn't believe his eyes. Just ahead of him, the scrub began to turn into full–size trees. Lying partially in those trees, his feet stretched out towards Ore, was a man, certainly the assassin. Just as certainly dead.

Ore looked up into the trees ahead of him. He still couldn't detect the presence of anyone else. Either they were really good, or they had done their job and left already. He carefully moved to crouch next to the assassin. It was him, He was still holding the staff in his hand, a surprised look on his face, a throwing spear pointing through his back.

Ore inspected the spear. It was disappointing. Whoever had been hired to assassinate the assassin was good. It was not only a single one–shot kill, it was with an unremarkable, untraceable weapon. Ore searched the body, but it had already been searched and cleaned out. No evidence at all. And he didn't recognize him, so it wasn't a regular from his time in the underworld.

Ore looked around at the trees. The angle of the weapon said it had been thrown from above. From a tree of about...that distance away. Ore inspected the possible places. There was one with signs of occupation, but from there, evidence was very difficult to find. This assassin was at least as good as Ore was. The other one was clumsy by comparison.

He followed the tracks he could make out just long enough to see that they led west and south, instead of east–southeast towards Osterly or west to Tokumade. Whoever it was wasn't giving away where he was headed, either. Ore stopped and chewed on a thumbnail. Putting his life in danger wasn't on the approved list of things he could do, and it wasn't likely he'd get anything out of this new assassin, even if he did find him. There were other ways to find out information of this kind, if it was possible.

Ore returned to the original assassin's body and stared down at it. He should probably take it back. Someone might recognize his face. But, why had he been left here to be found, in the open? That didn't seem like the assassin he *wasn't* following. He was too good to be careless.

Had it been part of his orders to let it be found? Was there another third party involved that wanted to incriminate this assassin's employer? And how had word spread about the accident if it wasn't this man? That would likely be an even harder question to answer.

Ore dragged the assassin closer to the side of the road, but kept the body hidden. He'd have the wagon stop and pick it up on the way back to Osterly. Then he headed at a good jog back to the murder site and his Mistress. It wasn't likely the second assassin would double around, but it was better to be safe than sorry, especially where she was concerned.

As Ore jogged back, he thought back to the woman in the carriage who had ended up wounded but not dead. Maybe she was part of that third party? He shook his head. It didn't seem likely, but he wouldn't completely discount it yet. If she was a part of Earl Shicchi's household, and she'd recognized him, who was she?

His thoughts went to one person, all unbidden. It couldn't be, could it? She was the right age. She shouldn't recognize him, should she? She was younger than he was, after all. He wasn't sure she would still be alive regardless, although who was he to say. *He* shouldn't still be alive. And the look had said, *what are you doing here?* not *why are you alive?*

Ore took a shuddering breath at that. Not only had she recognized him, she knew where he was, or where he was supposed to be. If she knew him and his movements, did the Earl as well? Or was it the third party again? Ore struggled to calm his heart. For now, she wasn't talking. He'd stick close, though, and make sure he was the one who heard what words she had to say.

-o-o-o-

The Osterly garrison field surgeon, Bonner, a greying man in his fifties, stepped out of the small room he'd been using as a surgery. He was feeling today like he really should have retired and settled down with a sweet plump woman somewhere warmer and quieter.

Wiping his rinsed hands on a clean rag, he looked around the open area of the lodge that served the village of Osterly as town hall and celebration center, and in the long cold winters of the north as the market place. Currently this corner of it was an infirmary, coroner's office, and mortuary.

Mizi and the village midwife, each followed by a young lady assistant, were going through the few bodies, straightening them, washing them as best they could, and generally preparing them for delivery to Earl Shicchi. It was a little surprising to see that the young court healer was keeping calm and working efficiently. While watching the young miss from the foreign country of Yamanzar who'd caught the eye of the Ryokudo royals, he could hear Leeds wrapping up his report to the garrison captain.

"...Lady Shicchi, her two ladies–in–waiting, the two mounted guards, and the driver all dead by the time we found them. The horses as well. Miss Ilena was thrown from the carriage and is the only survivor. But a huge boulder has crushed her hip and the surgeon —"

"— Thinks she'll survive." Bonner had moved over to join the conversation. Both other officers nodded acknowledgment of his arrival as he continued. "I've cleaned the wound and set the bones as best I can at this time. There's quite a bit of swelling of course and many of the pieces of the bone are no more than fragments. I expect some amount of infection and will likely need to perform more surgery later."

"But you think she'll survive?" The young female voice at his elbow told him the court healer had also come to hear his report. He nodded once. "That's good. Will she be able to walk again?" Mizi looked genuinely concerned for the long term welfare of the survivor.

"Lady Mizi, it's fortunate that this accident happened so close to this garrison," Leeds told her somewhat proudly. "Our field surgeon here is the best in Suiran. He's set and repaired the bones of many a soldier that otherwise would have left them crippled for life. If there is anyone in all of Ryokudo who can help Miss Ilena walk again, it's Field Surgeon Bonner of Osterly garrison!"

"*Hrmmph.* I'm not so sure about all of Ryokudo, Leeds, but I'll certainly do my best, Lady Mizi. After all, the Earl greatly values his steward."

"His...stew–ard?!" a new voice broke in surprise. The little group turned to find Ore had silently joined them. It was apparent he'd just come from cleaning up after helping to carry in the bodies of the dead. "You said her name was...?"

"Miss Ilena, Sir Ore," Ore's expression remained one of great surprise.

Mizi interjected, also with surprise, "The Earl's steward is —? The Earl has a woman as steward of his household?"

"If you could call that one a woman," muttered Leeds. The field surgeon studiously looked down at his hands and wiped some possibly imaginary dirt off them with the rag he was still holding.

Captain Grey threw the lieutenant a cautionary rebuking look, "Miss Ilena has worked very hard to become someone the Earl can trust completely, something he doesn't grant to anyone else. She is an exemplary servant to her lord, and equally, she serves all the members of the House and Earldom with equity and firmness. She is highly qualified for the position even given her young age."

He continued apologetically, "Unfortunately, the Earl is known for his sudden bursts of anger and sometimes...erratic behavior. Miss Ilena has become expert at deflecting his outbursts and repairing his.... Well, let's just say that after observing the earldom for fifteen years now, the seven years she's stood by his side have been much more stable than it ever was before. For the earldom to lose her would be a great blow, in my opinion."

Grey turned to Ore, who was still looking mildly surprised. "I would like your opinion, Sir Ore, as to whether or not you suspect or found evidence of foul play. It's unlikely that the Earl would have allowed his steward's life to be threatened, but it was common knowledge that his wife was a thorn in his side, although it was not all her fault by any means."

"You assume it was the Earl himself who ordered it, and not outside assassins?" Ore raised his eyebrows, then frowned. "Or even the steward herself? It sounds like it would have been a good way to remove a potential rival."

All three men shook their heads. The reputations of all parties involved were well established at this garrison. "The Earl is not very...creative, and he was bound by the oath of his marriage vows. Although there have been rumors in the past about the Earl and Miss Ilena, they do not bear out. Their relationship is strictly as it should be.

"The Lady's father's House will likely complain bitterly that it was spousal murder, but because he's such a minor lord, in the end he won't be able to receive redress. Miss Ilena wouldn't involve herself in such activity. Rather it is she that does her best to dissuade the Earl from entering into such wicked schemes, at least as much as she is able."

"How do you know?" Ore asked, frowning in disbelief.

"Well, confidentially mind as it's part of our being able to maintain the peace here in Tokumade without direct conflict with the Earl," the captain lowered his voice sufficient to exclude all but those directly around him, "but Miss Ilena has on important occasions managed to get information to us that has allowed us to prevent somewhat nefarious deeds from being perpetuated. Of course she's extremely limited in her capacity, having to remain trustworthy in the eyes of her lord, but she is able to turn a blind eye towards our secret investigations."

At this, Leeds nodded. "It's creepy, actually, how she's able to know when there are spies about, where they are, and even who they are. She's called me by name when my own mother and father wouldn't have recognized me...if they could have even spotted me, although she never gave away my position."

"The rumors she's a witch or a ghost are quite false, I assure you," Bonner interjected dryly. "After all, ghosts don't get their hips crushed and bleed that much and a witch would have been able to escape unscathed, if such creatures existed." Ore slightly raised an eyebrow.

"Besides," continued the captain, returning to his defense of the steward, "she was here with the Lady, which is very unusual. It would be like the Earl to think that because they were together he could say he couldn't have been the one to have ordered the murder of his wife, as that would have put his precious steward at risk."

"But she very obviously jumped from the carriage before it was buried under rocks, based on where we found her," Ore objected. "Would she have allowed the assassination of the Lady if she's as upstanding as you say?"

"I don't know why she jumped, Sir Ore, but she and the Lady were here for nearly three months. That's plenty of time for the Earl to have planned this murder without her knowledge. I don't believe she would have allowed it to happen if she'd known about it."

"There is one other clue, Captain," Leeds added. "Miss Ilena was only partially buried under small and medium rocks where we found her, but below her was one large boulder that we believe caused the damage to her hip. Above her we found traces of blood and marks on the rocks. It's possible that the carriage driver's head wound was caused by a staff that was then used to send the boulder down on her."

Grey pursed his lips. "Well, I admit to being puzzled as to why Earl Shicchi would be willing to place her life in danger, or even to end it. But either way, it's fortunate she's alive."

Ore nodded. "Indeed. It will be interesting to hear what her answers are when she regains consciousness. I'll expect her to be guarded at all times and to be informed when she awakens. If the Earl comes for her himself, he's not to be allowed to see her nor to regain her until Regent Rei is satisfied that the investigation is complete." The soldiers, used to hearing and obeying orders, straightened as they received his words. "When will she be able to be moved into the garrison?"

Bonner looked into the distance as he considered the state of his patient. "It would be best to leave her here in the lodge for at least three days, and maybe for a week, at least until I'm able to complete the second surgery. To move her any more than we already have at this stage would once again place her life in critical danger. Even moving her after the second surgery wouldn't be advisable. I believe at minimum a one week period will be necessary for her to reach sufficient stability to be transported to the garrison."

"How long for her to reach sufficient stability to be moved to Castle Nijou?" Ore asked.

It was the soldiers' turn to be surprised. "Do you really think that will be necessary, Sir Ore?" asked Grey.

"If, as you say, she knows what the Earl's been doing, I don't think he'd take kindly to having her questioned in an official investigation. I think it would be wise to assume that he'll try to have her removed. While it can't be helped that she can't be moved rashly, I believe it will be necessary to take her to the castle as soon as possible."

Bonner answered, "To move her even that distance...three weeks at least would be best — and then only if the wound is sufficiently restrained so that it doesn't shift. She must lie flat on her back for five weeks, only beginning to rise slightly at four weeks, for the hip bone to repair itself sufficient to be walked on again."

He paused a bit, then added, "However, there's one complication. Three tendons in the hip have been torn, two partially. The third, which attaches the main front leg muscle to the top of the hip, has been torn completely. I can repair the bone and the first two tendons sufficiently, but the third one I may not be able to correctly repair. If not, while she'll be able to sit in a rolling chair for some limited mobility, Miss Ilena won't be able to walk again."

-O-O-O-

"Mistress?" Ore knocked at the guarded door of Ilena's recovery room, then entered.

"Oh, Ore! You've returned." Mizi looked up from the table where she'd been working, her red hair reflecting the candlelight in front of her in golden bursts of highlights. It was that hair that was so unusual in Ryokudo that had brought them together and then had kept him at her side at Rei's request. Too many people with nefarious thoughts kept wanting her and that hair for themselves. Ore made sure they were severely disabused of their ill–thought ideas.

Examining her closely, Ore smiled wryly. "You've been working hard again." He knew Mizi wouldn't be able to rest if she wasn't allowed to help. Her natural instinct to help anyone in need that she had the power to help was often bringing them to detours along the road, but he loved and honored her for that, among other thing. *She's always pushing herself forward*, he smiled inwardly.

"Well, it isn't as if there's much I can really do," Mizi admitted. To Ore, she was looking rather disappointed. Typical court medical cases were resolved in a few hours to days at most. Sitting for the length of time it would take surgery and bones to heal would be different. Regardless, he knew Mizi wouldn't give any less of herself to the duty she'd claimed, even though it might be a bit misplaced. Of course, it wasn't his duty to tell her that, right?

"It's evening already and the dinner meal long past." Noting the empty dishes beside her, he added, "It looks like you've appropriately taken care of yourself in that matter, at least."

Mizi glanced towards the dishes as well, following his look. "One of the village ladies came and brought the food, and also a bit of water for Miss Ilena. I seeped a few herbs in it to help keep down any infection and aid in the healing."

"Were you able to get any of it down her?" Ore wondered, trying to imagine it.

"Well, between the two of us — Alise and I, that is — we managed to figure out a way."

Ore couldn't help but smile at her determination yet again. "Then, teach it to me, too, and I'll help next time." As Mizi nodded he added casually, "But for now, you should get your rest, Mistress. After all, Master won't like to see your eyes so shaded when he arrives tomorrow."

"Eh!? Rei? He's coming tomorrow, here?" Mizi bounced up from her seat in shock and guilt. Rei was infamous among his aides for becoming sternly unhappy with them when they didn't take proper care of themselves. She knew better, but when she was caring for patients she had a tendency to forget herself.

Ore grinned at her, happy he could tease her. She always had the best reactions whenever Rei was involved. He loved both his master and his mistress, particularly when they were together, so he was also looking forward to the next day. "Since the castle is close, I thought it best to send my report immediately. Especially since Master would worry when we hadn't arrived to report our progress by evening. I've just now received his reply...by bird."

Mizi raised her eyebrows. The birds that were trained as messengers for the crown were still fairly rare and prized, particularly here in the cold north. They were native to a warmer climate island that was part of Ryokudo in the southwest sea. If a messenger bird had come to Ore from Rei, it would have been Rei's personal bird. He must have been worried by their lateness and at the arrival of a report, rather than two of the people he loved and called friends.

Mizi sighed, then asked, "Ore, why did you bring this case so quickly to Rei's attention?"

"Ah, even when tired, Mistress is still sharp, eh?" Ore attempted a slight deflection by teasing. He'd been looking at the still–unconscious Ilena and the question drew his attention back.

Seeing his mistress would not be quite so easily turned from her quest, he continued vaguely, "Well, such things as lords who will not act as lords are things Master wishes to directly address himself, and we have here a valuable informant full of proofs. I should think if I hadn't done it I would have received a super scolding when we returned. While I do like Master's scoldings so, his super scoldings are a bit ...severe." Ore shuddered remembering the few he'd received — most of them because of Mizi herself, but she didn't need to know that.

"You *like* his scoldings, Ore?" Mizi asked, her eyes wide enough for the brilliant green irises to glint in the candlelight.

Ore grinned back. "Of course. They let me know Master loves me." He continued to grin, seeing he'd managed to confuse her yet again. Plus having the hidden distraction win out was always a pleasure.

Mizi was still so innocent, even though she and Rei had promised themselves to each other, *what is it now...four years ago? Isn't that too long to keep the innocence going, Master? Will you really make me force your hand in this matter?* Ore had threatened, only half–teasingly, on more than one occasion to steal Mizi away from Rei because of the slow deliberate machinations of royalty and lords.

But, really. Rei was going to get forced into marrying some girl he neither knew nor cared for, likely within a year, if these two didn't pick up the pace. *Actually, I'm surprised it hasn't already happened*, Ore thought unhappily, his good mood gone again. He sighed inwardly. *Really, I can't leave their sides, but there are times that it's such trouble.* "Well, Mistress seems to enjoy his scoldings as well," he put a knowing smile on his face as he responded to her.

Mizi put her hand over her heart, her hand slightly clutched — a subconscious defensive move she made whenever she felt insecure or frightened. "No, not really," she said weakly.

"Well, then," Ore put his hands behind his head, interlocking his fingers, and stretched. Leaving his hands behind his head he looked at his mistress from the corner of his eye, "I guess Mistress had better take the other bed. Ore will take the chair and keep watch over both Mistress and Miss Steward. We weren't expecting to stay overnight anyway so nothing's been prepared. This should be sufficient if Mistress approves."

Giving her the reward of remaining close to her patient seemed to do the trick. Mizi nodded once and obediently climbed into the second bed, only pausing to take off her shoes. "Wake me if anything changes, Ore."

"Sure thing! Good night, Mistress."

"G'night," she managed to mumble before falling quickly to sleep. Mizi had learned to fall asleep quickly while working odd and long hours on her research thesis at the university in Kouzanshi in the far northwest of Suiran, Ryokudo. Ore knew it well.

It wasn't like they slept in the same room often — in fact it was rather the opposite as Rei would have killed him — but Ore had always found it difficult to sleep. It had started when he was very young and it had been reinforced by his time in the underworld. It still hadn't really changed since he'd given his reins to Rei. Castles made him nervous, and when he and Mizi were away, there was only him to watch over her.

When they were out of the castle he often stayed awake, or relied on the nightwalker's trait of being on alert while sleeping, and he always took a room next to hers. With the precise catlike hearing that went with all of his other cat–like traits, he had memorized and categorized all the sounds she made as she prepared for bed, slept, woke, and prepared for her day. That way he would always be alerted if anything odd would happen in her room and he be needed immediately.

This room might perhaps be the most dangerous room they could stay in, since the Earl would be likely to send in assassins at some point. But tonight Mizi would sleep easier close to her patient and he would be more at ease being able to keep his eyes and ears on both young women.

It was going to be an uncomfortable night, however. He was too nervous to be in the same room with Mizi, chaperoned by only an unconscious body, to even unlatch his buckles on his familiar brown jacket that was as much emotional armor as physical.

-o-o-o-

Ore slid immediately from light sleep into still alertness. A muttering noise nearby had awakened him. He waited without motion for the sound to repeat itself, noting that his booted foot under the other had gone numb. He silently lifted the top foot and flexed the numb one, wishing briefly he'd thought to take the boots off, then remembered just how cold floors got in the winter and spring.

He glanced at Mizi to make sure she was still warmly bundled up under her blankets since there wasn't a fireplace in this small room. Three bodies kept it sufficiently warm for him. The candle was out, of course, but there was faint light from the town hall room seeping around the edges of the door. It was enough for him to see that everything in the room was as it had been when he'd dozed off.

He heard the two guards at the door shift slightly to relieve tired cramping muscles. Still third watch, then. Probably the early hours, maybe two or three hours after midnight. A faint groan — *coming from Miss Steward, Mistress doesn't make noise when she sleeps* — was followed again by a mutter like what had woken him.

Allowing his knife–edge awareness to ease, but keeping carefully alert, Ore slipped one of his throwing daggers silently into his hand and carefully crept up to the bed Ilena lay on. He listened closely as she slipped further into this state of talking quietly in her sleep.

"No, Master, please! ...Please, stop. ...Please...!" Her face held pain.

Well, the pain wasn't that much of a surprise. She probably was in quite a bit of pain, which was surely causing her sleeping mind to remember a thing she would rather forget. Ore replaced his dagger and waited, but no further words were forthcoming. Then, he noticed Ilena's breathing was a bit ragged. He shifted so the light from around the door reflected better off her face. There, shining on her face....

If anyone had been able to see it, on his face they would have seen cold, hard anger. But the finger that reached out and brushed away the tears from her temple was infinitely gentle. Ilena's mouth moved, but no sound came from it. Then she was still, once again succumbing to unconsciousness. The remainder of Ore's night was restless and full of his own dark thoughts.

-o-o-o-

Rei reined in his white horse at the top of the last of the rolling hills between Castle Nijou and the beginning of the snow covered northern rocky mountains. He'd outrun his aides and the now–required security detail, but he could see they were just coming out of the valley and heading up the slope behind him. He was glad to see that his close aides and personal knights, Andrew and Mina whom he considered friends, would reach him ahead of the security detail.

He scowled. It had always been his way to escape when frustrated, but it was even more difficult now that he held the position of Regent of Suiran. Even a short one or two day trip required more than just the two aides, who had been all that followed him since he'd been given Andrew. It was suffocating sometimes, having to follow protocol. He would have liked for at least this trip to have been just the three of them.

Mina had arrived back at his side within the last week while Mizi had been away on her university business. Five months ago he had lost Mina's constant support. He'd already by that time kept her over the originally agreed upon time by nearly three years, but even so, it was still difficult to let her return to the duties to which she was required to go.

The agreement for now was that during the deep frozen time of the winter, when travel was severely restricted by the weather, Mina — as heir — would go to her father to be trained in the duties of becoming the lady and administrator of their Earldom, Yosai, east of the castle lands. During times of nicer weather she would travel between the two so that when Rei had need he would have both of his quite capable knights by his side but her father would also have her to introduce her to the land of Yosai and its people.

Glancing at them one more time before turning to face the valley and its village on the other side, Rei wondered once again what had been the agreement between Andrew and Mina. They had been partners at his back for so long they trusted no one else, really. While Andrew was really dense when it came to matters of the heart, and Mina severely restrained, it had been no secret to him for quite some time that Mina loved Andrew and intended to make him her lord husband, even if he might refuse the title of Earl.

Andrew had been given to Rei when he was in the rebellious stages of his childhood by his lord brother, then–First Prince Sasou, and turned him around. Andrew would not willingly, nor easily, be pried from his position as top aide and second big brother and shield. Rei was grateful to have Andrew by his side, a steady, calm influence. Rei also wanted his two closest friends to be happy together. It was hard to know how to reconcile the two.

Rei had been surprised to stand up from his desk only this morning to realize that he'd had another growth spurt sufficient to be standing almost eye to eye with the tall aide. Rei wasn't sure he'd ever get as tall as his brother, who was another half–hand taller than Andrew, but he might slightly surpass Andrew by the time of his own next birthday — only his nineteenth. He'd surpassed Mina a few years ago and Ore this past summer.

The Touka family genes ran to tall, lithe, and understated strength in body; beauty in face and features with stunningly brilliant blue eyes and very pale golden hair that lightly curled naturally. While Sasou kept his hair just past shoulder length, Rei himself favored keeping it short so that the curls couldn't be seen at all. He was a bit stockier than his mother and brother, carrying enough of his father's genes to have a bit more girth to him and a slightly wider jaw that only served to add nobility to the beauty.

His girth wasn't all that noticeable really — not when he kept sprouting like a weed every few months. Really, the castle tailors were going to sigh at him once again when he showed back up the next day for a remeasuring. It kept surprising him that he wasn't literally looking up to Andrew any longer, although figuratively he probably would for his entire life.

Although it would be difficult to have both of his knights leave his side if Andrew chose to walk with Mina more formally, what really mattered to Rei was their happiness. He wasn't sure they were that right now. Rei had only been able to assume it had been a neutral parting at best before winter set in. Mina had kept her emotions locked tightly away as usual when they left her with the Earl on the way to the castle for Rei to take the position of Regent, although she had surprisingly embraced them both before sending them off.

When they arrived at Castle Nijou, Andrew had thrown himself, alongside Rei, into the work of beginning in a new place. He still hadn't said anything. Occasionally Rei caught him staring into space with a perplexed expression, muttering to himself quietly, so potentially the partners had at least talked.

He actually hoped it wouldn't be too much longer before Andrew made a decision and talked with him. Andrew at twenty–seven was getting old, and Mina at only a few years younger was already almost past the age most parents would wait patiently for their willful children to agree to marriage. It wouldn't be long before Earl Durand forced Mina into some sort of marriage arrangement herself.

A slightly queasy feeling of unease came over Rei as he looked down upon the village of Osterly below him where another relationship was a bit unsteady. Mizi hadn't minded that he was in the main too busy to spend much time with her. That was nothing new for the two of them. They were both glad they'd been assigned together to Nijou Castle. She'd been busy getting used to the new medical department arrangement, eased by the fact that she was still working with her one–time trainer then research partner, now boss, Nijou Head Court Healer Ryan.

It was Rei that was the problem, really. Not only had he been trying to get the lords of Suiran to fully accept him, train up new aides to replace Mina (it was going to take more than one to replace her efficiency, apparently, and he was having difficulty finding anyone that was a good match for him and Andrew), but he was having trouble coming up with the next step in making it possible for Mizi to be able to stand by his side as an accepted Princess of Ryokudo (or even Suiran).

He was determined to make it happen, and his older brother Sasou, now King for over three years, had been his ally in having Mizi perform tasks that put her in front of the lords of Suiran. So far that had been only in the capacity of court healer, the path Mizi herself had chosen. Sadly that wasn't sufficient for the lords to be willing for her to be added to the list of acceptable potential wives that still sat inside his desk.

The pressure was again mounting for him to at least begin having marriage interviews with the ladies on the list. If he couldn't come up with the next step in strengthening Mizi's position, he would have to submit. Really it was very complicated, this part of being a Prince.

His brother had married for convenience half a year after his coronation quite obediently. Aryana was a woman of good pedigree, training, and beauty great enough to match Sasou's own radiance. (It was often said when they were together that they were a match so pleasing on the eyes one couldn't look at them together very long.) From what Rei could see, that was all that it was.

Maybe his brother was being soft on him in letting him try to marry for love, but that didn't mean the King could wave his hand and make it happen by ordering the lords to accept it. But what was the next step? Sasou was surely waiting to see what move Rei would make, testing him yet again to see if he was still serious about his commitment to that path. What should he do next? *Argh! It's so frustrating!*

"That's quite the scowl, Rei," Mina said, pulling her horse to a stop beside her young liege, everything still severely in place, including her dark brown hair held back in its ponytail, even though they'd been riding for over six hours. "You'll scare the guards."

Rei pulled a face at her as Andrew came up to a stop on his other side. "Was the run not sufficient, Rei?" Andrew's question was spoken blandly, but for Andrew it was a cold comment. Normally he would have begun his kindly scolding before even reaching Rei's side. Rei, seeing the other guards rapidly approaching, looked at Andrew with barely recognizable mild surprise, wondering what his two aides might have said to each other after he kicked his horse into a gallop and left them behind.

They'd all been together long enough that Rei recognized that Andrew's anger was not really because Rei had run off ahead of the rest. Andrew had come to expect such things out of Rei from a long time ago. It was the only small rebellion Rei still allowed himself, and he had been learning proper restraint. After all, he'd stopped at the top of the hill, still within sight of his guard, rather than continuing on into the village as he would have before and during the early years that Mizi was with them.

Andrew closed his eyelids over his brown eyes, hiding his unwelcome emotion, and gave Rei a half–bow from the saddle, showing the top of his short cropped light brown head. "My apologies, Rei."

Rei looked from Andrew to Mina and back again. "I hope the two of you can resolve this soon." Both aides looked down meekly, unwilling to look at each other or him. Rei sighed, turning back to face Osterly. Such open repentance only meant they'd actually argued, even if it had been only a few words. His mood was certainly not improving much, even for all he was out in the open world and had been riding for more than half the day.

He shrugged one shoulder, an expression his aides recognized as irritation bordering on anger, and urged his horse down the hill towards the village and the mountains rising up behind it. "Let's go."

-o-o-o-

Mina commanded her horse to follow after Rei, naturally falling into her usual position. She snuck a brief glance at Andrew. His stiff back, riding half–way between her and the Prince when he would normally be in stride with her, his cold comment to Rei, and his silence. All these things telling her loudly that she'd offended him by her comment, even though no offense was meant. Rather she'd been trying to tell him that she missed being with them. She stifled the sad sigh that threatened to escape.

With the guards there, they were all three wearing their public court faces. The ones that gave little to no true emotion away, yet spoke volumes with the faintest of expressions. Those masks Rei and she had learned from birth and Andrew had learned standing behind Rei.

If anything was the most frustrating for her, it was that it was obvious there was little opportunity for Rei to be just Rei with the people he cared about the most. With the additional guard required when he left the castle, the additional people being trained who either couldn't or wouldn't accept his preferred casual manner in his office, and all of the worries weighing on him, he just wasn't being able to find moments to relax.

Normally Mizi would have been a place of refuge for him, but Andrew had confided to Mina earlier that week in a rare moment they'd been alone. She'd asked after Mizi and Andrew had told her that just before Mizi left on her current assignment, Rei made one complaint too many to her and she'd snapped, firmly telling him that, "If you have the time to complain to me so much about the people around you who are trying to do their best for you, you have the time to properly train them."

Such a harsh statement from Mizi to Rei was rare as Rei spent a lot of time trying to live so as to avoid them — a good thing from his aides' perspectives. That he'd slipped up and said something to earn it meant he must truly be nearing wit's end. It wasn't too hard to guess that Rei had probably hung onto his pride, at least for a day or two if he still wasn't.

Not that it wasn't reasonable. There were times when it would be appropriate for the one he loved to show sympathy for his difficulties so that he could for a brief moment lay the burden down. Well, it was likely the same problem for both sets of couples. Things were changing around them and unsettled, but they stumbled in their ability to talk properly about them. *Ah, I'm in complete agreement with Rei. I hope this can all be resolved soon, too.*

-o-o-o-

Ore had managed to coax his mistress out of the little room long enough for them to breathe fresh air. He'd been afraid she was about to walk on top of him for pacing, although she had been restraining herself. The room was rather small for such a thing as pacing with two beds, a desk, and chair taking up most of the space, along with three bodies. He'd alternated between being in the room to check up on her and Ilena, and talking with the soldiers of the garrison and villagers who came to visit together in the hall.

Mizi had remained in the room, studying her current herbal book after making up another infusion to coax down Ilena's throat. Ore had watched closely so as to learn how she managed to get liquid down the throat of a person flat on their back and unconscious — normally a dangerous idea. It had been mostly a process of infinite patience as only tiny amounts of liquid could be dosed at a time.

As Mizi stretched her arms above her head and took a deep breath of the spring mountain air, Ore called out. She turned to see him looking away from the majestic mountains, his hand shading his eyes.

"Is that Master and his men?" He pointed to where he was looking. "There, just coming down the hill?"

Mizi strained to see. "I guess it could be," she frowned, not really sure she was seeing horses moving on the hill or just wishful thinking. "You have very good eyes, Ore, if you can see them from this far." She turned back to look at him and her eyes popped. "Ah! Rei!" She froze for a moment her face going pale, then red. "Ore!" She turned an exasperated expression on her teasing friend.

"Oh. My bad." He raised his hands with a teasing twinkle in his eyes. "Here they are." He turned to Rei and the guards following him, a smile on his face, watching as they came across the open space between the stables and the town hall.

Rei was in his pale gold casual uniform with darker gold piping, and his white riding cloak which was similar to the soldier's white cloaks only of finer make and with the Regent's mark on the right breast. Mina and Andrew were in their usual Royal Guard black uniforms — the casual ones not the formals — and the same style black cloaks Mizi and Ore were wearing in the cool spring afternoon.

Mina refused to wear skirts while on duty, choosing the pants uniform of the men, although Ore had seen her in a dress once or twice when she'd had to fulfill her role of daughter to the Earl. Ore only wore either of the black uniforms if he had to, preferring his better fitting common brown nightwalker clothing so he could protect Mizi better.

There were swords at the sides of all three that never left them so as to keep Rei's life protected at all times. Rei's white sword belt and sheath was marked with the golden seal of the Touka royal family, modified with the First Prince's emblazon, received since his brother had been crowned King. The knight's swords in their black sheaths on black leather belts were marked with the same seal that showed they were personal knights to royalty.

Ore had one as well, but it was a short sword because he was more used to a knife given his past. He still reached for his throwing knives or used his fists and feet before he sought out the sword. On his side it was a mark of his place behind Rei.

Rei's gaze was as hungry as usual when he looked at Mizi, but his face was still darkened. Ore pasted his open smile on his face for all he was worth, but worry crept into his heart. If Rei was still angry with Mizi this meeting would not go as well as he would hope. The worry relaxed a bit as Rei's eyes moved to look at Ore and a light came across his face.

Ah, good. If it wasn't possible for Mizi to calm Rei, at least Rei was willing to be cajoled by Ore. That meant it wasn't all lost, just that Rei was sufficiently burdened that a happy friendly face was a rare joy today.

Well, but really, it isn't good for Master to look at me like that and not Mistress. "Welcome, Master. If you keep looking at me like that, I'll have to steal you away from Mistress. Would you like a hug?" Ore spread his arms wide as if to embrace Rei, Andrew, and Mina all at once, and tried to look alluring.

That definitely got the reaction he wanted. Rei stopped in the midst of his stride, unable to restrain his usual look of pleased revulsion whenever Ore teased him that way. *Pleased because he's happy the hug was offered. Revulsion because Mistress is the only one he sees that way.* Ore sighed sadly and began lowering his arms. Before he could complete the motion he was totally caught off guard. *Some*one had thrown their arms around him.

"*Pfft!*" Rei was holding his hand over his mouth "Your expression, Ore!"

But Ore wasn't liking the expression he was seeing on Andrew's face. He put his hands down on the shoulders in front of him, gently pushed away the person holding him, and looked down. Mina was the second smallest of the group after Mizi, and this was most definitely Mina having just done a very uncharacteristically Mina action. She was smiling her slight smile and her eyes were bright. *Tears?! That is even less Miss Mina–like!*

"Your expression is indeed most rewarding, Ore," Mina said.

Ore allowed his surprised look to fade into wariness. He stepped back and made a show of looking her up and down. "Is this really our Miss Mina, back from the barrens of her home? What a strange thing to have happen to this poor heart. And here I thought you hated me."

Mina gave him a proud look and raised her head slightly. "And shall I never do it again, then?"

"Ah," Ore raised his hands in negation and defense. "Well," he looked up and around her at Andrew again. "I think that perhaps you should reserve them for the one who really wants them, eh?" *That isn't a good thing. A cold shock to the system, followed by feigned indifference. Ah, Mister Andrew and Miss Mina. What are you two doing?*

Thankfully the interaction was interrupted by Mizi flinging herself into Mina's arms with a cry of delight. "Mina! It's so good to see you again!"

Ara! Is that really better, Mistress? Mizi was also not known for demonstrative acts of affection. It looked like Rei had just received a punch at the belt–line.

Rei recovered with a shake of his head and a small smile played on his lips. "I got it, you three. Good grief, I *must* be in a state to make even Mina and Mizi join in on Ore's jokes."

Hah, Ore sighed inwardly. *If only it were that simple. I don't think the ladies are joking so much as you might think.* But at Rei's words the whole atmosphere seemed to become less oppressive. *As is often the case, Master can calm the seriousness that rises all too often in Mister Andrew.*

Rei placed his hand on Mizi's hooded head. "It's good to see you again, Mizi. Have you been well?"

Mizi smiled up at Rei. "Yes! It's good to see you, Andrew, and Mina again." Ore and Mizi had been gone from the castle for a number of weeks now for Mizi's continuing research.

There's the light I was looking for! Ore smiled to himself as he drank in the sight of the pair greeting each other in their usual happy but awkward and restrained manner.

As Mina leaned in to talk quietly to him, Ore braced himself for one of her typical biting comments. Instead she shocked him again. "Thank you for being here for Rei, Ore." He stared at her, seeing her face was soft, giving truth to the statement and for a moment her eyes were bright again before she turned away hastily.

He looked once more at Andrew, but the man was warmly returning Mizi's welcome and hadn't seen. Was there more going on at the castle while they were away than he would have thought? Certainly, the stress and cabin fever had been bad there just before the spring thaws had released them from its confines.

Or was there something more going on? He would definitely need to corner Mina when Andrew wasn't watching and press her for information. At the very least to understand where her tears came from, since Andrew wasn't at all capable of it.

As for himself, he felt the usual calm from being in his master's presence well up in him again and settle like a warm blanket over his own dark worries. They didn't calm completely. Although Rei had never demanded that Ore tell him words about his past, he would have to find the courage to speak them, he knew. Else they would eat at this happiness he'd finally found.

Rei turned and looked at Ore, his face recomposing into the careful neutrality he carried everywhere he went in public, but his heart seemed lighter finally. "Ore, I would like to see Earl Shicchi's steward first, please. Then we'll go speak with the garrison commander."

"Yes, Master," Ore bowed slightly and gestured with his hand towards the town hall and it's room with two attendant guards. It wasn't all that unusual to the five to have this kind of interaction when meeting, so they weren't affected by the fact it had been in public, but several of the onlookers, including garrison soldiers, were having difficulty keeping their eyes in their sockets, or the grins off their faces. "I'm sorry, it's a small room."

"That's fine, Ore." Rei nodded at the guards as he passed them to enter the room Ilena was recovering in. Ore followed him in.

"Mina, did you know that Earl Shicchi's steward was a woman?" Mizi asked Mina as the two of them followed Andrew into the room. It wasn't common for females to be in positions of high responsibility.

Ore twitched at the question. Rei turned kind eyes to Ore. Deciding to hang on to those brilliant blue eyes as his life preserver, Ore ignored Mina's answer. However, because he was focused on looking at his master's eyes, he missed seeing the shadow of concern that came over Rei's face. "Ore," Rei's calm voice was reassuring, "what's happened here since you sent your report to me?"

Standing at relaxed attention, the bed containing Ilena to his right, and continuing to stare only into Rei's eyes in an unfocused way, he gave his report smoothly. He hoped it came across as militaristically trained, but as he spoke he could only feel the way he'd often felt when giving reports of completed jobs while standing in front of a person he'd received much darker orders from.

Divorce yourself from your emotions. Don't see the person on the other side. Expect swift payment or punishment at the end. Show only a relaxed exterior that's proof of internal strength and confidence, but doesn't provoke. It was a brief report. Even the further questioning he'd made of the villagers about their overlord hadn't revealed much more than the garrison leaders had said the day before.

"Thank you, Ore," Rei said when the report was completed. Ore bowed slightly, his right hand coming to his breast formally, then returning to his left hand behind his back.

Rei turned to Mizi. She looked guilty and he smiled gently for her. "Mizi, it isn't good, nor necessary for you to sleep here. Mina and Andrew will go with you to the garrison and requisition sleeping quarters for you and Ore. That is, if you wish to stay. I'll have Ore stay for the two weeks it will take for Miss Ilena to be moved to garrison quarters, and maybe for the two weeks more to move her to the castle, but you could return with us." Ore relaxed just slightly. That was a solution he could favor.

"Ah, well." Mizi's guilt and desire warred within her, and therefore in her eyes and face. "I realize that I'm not a surgeon, nor really in a position of responsibility here, but I already would like to continue to do what I can here. Ryan is —"

Rei lifted a hand to interrupt Mizi. "Ryan is handling the castle Medical Department easily with the assistants he has now. With the spring release the number of cases is diminished." At Mizi's wide curious eyes, Rei smiled. "I spoke with him last evening. Ore made it fairly clear in his report that you would likely wish to see this through to the end. Ryan sent you a packet of herbs that Andrew's holding for you."

As Mizi took the package from Andrew, she smiled happily at him and Rei. "Thank you, Rei." She bowed slightly. "I will do my best here, then."

Rei nodded at her, still smiling gently. This determination and care of hers for others was an endearment for them all. Andrew deferred to Mizi and allowed her to exit the room first, before him and Mina.

CHAPTER 2 A Person Ore Once Knew

At the sound of the closing of the door, Ore's expression began to crumble. "Ore," Rei called softly, placing his hand on his sworn man's shoulder, feeling the trembling that was no longer controllable.

Ore looked at his master with a torn expression, still looking for safety in the blue eyes he loved. "Master," his voice was rough but soft, "I left her behind. I abandoned her!"

Rei could only watch in amazement as the man who'd stood strong in even the most agonizing situations began to cry. His tears were silent and unnoticed. There was only agony and a silent cry for salvation. Rei moved forward, wrapped his arms around Ore, and held him. Only then did Ore begin to sob into his master's shoulder, his body wracked with deep grief.

Confusion roiled within Rei. Ore was the sort who'd always hidden his true emotions behind steel walls, even though some of them leaked out every now and again. He'd never shown any signs of grief before, other than his darkly burning anger when hunting for Mizi after she'd been kidnapped four years before, shortly after becoming an apprentice court healer. For Ore to completely succumb to this grief.... Rei was glad he'd come right away.

Who was this young woman, roughly in her mid twenties, who could cause Ore's emotional resolve to crumble? What was their background and relationship? And...what was he supposed to do now? How long should he hold and comfort his friend before it became an embarrassment to them both?

Of all the things...! Rei rolled his eyes at himself. He was only really asking the question because Ore had to keep teasing him about just such a situation — like only fifteen minutes ago. Just that had caused him to briefly doubt his own judgment.

Ah, yes. There's always a little bit of truth to all Ore says, even if it's teasing. But had I hugged him then, that would have been a bad time given his fragility in this place. Maybe it was no wonder the panic on Ore's face was so desperate when Mina grabbed him out of the blue.

Always he's thinking about others in what he says and does while deflecting them from himself. In his own way, Ore had his own depth of tenderness, like Andrew. It was likely this woman, at some point, had a place within those same depths. Rei felt Ore begin to relax and gently let him go, but left one hand on Ore's shoulder as they'd begun.

Looking at Ilena while waiting for Ore to fully regain his composure, Rei realized that their dark features were similar. Black straight hair, a slightly darker complexion than most citizens of Ryokudo, a face, even in repose, that spoke of many hidden secrets she never let anyone see. She was covered with a rough wool blanket, save the arm lying outside of it that had a light shirt sleeve covering it. Might she be a sister, or beloved cousin?

Being a high ranking member of the household she might be such a thing as a distant cousin, but it would be strange for a daughter of the House not to be married out. Besides, after doing his research on who Ore was, he knew there was no daughter of the House of Shicchi that would be this age. Ore shifted slightly under his hand, bringing Rei's attention back to his friend.

Ore was looking at him again expectantly, his demeanor much calmer. Rei smiled gently. "Shall we sit, then?" He moved to the one chair, turning it to face the center of the room. He'd expected Ore to sit on the empty bed, the way he would sit on the settee in Rei's bedroom on nights he couldn't sleep and Rei was still awake.

Not finding Ore there, his surprised eyes continued to travel around the room until they found him perching carefully on the edge of Ilena's bed, tucking one leg under the other that he dangled towards the ground. Now that Ore had let the wall crumble, it looked like he didn't want to be too far from her. Well, perhaps that was a reaction to the cause of his grief. Likely it would take some time before Ore was recovered from this nearly unconscious need to be near Ilena.

Rei could relate. He'd also found it hard to be far from Mizi after she'd been recovered from her kidnapping. It looked like his earlier decision to have Ore stay near Ilena, as well as his understanding that Mizi wouldn't likely leave her either, meant that the arrangement already decided on was sufficient.

Remembering the chair in his hand, he looked at it briefly, then settled it so he was facing Ore and sat down in it resolutely. Ore needed his strength as a master now, not as a friend. Sitting up straight, he looked Ore in the eyes and ordered firmly, "Let's have it, then."

Ore took a breath and rubbed the back of his neck. "I don't know everything about her or her past, only the parts I was involved in, of course." Rei nodded. *Of course.* "I don't remember much about her parents, only that they were distant relatives, through her father, it seems. They'd come through and stopped by for a visit when she was about five or six and I was about eight.

"It was short, I think just overnight, but as soon as she saw me she grabbed hold of me and wouldn't let me go. She kept telling everyone I was 'hers'. That's all I really remember of that event, because I was annoyed at being claimed by a little girl I didn't even know, although I had to be polite to her — in public anyway." Ore grinned wryly, putting his hand back in his lap.

He looked at it for a moment, then curled his fingers into a slight fist, his grin fading. "The next time I saw her was about three years later. She arrived at the earldom manor with only a maid this time. My grandfather was still lord of the House at the time, and the maid spoke privately with him. After that, the two lived with us. The circumstances of why or how it came about were never explained. It was just the old man's decision and the rest of us lived with it."

Ore took a breath, briefly closing his eyes. "It was one of his last decisions before he died a short while later, finally giving in to the poison administered by my father. While the old man was harsh, at least he wasn't mean–spirited. After his death, Ilena was the only thing that kept the household — and me — going.

"There were many that would go to her when they'd been punished, when they couldn't see a way to live any more. Always she helped them return to life, somehow." Ore looked up at the ceiling past Rei's head, remembering.

"Although she never brought up that she'd claimed me years before, the first nights at our place she would always find a way to be near me, by my side if she could, even going so far as to reach out and grasp my sleeve at my Grandfather's funeral."

Ore shifted, looking at Rei. Finding strength in his master's straightforward expectant expression, he continued. "Ilena had an inner fire, a strength, then, that was above and beyond her years. She also had this way of seeing to the core of people, ...things, ...issues. She wouldn't ever complain about being lied to, but not even my father could withstand her eyes that could see through to the truth. He banished her from the main house, unable to live with those eyes following him everywhere." Ore shrugged. "For myself, I followed those eyes.

"The first time she saw me flee from the main house after I'd been punished by my father, she sought me out — or rather hunted me down. I had the best hiding places." Ore closed his eyes, a faint smile on his lips. "I watched her pass me about ten times from my hiding place without her ever knowing I was there. Then she stopped, looking at the tracks, and the area around her, and closed her eyes." Ore's eyes, although closed, were transfixed on his vision of the young Ilena. "She said, quietly so we wouldn't be discovered, 'Kase, I will find you. Don't come out. No matter what, I will always come find you'."

Ore's breath caught. "Ah, she's done it again, hasn't she." He ran one hand through his hair and held his head. Rei waited patiently while the pain rose again in Ore, then subsided.

"She slowly scanned the whole area. I knew as soon as she'd seen me. For some reason, I couldn't move, could hardly breathe, as if I was her prey and she'd targeted me. But it wasn't a thing to be afraid of — rather a pleasure to have been finally discovered. She made sure there was no one in the area to see where she went, then she walked away and disappeared.

"I was so disappointed. I put my head down on my arms and vowed to not come out until past dinner. Then, suddenly, there was a pair of arms around me. Ah!" Ore stopped and laughed. "It was a lot like when Miss Mina grabbed me today." Rei allowed himself a small smile.

Smiling a little sadly at the memory, Ore continued. "The shock of the surprise and my relief that she'd kept her promise, and even kept my hiding place a secret — her hair was filled with leaves and the dirt on her elbows and knees told me she'd found where I'd come in from and how I'd gotten there — like with Master today, I couldn't hold the tears in. The pain came rushing out of me, into those small arms, their warmth replacing it in my broken heart."

Ore looked away from Rei. Softly he said, "Master is very much like her." Then he looked back down at his hands and took another breath. It looked like he was working up the courage to finish the story.

"It's not that I want to excuse myself. I know I made the wrong decision that day to not find her and take her with me and I have that to my regret." Ore's tawny golden eyes, dull with his thoughts of self–recrimination, came up to meet Rei's.

His following words were delivered simply, as if giving one of his reports. "Even before she came, I was having great difficulty under the oppression of my family. All the men of the Shicchi line have an inborn brutality and no one is spared from it. After she came, I was able to survive a while longer, but then came the death of the only protection I'd had in my Grandfather.

"My eldest brother finally lashed out at my father just over a year later, killing him in a surprise win that shocked even my brother. He threatened the whole household with death if anyone breathed a word against the tale that it had been a sudden illness that killed our father. Even though everyone swore over and over to him, even myself, eventually a madness overtook him. In particular he seemed to believe that his brothers were plotting against him, though I, at least, had no intention of ever running that House. The position had come to mean a curse to me."

Ore tensed slightly. "The night he entered our second brother's room and killed him as he slept next to his new bride was the night I escaped out my window and left to never return. I knew instinctively that if I didn't move immediately, I was next." Ore closed his eyes again. "I had thought I would never see my one source of warmth again. She who'd tried to be my strength, and the strength of the whole household. One small pair of shoulders that kept choosing to carry such a burden. I looked back once, wishing I could have brought her with me, knowing I couldn't return." He paused for a breath.

"Many times during the following dark years, as I lived out the family curse myself, I would rest my head in the darkness of night on my arms and feel those arms around me again. And when they'd held me long enough, I could finally sleep, even if only a little.

"I didn't believe she could continue to survive there. No one really did for very long, although close family was more likely to die than the servants. So at times it really felt to me as if she had died, and was finally free to come to me. I suppose it's a rather perverse pleasure to think that she might have been given a way to escape, even if it was only in death." Ore shuddered. "But...."

He turned to look at Ilena and ran a thin thread of her long black hair lightly through his fingers, as if to confirm the reality of her presence. Quietly he finished his thoughts. "I can't say her real name, but I know it isn't Ilena. Like I am Ore. Her nursemaid's eyes would always follow after her, with great sadness in them. Always she was obedient to Ilena, though also her support. Ilena went to great lengths to ensure the nursemaid was protected from the rest of the House.

"Perhaps it was in learning how to do that that she learned how to protect the rest of the household, as the Captain has said she's done for the last seven years. That would mean that she's been my older brother's right arm since she was roughly seventeen. Given how the family blood runs, and her inborn strengths, likely she was influencing him for many years before that. Or at least learning how to." Ore dropped his hand to the bed, shaking his head incredulously, then turned back to Rei.

Ore said resolutely, "I believe that it's impossible to predict Earl Shicchi's intentions towards Miss Steward. Because of the way the family madness works, he'll at one time be intensely protective towards her, then at another time he'll declare that she's a hindrance and should be cast off, which in the language of the family means death."

He frowned. "If he feels his position is threatened excessively, he won't hesitate to burn even this building down in order to prevent her from speaking. If you wish to be able to hear the words she has to say to you, then the most careful protections must be set."

As Rei considered Ore's words, there was an intake of breath and a groan from Ilena. As they both turned to look at her, they could see her trying to open her eyes. Ore quickly poured up a glass of water and gently lifted her head just enough he could put the cup to her lips and dribble small amounts of water into her mouth. Ilena swallowed greedily, then turned slightly away from the cup. Ore handed it to Rei to set on the desk then gently lowered her head back on the bed.

"Who?" it was a croak of a whisper.

"You're in the village hall of Osterly. You were brought here yesterday after a rock slide took your carriage. Do you remember?" Rei answered her, wondering that she should be conscious.

Ilena blinked tawny eyes the color of Ore's a few times, as if to see him better. "Eh? ... Dead. Must ...be ...dead." Her voice came out a faint whisper.

"Eh?" Ore reacted to her odd words at the same time as Rei asked in surprise, "What?", her words unexpected.

Ilena slowly raised a weak hand and stretched it out towards Rei. He glanced at Ore, who looked back, suspicious. As the arm began to fall, Rei caught the hand in his. "R–e–i." Rei's eyes narrowed at her, and he gently gave the hand to Ore, who was closer to the bed.

Her eyes swam and began to close, but weakly, quietly, she said, "Ka–se." Her eyes closed. "I'm...home."

Ore slowly and carefully put Ilena's hand back down on the bed, lightly caressing it as he let go. He wiped the tear streaking down her temple with his thumb. Without looking at Rei, Ore asked, "Master, do you know why she calls your name?"

Rei shook his head, wondering the same thing. "I've never spoken to Miss Ilena in my life, at least within my memory."

Ore frowned. "She's said to be an exemplary servant. Even if she only saw you from a distance, to recognize you isn't a surprise. But to say your name familiarly.... I think caution is necessary, Master. Things about this case aren't right. While I knew her as a child, I can't know what she's actually become. I've never known anything good to come out of that place."

"You did," Rei said simply.

Ore's golden cat–eyes glinted in anger at the perceived lie. "Master —"

Rei held up a hand and interrupted. "I know what you did, Ore, but I also know what you've done since then and know your heart. You are good, Ore. We'll have to wait and be cautious, certainly, but I think if she helped you, and if she's been helping others, it's too early to judge her as being other than the same. I don't believe time changes the fundamentals of a person's heart."

"You are too kind, Master," Ore said, standing up. "Oh, yes, and she talks in her sleep, although I don't know to what extent yet."

"Did she last night?"

"Briefly."

"And?"

"...She was remembering a past pain. There was nothing of significance."

Rei could see Ore was thinking of the things he'd seen for himself in that place. "I see."

"Shall we return to Mistress and the others, Master? Miss Steward will likely not wake properly for another two days at least, or so the field surgeon said."

Rei nodded and Ore let them out, leaving the puzzle of the wounded steward behind them for now.

-o-o-o-

Rei and Captain Grey discussed the matter of Ilena's safety, with Rei impressing upon his subordinate that he felt it was very important to ensure that she be able to at least give some testimony as to who she thought might have been involved in the assassination, if it was one. "It may be, Captain, that she saw who caused the landslide and rolled the boulder onto her. I'll be leaving Sir Ore here to receive her testimony when she's awake enough. Lady Mizi would like to stay as well. I'm inclined to allow her to stay, particularly as Head Court Healer Ryan has allowed it. She should be a better choice to change the dressings and poultices for a female patient than a male field surgeon, no?"

Rei smiled at the captain. They both knew it was an excuse to let Mizi do as she pleased. "However, because there's the possibility of foul play, I'll be sure to let Mizi know she's not to be there overnight again. I'm sorry to trouble you."

"No, Prince Rei, it's no trouble. We'll be sure to protect the lady for you," Grey left the "who" vague on purpose. "With Sir Ore here as well, I'm sure all will be well." While it might be annoying to be babysitting multiple people, things were quiet in general at the moment, and having interesting guests would help the soldiers pass the time in a slightly less rowdy manner than usual.

"Well, then thank you for your service, as always." Rei left Grey and walked with Ore to find Mizi, Andrew, and Mina. For this night, he, his aides and his guards would also be bunked there. The trip between the garrison and the castle was less than one day, but it was too far for an easy single day trip.

Rei used the opportunity while he was at the garrison to do one of his usual inspections. He invited Mizi to go with him so they could also spend more time together while they had the opportunity.

"*Hah*, a working date...," Ore sighed ruefully as he walked behind them with Andrew and Mina.

"I suppose it's better than no date at all," said Mina in her dry manner.

"Hm...I suppose." Ore saw that Rei and Mizi had stopped to talk to one of the soldiers. It looked like it might take long enough. He lagged behind, gesturing to Mina to stay with him and let Andrew go on.

They stood where they could see the others, but far enough away that a quiet conversation wouldn't be overheard. Ore asked Mina, not sure he would get anywhere with the taciturn woman, "So, what's going on that Miss Mina feels the need to jump into Ore's arms with tears in her eyes?"

Sure enough, Mina's expression turned hard. She was a tough nut and when she cracked, if she ever did, it wasn't to Ore. But then, looking at Rei, her face softened slightly and her eyes creased ever so slightly with worry. "He hasn't been getting any rest at all, has he?"

Ore looked at Rei as well. "No? Not really, I suppose. It's always difficult at the beginnings of things, though?"

"Andrew took offense at a comment I made that he normally would have understood, too." She looked a little sad. "I don't think he's been getting any rest, either, and that isn't like him."

Ore was surprised and took another look at Andrew. "He's seemed normal to me. ...Except he keeps having only the air to talk to and it seems he can't find something he's looking for occasionally."

"Yeah, I've been missing everyone, too."

"That was surprising. It sounds like Miss Mina has been missing Ore, too."

Mina looked at him out of the corner of her eye, like she did when she made snide comments. "Yeah, I have, actually. Mizi, too."

"Now, really, are you sure you're Miss Mina? Ah, I'm sorry," he held up his hands. He'd made her mad with that question.

She let it pass. "It's not that I mind the work of learning to be an Earl. And I'm not considering running away from my duty."

"It's just lonely, huh?" Ore said insightfully.

"Well, I guess that's it, isn't it," Mina agreed.

"Hmm. ... What did Mister Andrew say?" Ore clasped his hands behind his head.

"Eh, when?"

"When you talked to him before you left, of course." Ore wasn't going to let her wiggle out of understanding.

Mina was silent for a moment and to Ore it looked like she was trying to not cry again, though... *it wasn't likely that, right?*

"He said, 'Let's talk later, when things have settled down'." Her words came out somewhere between neutral and cold.

Ore sighed. He could imagine it was certainly said in Andrew's kind, I'm–trying–to–be–helpful voice. But.... "He really just doesn't understand, does he, Miss Mina? Only having eyes full of Master is kind of sad when there is something to see right here."

Mina looked at him, the hard blue–green eyes she showed the world still looking like they were fighting tears. "How do I make him see without hurting him?"

"Hmm?" Ore thought about that for a moment. "I think maybe you're thinking too hard. He's not someone who can be easily hurt by that."

"Ore!" Mina was mad again and Ore was surprised by that. "He loves Rei. How can he not be hurt by being asked to leave his side?"

Ore looked at her, confused. "But, he loves Miss Mina, too."

Mina immediately went red and turned away from him. "No, he doesn't. Not that way." She paused for a moment, then walked away, ending the conversation.

Ore looked after her sadly for a moment before following her to catch up with the others. Apparently Mina was as blind as Andrew. What a sad state they were choosing to live in.

-o-o-o-

After having dinner with the garrison soldiers, Mina challenged Andrew to a practice bout at the list. Mizi, not one to shirk her duties, wanted to go visit Ilena one more time before retiring for the night. Rei was torn between accompanying her and staying to watch the bout. Mizi turned towards him and said, "Rei, you can wait here. I won't be long. I have to change her dressings, and, well...," she blushed.

Rei looked at her puzzled a moment, then saw Ore's smirk. "Ah! That's all right!" Rei held up his hands, finally understanding that it would be an awkward modesty moment if he went.

"I'll go with Mistress," Ore said, as if to the air. By now, if he'd have not just walked off with her he'd have been worse than super scolded. Even though he missed Rei, he wasn't likely interested in being scolded like that tonight.

"We'll be back soon!" Mizi promised again.

When they reached the guarded door in the village hall, the guards said that the village girl, Alise, had already come to take care of Ilena and had left about a half–hour earlier. Mizi and Ore went in to check on her anyway. Mizi confirmed the poultices had been done sufficiently well and in the end was satisfied with the job Alise had done. It made her feel superfluous. *Maybe I should go back with Rei.*

She looked around to see if there was still a cup for water in the room so she could make the herbal infusion. There was, but the cup was empty. She was about to ask Ore to go refill it, when he suddenly leaned over Ilena with his ear over her mouth.

"Mistress! Does Miss Steward have a heart beat?"

"What?" Mizi quickly stepped back to the side of the bed and picked up Ilena's hand, feeling for her pulse. They held their positions for quite some time, then looked at each other somberly.

"One breath per four seconds and it feels like they're slowing," reported Ore.

"Roughly forty–five beats per minute and decreasing," agreed Mizi. "What made you check, Ore?"

"She was too still."

Mizi stepped back and looked at Ilena again closely. Ore was right, she looked like she was entering death. Mizi looked back at the empty glass, picked it up and took it out of the room to where there was more light. There was still a tiny amount of liquid inside.

It was hard to tell, but it looked like it was a very pale yellow. She sniffed it. There wasn't much of a smell, perhaps slightly like a dry herbal wine. She dipped her finger in and was about to taste it when Ore's hand interposed itself between her finger and her lips.

"Mistress, do you already know what this could be? Is it a poison?"

Mizi paused, running through everything she knew. "It isn't from any combination of herbs I know of. But, while it is mimicking a poison," She lifted the glass to the light again tilting it back and forth slightly, "It isn't one that I know of. There isn't any sheeting on the glass, and almost all of the known poisons do that. The ones that don't aren't this weak." She frowned, slightly biting her lip. "It could just be a local herb I don't know of."

Ore looked doubtful that there should be such a thing. "I'll call Miss Alise and you can ask her. Wait with Miss Steward for a moment." Mizi went back into the room while Ore ran off to fetch Alise.

Mizi felt for Ilena's temperature. It was a little cool, as one might expect with the decreased blood flow. Measuring the heart rate she found that it was indeed decreasing. It looked like at a rate of one less heart beat per five minutes or so. If it wasn't going to cause death, it looked like it was at least having a hibernative effect. Mizi continued to check Ilena's pulse, breathing rate, and temperature every five minutes, documenting the decrease of all of them, hoping to find that it would stabilize at a baseline rate.

Ore finally returned to Ilena's recovery room with Alise. "Alise, do you know why Miss Ilena has entered a state of hibernation?" Mizi asked.

Alise's eyes went round. "No, Lady Mizi, I don't."

"What did you do when you came here earlier?"

"Well..., I just did what we usually do. I changed the poultices and cleaned the wound. The swelling of most of the bruises is decreased, so I was thinking that things were going well. Isn't she just sleeping?"

Mizi shook her head. "Her pulse and breathing rate have been decreasing steadily." She picked up the glass on the table. "What did you give her to drink?"

"Oh, no, Lady Mizi! Please, you don't think I gave her something? It was just water, really, as usual! I promise!" Alise became frightened. "I really wouldn't...!"

"It's okay, Miss Alise," Ore said reassuringly. "Mistress is just trying to figure it out. But if you could, maybe you could take us to where you got the water from?"

"Y–yes! Of course." Alise was holding her hands tightly in front of her chest.

"Wait just a bit," Mizi said. "I'd like to see if the rate of decrease has stopped yet."

Ore and Alise waited with Mizi as she continued to check the statistics for another fifteen minutes. Mizi wrote some final notes in the medical diary she was keeping on her desk, then rose.

"Let's go then, Miss Alise," Ore held the door for the two young ladies.

Mizi said as they walked, "The heart rate stabilized at about forty beats per minute and the breathing at one breath per five and a half seconds, roughly. We should come back and check on it again." Ore nodded.

Alise led them to a small home not too far from the village hall and invited them into the kitchen. There, she showed them a bucket one fourth full of water next to the sink.

"May I have a glass of the water?" Mizi asked. Alise nodded and hurriedly dipped out a glass of water and handed it to Mizi. Mizi looked at it through the glass. It did have a faint yellow tinge to it, not too unusual for water that had been drawn from a well and sat in a bucket since morning. She smelled it. Again, it had that faintly herbal wine smell.

This time, as it looked like she was about to drink it, Ore slipped it neatly out of her hand. "Here, Miss Alise, you wouldn't mind tasting it first, would you, for me?"

Alise looked at him, frightened. She shook her head and held her hand out for the glass. Ore handed it to her and she drank several gulps from it and handed it back. Ore took the opportunity to look at it closely and smell it as well, then took a small sip. After thinking about it for a minute, and watching Alise's reaction, he handed the glass back to Mizi. "Tastes like water to me," Ore said.

Mizi set the glass down and looked more closely at the bucket holding the water. The slightly wine–like smell was coming from the bucket itself. "What is this bucket made out of?" Mizi asked. "And where did you draw the water from?"

"Eh? Um...well...I think one of the local trees, but I don't know which one. It was made by the village woodworker. You could ask him. His name is Tyler.

His house is the one near the woods just before you reach the garrison. And the water is just from the village well, there outside the hall."

"Hmm. Shall we pay him a visit on our way back, then, Mistress?" Ore asked. Mizi nodded. "And you'll stay here, like a good girl, yes Miss Alise? I'd hate to find it difficult to find you tomorrow."

"Ah...ah...of course!" Alise's voice squeaked up an octave in fear. Ore's stern eyes were rather frightening, as the pupils tended to contract vertically rather than circularly.

Ore patted her on her head and smiled. "Good, good."

They stopped by to take Ilena's pulse and her breathing rate again and record them. Mizi was relieved that they were still the same as when they'd left. They stopped by the well and Ore drew up the bucket. Mizi dipped her cupped hand into the bucket and tasted the water cradled in her palm. It only tasted like the water of the area, lacking the hint of herbal wine. "The water is water. The difference does seem to be the bucket."

"Then shall we be going to visit this Tyler?" Ore escorted Mizi away from the well.

After asking at one of the houses near the woods, they were directed to the woodworker's house. He was cordial and explained that the tree he made buckets from, preferably, was a yellow hawthorne, and that it did tend to leach small amounts of its yellow color into the water over the course of a day.

The villagers had been drinking the water from his buckets for over twenty years but this was the first he'd heard of such a thing as a person going into a state of hibernation. They thanked him and left. Mizi paused outside Tyler's home, wondering if she should go back to Ilena and check on her once again.

"Mistress, Master is waiting," Ore reminded her. "Let's return to him and report what's happened. Then I'll return and sit with Miss Steward and make sure she doesn't slip into further danger." Mizi wasn't too surprised at the odd nickname Ore had taken to calling Ilena. He called people whatever he wanted to call them, and she and Rei bore with it since it was usually at least polite.

Mizi bit her lip. She didn't want to get Rei worried and they'd already been gone longer than she'd expected. Plus, he'd been stern about her not sleeping in the hall again overnight. She nodded, and they went on to the garrison.

When they arrived, Andrew and Mina were still bouting on the list. Rei stood when they walked up. "It took longer than I expected, I'm sorry, Rei." Mizi said when they arrived.

"That's okay," Rei said smiling.

"Andrew and Mina are still practicing? How many matches have they had?" Mizi asked, looking at their precise forms. Both seemed to be sweating quite a bit, their shirts sticking to their muscular forms. The bout seemed a little odd in another way and it took a bit before Mizi realized it was because the swords were attacking from the same side because Mina was left–handed.

Rei and Ore stared at Mizi. Ore put his hand on his hip and said, "This is Mistress' first time to see them?"

Mizi answered innocently, "Yes. They seem very graceful together."

Rei laughed. "Well, if that kind of thumping and banging can be called graceful, then yes, they are. That's still the first match from the beginning."

"Eh?! They haven't rested, or stopped?" Mizi was amazed.

"Well, they occasionally part to breathe and then move into the next attack," he allowed. "Mina's been giving it more than usual at the beginning so is wearing down faster, I think."

"You think there will be a winner this time?" Ore asked him, looking closely at the combatants. "Why does it look like Mister Andrew is just willing to be the partner in this, instead of the opponent?"

"I think he's trying to apologize for getting angry at her earlier today." Rei was looking at the partners, a little frown of worry between his eyes.

"Ah, so she's angry, is it."

"I don't think she was until it was obvious he wasn't going to fight seriously." Mizi failed to see how having a bout for longer than a half an hour wasn't being serious.

Suddenly, when they'd just parted to begin a new sequence, Andrew put his knee down on the ground, and rested his wooden practice sword tip down on the ground in front of him. Mina stopped, lowered her practice sword, and they just breathed hard for a moment.

"That's how they end all their battles. If Andrew, or Mina, didn't yield in the end, Mina and he could go for hours, probably. They're that evenly matched and know each other's skills so well." Rei explained to Mizi.

They watched while Mina extended her hand to Andrew to help him up. "Will you get more proper rest from now on?" Mina asked Andrew as he looked up at her.

He grimaced back. "Yes. I'm sorry, Mina. I shouldn't have snapped at you." She pulled him up.

As they walked towards the other three, she said, "You two need to learn to pace yourselves better. There's no sense in beating yourselves when all it means is your strength is lessened."

"Ah," Ore said, "Mister Andrew had to take Master's beating too, huh?" Mina looked at Ore stonily.

Rei looked sheepish. "Sorry, Andrew, Mina."

Mina looked at him, not quite content, "...and...?"

Rei looked at her unsure. Mizi shifted slightly, and he got it. "...and Mizi. I'll get proper rest from now on."

"See that you do."

They all walked with the sparring partners to where they could wash up and collect their jackets, set aside for the match. On the way Mizi told Rei what was happening with Ilena and what they'd discovered in their research. Rei's brow creased. "But you think she's okay?"

Mizi ran her hand through her hair and breathed an exasperated sigh. "I don't really know whether to think that or not. Ore, I want you to keep documenting the rate of change of her vital statistics. If either starts to become erratic or drop too low, please send for me or the field surgeon. As long as she appears to just be sleeping, she's likely okay.

"Also, I've been keeping track of her temperature. If she starts to come out of the hibernative state she should begin to warm up. If her other vitals increase but her temperature drops more, that could also be a sign to send for one of us."

"Yes, Mistress," Ore obediently accepted his orders.

-o-o-o-

Ore sighed. He'd really wanted to spend more time with Rei and Mizi tonight. He would have eventually gone to sit with Ilena, of course. He wanted to know if she would sleep talk more, or if that had been an unusual occurrence. This was a rare night where the young couple would have been fun to observe from the shadows. Their awkward romance both made him warm inside and made him want to berate them in frustration: *just get together already!*

Well if it was any other pairing, they probably would have. Mizi respected Rei's position highly and he, because of his position, respected her just as highly. Maybe it was okay to be here with the unconscious steward instead. At least *she* wasn't going to make him want to strangle anyone, right? And he'd managed to finagle a couple bottles of wine out of the garrison kitchen, saying, "because the Prince is here." So that was alright.

Ore was generally sitting in the chair, his feet propped up on the desk. Every ten, and then after an hour, every fifteen minutes he would take Ilena's vitals. By midnight, he'd finished off the bottles of wine and had moved to the second bed. He was considering lengthening the time for vitals so he could actually get some rest. He decided to check one more time first.

Eh? Hmm. Both heart rate and breathing rate have increased, though not by much. Temperature, then. About the same, so at least not decreasing. I'm not going to be able to go to thirty minutes then, eh? You're almost as much trouble as the rest.

At the next fifteen minute mark Ore jerked awake. *Ah. I'm going to have to go to ten minutes so I don't sleep for an hour and miss important things.* He checked Ilena's vitals. A definite increase again, and this time the temperature was up as well. As he recorded the information, he could see from the records that it looked like from the beginning of the drop of vitals to the beginning of increase was about six hours.

Hmm...that seems rather regular. Like it's a set timing from when she was given the water...if it was just water. I've not noticed her in a state like this before...but I'm not sure I was here to see it. And Mistress didn't notice it until I pointed it out to her. ...And maybe it's just Miss Steward's normal sleep pattern.... Ore snorted at himself. He'd never be able to believe that.

For the next two hours, Ilena's vitals increased slowly but steadily until they seemed to balance back out at a steady rate that was more like the sleeping rate he would expect. He was finally relaxing into the bed, having given himself permission to sleep, when he remembered that it was about this time the night before that she had murmured in her sleep. He mentally shrugged. He'd hear her if it happened again, but it didn't seem too likely.

"You can't!"

Ore jerked awake and froze. *I can't what?* He breathed a bit. *Oh, not me.* Lying still he waited. Ilena was clearer tonight than last night.

"You can't have him! He's been mine since forever ago!"

Have who? Ah...likely me — Kase, ...unless it's some stray dog.

"I hate you, stupid Pakyo."

Pffft! No way! Did you really say this sort of thing where he could hear you? Or were you protected enough in your own room it was okay? Or did you say it to his face on a regular basis and he laughed it off? ...Not likely. Not when he hates his name.

"I hate you. You made him go away."

....

"It's okay, Kase. I'll protect you. He won't get you. Ever. I won't let him."

Eehhhh....

"You have to stay alive or I'll die. Stay alive, Kase. Get stronger, ... promise me. Promise ...." Her voice trailed off.

Ore waited to see if Ilena would continue, but she didn't. Although he was holding his heart and emotions with his iron will, he couldn't shake a sudden restlessness. He sat up on the side of the bed, resting his arms on his knees, hands lightly clasped.

He finally moved to the table and relit the candle stub. He needed to write down in the book that this was part of the pattern. As he was finishing writing, he turned to check her vitals one more time. *May as well record them as well.*

Sniff. "Hah! Haaa—ahhh!" Ilena's cries pulled Ore out of his seat faster than he had been intending to move and he nearly fell on her. He couldn't see her well enough. He went back for the candle and held it carefully over her head so he could see her face. Her breathing was ragged and she was obviously in pain.

"Ahhh! *Haaa...haah....*" She was alternating between crying out in pain and breathing as if breathing was painful, her body slightly arching as her back muscles tensed against the pain.

He held the candle carefully out of the way, then put his ear to her chest and listened to the air as it moved through her lungs. It was a bit raspy, but he couldn't decide if that was anything to be concerned about or not. They did seem to be filling well enough.

"Ahhh!" Her hand reflexively clutched at the blanket. "*Haaa... haaah....* Rrgghh." Her mouth and jaw clenched as a shudder went through her. It looked like she was fighting some internal monster. *Wait. That's what it looks like. I've seen something like this.... Gods, no.*

Ore fell into the chair wanting to put his hands over his eyes, but knowing he had to look, had to see... and he did. There, as the fight with the demon inside began to subside somewhat: tears. Tears of the weariness and pain of the fight slipped down Ilena's temple. Last night, she'd cried too, after sleep talking, but the symptoms had been much lesser then, likely due to her being mostly unconscious to begin with right after her injury.

His heart sank. He'd seen this years before. His hand unconsciously touched his chest where he'd been cut deep enough to nearly lose his life.

The Little Death. He'd had compatriots who'd gotten into the stuff. It made them not feel the pain so much. The pain of the world, the pain of the fights. But it's price came at the beginning: a death–like state, sleep talking, then what they said was real pain, burning inside. But when it was over and they woke, the pain they felt was cut by however much they'd taken. Those who took too much felt no pain, but the price for that was death. Only the desperate went that far.

He touched his scar again, taking a ragged breath. He didn't want to believe it. He didn't. But the pattern was the same. Was there anything else, some other symptom to say if it was or wasn't? He tried to remember.

"Kase?" The thin voice whispered into the room.

Ore's head jerked up. Ilena was looking at him with her tawny gold eyes that matched his own. *Oh, yeah. They wake up for a short while, completely alert, then suddenly fall asleep again.* The agony in his heart made it to his face. She was reacting to it just as the candle stub, finally at it's life's end, snuffed out.

"*Haaah*," Ilena sighed. "Well, I'd ask if it was a dream, that was so short, ...but I know what state I'm at, ...so it's not. If you've got questions you ...can manage to get out, ...you'd better do it quick. My hip hurts so bad ...I'm not likely ...to be awake long." The voice was more weak than pained, but then the Little Death should be taking care of that soon.

"How badly does it hurt?" *Why was that my first question?*

"Like ...it's got a small fire in it. Like I want to ...twitch it to cast the coals off, but ...I can't move."

"And you shouldn't. You have to lie still for five weeks, the field surgeon says." Ore wanted to make sure she understood her situation.

"*Haah*. That's a long time."

"Who caused the landslide?" He ought to get as much information as he could.

"Earl Shicchi," Ilena answered promptly.

"How do you know?"

"He didn't tell me. Just told me ...to stay alive ...if I could, ...and laughed as he sent us off. It was one of his bully men ...who made sure ...the driver was dead ...and dropped the boulder on me."

"You saw him?" Ore was hopeful.

"Yes, but not clearly. ...I assume everyone else died?"

"Yes."

A gentle sigh. "Sorry."

"About?"

"I couldn't prevent that," Ilena said sadly.

Ore didn't have anything to say to that. He couldn't know whether it was a lie or not. "Why did you take the Little Death?" he couldn't quite keep the sorrow out of his voice.

"*Haaa...haaa....* I'm afraid ...I'm ...going ...to ...*haaa*–have to tell you ...next ti–m*mmm*." Ilena breathed in pain a few more breaths, although each one slower than the previous, until she was breathing the breaths of deep sleep.

Ore sat there a bit longer, then tiredly set the forgotten candlestick on the desk next to him and crawled into the second bed. She knew she'd taken it, the Little Death. If she didn't get more, if she'd done as the others he'd seen, even her fate would be death regardless of what the surgeon and his mistress were doing for her. He curled up into a ball and the child inside him cried itself to sleep.

CHAPTER 3 The Little Death

"Ore. Ore!"

Ore slid slowly out of darkness. "Hmm?"

"Goodness, I've never seen you sleep so soundly. Was it such a long night?"

"I'd prefer to not have to remember it," he said sourly.

"Eh? Was it so bad? I'm sorry. ...But by the record you made, it looks like everything was okay. She returned to stable by two hours after midnight?" He could hear the rustling of the pages. "Was there anything after the sleep talking? There's nothing written."

"The candle burnt out." He closed his eyes again, wishing he could go back to sleep and really not have to remember the rest.

"Ah, I see."

Ore's eyes suddenly flew open and he turned to see Rei standing next to him, looking down at him, his arms folded in a scold. "How did you do that, Master?"

"What?" Rei asked innocently.

"Sound just like Mistress?"

Rei tilted his head. "Did I?"

Ore considered throwing a curse at Rei, then decided to just let his displeasure show on his face. He wasn't up to using that much energy. Slowly he sat up, rubbing his face. He rested it in his palms, his elbows on his knees, his back pressed against the wall. "Why did you come, Master?" he yawned.

Rei raised his eyebrow. "You're the one that doesn't want anyone to know who you are. I figured you'd like to give your report in private?"

"Ah...right. ...Are you sure it's morning?" Ore couldn't quite get to the state called "awake".

"It's after ten in the morning, Ore. Mizi's already been in and out some time ago. I've got to leave soon, though."

"Oh!" That shock was enough to wake Ore up. He probably hadn't had a sound six hours of sleep in years.

"Yeah. That's what I said!" Rei smiled.

Ore made a sour face again. "Well, one good thing from a bad, then, I guess."

Rei looked at him expectantly. "So...what isn't written?"

"Ha...let's see," Ore leaned his head back against the wall. "The sleep talking: she was protecting Kase from Earl Shicchi. She told the Earl he couldn't have Kase because he was hers from a long time ago, and that she hated him. — That was funny. If she was saying stuff like that at the earldom she should have died a long time ago. — She told Kase to stay alive and get stronger so she could stay alive."

"Was that all?" Rei asked after a pause.

"That was it for the sleep talking. I wrote about it in the book, then was going to go to sleep, when she started to...to cry out as if in pain. It looked like it was hard for her to breathe, so I checked, but it wasn't something I could tell." He closed his eyes. He didn't want to see the pity in Rei's eyes. "I was thinking of calling for Mistress, but then I remembered I'd seen it before. It was something that would pass, and if I wanted to make sure I was right, I needed to just stay and wait."

"Were you right?"

Ore opened his eyes and nodded once, the sour look back. "Shortly after the time of pain, they wake up for a short period and are very aware. I wasn't paying attention to her right at the moment of it, but she called me 'Kase'. I looked up in time to see she was very awake just before the candle snuffed itself out." Ore explained exactly what their conversation had been.

"I asked her why she'd taken the street drug 'the Little Death'." Ore looked into Rei's eyes, his face closed, seeing nothing but the brilliant blue that was focused back on Ore. "She said, as she faded back into sleep, that she'd have to tell me 'next time'. ...There was nothing else for it at that point but to sleep myself. She'd not only had every symptom, she'd admitted she'd taken it."

"*Haah*. The Little Death?" Rei was troubled. "What little I've been told about it, the police and military doctors can't find a way to keep the users alive long enough to question unless they give them more of it, and they have a hard time of doing that if they don't know what dose the user was on."

Ore nodded. "Even if she lives long enough to answer my questions, it's not likely she'll live long enough to make it to Castle Nijou. That's my experience with it ...unless she can tell us her dose and the field surgeon has some here we can give her."

"Could you tell how long she'd been off of it?" Rei asked.

Ore paused, thinking. "She'd been given it that evening. I'm positive of that. Either Miss Alise was a good actress and lying, or someone else slipped in and gave it to her. The timing is right for it to be Miss Alise."

Rei looked thoughtful. "Well, I'm not sure I like the idea of her being involved, instead of locked up for questioning, but until you can get Miss Ilena to tell you her dose, maybe pretending to believe Alise for now? Since she already knows the dose."

"Maybe," Ore said slowly.

"There's a problem with it?"

"At the highest dose, death follows without fail. They can take it three, maybe four days, but it kills the body — the night pain. If Miss Alise gives her that high a dose to take her out, then that's it."

"Did it seem to be that level of dosage last night?"

Ore considered. "No...it seemed to be a rather light dose, actually. She didn't cry out loud enough for the guards to get concerned with me in here with her."

Rei nodded. "Try to get the dosing from Miss Alise tonight. Once you have it, have her arrested for questioning. As long as they seem to be wanting to keep Miss Ilena alive we'll play along."

Ore nodded, his face neutral. "Do you want us to keep her on it until we can get her to the castle for her testimony or do you want me to just get as much evidence from her as possible here?"

Rei paused. "If it's a low enough dose, there's a possibility she can stay alive and be weaned off of it. I'll talk to Ryan about it when I get back and see if he can figure something out, or if he's seen more research on that than I have. But to make sure, do learn from her what you can.

"Also, I want her in the barracks sooner now. At the first possible opportunity, move her. Use the excuse of death by drug withdrawal if you want. If she's already on it, the Earl probably knows, and might be actually expecting to hear of it. It might protect her a little longer to let him think it."

Ore nodded, getting angry again because he knew his brother. "He very well may have been the one to make her take it, actually. If he really relied on her, then that means he didn't want her to be leaving whenever she wanted. If she had to come home to stay alive, that would have been very convenient for him. ...Of course, if he's told them to be keeping her alive now, then she might be just a plant to feed us lies and partial truths."

Rei agreed. He held out his hand to Ore. "Let's go back to the garrison. I want to talk to the Captain one more time, then we need to go. You need to eat, and tell Mizi and Dr. Bonner about Miss Ilena's hip pain."

Ore took his young master's hand and pulled up to standing next to him. He was glad to have these shoulders to lean on today. It was much more easy to take orders and not think. Every experience he'd had with the Little Death had only made him hate it. Learning Ilena was on it put him into too much internal conflict.

-o-o-o-

Rei looked at Mizi. It was kind of odd. It was the first time he was leaving her to take care of Ore in his place, rather than the other way around. He'd called her out to talk to her, leaving Andrew with Ore at the table, eating in the garrison dining room. Mina had come with him and was looking, for her, concerned. "Mizi, ...can I leave Ore in your care?"

"Ore!?"

Rei paused an awkward pause. He couldn't explain it enough. Would she accept that? "Ore...is facing a difficult thing here in this place. Will you help him?" Mizi looked from him through the door at Ore, who was mechanically eating, then back at Rei, surprise and concern written all over her. "It isn't mine to tell you what it is," he shook his head. "I can't stay. Will you, in my place?"

"Of...of course!" Mizi had put her closed hand over her heart and now she clenched it in determination. "I'll do whatever I can!"

Rei reached out to put his hand on her head, then changed his mind and pulled her into a one–armed hug instead.

"R–Rei?" Mizi moved her hands to wrap her arms around him and clutch the back of his cloak.

Rei held her until the emotions in him settled. It was a combination of worry for the man who loved him and had given himself completely to him, even though Rei had bridled him, and a reflexive feeling for how he himself felt whenever he thought of losing Mizi. Even if Ore hadn't seen Ilena in many years, it was obvious from his tears that he'd once loved her. Loved her enough that, seeing her again now, those emotions were still tender and raw.

The one thing that Ore had confided to Rei when he'd first agreed to watch over Mizi was that in House Shicchi was someone who was very dear to him — dear enough that Ore would leave even Rei and Mizi's side if it became necessary to protect that one. This one fit that level of concern, but it had become a complex thing suddenly. It wasn't going to be easy for Ore for a while.

"Thank you," Rei said into Mizi's ear, so close to him. How he longed to have her here whenever he wished. How was he to help that move forward?! His own emotions felt as tender and raw as Ore's. He buried his face in Mizi's hair, momentarily holding her tighter, then he took a deep breath and slowly released her.

As he moved away from her, his right hand slipped down her left arm to catch hold of her two smallest fingers and hold on to them gently. He lifted his left hand to catch hold of a strand of her blazing hair and let it slide lightly though his fingers until he held just the ends.

"It's grown to a beautiful length, Mizi." He smiled, remembering the day they'd met. "It seems longer than the strand I cut for you so you could be free of the brambles." He saw in his mind's eye the same strand, now sitting in a box tucked into the middle drawer of his office desk. "Is it?" He looked into her startled green eyes.

"Eh? Ah! Yes, yes it is. Or rather it's about the same length, I think? I've never been able to grow it much more than this, for some reason, but I don't mind it. To have it too long, it would get in the way of my work, I think."

For some reason Rei's heart twinged. He slowly let the strand slip from his fingers, the smile slipping from his face with it. He pressed more tightly the fingers of her hand he was holding and looked over to Ore. It was time to be going. As it was they wouldn't arrive at the castle until after nightfall.

-o-o-o-

Mina looked at Rei's back as they rode down the hill away from Osterly. He'd paused briefly to look back at the village when they reached the top of the hill, waving at the two specks still standing in the village square where they'd parted. It was more relaxed, but a new worry sat there.

She sighed, then looked over at Andrew who was riding beside her again. He looked over at her, a question on his face. "He asked Mizi to watch over Ore this time," she answered the look.

"Eh? He did?" Andrew was surprised. Mina nodded a brief nod. "Hmm." Andrew looked absently at Rei's back, briefly pondering, then looked back at Mina. "Ore knows the Miss, then?"

Mina nodded again. "It looks that way."

Andrew pondered longer. "For Rei to ask Mizi such a thing.... The Miss and Ore, they look very similar, don't they?" He looked back at Mina. "Do you think it could be family, then?"

Mina looked away from him. Her own heart hurt. "It's a possibility."

-o-o-o-

Mizi and Ore waved one last time to the figures on the hill, and then they were over the other side and lost to view. Mizi sighed and clasped her hands behind her back, staring unfocused at the top of the hill. The brief visit with Rei had been rather normal, and just as normally brief. It was hard to have that still be normal, for all she was glad he was talking to her again.

To distract herself, Mizi turned her eyes to inspect Ore. He'd been a little more subdued than usual, but he also kept yawning. "Was it a long night?"

Ore was just coming out of a yawn. "Eh, what?"

"You seem particularly tired today. Was it a long night?" She kept her voice light and a smile on her face.

"*Hehh.* Well, having to wake up every ten to fifteen minutes is rather difficult, isn't it, Mistress?" He looked at her with one of his sideways smiles. "Just when your body thinks it can rest, you're getting it up again."

"Yes," Mizi smiled. "It can be a difficult pattern to learn. Ah! I know. Why don't you rest in your room for a while. There isn't very much for us to do anyway."

Ore looked at her in surprise. "Then what will Mistress do?"

Mizi laughed a little laugh. "What I always do, Ore! Sit at the desk and read."

"That isn't a healthy thing to be doing, Mistress," Ore frowned, "to be sitting in the dark hunched over your desk all the time will make you into an old lady too soon."

"Ah, then, ...I'll sit out in the courtyard. I know you're supposed to see I'm safe, but where soldiers can see me should be safe enough, don't you think? I promise I won't wander off without taking a guard with me." She started them walking towards the garrison. Ore considered her. She was trying too hard, but it was as she said. He was too tired.

She threw out her last gambit. "Besides, you're going to have to sit next to Miss Ilena again tonight, aren't you? Since Rei has said I mayn't." She frowned just a little. She'd do it just to help Ore if she could. "So you need to rest today during the day. If the same thing happens again, tonight will likely be just as hard. I think it took me five nights in a row to be able to learn that pattern of monitoring a patient."

She watched Ore closely. He'd put on a disinterested air, as if it didn't bother him that much, but he wouldn't look at her. "Well, I am used to not sleeping much, after all," he said, "but if it will make Mistress feel better, I'll rest some more. After all, Ore is also naturally lazy as well."

She smiled a rewarding smile at him. "That's not true. Ore is always working hard. If he doesn't rest, Rei will get angry." She paused and looked at him threateningly, "And so will I."

"Ah, ah! Mistress! I'll sleep! I don't want you angry with me." Ore waved his hands at her, laughing, trying to erase the threat.

They'd been given rooms in the wing near the surgery, not too far from Doctor Bonner's own room. The rooms were patient recovery rooms with two beds each. Mizi had requested it so that they could be close to Ilena when she was able to be moved there. Ore hadn't been in his yet, the need to have someone watching over Ilena having prevented that.

"Look, Ore!" Mizi said brightly as she entered his room, "They gave us adjoining rooms." Ore looked where she was pointing. Sure enough, there was a door connecting the two rooms. "Call me if you need me, okay, Ore?" she said.

"Isn't it supposed to be the other way 'round?" Ore protested.

Mizi put her hands on her hips. "Good night, Ore. I promise I'll be good."

Ore smiled at her sheepishly, one hand behind his head. "Good night, Mistress. Call me when you're ready to go and do the evening check."

"I'll call you for dinner. You have to eat right, too." She mock frowned at him as she paused, ready to close the door behind herself for him.

"Yes, Mistress," he said obediently as he lay down on the bed.

The door clicked closed behind Mizi. Ore curled up into a ball again and quickly fell into the darkness that had followed close beside him since his master had called him awake. He felt grateful his mistress had forced him to obedience. The light of day was a little too painful at the moment.

Mizi frowned. Ore had been his usual teasing self, but behind that front he wore it seemed there might be something else there. What did Ore need? Her circled hand went to her heart. It wasn't good that she hadn't been able to see on her own that he needed something. She was too used to being taken care of. Her fist clenched. She would have to do a better job from now on, of being aware of Ore.

When Rei had returned to the garrison that morning with Ore, Ore had been rather stiff and formal, but Mizi had assumed it was because Rei had given him the order to talk to Doctor Bonner and her about what had happened that night and he was giving his report. He always gave his verbal reports in a formal manner, particularly to outsiders.

But, now that she thought about it, he'd given Rei his first report in Ilena's recovery room just as formally. That wasn't normal, was it? And then Rei had sent the rest of them from the room. Her stomach clenched. Rei had known just from Ore's written report that had brought Rei here. She was definitely going to have to work harder!

Mizi leaned against the wall outside their rooms, her hands clasped behind her, and looked up at the walkway ceiling above her, thinking. How far back? Ore had seemed very surprised to hear that Ilena was the Earl's steward. She had been, too, so hadn't remarked it.

After a few minutes of consideration, Mizi shook her head and pushed away from the wall. There really hadn't been anything odd in Ore's behavior before he'd learned Ilena's name and position. Since then, he'd seemed somewhat restless, but other than that fairly normal. Until Rei had come. She paced down the corridor a few doors then back, not wanting to go too far.

Mizi thought about the young woman they were watching over. The captain had said she'd been the steward of Tokumade for seven years. Based on how young she looked, that meant she had to have been still in her teens when she began. Given the reputation she'd been hearing about the Earl, that was not a small achievement. Ilena must have worked very hard from a very young age. ...That might make people who knew the denizens of the Earldom know her, but how did Ore know her?

Mizi frowned. She knew nothing about Ore's past, except the one time that they'd run into a colleague of his who was a bounty hunter. That was it. If ever she asked about it, he only laughed and said that it wasn't the path he followed now, so to pay it no mind. It seemed like it might have been shady, but Ore himself didn't seem to hold much emotion for that part of his life. But for Rei to have taken his reins, Rei would have had to know something about it.

Being an orphan most of her own life, until they discovered that her father was in hiding for opposing a corrupt lord and was the leader of the Raionmure of Yamanzar, Mizi had assumed that Ore was an orphan as well. Maybe he was, but that didn't mean he didn't have family. Was Ilena family to him? Like with her, who had never expected to see any of her family again, had he suddenly been presented with evidence that one was still alive?

Mizi nodded. That would make sense. To first see Ilena again in such a state of near–death would likely have been really shocking. Well, if that was the case, he wouldn't have to worry about her while he was worried about Ilena. She would see that they both recovered.

-o-o-o-

Mizi woke Ore for an early dinner, thinking that it would be wise to be at Ilena's side before Alise arrived there. After dinner Ore suggested they go by Alise's place and pick her up. She was at her home, but terribly nervous. Mizi said kindly that her help was very much appreciated, that the woodworker had been helpful, and would she please come help again? Alise was self–deprecating in return.

Ore finally said, "Go ahead and bring the usual beverage along. It's been approved."

Alise's eyes got misty. "Thank you very much," she bowed deeply. She retrieved a small closed wooden cylinder from the kitchen.

Ore found that response very interesting. If Alise knew what the liquid was, it was a little odd that she would be so tenderly caring of Ilena. Unless this particular person didn't want Ilena to suffer death. If that was the case, then — just maybe — it would be alright. "You wouldn't perhaps be able to tell us how much she's taking, so we can take over, could you?"

Alise squeaked and denied any knowledge, only saying she'd been given it by delivery, and knew nothing else, other than Ilena would die if she weren't given it. Ore frowned a bit, but there wasn't much he could do otherwise for the moment. He refused to answer Mizi's curious looks that went between him and Alise, not willing to even look in her face.

They went to Ilena's recovery room for the usual evening ritual. Mizi said that Ilena's wound felt a little warm, potentially indicating some level of infection. She asked Alise for the 'water' to infuse some of the infection fighting herbs in, and Alise poured it into the glass.

Ore picked it up and looked at it closely. It really did look just like the water they'd seen in Alise's house, and smelled like it too, but he didn't taste it, and he didn't let Mizi either. Was it just such a low dose that there would be no clue other than the night reaction? He'd never actually seen anyone take it previously, after all, just had to live with the night effects later.

Alise was looking nervous again, but he ignored her and told Mizi it was okay to use, handing her the glass. Alise relaxed a bit. Ore turned and looked at Alise. "I'll be staying the night again — and expecting to be able to find you at home in the morning." Alise gulped and nodded, her eyes wide, her hands clasped in front of her chest.

This time, all three of them stayed in the room until Ilena had reached her hibernation plateau, then Ore walked both young ladies back to their respective sleeping places. "See you tomorrow, Miss Alise," he waved at her as they left. The grin he gave her was more predatory than friendly. She bowed and closed the door.

Mizi sighed. "I understand that you still think she needs to be under investigation, but I do wish you didn't have to be so frightening towards her."

"Mmm.... Sorry if it bothers you, Mistress. I thought it better than just summarily locking her up," Ore deprecated.

"*Haah*. Well, I suppose that wouldn't be kind since I don't really have any evidence she's done anything wrong."

"Well, within a few days, we'll probably know, eh?"

As Ore and Mizi walked back into the medical wing of the garrison, she frowned. "Let's go talk to Doctor Bonner about Ilena before we end the day." Ore followed her obediently, always content to follow where she wanted to go.

The doctor was in his quarters, preparing to end his day, but he let them in cordially. "Doctor Bonner," Mizi said, "I'm concerned. The hip was warm to the touch this evening. I've given Miss Ilena some more herbs to help fight infection, but she's having a repeat of last night's odd hibernation. Her temperature has dropped quite low and I'm sure that doesn't help her body fight off infection. I'm concerned it may blossom quickly."

"Hmm...that could be very likely," Dr. Bonner stroked his chin. "You'll be staying with her again, Sir Ore?"

Ore nodded. "Master asked that we move Miss Steward into the garrison as soon as possible. I was wondering, other than the strain of moving an ill patient, what was your reasoning for keeping her in the village hall?"

Bonner raised an eyebrow. "In order to keep the hip from moving so that the bones have time to knit back together."

"You said that you would likely have to do another surgery, is that right?"

"Yes, that's right."

"Then would it be possible to move her to this location here to perform that surgery? You would be able to reset any bones that moved during the transport at that time."

Bonner tapped a finger on his chin in thought. "That might be a possibility. I suppose we could even move her tonight, since it's looking like it will have to happen soon anyway."

Ore considered the possible plans. "Master wants it to look like she's died somewhere around that point, so as to throw the Earl, or whomever killed the Earl's Lady, off the trail of trying to remove Miss Steward."

"Well," said Bonner thoughtfully, "now, while the blood flow is reduced, the infection won't spread. It would be best if we completed the surgery before she comes out of the hibernation stage."

Mizi nodded. "I'd like to help, if I may."

Bonner raised his eyebrow at her. "You don't shirk at the sight of blood, Lady Mizi."

Mizi shrugged. "I can't do my work if I were to do that, Doctor Bonner."

He smiled at her pluck. "Well, then go and get changed into very clean, simple clothes, and meet me in the surgery room. The less dirt we add to the wound site, the better."

Mizi nodded and crossed the hall to her room. Bonner turned to Ore, a very serious expression on his face. "We'll need to take Miss Ilena off the Little Death, Sir Ore. Lady Mizi is correct. If we continue to allow regular temperature drops, even with the surgery to remove any further foreign objects, she may still die of infection. Is the dose low enough?"

Ore shrugged, worried. "I don't know for sure. I was supposed to find out tonight when she wakes up if she knew herself. But if the liquid Miss Alise brought tonight was indeed the Little Death, it was so faint as to be undifferentiated from water. Miss Alise claimed to not know it either."

Doctor Bonner thought carefully. "It's likely that if it's low enough she should be able to survive for at least a few days, and maybe wean herself from it without any further aid from us at all. If you could get the dosage, that would certainly help matters, but I don't want to keep giving it to her."

Ore looked at Doctor Bonner quizzically. "Do you have some of it to give her?"

Doctor Bonner nodded. "The Captain confiscated some a few months ago. Regent Rei asked him to give it to me to aid Miss Ilena."

"I'll do my best," Ore said. "I'll go and have a wagon prepared to bring Miss Steward here and come with her."

"Alright. We'll meet you in the surgery room." Doctor Bonner went back into his room to change back into appropriate clothing and Ore headed to get the transportation started.

Before stopping at the garrison stables and requisitioning a wagon to transport Ilena, Ore stopped by the office of the Captain to briefly explain the plan, including the farce that Ilena should 'die' on the operating table, and to ask for additional soldiers to accompany the wagon to protect Ilena.

Grey raised an eyebrow. "Then what excuse will you and Lady Mizi give to remain here at the garrison?"

"Ah," he hadn't thought of that. "Is it something the men can keep quiet?"

The captain nodded. "But if you leave the garrison, the villagers will know, and it would be easier if only a limited number of men actually knew you were here."

Ore agreed. "I guess it will be enforced imprisonment by choice for Mistress and me in the medical wing then, won't it?"

The Captain gave him a searching look. "Not by order?"

Ore smiled his practiced disarming smile at him, learned to divert people from focusing on him. "Nope." He waved and left for the garrison stables.

-o-o-o-

Inside Ilena's room, she was still in her deep sleep. Ore checked her vitals. They were still low, but the heartbeat seemed just a little irregular. He moved the covers off her wound and checked it. It was looking more raw and red than it had when they'd left earlier that evening and it was warmer to the touch than the rest of her body. He covered her again, then made her and the bed ready, pulling the bed sheet out so that the soldiers could lift her by lifting the corners of it.

Securing the medical record and other items that pertained to her being in that place, he opened the door and ordered the soldiers in a loud voice to send for the field surgeon, that Miss Steward was suddenly doing very poorly. One of the guards ran off towards the garrison. The other stood carefully alert, and even Ore held his throwing daggers at the ready. This would be a perfect time for an ambush, if one was ready.

In short order, the town hall was emptied and surrounded by soldiers. The guard came back and told Ore that the wagon was nearly there. Ore looked worriedly at Ilena. She had a faint sheen of sweat on her brow now. He quickly took her vitals again. The heartbeat was more erratic and her breathing, while still slow, had increased and was becoming ragged, and she was clammy and cooler.

"Get them in here as soon as possible. She may not make it to the surgery room," Ore said. The guard got it, and yelled to the guards at the door to have them hurry it up. There was a small flood of guards entering the hall with a stretcher, and then they were in the room. Quickly they moved Ilena to the mobile bed then they were sprinting to the door.

The ride to the garrison was short but chaotic. Ore rode with Ilena and watched her closely. Later, Captain Grey told him that there had been a brief clash with a small number of rough looking men, but it had seemed like they were more interested in confirming if the passenger on the wagon was Ilena than in doing her in. Once they'd confirmed it, they'd broken off and fled as a group.

The few captured claimed they weren't there to fight, just to confirm whether Ilena was alive or not. "All for the sake of poor Earl Shicchi, who was so grief stricken at the death of his wife and the life–threatening injury to his faithful steward that he was unable to rise from his bedchamber." Ore could only remember that he held on to Ilena's wrist, constantly feeling for her pulse, and watched her chest to count her breathing, willing her to live.

As the guards carried her into the outer surgery room, Ore shed his boots and his jacket. The surgeon tossed him a long medical coat that he threw on over his other clothes and he tied a large handkerchief over his hair. He quickly washed his hands thoroughly and entered the surgery room.

By then, Mizi was helping Bonner prepare Ilena. Ore took up residence next to Ilena's head on the right side to be out of their way. He went back to holding Ilena's wrist and counting her breaths. Once he had the current baseline, he called it out to them, then started counting again.

Bonner raised an eyebrow. "One would think you two had been in the surgery room before."

Mizi nodded. "Not much, but a few times in Kouzanshi. We learned clean room procedures there."

Bonner held the tools of his trade over Ilena and took a breath. "Well, let's get started, then, shall we?"

The surgery was detailed and meticulous, with lots of washing out of the wound to remove the infection and loosen any more rock and bone particles. They were easier to find now that the body itself had attacked them, marking them for what they were. Bonner shifted the hip bones just slightly, pleased with the progress they were making. Then it was time to look at the tendons again.

That was more tricky. He'd set the two outer tendons right, but couldn't decide how to handle the main tendon. He finally decided on trying taking a portion of living tendon from the the back side of the hip, wrapping it over the hip bone, and stitching it to the part of the tendon that was still attached to the main leg muscle.

It didn't look like it would work, but it might and he needed to try something. Bonner put the rest of Ilena back together again, making sure that when her heartbeat was strong again it wouldn't cause the wound area to fill with blood, and stitched the outer wound closed. "Well, that's that," he sighed. "Now it's wait and see what her body does."

"Do you think your trick for the tendon will work, Doctor Bonner?" Mizi asked. She applied her poultice to the wound and bandaged it while Bonner cleaned himself and his tools. After watching the surgeon, she was glad Ilena was in a state of deep unconsciousness. It all looked very painful.

"No," he answered bluntly, "but a lot of surgery is experimentation and doing what one can. Typically, when the tendon has torn off the bone like that, there's nothing that can be done. But I'd rather try something that has even a slight possibility of working than not try anything at all. That's how we learn, after all."

Mizi nodded. That was how a lot of things had gotten done at Kouzanshi, the center for research in Ryokudo, too. Study, educated guesses, trial and error, repeated over and over until a thing was found to work. "Do we keep Miss Ilena in here tonight?" she asked.

Bonner looked at his patient thoughtfully. "For now. ...How much longer do we have, Sir Ore?"

Ore asked him what time it was, having lost all sense of it in his focus on the timing of Ilena's breaths and heartbeats. After he was told and calculated, he answered, "We have about an hour or less until she begins to rouse. Two hours to come out of the hibernation state, if it holds true. ...Another half an hour before the screaming starts, if the pain from the surgery doesn't start it at the three hour mark."

The field surgeon nodded. "It likely will. We can't give her anything to kill the pain of the surgery until she gets to the awareness state. It simply isn't possible."

"*Haa*, that's four hours out still."

Ore and Mizi looked at each other. It was obvious they both wanted to tell the other to go get rest. Bonner raised his hand. "Don't fight. It isn't possible. Just both of you stay here. Doze in your chairs if you need to, but be prepared to have your hearts ripped out by her screaming. If you've never heard the screams of the dying it will be more than you're prepared for. ...And when it's a woman, it's the worst.

"I'm going to bed. Her screams will wake me, but I'll stay there unless you come get me, if it's all the same to you. Sir Ore, you know the sign to look for. Lady Mizi, prepare the pain killing medicine between midnight and one. Sir Ore will let you know when it's time to give it to her." Ore and Mizi nodded their understanding.

"We'll move her to Sir Ore's room when we declare her 'dead' and announce that we're keeping the body in cold storage for further investigation. At that point, you two are under house arrest, so to speak, if you want her kept safe."

Ore shook his head tiredly. "I've got one more thing to go do in the morning — as part of the investigation it won't look strange — and I need to bring my horse to the stable here. Then we'll have a couple of guards ride off, as if us, or something." That detail was too blurry to think about tonight.

Bonner nodded, "Well, then, good luck tonight." He left for his room and distance between him and the screams still to come.

Ore and Mizi looked at each other for a long moment, then sighed. "Well, he is right. It's no use, is it?" Ore said.

Mizi nodded, "And he did say it will take both of us to give her the pain medication."

Ore nodded back. "Well, then, we should at least rest while we can." He stood up from his chair and stretched. He'd gotten rather cramped sitting in one position for over an hour. He fetched a chair for Mizi and set it down where she indicated when he asked her where she wanted to be.

For a while it was quiet while Mizi caught the medical journal up to date to their current time, then she handed it to Ore, who made his notations in it. They sat quietly for a while after that. Finally Mizi ventured, "Ore...is she...family to you?"

Ore looked at her out of the corner of his eye without moving, slightly surprised at the question. "Did Master talk to you?"

"Only to say that he was concerned and ask me to watch out for you," she admitted, chagrined. "I'm sorry I didn't notice before."

"You weren't supposed to," Ore said a little coolly. Mizi was sorry she'd asked.

Ore looked away from her, up to the top of the wall opposite them. "A distant cousin," he finally answered. "I haven't seen her since we were very young. I'd prefer if she didn't learn who I was."

"I'm sorry, Ore. ... But...that seems very sad." Mizi had been very happy to meet with her father.

"It will only bring us both lots of trouble in the end. She doesn't know the name Ore, so it shouldn't trouble you much."

"Alright. If that's what you want."

"It is."

-o-o-o-

Ore was dozing when his senses went on alert. He was still subconsciously counting Ilena's breaths. They'd risen to near normal and were sounding harsh. Mizi was resting her arms and head on the bed next to Ilena. He shook her until she was awake. "It's time to prepare the pain relief medication, Mistress. Miss Steward will begin her pain sequence soon." Mizi obediently went to the small side table she'd set her supplies on and began preparing the medication.

Ore watched Ilena closely. He could see it coming. What would she say today, if anything? Or would it go right to the pain?

"My lord!"

Mizi looked up startled. "What is it, Ore?"

"It's alright, Mistress. It starts with dreaming and talking the dream out loud. If she can do that without screaming —"

"Aaahhhh! Please, my lord!" Mizi was paralyzed. "Please, my lord, I don't know. *gasp* I really don't know! Aaahhh!" Ilena's body arched and Ore leaped up to stabilize her lower half so she wouldn't throw the pieces of hip bones back out of alignment. Ilena breathed hard for a few breaths, then it began again.

"He didn't...I swear he didn't! I haven't seen Kase since dinner, my lord. I swear it! ...Aaaahhhh!" She fought to arch again. Ore held her weakened body still, although the pain gave it some strength. He couldn't look at her face, instead choosing to look at his hands, working hard to control his fierce anger and hide his guilt.

Ore held Ilena as her screams continued, occasionally punctuated by dry sobs, each one punishing him for leaving her behind. She didn't speak again, though. He knew she hadn't been allowed to. Punishment was merciless when the Earl was angry. Then she was still, her ragged breathing very loud in the sudden quiet. Ore was about to let her go when she chuckled lightly. He froze, and looked up into her face. Was she awake already?

She wasn't. *What's this?* Ilena laughed, as if to herself. "You bastard. You've done it to yourself. He's finally free. Like I'd ever tell you where he was, even if I knew. I'm glad of it.

"And I know you. You've left me alive, you'll keep me alive forever, now, just in the hope of getting him back. That's all the space I need to bring you crashing down. I've learned what patience can do to a House, how it can canker slowly from the inside. I can be patient for as long as it takes."

Ilena laughed. "I've won already, bastard Pakyo. Kase has freed himself so that I'm now free to move against you. Free...," she faded out.

Ore stared at her in shock. One crazy thought finally made it through. *Wasn't she, like, only eleven at the time?*

Mizi's hand thumped to the table. Breathing as if for the first time in a while, she fought herself. "Was that it, Ore? Is it time?" Her other hand was curled at her heart.

Ore shook his head. "No what's to come will be worse, most likely."

"Worse!?"

Ore risked a glance at her and nodded. "But no talking. All screaming." His face was grim. Mizi shook, then as determinedly as she could began working on her medication again. It had to be done by the time the next set of screaming was done.

It took more strength this time to keep Ilena still through the repayment pain of the Little Death with the addition of the pain of the surgery, but it didn't seem like Alise had given her a larger dose than before. When it had gone on for about the same amount of time as it had the night before, Ore started watching Ilena's eyes closely. "Mistress it should be about time."

Mizi jumped. She'd finally closed her ears as best she could, losing her mind and focus into her work, putting the screams into the background as much as possible. Ore's words surprised her back into reality. "Ah, ah, right." She quickly poured out the medication into a small cup and took it to stand next to Ilena's head, ready to give it to her, trembling slightly.

"As soon as the tears drop from her eyes, you'll have a few breaths, then she'll become conscious. Look for the fluttering of the eyelids. At that time, you can lift her head and give her the medication." Ore released Ilena's hip, but stood ready to hold it down again, if necessary.

Both battered nurses watched Ilena closely. The screams had subsided, but her whole body was obviously still wracked with pain. Then she began to relax little by little and the tears began to leak out of her eyes. Mizi leaned down close to Ilena's ear. "Miss Ilena. I'm Mizi, Court Healer for Regent Rei. I have some pain medication for you. Please, drink it. It will help ease the pain of the hip surgery."

Ilena sobbed once as Mizi lifted her head and began to help pour the liquid down her throat, going slowly so as to allow Ilena to swallow it. When it was gone, Mizi lay Ilena's head back down on the mattress. She was so worn out from the efforts of fighting the pain, Ore wasn't sure the awareness period would last long.

"Rei?" Ilena asked hoarsely.

"Regent Rei has returned to the castle, Miss Ilena," Mizi said. "I'm staying at Osterly barracks with you."

"Then who?" Ilena asked, turning her head towards Ore's direction. It looked like her eyes weren't capable of seeing tonight.

Ore reached out, his head bowed, and touched the back of her hand with the back of his hand, his middle finger wrapping around her middle finger. "Ah." Ilena sighed. "Kase. ...Thank you."

Ore was quiet for a while, then said, "Mistress, she's sleeping again, and will sleep until morning, or longer given her state. We may rest now." He released Ilena's finger and placed his hand on hers instead.

Mizi slumped. "Doctor Bonner wasn't kidding. That was probably the most difficult thing I've had to go through, other than when I was kidnapped."

Ore, still looking down, said warningly, "It isn't over, Mistress. I'm sorry."

Mizi's head lurched up. "What?" she breathed.

"This is the nightly progress of a terrible street drug called 'the Little Death'." He spoke as if giving a small lecture, devoid of emotion. "Taken in it's normal doses, if a user doesn't keep taking it, they die. The night pains get worse until they tear up the body if they try to stop using it. The higher the dose they use, the faster the night pains kill them. As near as I've been able to determine, Miss Steward is taking a light dose." Mizi's eyes bugged out to have it called only a *light* dose.

"It has to be given every twenty–four hours. The only one who could have been giving it to her is Miss Alise, as the progress begins within a half hour of dosing. Master required of me that I make it clear to Miss Alise she was to continue with the dosing for the time being. In the morning I'll visit Miss Alise to try to get from her again, if I can, the dosing she's been making.

"It's required knowledge if the surgeon is to help Miss Steward survive the coming days. If she can be successfully weaned off the drug, then this nightly process will fade away. If she can't, the surgeon will either have to put her back on the drug and they'll continue nightly for the rest of her life, or she will die."

Ore looked emotionlessly at Mizi. "The night pains will continue, but the pain of the hip surgery will heal and pass with time, so not all of the nights will be as bad as this one. For probably a couple more, at least, I would guess, we'll have difficult nights. I'm sorry I wasn't to tell you until now." Ore was very tired.

Mizi sat down with a thump in the chair Ore had occupied earlier. This was a lot to take in after everything else. That it was going to continue...*nightly!?* Finally she put her hand to her temple. "I'll think about this in the morning. It's too much tonight."

Ore nodded. He replaced the covers over Ilena neatly while Mizi cleaned up her tools and herbs she'd made the medicine with. She paused and looked at Ore, "Would it help to give her the pain medication before she goes into the Little Death?"

Ore shrugged. "I don't know, Mistress. Maybe Doctor Bonner knows." Mizi nodded. She'd ask him in the morning. "Let me walk you to your room, Mistress. I have one more thing I must do."

Mizi wearily walked to the door, trailing Ore. "Oh, the book."

Ore looked at it. "I'll get it later" he said, opening the door. Ore walked Mizi to her room, then leaned against the outside of the door, listening until she'd climbed into her bed. He went into his room. They'd given him a two-bed room. He removed the top sheet and blanket from the bed on the wall farthest from Mizi's room. He hated to have Ilena's screams that close to her at night, but he was ordered to have Ilena with him.

When he was satisfied, he went out to Doctor Bonner's room to report briefly and tell him that he was going to move Ilena to his room now. Bonner nodded sleepily. "Did the Lady make it okay?" he nodded his head at Mizi's room. "It didn't sound as bad as it could have."

"She's shaken, but she'll be okay in the morning," Ore said tiredly but confidently. He knew his mistress.

"Well, call for four to lift and carry Miss Ilena on the stretcher. I don't want to have to go in again." Ore agreed wholeheartedly.

It took another fifteen minutes to get soldiers gathered and move Ilena into his room. He swore them to secrecy and made them the guards on his room and on the entrance to the medical wing for the rest of the night. Putting the medical record book on the little desk in his room and pulling off his boots and jacket again, he fell into his bed and deep sleep for the second night in a row.

CHAPTER 4 The Steward is Dead

Ore woke in the morning feeling a bit like he had a hangover. He wasn't sure since he hadn't had one since he was very young. Alcohol had always been the drink of choice for the Shicchi family, even for the young.

He sighed and rolled over to sit on the edge of his bed, rubbing his face with his hands. Dropping his hands to rest on the bed beside him, he looked over at the bed on the other side of the room. Ilena was still breathing at least. He got up, washed to finish waking, and dressed for the day.

"Well, now," he said to the sleeping form of Ilena, "to take care of you." When he'd confirmed the state of the wound, he took her vitals and updated the medical record, mechanically writing quickly. He knocked on the adjoining door to Mizi's room, and hearing nothing, peeked his head in. She was still sleeping soundly.

He quietly entered the room and dropped the medical record on her desk, then left just as soundlessly back to his own room. It wouldn't do to have the guards see him leave Mizi's room. That would get him in trouble with Rei.

"Stay there," he told Ilena. "I'll be right back." He wondered if she was conscious enough to be laughing inside. Probably not. It wasn't that good a joke anyway.

Ore headed for the garrison dining room first, grabbing up an apple and a hunk of cheese. Munching alternately between them, he walked through the garrison and headed for Alise's house. It looked like it was mid–morning. That worked, although he didn't know if Alise would be home. *Wonder what she does during the day?* The thought was idle.

His eyes were sweeping the village, catching every dim shadow, every furtive movement. In particular, he wanted to see if someone was entering or leaving the area of Alise's house, or if it was being watched. He was certain he'd picked up at least one tail, and every idle shadow–hugger watched him as he walked. This little village wasn't big enough for this many of them. Someone definitely wanted to know what was going to happen next.

The problem was, Ore wasn't sure himself. He couldn't quite work up the energy to put on a show of being angry or upset at the moment, which was probably the right way to go about it. He finally settled himself with leaning against a wall, one foot up on it, his arms crossed, looking broody.

From here, he could see Alise's house from the side. That way he would know if someone came or went from the front or the back. It was an obvious stakeout, for the sake of his tails, but really he just wanted time to think. If he got to see something useful, well, so much the better, but he doubted it would happen.

Finally he sighed. Nothing was coming to mind. Well, cold expression-lessness was often just as useful as hot anger. He knocked on Alise's door. *She actually answered it*, Ore was mildly surprised. He slowly lowered his hand that had been about to knock again. "May I come in?"

"Master Ore. Y–yes, please." She ushered him in, closing the door behind her. The front room was small and simply furnished.

Ore did his automatic sweep of the room and the house. One person upstairs in a bed. Maybe she took care of an older family member and that was why she was home. One person hiding very quietly in the kitchen. Had that person been waiting since morning for him to come? Well, that made the task easier then, didn't it?

Ore set his back to the door, standing close enough to it to run if he needed to, although there wasn't a sense of a threat, just of observation, coming from the kitchen. "Miss Alise, what is the dosing of the Little Death Miss Steward was on?"

Alise took in a sharp breath and tightened her fists, which were clutched in front of her skirt. She looked directly in his eyes, her eyes pleading. "I'm very sorry, Master Ore. I don't know."

"Does the person in the kitchen know?"

Alise startled quite badly, but Ore didn't move. She shook her head violently. "N...n–n–no, Master Ore."

His eyes narrowed. "You're very certain?"

"Y–y–yes, Master Ore. We're only delivery persons."

"But the person who makes it knew I would be coming today to ask." He stated it as fact and her body didn't deny it. "Why didn't that person tell you?" He could feel the panic of the person in the kitchen rising as that person's breathing rate increased.

"I...I don't know, Master Ore," her shoulders slumped in defeat and tears started to well up in her eyes. "I don't want Mistress Ilena to die, Master Ore. If I could help you, I would."

"Have you received today's delivery?"

"Ah...yes." It was almost a whisper.

"I'll take it," he ordered her. Alise curtsied and turned quickly to the kitchen. She returned shortly with a canister like the one she'd brought to the recovery room the night before.

"See you tell them not to deliver any more," Ore ordered her as he took the container.

"Why? Won't Miss Ilena be needing it?" He could see that Alise was very afraid, but she had enough courage to look him in the eye when she asked it.

Ore was coldly silent for a moment. "The steward died because of the Little Death last night. It interfered with her healing. She will not return to the Earl."

He stared at Alise a moment longer as her eyes went very wide and then tears started to fall. He turned and walked out the door, closing it behind him. He could hear her sobbing into her hands and the faint footsteps of the person in the kitchen quietly coming to comfort her. He raised his head to the sky and breathed out a deep breath, closing his eyes briefly.

Well, that was done, and it went about as he expected. He tucked the canister into his jacket and walked slowly to the village stables where he collected his horse and paid the difference he owed. He led Fenrier past the village hall without looking at it — really without looking at anything, aware only of the people in the shadows watching him, the people in the light moving out of his way.

When he was at the garrison, he left Fenrier with the stable hand there, asking for him to be prepared for departure, and returned to his and his mistress' quarters. Word started to spread that Missus Ilena, Steward of the Earldom of Tokumade, had died and Master Ore, rumored missing heir of the same, was heartbroken.

-0-0-0-

"Mistress! Mistress!" Ore knocked on Mizi's door from the outside hallway. "Have you woken yet? It's nearing time to leave."

He heard stirring on the other side of the door. "Time to leave?" came muffled through it.

"Yes, Mistress. Master will be waiting for us. We shouldn't be arriving too much after dark or he'll worry."

"Ah, just a moment," he could hear Mizi throwing on some clothes and washing her face quickly. Then she opened the door, her eyes wide, "Ore? What...?"

He put his finger to his lips. "May I come in briefly and help you pack, Mistress?"

"Eh, ah...yes, please," Mizi answered, letting him in. Once the door was closed behind her she asked, "So...what are we doing?"

Ore sighed. "Somehow we are going to leave with everyone noticing. Then we are going to arrive without anyone noticing. I'm afraid I have to admit to not being able to consider it properly at the moment." He yawned.

"Ore, that was a *very* big yawn," Mizi scolded. "You didn't sleep properly, did you?"

"Perhaps it is that I slept too much," he yawned again. "I'm not used to sleeping so deeply as I have the last two days."

"If we're 'ready to go', does that mean you've talked to Miss Alise?"

"Yes. She was unable to tell me anything, but she did give me today's dosing," Ore answered, handing over the canister, "but I didn't think she would be able to. She did tell me that there was a middleman who delivered it to her from the person who made it, so there are probably several layers of persons between to make it difficult to track down the person who really knows.

"Miss Alise, herself, doesn't want any harm to come to Miss S...Miss Ilena, but isn't capable of helping beyond what she's been able to do this far." Ore sighed, "So I've sent back up the chain that the Steward has died to the Little Death last night and won't return to the Earl. It will be up to Mistress and the surgeon to keep Miss Ilena alive for Master's sake, ...but he did ask the little Mister to help."

"Oh, he asked Ryan?" That was a ray of hope for Mizi, who was feeling a bit helpless about a drug she'd never heard of before that previous night.

Ore nodded. "Also, Master ordered the surgeon to provide whatever you need of the Little Death the Captain confiscated some time ago in order to keep Miss Ilena alive long enough to bear testimony against the Earl, if it's possible."

"So we have access to some? ...Ore," she said very carefully, and his warning bells went off and he went on alert, "how is it that I, who need to know these things so that I can be of help because I am here in the place to be of help, know these things last? Surely a task of such import and difficulty should not generally be left until the last minute to comprehend and complete."

"Ah...!" He fished for the right way to respond. Abject humility was the only way. He bowed deeply. "You are correct, Mistress. I'm very sorry." He would have to be very sure this righteous anger of Mizi's was conveyed in his next report to Rei...after all, he should also be prepared for her anger the next time they met. This was not a small matter for her.

"Go check on Miss Ilena. I'll go speak with Doctor Bonner," she ordered, picking up the medical record book off her desk. "I'll come for you after that."

"Yes, Mistress." Ah, he was being sent to his room for being naughty. Mizi even pointed at the door between their rooms and waited until Ore had bowed himself through and closed it.

He heard her sigh a frustrated sigh and exit her room. He leaned his forehead against the door between their rooms, listening to her walk down the short distance to the surgeon's office, knock, announce herself, and be admitted. He turned his head slightly so he could just see Ilena. "You know, you're getting to be quite troublesome," he told her. "For all our sakes, I hope you stay alive."

"I'm sorry. I plan to."

Ore jumped. Up into the upper corner of the room where he'd been standing, holding himself in position as if waiting to land on the next person to walk through the door. His unconscious reactions had him back on the floor again in a crouch before his mind registered that he'd even scanned the room for attackers and seeing none, had let himself drop.

Ilena had an amused smile on her tired face. "That was an interesting reaction. I think I might need to be grateful that there aren't several daggers sticking out of me as well." He'd seen her face and she'd been looking at him when he was up on the ceiling, but now that he was on the floor she could only see him slightly by turning her head.

Ore took one long slow breath, willing his heart to calm, sliding his throwing knives back into their sheaths. "Indeed," he said coldly. Standing, he stared at her, his eyes hard. "Next time, you will."

"Understood," her voice was apologetic, but it was also still tinged with amusement.

For some reason, the first contact he'd had with Rei's older brother rippled across his memory. He'd been running an errand for Rei, when a foot out of nowhere had tripped him. He'd caught himself though he'd come down wrong on one ankle, but he'd not seen the attacker before or after. It had been Rei who'd told him it had been his older brother, testing him. It rankled that it felt like Ilena had just tested him and he'd passed it just as badly, by his own standards.

"Why are you awake?" Ore asked Ilena, walking to her and lifting her arm to take her pulse.

"It doesn't hurt? ...What are you doing?"

"Measuring your heart rate. One of the odd jobs your presence has required is that I'm now a nurse."

"Oohhh." She waited quietly while he counted and calculated, and then measured her temperature.

"It really doesn't hurt?" Ore asked neutrally.

"No, but then the court healer did give me a painkiller on top of the painkiller I'd already taken. I shouldn't think it too odd."

Ore turned the desk chair and sat on it so that he was leaning over the back of it to talk to Ilena. "Let's talk about that second painkiller, shall we?"

"What would you like to know?" Ilena asked obligingly.

Ore started to ask a question, then stopped. There were rather a lot of things he needed to know about and several he wanted to know. What was the most important? They didn't really have a lot of time at the moment, but would, or potentially could, have more later. *It's that then, isn't it?* "What dose are you on and how do we get you off of it altogether?"

"Hmm... I'll tell you, but go open your door first."

?? But her eyes were closed. Ore got up and opened the door to find Mizi just walking up to it, her mouth open to request entrance from the guards outside. They looked at each other briefly, both astonished. Ore recovered, "Mistress, please come in." He bowed her in, closing the door behind them, remembering she was probably still angry. "Please have a seat, Mistress."

In looking for the chair, Mizi couldn't miss Ilena's open eyes, looking at her. "Ah! Miss Ilena! You're awake?"

"Yes, Miss...?"

"Mizi," the subject supplied as Ore turned the chair around and Mizi sat down.

"Lady Mizi. Thank you very much for taking care of me last night. I apologize for the ordeal I'm sure it was." Ilena's voice was quiet and her face tired.

"I think, as an appropriate apology, I would like to know how it is I'm going to help you," Mizi said. Ore, hearing this, had his heart sink. She was still angry.

"Of course. I'd be happy to tell you the process, if you'd be so kind as to take the dictation."

Mizi paused, her hand lifted. "*You* know...the *whole* process?"

"Yes, Lady Mizi," Ilena said soberly. "However the story of why needs to wait for another time. It is rather longer than I have the energy to tell today." The 'why' was one of Ore's burning questions, but even he agreed the other was most important now.

Mizi blinked, then took out her pen and opened Ilena's medical record. "Very well. I'm ready."

Ilena glanced at Ore, then turned her head to look at the ceiling and closed her eyes. "Please be aware that I've already received the first two doses, but I'll give them to you for completeness sake." Mizi nodded, making notes.

When her pen paused, Ilena continued. "The Little Death comes in grains. Typically in the underworld a few grains are placed on the tongue and allowed to dissolve. This is very dangerous. Please don't do such a thing to me." Mizi made another note, her pen scratching on the paper.

When it was quiet, Ilena continued, "Three grains only, seeped in a liter of water. Do not stir. At five minutes, take only the top measure of three drams, careful to leave the grains behind. Discard the remainder. Repeat for the second night. These two doses should be given at the typical time the user takes their dose." Ilena paused again until the scratching stopped.

"The following two nights, two grains only, seeped in a liter of water, do not stir. At five minutes, take only the top measure of three drams, careful to leave the grains behind. The dosing for these and the remainder of the course must be given at the appropriate time." She paused again, waiting for Mizi to catch up.

"The appropriate time to dose for the remainder of the course that I'm to take is at the time of lucidity, just after the tears flow. The timing of the night wakefulness is consistent throughout. However, administering becomes difficult as the length of time for lucidity shortens nightly until it's so brief that your only clue to the dosing time is the few tears that fall. In my case, if you're holding my hand at that time, I'll squeeze your hand to let you know the time is right."

This time she waited while Mizi figured out how to write it down. "Ready," said Mizi when she was done.

"The remainder of the course is this: the fifth night, two grains only, seeped in a liter of water, three minutes. Take only the top one dram. Discard the remainder. Repeat thereafter nightly, until the patient no longer cries in the night. Even silent tears require this dosing. Waking the following morning after the course is complete will be normal with clear eyes."

When Mizi was done writing, she read it back to Ilena, making a few minor clarifying notes as she went. "So in your case, tonight we'll wait until the time of wakefulness and give you the first of two nights of the two grains seeped in a liter of water, taking the top measure of three drams at five minutes."

"Yes, that's correct."

"Can we use this for other people who've been using the Little Death?" Mizi asked hopefully.

"No. I was on a very minor dose, sufficient for our needs. The process is different for others."

"Do you know it as well?"

Ilena paused. Ore perked his ears up. "There's a research paper being written with the process in it. It's not mine to say at this time."

Mizi's mouth formed into an "oh" and Ore's eyebrows raised in surprise. They understood the importance of research, papers, and publications to the individual researchers from Mizi's time at Kouzanshi, but this was an unusual topic. "It isn't your research?" Mizi asked.

"No, my lady. I haven't time to devote to full–time research." Ilena's breathing was becoming a little labored.

"Are you in pain?" Ore asked her.

"I'm...tired. Perhaps the pain...is translating to ...weariness."

Mizi looked curiously at Ore, and he explained, "She told me when I came in that she was awake because she wasn't feeling pain. It's likely a combined effect of the pain medication you gave her and the pain reducing effects of the Little Death."

Mizi nodded and annotated the medical record, deciding that that information was also significant. "Then, Miss Ilena, —"

"She's asleep, Mistress," Ore said quietly.

"Eh? Oh." Mizi nibbled on the end of her pen. "Well, that was a surprising source of help, wasn't it?"

Ore nodded. It was also suspicious. Was Ilena the one who'd supplied Alise with the proper dosages before leaving the village? Again things pointed to Ilena being the culprit of the death of the Lady wife of the Earl. Not that he could rule out coincidence or the hand of the Earl.

There were still too many unknowns, but if Ilena was now guaranteed to remain alive, he'd have the time to hear what she had to say for herself. In the meantime, "Mistress, it really is time to go if we're going to carry out the farce that Miss Ilena is dead."

Mizi nodded, setting the medical record down on the table. "Let's go then, and return when we can."

"Okay, Mistress, then if you'll kindly pack your things, I'll pack mine, then we'll go say our farewells to the Captain. There should be time to write our reports to Master while we wait for the plan to be readied. We can send them with the soldiers who go to the castle in our place."

-o-o-o-

The next three nights they were able to sleep earlier in the evening and awaken shortly after midnight in preparation for the Little Death side effects to occur. The sleep talking periods were continuously embarrassing and difficult for Ore to listen to, but since Ilena only ever called Kase's name, Mizi continued to remain oblivious.

Mizi experimented with giving Ilena the painkilling medicine at various times each night, attempting to get the pain of the hip reduced sufficiently that her cries were only from the repayment pain. She also hoped it would reduce those pains somewhat, thereby reducing the pain of the listeners. By the end of the third night, she felt like she had a rudimentary idea of the best timing combination.

The time of lucidity was definitely decreasing. Ilena had talked to them briefly the first night, had reacted to their talking to each other the second night, and on the third night, just to be sure, Mizi had held her hand. She'd spoken briefly, just to say "now" and squeeze Mizi's hand. Then, each night, she'd faded into sleep and the two caretakers had made their medical notes and returned to their beds.

During the days, Ore fretted and Mizi studied until she sent him off to disturb Bonner, who on the third day sent him off to disturb the captain. There, Grey handed him a set of papers. "I've received these yesterday and today. I thought it best to wait until you came to get them rather than expose you to more soldiers than need to know you're here."

"Thank you," Ore said, taking them. He decided to read them there so that if an immediate response was needed he could leave it with Grey for delivery.

Two were for him, and one for Mizi. He opened his two, put them in order of delivery, then began to read them. The first was just a general response to the report he'd sent with the fake Ore. The second was orders. He wondered what had happened at the castle in one day to make Rei suddenly go from patient to impatient.

As he didn't have anything to report back yet, he tucked the three letters into his jacket and said goodbye to the captain, stealing an apple off his food tray on the way out. He took the roof route and took some time to sit out of sight where he could look east out over the hills towards the castle, enjoying a brief view of freedom while he contemplated his most recent orders and what exactly to do about them.

-o-o-o-

Mizi sighed and put down the letter Rei had sent to her. "Was Master properly apologetic, Mistress?" Ore asked her. She chose not to answer. *Oh, dear.* "Well, perhaps he feels it best to properly apologize in person, then, Mistress?"

She gave him a look that said, *Don't push it*, and he backed off, but that told him the tact to take. "Mistress, Master has sent me orders that arrived this morning, a day after he sent these letters. In order for me to carry out his orders, I need to ask that you please let me take care of Miss Ilena alone at night until she's completed the course of her recovery."

Before Mizi could get angry about being cut out of the loop again, Ore hurried on, "Master would like to know if using this low dose of the Little Death can be used for interrogation reliably. While there isn't much time left in Miss Ilena's case to experiment, our past relationship is such that I'll know if it's possible based on the answers she gives to my questions during the sleep talking phase of the night. I would ask that you not be present as the information she and I will talk about is personal to myself." There, he'd been as open as he could.

Mizi sat quietly for several moments, balancing her need to continue to be in control of her patient during a touchy time with her desire to be a strength to both Ore and Rei. Although, when it was put that way....

"I'll make up the appropriate dose each evening for you, then, and give her the appropriate painkilling medicine at the right time myself. Please continue to keep the medical record updated precisely and let me know when she's completely recovered. If there's any difficulty, you're to tell me immediately."

"Yes, Mistress," Ore bowed slightly. "Thank you."

That night, Ore was oddly nervous. It wasn't like Ilena was going to be awake or remember the brief conversation they might not even have, but he still would have to, on some level, admit to her who he was. That went entirely against his self–preservation instincts.

He lay on his bed, hands behind his head, one leg propped up on his other knee, wondering just what he should ask. It should probably, for this first one at least, be somewhat related to whatever her dream was. It would be easiest to steer the conversation where he wanted it to go if he started wherever she was, but that made it difficult to prepare a question set ahead of time.

He dozed off lightly at some point, coming back awake when Ilena's breathing switched to the more ragged breaths that indicated the dreams were about to begin. He sat up cross–legged on the bed, relaxed and waiting for her to begin.

"Here you are, Kase. See, I've found you. I'm here." She was dreaming of one of the times he'd been punished and gone into hiding and she'd come to find him. "What happened? Will you tell me?"

"You've been hurt because of me." Ore answered her, hoping he'd been faster than the dream Kase, glad to have an easy opening at the beginning.

"It's of no consequence, Kase. I can bear all things if you're free." That seemed to follow his comment.

"But why? Why are you willing to bear such horrible things because of me?"

"...Because I love you."

"Do you still love me, even after all these many years of pain and effort?" This was a change of time. Would it work?

"Yes, Ore, I do." Ore leaped up to see if Ilena's eyes were open and she was awake. She wasn't. He shook.

"Why?!" It was the only thing he could find in his shocked mind to ask.

"Because you are mine, and I've been waiting for you to be strong enough for me."

That was the answer he was expecting, but..., "How is that 'loving' me?"

"Because I can't give myself to you until you're strong enough to bear the burden that is me."

Wha...? What kind of an answer is that?! "What is the burden that is Ilena?"

"...I can only answer that question ...to Rei."

Ilena was gone from the dream state. Ore prepared for the payment of pain state, making sure the next dose of the drug was at hand, setting aside his reaction to the session during the time he needed to focus on getting the timing right. Thankfully he didn't have to hold her down due to the level of pain being somewhat reduced by the painkilling medicine.

He did gingerly hold her hand so that he'd be sure to give her the draught at the right time. The tears began, although there weren't many, then she sighed. Ore immediately raised her head and gave her the dose. "Thank you," Ilena said faintly, then she was gone, asleep for the remainder of the night.

Ore recorded the medical information in the journal, then lay down in his bed, trying to put it all together in his head, as if he was writing the report to Rei. *The subject will answer questions. It's possible to redirect the dream to the topic you wish to talk about.* *Did I wish to talk about that? ...Well, more like I didn't wish to hear about it.*

She was honest and consistent in her answers. *Well, consistent, at least. "Honest" may be just guessing on my part.* Time frame can be modified to the present if they're dreaming about the past. *She called me Ore for the first time ever when I redirected her time frame. Does she know already that Kase became Ore? How!?*

And...there are things she has control of, that she won't speak about while she's dreaming, or will only speak to specific persons. This may be peculiar to her, not applicable to other users. *Again, she refers to Master familiarly, as if she knows him. And this time she says there's a thing she will only tell him. What is it and why?*

Ore frowned. He'd received useful information, but there were still plenty of questions Rei would have that Ore could see wouldn't be answered by just testing Ilena alone. That matter of honesty was the hardest one. Was there a way to verify what was said?

Ore yawned. Well, he still had a whole day to think of it, and who knew what tomorrow night's dream would be about? There really wasn't enough time to try everything. He'd just have to do the best he could. Still...he didn't fall asleep easily. His nightmares kept resurfacing.

-o-o-o-

Ilena woke to the sound of a pen scratching on paper. That was new. Usually it was silent the rare moments she woke. Except for that time when ...it *was* Ore, right?... had come in after talking to Mizi and she'd badly startled him. That was funny, but frightening at the same time, his reaction.

Well, on the off chance this was him and not the healer.... She took a deep breath, then was surprised by a sudden yawn that overtook her. By the time she opened her eyes from recovering from the yawn, Ore was standing over her, his golden eyes dark with suspicion, the pupils narrow, his face closed. She could look at those eyes forever. She'd forgotten until just then.

"How long have you been awake?" he asked.

"Mmm, just now." She blinked at him, then lifted a heavy hand to rub her eyes. "It is Master Ore, right?"

He considered his answer. "Yes."

"May I please have some water, and perhaps a little something mild to eat?"

His eyes widened slightly in surprise. "One moment," and he disappeared from her sight.

Ilena sighed. It was going to be hard being on her back for five weeks — not being able to see the little world around her, let alone move about as she was used to. It was nice being able to rest for once. *If only it didn't include all the pain here at the beginning. ...But then I'd not lie still at all, would I?*

Ore returned with water and helped her drink it. She firmly pushed her emotions down. Now was not the time to be thinking about Kase. She was a suspect in a murder investigation, and this was not Kase — at least, not any more.

"Do you think you'll actually be awake long enough for the kitchen to make you something to eat, and then eat it?" Ore asked her, a bit skeptical.

"Ah, well, ...I guess I don't know that. But, I am hungry a bit."

"Well, hunger is a good sign of healing...," he paused to think about it. "I'll let Mistress know you're asking."

"Thank you," she could at least be polite.

She heard Ore move to the inner door, knock, and be called in. She also heard him talking to Mizi, although he spoke quietly. Ilena had been on hyper alert for so many years her hearing was no longer normal, or so the earldom support staff had always said. "Mistress, Miss Ilena is awake and asking for food. I've given her some water to drink already."

"Oh? Already? That *is* good." Mizi paused for thought. "I'll prepare an herbal tea that has restorative properties and some nutrients in it. That should be sufficient for today, and not take too long to prepare. It's not likely she'll be awake long enough for the kitchen to prepare anything. We can let them know to have something on hand for tomorrow."

"Thank you, Mistress. I'll return to sit with her," Ore said.

He walked back into his room, leaving the door open slightly as an invitation to Mizi to come in when she was ready. Ilena could tell because the door didn't click closed. She closed her eyes and took a deep breath, calming herself. She and small rooms did not get along well.

"Asleep already?" Ore said over her.

She opened her eyes. "Was that a joke?" Ilena was seriously curious. It had actually sounded like he'd had a bit of teasing in his voice.

"Perhaps," he said noncommittally.

Amazing. "I...," she closed her mouth. What she had to say wouldn't matter.

"What is it?" he asked her, not letting her get away with it.

Ilena changed what she was going to say. "I think you have some questions for me?" It didn't fool him, she could see, but he went with the flow.

"I have lots of questions, of course," Ore settled into his chair and she turned her head to be able to see him. "However I'm never quite sure how long you'll be awake. Do you know this time?"

Was he stalling for time to figure out which question to ask, or did he want to see what she would volunteer? "No," she answered obediently. She really was still at a point where she could only let her body do what it was going to do.

"Then let's start with: who prepared and gave Miss Alise the Little Death to give to you?"

Investigation, then. How to answer honestly without the details.... Would she be able to stay awake long enough for the full answer? Probably not, it was a long story. "The Earl's physician."

"I found the assassin dead by the hand of yet another assassin. He wasn't hard to find, so I assume he was left findable on purpose. Who is the third party that hired the second assassin?"

That was a surprising question. Ilena considered the options. "There are several possibilities, I guess. The Earl has more than one...associate who would like to see him fall."

"Are you one of them?"

Ilena allowed the surprise to register on her face. "I'd think you'd already know the answer to that. I don't hide my hatred of him, particularly at night. However, it wasn't me. As I said before, I wasn't privy to his plans, so couldn't prepare an appropriate counter–defense."

Ore tilted his head. "How long have you been on the Little Death?"

"Mmm...just over seven years, approximately?"

"Seven...years!" Ore was visibly shocked.

"Seven years for what?" Mizi entered the room, carrying a slightly steaming cup.

"She says she's been on the Little Death for approximately seven years!"

Mizi stopped and the cup almost slipped from her grasp. "Seven...ye–ars. ...Oh, my." Ore swiftly and carefully took the cup from Mizi, set it on his desk, and gave her his chair.

Ilena sighed internally. It looked like she was going to have to try to give the full story. And whatever was in the cup smelled good, too. "Why aren't you dead from before?" Ore asked his next question. It looked like it had been a burning curiosity for some time.

This time, Ilena actually sighed. "You're asking for the long answer. I can't guarantee I can stay awake for the whole thing."

"Please try," this time it was Mizi. She sounded like she'd just, for her, given an order.

"Very well. May I please have a little of the tea, first, then?" If she didn't ask for some now, she might not get any. Ore obliged, giving her a few sips to the equivalent of a large gulp. She looked at them both, taking in the sight of them while waiting for Ore to set the cup back down.

"When I was fifteen, Earl Shicchi went with a small number of his men to Kouzanshi, taking me with him. He'd heard of a man who was a surgical researcher. To this day I don't know if he had a particular use for the man in mind or if he was just intrigued by the concept that there was a man who would cut up cadavers for fun. Perhaps he thought that if there was such a man, he would be more trustworthy — in the Earl's eyes — to handle the medical needs of the household, in that he wouldn't complain about the Earl's own...lifestyle.

"I wanted the researcher for my own purposes as I needed an ally to help the people of the household. So when he rebuffed the Earl, I approached him alone and told him that directly. I asked him to allow Earl Shicchi to be his patron in providing a place, and plenty of bodies to research on, but to allow me to be his patron in that I'd provide myself as a shield for him against the worst of Earl Shicchi's requirements.

"I'd also provide in myself a living specimen for the final phase of his research — that is taking his theory to practice — provided it wouldn't result in my own death nor interrupt my own purposes. In return, he'd be a shield with me between Earl Shicchi and the innocent members of the House who couldn't protect themselves. I was relieved to see him enter the inn the next morning with his bag of instruments in hand. In this way, Doctor Elliot came to Tokumade and became my ally in behalf of the household."

Ilena paused to rest. Yes, this story was going to be too long, but she'd give it her best. She felt hands on her and was surprised. Mizi was holding her head and offering her the cup again. She drank a little more. "Thank you," she said when Mizi let her go again and replaced the cup on the desk.

Mizi nodded, "Please continue if you can." Ilena noticed Ore had an interesting soft look on his face as he looked at his mistress. *Ah, he loves her. She must be kind frequently. That's a good thing.* Ilena took a deep breath and continued.

"Because Earl Shicchi's distrust of those around him is the cause of most of the damage to them, I asked the surgeon to help with that. After some time, he came to me and said he believed he'd found a potential solution and invited me to visit him at night.

"At the time, the Little Death had been recently introduced into Suiran, and a number of the Earl's men had begun taking it. Doctor Elliot showed me how those who take the drug talk in their sleep. He explained that if given daily, they don't die, but continue to talk in their sleep. At the time it seemed very extreme to me.

"He believed that if it were taken as an infusion the severity of the symptoms would be lessened. If Earl Shicchi could hear each night what his household members thought about, wouldn't that help to decrease his distrust, and calm him? Particularly if he believed that the unconscious words were truth.

"As I could see how to get Earl Shicchi to believe it, and we hadn't yet found any other possibilities in nearly an entire year, I decided that we might at least try the experiment. I confiscated all Little Death that came into the house and gave it to the Doctor. If the men wanted it, they had to participate in the experiment.

"After nearly three–quarters of a year of research to find just the right dosages for the sleep talking to be manifest with the least amount of other side–effects possible and the correct dosing for withdrawal without death, we spent the remainder of that year experimenting on me. I'm afraid that was a difficult thing for poor Doctor Elliot." Ilena closed her eyes, remembering.

"You've been on the Little Death ever since then?"

"In the main." Ilena paused again. She could feel she didn't have much time left. How much more should she tell? "When we were ready, I approached Earl Shicchi and asked him, 'If I were to give you a way to know what I was thinking, would you find peace?' He was disbelieving but intrigued.

"I explained that because I would be taking a drug, and talking in my sleep, he could have confidence that I wouldn't be in control of what I was saying. He could then listen to me during the sleep talking phase and know what was in my head. He liked the idea and agreed to it. I believe that first night it was more that he was thinking it would at least be a fun diversion.

"That evening, Earl Shicchi watched as the Doctor gave me my dose of the drug. He stayed in the room with me that night, but in the morning he was gone. When he came to the table late in the morning, he said, 'It's as you say, you love my little brother and hate me. The best part was getting to listen to you cry out in agony when the drug punished you after you told me those things.' He coldly ordered me to continue to take the drug. For many nights thereafter he was in my room every night at the time of the symptoms, waiting to hear what I would say."

"I've heard what you say in your sleep to and about him. How is it he didn't kill you?" Ore asked his burning question again.

Ilena smiled a tired smile. "Indeed. I did keep waiting to die, but I continued to awaken each morning. He didn't like hearing it night after night, but because it didn't change, it began to soothe his heart, as we'd hoped, and his daily language and attitude towards me became less threatening.

"Then came a day when he was furious at one of the men of the household and condemned the man to punishment. The man, innocent of the accused deed, pled with Earl Shicchi that he be allowed to take the same drug I'd been taking to prove his innocence, rather than to be punished. Earl Shicchi allowed it. I was pleasantly surprised that he was able to rein in his anger and consider the option. He was content after a few nights of listening to the man.

"After that, household members condemned to punishment began to plead for the new option regularly, until many were, on their own, going to Doctor Elliot or myself and requesting that they be able to take the drug before coming under Earl Shicchi's displeased eye.

"We strove to find the best doses for the young and aged who came to us, and we were sure to never give a stronger dose than necessary to any of them, in the main keeping the dose low enough to cause a minimum amount of pain. Though I worried for them, they said the pain of the drug was worth the cost to prevent the pain of the Earl's punishment."

"The Earl's punishment is worse than the pain of the drug?" Mizi was disbelieving.

"Yes, Lady Mizi, very much so," Ilena answered soberly.

"Mistress, the first night you experienced this drug Ilena was reliving her own punishment by the Earl, ...by what she was saying in her sleep talking that night. If you recall, her pain that night was severe." Mizi nodded, going a little pale.

Ilena paused, resting and putting the remainder of her thoughts together. "As more and more people chose to 'give away all their secrets' at night, and Earl Shicchi could enter any room at night to hear what they were, he became much calmer and the household began to function more ably as a result.

"After a time, he began to order certain people to stop taking the drug. He no longer wished to hear their 'babble', as he put it, and he knew he could make them take it again anytime he ordered it. Eventually most of the household was quiet again.

"He didn't allow me to ever go off the drug, however, nor did I ever request to. In this manner we were able to maintain a sort of truce. He could trust me as long as I took the drug, and I could control him to a degree as a result. However, he's finally cast me off, and I may finally be rid of the drug." She smiled at Mizi. "Thank you for helping me do so."

"You're welcome," Mizi answered, almost automatically. She looked at Ilena, who was fading. It had taken a lot to tell that story. "Are you able to finish the tea, Miss Ilena?"

Ilena roused slightly. "I would like that, please."

Mizi lifted Ilena's head again and gave her the last of the restorative tea. "We'll have some pottage ready for you when you wake again. It will be good to have you building up your strength again."

"Thank you." Ilena was very quickly asleep thereafter.

-o-o-o-

"What an amazing story, Ore," Mizi looked at him, her eyes wide.

He nodded, "Amazing enough to make you wonder if it's really true."

She shook her head, almost upset with him. "Ore, you're too distrusting. She wouldn't have told a story that long and involved if it weren't true. She's too weak and tired still for making it up. I don't think a lie would be worth such effort."

"You're right, of course, Mistress. I'm sorry." Ore was quick to apologize. Almost too quick. It made Mizi feel like she was being pandered to and she glared at him. When he noticed her glare, he changed the subject. "Ah, Mistress, speaking of being hungry, it's time for our lunch. Shall we go and find it?"

While she wasn't done being upset with him, she didn't see that continuing would have a point. She put her hood up to hide her hair and they left the room. As they walked to slip into the kitchen unseen by the soldiers just drifting in for lunch, Mizi remembered that Ore and Ilena were likely family from a young age. She wondered if he'd been in that household as well. He'd talked as if he understood about the pain of the "punishment" of the Earl.

After they'd put in their request for some pottage to be ready for the next day and collected their lunches, they returned to the surgery wing to eat their lunch in the small courtyard that was surrounded by the halls of the wing. It was one of the few times they allowed themselves to get out of their rooms. Finally Mizi worked up the courage to ask, "Ore, were you ever punished by the Earl?"

He was silent for a while, but she hadn't really thought he'd be willing to talk about it. He finally answered, though. "Yes, and by his father multiple times." She turned to him in surprise and dismay, but he put up a hand forestalling her.

"Miss Ilena has always been that way, from the time I knew her." Mizi held still, amazed Ore was willing to talk to her about it, scared if she moved he would stop. "The pain from those times no longer exists for me because she was there to remove it, so Mistress doesn't need to worry for me." He smiled encouragingly at her.

"Ore...so you believe her story?"

He was thoughtful and perhaps a little...sad? "...Yes, I think I do. It isn't unlike her character, as I knew it then, to wish to help the people of the household and protect them. Many of the other things she describes about the Earl hold true to my memory and understanding. I think it's that I don't wish to believe the method she and Doctor Elliot chose to use. The Little Death is not a drug to be used lightly."

Mizi didn't think they had used it lightly, and likely Ore didn't believe that either. It was something else. "It's hard to know someone you care about has had to go through great pain and difficulty." She wanted to reach out and touch his pain away, but withheld out of respect.

Ore looked at the ground. Mizi wanted to support him, but what could she say? "Miss Ilena will be off of it finally very soon, and Rei will place her where she can be safe from it happening again. I'm glad, for your sake, you're able to be a part of helping release her from that pain she's carried."

Ore looked up at her, then smiled, "Thank you, Mistress. You're always too kind." He stood up and stretched. "Well, I have a lot to write about to Master now. Poor Ore's hand is going to fall off." He held out his hand to her to help her up from the ground. Mizi accepted it, standing. As she did so, she hoped he understood that she did care for him and wanted to see him happy.

-o-o-o-

Ore saw his mistress to her room, then returned to the courtyard. He stood there briefly, then went up on the roof to the place where he could look out over the hills towards the direction of the castle. *Master, what am I to do?*

He sat and thought of a lot of nothing for a while. His orders held him still, but his inner confusion called to him to run in the direction he was looking. *Am I too close to this to be of use to Master? If my emotions can't be controlled, how can I be effective?*

Finally he sighed and stood in preparation to return to his room. He would just have to tell Rei what had happened, how it affected him, and let Rei decide. He would interrogate Ilena again tonight during the sleep talking and then send his report.

CHAPTER 5 Rei and Mizi Tie Ore to Ilena

Rei set Ore's report down. He wasn't the sort to keep important reports from his close aides. He also wasn't the kind to be callous for the sake of convenience. He'd settled on reading it aloud to Andrew and Mina as a compromise.

"So, Ore knows her...," Andrew mused aloud the confirmation Ore had given to their guess.

"I take it you left out the personal bits, then," Mina said.

Rei nodded, looking back at the last part of the report. Ore had "interviewed" Ilena again the second night, only that time she'd dreamed about Earl Shicchi. Ore had tried to get her to talk about something completely different, but she couldn't be turned from the topic she'd started with, and the sleeptalking time period had ended short as well.

That didn't bode well for what he'd been hoping to use the lesser form of the drug for, although from the first experiment the night before that, it looked like it might have some potential. He sighed, wondering if they might get another chance to experiment with it. If it didn't have to come at the cost of death for the one being interviewed, it could be very useful.

Then there was the researcher who already had the data. Could he get hold of that person and his research paper first? If he could, he'd put him to work to get the answers Rei was looking for.

"Well, it looks like the research for using the Little Death as an interrogation drug will have to be put on hold for now," he said giving voice to the summary of his thoughts. "I'd like to go visit Miss Ilena myself within the next week or so to see what she'll tell me directly. I believe it could be highly productive if it's as Ore reports: that she's always been pushing back against the Earl from the beginning.

"I'd like to keep our investigation going at this end so that I can confirm her willingness to help. Please put the visit into my schedule, Andrew." Andrew nodded and pulled out Rei's appointment book.

Mina gave her testing look to Rei that covered her own worry for her friend. "What are you going to do about Ore?"

"He'll have to work it out himself. I need him there and I trust his judgment, regardless." Rei remained calm.

"Hmm. Yes, he is rather the naturally suspicious sort, even if it is himself he doesn't trust, but do you really think he'll stay there and not come here?" Mina pressed Rei.

Rei pondered Mina's question, rolling his pen between his fingers. "No, I don't. Not if we wait too long to go. I do trust he won't leave if staying's important."

"As long as he has orders to keep him busy, staying is important," Andrew said matter-of-factly, looking up from putting the appointment book away.

Rei nodded. "I want him to find Doctor Elliot."

Ore stared at the order in his hand, his stomach doing flips. How was he to find a man, when the last place he'd heard that man belonged was a place that for Ore to enter meant death? But...he couldn't refuse an order from his master.

To make his mood worse, he'd been unable to make any progress with Ilena last night again. She was utterly refusing to talk about how it was she knew Rei. How could such a thing really be possible when she was asleep? Shouldn't her mind be more susceptible to suggestion then? He crumpled the paper in his hand. Was Rei really trying to make this difficult?

"What is it that makes Master Ore so cross? Is it a matter I may be of help to?"

He turned his head and looked across the room. He'd fled to his room after receiving and reading the order, as if fleeing to his safe hole, and was lying on his bed in his thinking position: one hand under his head, one leg propped up on the other raised knee. "I've been told to find a man in a place I may not go to," he grumpily told the recently awakened Ilena.

"Hmm, that does seem like a difficulty."

He blinked. Although she'd said Doctor Elliot worked for the Earl, she'd also said he'd provided the first three days of the drug to her. "Where is Doctor Elliot?"

"Knowing such a thing will ease Master Ore's mind?" He didn't answer. Ilena looked up at the ceiling. "I can't tell you where he *is*, but I can tell you where he *is not*." She looked back at him. "He isn't at Tokumade manor. No good thing remains there. It could be altogether burned down with its current occupants inside and there would be none who would cry."

That was harsh, but Ore felt momentarily like he would like to just go and do that. "You said he provided the Little Death for you your first days after the accident, and I presume he did so before that as well?"

Ilena was shaking her head. "We'd parted ways already and I was preparing my own doses while the Lady and I were here. If he provided those doses it was because someone sent word to him I was injured and unable to help myself. It's likely he prepared them and sent them back with the messenger, but didn't come himself."

That bore out based on his previous investigations, but it meant someone knew how to find him. "Did he return to Kouzanshi?"

"No. There's nothing there for him."

Ore was beginning to feel better. Doctor Elliot wasn't at Tokumade, nor had he traveled the great distance to the west to Kouzanshi. He was a researcher, and researchers needed patrons, money, and supplies. It was a good bet he'd gone to a place with many people where he could hide and search for a new patron.

If he was still close enough to call upon to aid Ilena, he was in all likelihood at Nijoushi, the city attached to Castle Nijou. That was a place Ore could go.

If Doctor Elliot couldn't find a patron, he would leave there and go elsewhere, maybe even south to the capital of Ryokudo, Ichijoutsu. Ore would have to move fairly quickly if he didn't want him to leave before he found him.

"Master Ore," Ilena called to catch his attention. "Your gloom has cleared. ...May I please have my promised meal now?" She was smiling as if she'd made a joke.

"Ah," he sat up, having been reminded that she hadn't woken up the previous day. He smiled teasingly in return. "Hoping for a reward for good behavior, eh? I suppose that can be arranged."

He went to Mizi's door and requested if she would be willing to fetch the pottage. He wanted to ask more of his other questions while Ilena was awake. As he walked to stand next to her, she reached out and grasped his sleeve. The look she gave him was very serious.

"Doctor Elliot is a very important person to me. Please promise me you'll treat him well. He is still someone I'll protect." Ore nodded. Rei didn't intend to misuse the Doctor. "Then..., he'll be willing to do as Prince Rei directs. But...don't go looking yet, Master Ore," her eyes were pleading and she clutched at his sleeve tighter.

"Why?" he asked coldly, suddenly suspicious.

"As long as I'm believed dead, you won't find him. When Rei is willing to acknowledge I'm alive, then he'll be made easily available to you."

He twitched his arm and she let go of his sleeve. "Why is that, Miss Ilena?"

"It's as I've said. It's my role to protect the innocent and the good of the House of Shicchi. As long as they're afraid their protection is gone, they'll trust no one, not even you."

Not even me? What does she mean by that? Do they all know who I was, who I am? That thought frightened him viscerally and he took a step back from her. "I will decide my own actions."

"Of course, Master Ore." He had the sense that if she'd been standing, she would have bowed. "I'm sorry for saying such unreasonable things."

He turned away from her, walking to the desk and placing his hand on it, giving himself time to recover. It really hadn't been an unreasonable request. Rather she was saying she suggested he just wait until he was handed what he wanted, instead of waste a lot of effort. That wasn't what was bothering him.

"Miss Ilena," he could tell he sounded dangerous, but that was how he felt, "There are yet a few remaining things that I need to have answered by you." He turned and looked her in the eye. She returned the look, passive yet receptive, the perfect steward's face. "Who do you think I am?"

"You are Sir Ore, personal messenger and third knight to First Prince Rei, protector of Lady Mizi, Prince Rei's beloved."

His expression didn't change. "Who do you think I was?"

"Kase Shicchi, third son of the previous Earl, heir to the Earldom Toku-made."

Hisssss. "Why do you think that?"

"Circumstantial evidence and personal belief."

"You have no solid proof?"

"No."

"Please refrain from such a belief. I am not he."

She stared at him, a look he remembered from long ago, one he'd never had cause to flinch from before. He forced himself to hold his ground. "As you wish, Sir Ore."

It was the tone of total acceptance and obedience, but he knew she didn't believe him, because never had he seen anyone lie to her and not be found out. It would be enough, because she'd also never complained about being lied to. But, somehow.... He squashed the thought. It would get him into trouble.

"And, finally, Miss Ilena, —" There was a knock at the door and Mizi entered with Ilena's pottage.

Mizi saw the dark look on Ore's face and stopped. "I'm sorry. I'm interrupting."

Ore, trying to control his anger that he'd worked so hard to learn to control, said, "No, please feed Miss Ilena, Mistress. I need to go out for a bit." He left quickly, leaving not only the ground but the garrison as well. He would return when he'd recovered his ability to stay calm.

-o-o-o-

"I don't think I've seen Ore so angry in a long time," Mizi said in awe and sorrow. She turned to Ilena. "Miss Ilena, what have you done?"

Ilena looked at her sorrowfully. "I've answered his questions truthfully." She paused, looking at Mizi, even through and into her for a moment. "I see that you care for him. Thus, I'll tell you: he isn't so much angry as he is afraid, because I know his distant past and his present and he never wanted the two to meet. Truly, Lady Mizi, I never wanted to cause him pain. ...He's refused me, saying he isn't the person I believe him to be. Therefore, to me he isn't. Please let it lie."

Mizi wondered just how it was that Ilena knew she was trying to come up with something comforting to say. So instead she asked, as she sat near Ilena, preparing to feed her, "Why is he so afraid of his past?"

Ilena swallowed the first spoonful, then answered, "Because that past was full of darkness and death. For anyone to know of his present connection to that past is to present to him his own death."

Mizi fed Ilena more spoonfuls of the pottage and Ilena ate hungrily. When she was nearing full, she paused in her eating. "You're still thinking on it, Lady Mizi."

"Yes," said Mizi slowly. "Are you a danger to Ore?"

"No, Lady Mizi. My only role in this life is to be a protector of others. I've protected Ore since we were very young. He won't die, and most assuredly he won't die because of me. If I can't help him understand because he will not, then I'll continue as I have before: protecting him from a distance without any acknowledgement. The one does not require the other."

Mizi thought on that for a moment, feeding Ilena a few more spoonfuls until she refused saying she was finished. "What is Ore to you?" Mizi finally asked.

Ilena looked at her with a little surprise, then said simply, "The man I love and wish to stand next to the remainder of my days."

Mizi sat in shock, the gears of her mind halting. Ilena waited quietly. When Mizi finally had her thoughts going again, she looked at Ilena, only to find she'd fallen asleep again.

Mizi put her hand to her head. "He's the man you love and you're willing to accept that he won't acknowledge you? Surely only the strength of love can allow you to abide such a thing. ...I think I'll let Rei know these things you've told me. Only he can see the entire picture and know how to help Ore."

-o-o-o-

For the next four days Mizi nursed Ilena and Ore didn't return. During that time Ilena was fully weaned off the Little Death, and was clear–eyed in the mornings. Mizi was glad to finally have full nights of sleep again, unfilled with cries of pain.

On the fifth day Rei came, Andrew and Mina at his back as always, bringing Ore with him. He first visited with Mizi in the courtyard of the medical wing. Mizi thought the way Andrew and Mina flanked Ore, he was there more as a prisoner than a returning guard. All three stood very formally along the edge of the courtyard near the hallway.

Perhaps Rei had punished Ore for leaving his duty and was making him return to it, but looking at Andrew and Mina, it seemed also likely that they were there to strengthen Ore during a time of weakness. It wouldn't be surprising if it was both.

"It is good to see you again, Mizi," Rei greeted her slightly more formally than his usual manner, including a small formal bow. "I apologize for my lateness in coming."

Mizi waited, her hands clasped in front of her skirt. She hadn't forgotten that he'd prevented her from performing her duties effectively. "Thank you for coming," she said formally after a moment.

"I'm sorry for not considering you seriously in the matter regarding the Little Death. It wasn't wise of me to put protecting you above your needs in regards to completing your work effectively." One of the things Mizi really loved about Rei was his ability to admit his errors, quickly and without deflection.

She'd also been considering what Ore had said to her when he'd been so candid about what Rei's order to him was and his needs. "I apologize for not trusting that your intentions were good, and for not remembering that there are times when it isn't possible for a Prince to say all the things that are within his mind."

Rei offered a peace offering. "Is there anything that you need at this time that I can be of assistance with?"

Mizi answered, "Miss Ilena is no longer under the influence of the Little Death, and her eyes are clear. However, I seem to be missing a companion you required should stay with me and assist me in the matter." Ore had shirked his duty far too long, regardless of his anger or fear. She was also upset with him that he wouldn't face his past properly, although she didn't know if she could force that.

Rei turned and called, "Ore."

Ore walked up to Mizi and Rei and bowed down on one knee before Mizi, his fist resting on the ground in his way of fully formal humility. "I abandoned you selfishly, Mistress. I'm sorry."

She looked at him calmly, her lips firmly pressed against each other, considering. Then she thought of Andrew and Mina. "Because you stand alone and partnerless, it cannot be forgiven lightly." She could sense the bewilderment and despair coming from Ore and the curiosity from Rei. She was stern, but not so often severe as that comment had been.

"...Will you, Ore, return and stand in the place Rei has put you, as you ought from now on?" He nodded his bowed head once. Mizi already knew Ore was completely devoted to his duty at her side. She turned to Rei. "I will accept Ore back to stand by me if you'll promise me a partner for him that will help remind him of his duty and will stand as a protection for him. One that I approve of."

Rei smiled a secret smile that lit his eyes. "And who is it you wish for me to prove, Mizi?"

"Ilena, the former steward of Tokumade."

Rei's smile moved ever so slightly to his lips. "You already approve?" Mizi nodded firmly. "You understand this will be difficult for Ore?"

"I understand it's only difficult because he won't face that which he ought to face from his past so that he may freely face his future." Out of the corner of her eye, she could see Ore's ears turn faintly red.

Rei nodded. "I'll test Miss Ilena. If I approve, and she's willing, you shall have her to stand by Ore." Ore's head bowed even further in resignation. While he'd earned it, it was a hard punishment to bear at this time.

Turning towards Ore's quarters, Rei said, "Ore, come with me." Ore rose, bowed to Mizi without looking up at her, and walked behind Rei, looking like he was going to the gallows.

When the door had closed behind the two men, Mizi turned to Andrew and Mina. "Thank you for supporting Rei and Ore," she said to them. Andrew and Mina nodded. "...And for supporting me," she added. They weren't sure what she meant. She smiled as she said, "I wouldn't have thought of that if it hadn't been for the two of you standing at Rei's back."

"Umm...Mizi, would it be okay if you didn't tell Ore that?" Andrew asked plaintively.

"Why ever not?" Mizi was puzzled.

The partners looked at each other, then Mina explained, "We would have been here at least two days ago, except that Ore showed up in his tree. Rei managed to get him to report, but he couldn't talk Ore down from his tree. He finally had to send us to get him forcibly this morning. He even threatened to tie Ore to his horse."

"Ah, it isn't you," Andrew hurried to reassure Mizi.

"Although he was afraid of that too," mumbled Mina.

Andrew continued, "He can't face Miss Ilena, even now."

Mizi sighed. "Yes, I know. Ilena explained to me why. It's as I said. It's because he won't properly face her and his past. He believes that to do so will bring his death, but he doesn't properly comprehend what she's done for him until now. Rei's taken Ore's reins but he's still a wild stallion. I believe she can help him in the ways we can't."

Mina looked at Mizi appraisingly. "Rei said as much as well: that Miss Ilena can touch Ore in places the rest of us can't, and because of that is likely to become his greatest strength. Even if you hadn't suggested it, he was already minded to test Miss Ilena and place her by Ore's side."

Mizi was relieved. She hadn't asked amiss, then. It made her feel good that she'd thought of a thing on her own that Rei had thought of.

-o-o-o-

The guards at Ore's door opened it for Rei. When Ore looked like he was going to balk at entering, they looked at him coldly, as if to say they would use force if necessary. They also were disappointed that he'd shirked his duty. He gave up his thoughts and meekly entered behind Rei.

They closed the door with a cold *click* that sent shudders up Ore's spine. He stood at formal rest attention just inside the door, waiting on the will of his master. Rei walked to stand near Ilena where she wouldn't find it difficult to look at him and speak with him.

"Welcome, Prince Rei," Ilena was the epitome of graciousness. A gift, considering she couldn't rise from lying on her back. Ore's lips pursed in a sour expression.

"Miss Ilena, I would have you tell me what you know," Rei ordered.

"Yes, Regent Rei," she agreed obediently. "Please have a seat. This will take some time."

"I should think so," Rei agreed neutrally. He sat in the chair that was already set by the bed, as Mizi had just left it when he'd arrived.

Ilena added, "It would be helpful if notes were taken."

Rei ordered, "Ore."

Ore moved to the desk and pulled it up close to the second bed. He pulled out paper and pen, then, using the bed as his chair for the desk, readied himself to take notes. Ilena didn't look at him, nor acknowledge him.

Ilena proceeded to tell Rei many things, from the beginning as Ore had told him about the deaths of Grandfather Shicchi and Father Shicchi, to Earl Shicchi's murder of his second brother and sister–in–law, to the chasing away of his third brother who fled for his life, to her own beating when he couldn't find Kase with her.

She then continued on, telling Rei chronologically of multiple instigations of various murders and crimes Pakyo had reasoned out and ordered through the years from that time on until the murder of his own wife. As she told of them, if they were performed with the aid of other Houses, or requested by other Houses, she included their names as well.

When she reached the end of listing the evil acts, she included the names of the Houses Earl Shicchi was currently allied with. "Bring me the list of names of allies, past and present, and a pen," she required.

Rei nodded and Ore stood and took them to her. She took them without looking at him, studied the list carefully, then made some marks on the page and handed them back to Ore. Ore handed the marked page to Rei and sat back down.

"I've marked five Houses with circles. These are the Houses you should explore first. Three of them Earl Shicchi ordered eradicated in order to keep his evil deeds secret. While he still believes that you're merely investigating the death of his Lady wife and her people, he won't be surprised with you also investigating old cases he's been involved with.

"In all five of the oldest cases, there was no finding against him. He won't care what you do, even if you explore them deeply, but he will pay attention. He'll be trying to understand if you've faked my death.

"I've marked four Houses with triangles. These are alliances that are ended. Both he and all the allied Houses will notice when you begin to more deeply explore them and become nervous. Earl Shicchi will begin to assume I'm still alive and will begin a slow but steady exodus into the mountains. Explore them second.

"The three X's are the current alliances. Please exercise great caution and speed when you're ready to deal with these. When you seriously investigate these cases all the roaches will scatter, the mice will pack their bags, and the evidence will begin to be removed, including my Children.

"Earl Shicchi will know I'm alive and have spoken to you, and will that very day disappear into the mountains, thinking to become a thorn in your side for many years to come. Adding decoy cases to your investigations will slow him down somewhat, if you feel it's necessary, and make him question whether I'm alive or not. But that is, of course, up to you."

Rei looked at the list, "What's the meaning of the one crossed out?"

"Please excuse my determination, but do not touch it! This alliance was instigated by the other party. Even Earl Shicchi was reluctant at first to take the side job he was given. I've given it to you only so you may have my full knowledge of all the deeds of the House of Shicchi. You'll have enough evidence to convict him with the rest. This House will bring you down and perhaps all of the House of Touka if it's exposed at this time."

She paused. "Please, rest assured the King is well aware of their dealings and has a plan already in place to deal with them. I beg you to not interrupt him." Rei looked at her in surprise, but didn't answer.

"The next topic, then, if it pleases you, Regent Rei?" He nodded. "Earl Shicchi has at least one double, and perhaps two. If you kill *an* 'Earl Shicchi' you're not assured of having killed *the* Earl Shicchi. If you don't find all of them, whomever is left will return and carry on his evil deeds. Indeed, one of them is more terrible than Pakyo himself." That was sobering.

"He's already set up three houses to escape to, all north into the mountains. It's likely that he and at least one other double will go there, and a third may remain at Tokumade Manor. The majority of his men will be split between the closer two houses in order to weaken any pursuers and, if possible, prevent them from reaching the third house. I wouldn't be surprised if he's already sent men into those places to watch that they're kept secret and safe.

"If you're able to have men in position at the farthest house before he arrives, without alerting him or the men stationed at them, you'll have a greater chance of success. Bring me a map of the borderlands north of Tokumade later and I'll mark where they are for you." Rei nodded.

"I'm sure you received the report that I'm the protector of the upstanding people of Tokumade who were under the harsh hand of the House of Shicchi. These people I call my 'Children'. I've sent all of them away from the House little by little, and none remain there. Some of them are further witnesses to these evil and traitorous acts of Earl Shicchi and his allies.

"I'm willing to loan them to you temporarily if you feel you require their testimony, and if you'll promise me that you'll see they're kept safe until after you've cleaned the House of Shicchi and it's allies, so that they don't lose their lives for that which they didn't have to.

"However, I will only do so one group at a time and at intervals so that their movements aren't warning signs to our enemies. When the final group is collected, it also must be done quickly and with great protections. Several of those witnesses are still within the Houses of our enemies. Their absence will increase the alertness of Earl Shicchi and his allies, although it shouldn't cause them to flee at first. Should they see the pattern, however, that will be telling enough and they may kill those who could have helped you, or flee prematurely."

Rei considered her words for a time after she was silent. "Thank you for telling me what you know. I'd like to promise safety for your 'Children' and request you do as you've said you'd do, so that I may have further testimony against the Earl and his allies."

Ilena bowed her head in acquiescence. "Then after I'm safely at Castle Nijou, I'll give you the first list. However, they won't go with anyone who comes for them. They'll only consent to come to you if Ore himself goes to retrieve them and tells them 'Mother has sent me for you'."

Ore's head jerked up in alarm. He was ignored. "Ore is the key?" Rei asked, a little surprised. Ilena nodded.

Rei pondered a little more. "Miss Ilena, what path do you wish to walk, now that you're no longer the Steward of Tokumade?"

Ilena's eyes lit up and she stared at Rei fiercely, reminiscent of a falcon that had centered on it's prey, "To stand by the side of Kase Shicchi — Ore; to protect Prince Rei; and to protect what Prince Rei protects. And if I cannot do that, to be set free to do my own will." Ore couldn't hold back a choked sound as she sealed his fate with her words.

Rei nodded and stood. "I'll consider it." He held his hand out for the notes Ore had taken. After he'd received them, he ordered. "You'll remain here." Ore bowed. It had to be the most depressed Ore Rei had ever seen, but he didn't let it enter his heart, and he let himself out.

Ore returned the desk to it's place, and the chair as well, then turned to face Ilena formally. She was looking at him. He supposed that might be better than having her feigning sleep. "Welcome back, Ore. I'm sure you're tired from your travails. Please feel free to rest until Mistress Mizi comes for the evening meal. I'll awaken you before she arrives."

He couldn't help himself. "Was this all planned out to your specifications as well?"

"No, Ore," Ilena answered calmly. "Mistress Mizi has done what she wished in her own heart and Rei has followed his own as well. If you can't accept your own fault, then lay the blame at the feet of Fate or the gods. It was not mine to know that you and I would ever meet again."

"No? Then why do you, and all of your 'Children', believe that I'm Kase and recognize 'Ore' as the same?" His voice was snide with his frustration.

"Because you're the messenger that follows Prince Rei. Even if you'd never seen my face, when it was time for the House of Shicchi to fall, isn't it you that he would send before him to see to it?" He couldn't deny it.

"And," he looked up surprised that there was more, "am I not the shield that stands before him, required to provide him all protections necessary to his remaining Prince of Ryokudo, Regent of Suiran?"

Ore's eyes went wide. He couldn't understand why, but he could see that Ilena had acted in that manner. He bowed his head in defeat. "I'll rest now," he said humbly, and climbed into his bed, turning his back to her and letting his troubled soul slip into the darkness.

Oddly enough, that darkness seemed to contain a spark of light beckoning him forward. He stared at it in confusion, not comprehending it, until he finally slept.

-o-o-o-

Rei walked out of Ore's room and rejoined Mizi, Andrew, and Mina. They were quietly talking, having already caught up while he was meeting with

Ilena. They looked at him quizzically. "She wants him," he said simply and shrugged. "We'll see if she can actually catch him."

"Have you already finished testing her, then?" Mizi asked him.

Rei paused, then shook his head. "I've merely begun," Mizi looked disappointed, "but, I've never encountered such a person, I think." He paused again. Then he brandished the notes Ore had taken. "Well, take a look at this and tell me what you think," he handed them to Andrew, and Mina read them over his shoulder.

Rei explained them in short to Mizi. She smiled, already knowing what kind of support Ilena could be, glad that Ilena had given Rei and the others more evidence of it.

Andrew and Mina looked at each other when they were done reading. Andrew handed the pages back to Rei. "That's rather impressive," he said carefully.

"Very thorough," agreed Mina, just as carefully.

"What?" Mizi was stunned at their reactions. Rei held up his hand, forestalling her, and she ceased, waiting.

The two aides looked at each other again. "She's listed all of the anticipated cases and confirmed the ones we weren't sure about," Mina said, beginning to list the points they'd been looking for. "She's listed all of the known and expected allies, as well as the ones we couldn't quite name, but could see traces of."

Andrew picked it up, "She's included information critical to the success of your goals, including strategy tips that are useful, but not extraneous. She's already prepared additional witnesses needed to complete the legal necessities. All these things were above and beyond what was expected, although we'd hoped for even a small level of the last."

"And, not on the notes," Rei added for their benefit, "she knows the movements of my brother in the workings of Suiran, or at least where it's connected with the Earl."

"What?" they asked together.

Rei nodded. "It's made me wonder if she's one of his agents." They looked at him, not knowing how to answer. "Except, ...that one of my brother's agents wouldn't request to serve me."

"She did?" Andrew asked. The head aide was so protective of the prince, no one got to serve Rei unless they passed Andrew's tests.

Rei smiled a small smile at him. "To be more precise, when I asked her what path she wished to follow now that she's no longer the Steward of Tokumade, she said to stand by the side of Ore and protect me and protect what I protect. Otherwise, she wishes to be set free."

"Ah, poor Ore," said Mina quietly, not really meaning it. "He's left no escape, then, is he?"

Rei grinned. "No. No, he's not. Not unless she doesn't pass the test."

Andrew looked thoughtful. "It doesn't look like that will happen, though, does it?"

"You think so?" Rei asked him mildly.

"I think," Mina said slowly, "that she's moving very carefully. Stepping lightly at the first to see that she reaches her goal, whatever it is." She turned her full attention on Rei. "I think it would be wise to give her enough time to show you everything she's holding in her hand before deciding."

Rei nodded. "That's how I feel. Until I've received all the information, I can't know what she truly wishes to have."

"But, she doesn't lie," Mizi said, worried.

"No, that's true," agreed Rei. "She neither lies, nor withholds information specific to the questions she's asked, but she also doesn't tell everything that could be told. Therefore, I can be sure she does want to stand by Ore and serve me, but there's likely more to it than that which she isn't willing to say.

"There are two questions that are still open." Mizi was puzzled. He held up his hand, counting them on his fingers, "One, why does she know me, with great familiarity, when I don't know her? And, two, why does she wish me to promise I'll set her free if she can't have Ore? What hold do I already have on her that I don't know about?" He looked back at Andrew and Mina. "I think...it will be very interesting to see what she still has yet to show me."

"I think Ore would be the first to tell you she's very dangerous," said Mina with a straight face.

"Then it's up to Ore to be sure she's contained, isn't it?" Rei answered mildly.

"We can certainly count on Mizi to continue to be her champion, isn't it so?" Andrew turned to her and smiled.

Mizi went to nod, then stopped, "Well, as long as she continues to be worthy of it," she said.

They all smiled at her. "You're getting stronger, Mizi," approved Mina.

-o-o-o-

Rei visited with Captain Grey briefly, long enough to create a plan to securely move Ilena to Castle Nijou when Doctor Bonner would release her to be moved there at her three week mark. Then he regretfully said his goodbyes to Mizi. While he and his aides would arrive at Castle Nijou after midnight, he couldn't afford to stay away for two days this time. On the way back, the three of them, surrounded by his honor guard, discussed what action items they would have now that they had this new and confirmed information from Ilena.

"Really, being a Regent is so much more work, it's difficult to learn how to pace it. Here we are riding home in the middle of the night just to get to more work. ...And right after Mina has scolded us for not getting enough rest." Rei yawned, punctuating his complaint.

They smiled at him. "My father taught me this winter that when that happens, the only thing to do is to add more hands to do the work," Mina suggested.

"Hmm," Rei considered it. "Well, then, I think you'll have to postpone going back to him until this is completed then?"

Mina slumped her shoulders. "Ah...well...I guess there's no helping it. But...you may have to excuse me from the battle, then."

Andrew looked stricken. "What will I do, then? I won't have my left hand to protect me! I shall surely die! Rei, you can't let that happen!"

"Oi, oi!" Rei waved his hand at Andrew as if shooing a fly. "Would you rather go back to four hours of sleep at night?"

"Isn't that better than being dead?"

"Well, considering that I'm not sure exactly who on the staff I can trust with the information presented to me today...it may be about the same either way," Rei said seriously.

Both aides got serious as well. It was true. If there were agents of any of the lords who were accomplices of Earl Shicchi within the castle and they learned of the hunt that was on, the board would be tipped very badly against Rei. "I'll need you two to focus on this matter. I'll have the others do the other work that needs doing. ...And if we really need to add another pair of hands or two, we'll see what we can do.

"In the meantime, ...do you think I can learn to sleep in the saddle?" He slumped down uncomfortably. "Next time, we come by carriage," he grumped, wishing right at that moment for even an uncomfortable carriage bench to be lying down on. Andrew and Mina grinned. They were glad Rei was in a good mood.

-o-o-o-

Thereafter at Osterly Garrison, conversations between Ore and Ilena were, in the main, brief and noncommittal. The exceptions to this were the daily grilling sessions that Ilena gave Ore, and occasionally Mizi. She seemed intent on understanding everything there was to know about life at the castle and the people who lived there before she arrived.

Once she'd picked their brains twice each on every subject she could think of, they wouldn't answer her questions any more. So she switched to quiz method, where she would tell them what she'd learned from them and they had to say if she was right or wrong. That didn't last too long either. They finally started staying away just a little more than they perhaps should have.

At some point, Mizi finally told her, "It's good you're working hard, but there will be a great distance between knowing the data, and actually experiencing it."

Ilena sighed, "I know Mistress Mizi, but I'll still have at least another two weeks or more before I'll be able to do that. I haven't been in a proper castle in ages. I'd like to not be too misinformed, if at all possible. That really wouldn't do for a guest of the Prince, even if it is a guest under house arrest."

"House arrest, Ilena?" asked Mizi.

"As long as Prince Rei is testing me, I'm not free to wander the castle and do as I please, am I? Whether or no I have a working hip."

"Nope," agreed Ore, who'd lived it himself.

"I didn't have the trouble," Mizi frowned, remembering that the only trouble she'd had was with one Marquis and Ore.

Ore sighed, "Mistress has always been different in Master's eyes." Ilena nodded, agreeing.

"Oh," Mizi blushed. She hadn't really considered it that way before.

"It's a good thing," Ilena reassured her, "but I certainly don't expect it for myself, and it really wouldn't be right to." Ore's expression agreed with her.

"You don't like to sit still, Miss Ilena," observed Ore.

"No," she agreed. "I've always been very busy. It's very difficult for me to have enforced quiet time."

"Does this mean that you'll get into trouble if you aren't kept busy doing good things?" He'd taken to teasing her as a means to let out his frustration.

"I'm quite capable of keeping myself busy doing good things, Ore." She always responded blandly, which made him more frustrated.

"Of course," mediated Mizi. "Doing your best to be prepared for where you're going next is certainly a good thing to keep yourself busy doing, and is certainly better than simply being lazy."

Ore rolled his eyes behind Mizi's back. "Please, don't encourage her today, Mistress. She's already spent the majority of it quizzing. Time to rest is useful as well."

Mizi sighed. She could only mediate so much between the quarreling pair. "Ore, it's nearly time for supper. Would you be willing to go and fetch it?"

"Yes, Mistress." He bowed himself out and was glad for the open air.

"Really, Ilena. Shall I come to regret asking to have the two of you paired?" Mizi was getting beyond her capacity to cope.

"I'm sorry Mistress Mizi. I'm not skillful at handling Ore's resentment yet. My usual response to the Earl when he said such hurtful things was to ignore him. ...Would that work with Ore? It seemed to me when he's ignored he tends to fall into the darkness that's within him and it becomes too difficult to reach him. I was not wishing for that. Is there something you can tell me?"

Mizi shook her head. "I'm afraid Ore is very different for you than for any other person that he knows. I can't say what will or won't work. I'm sorry."

"Well, perhaps, because he chooses to take the position of an adversary, I'll try to be as polite and obliging as possible. Though...I'm afraid he also oddly affects me. It make take some training and effort to maintain such a position."

"Well, it would be nice to have some pleasant conversations again," admitted Mizi. "I do hope we'll be able to soon enough."

"I would like that very much as well, Mistress Mizi. But, if it makes you feel better, Ore does sleep very soundly when he comes in to sleep."

"Is he still staying away until late?" Mizi was disappointed.

"Yes, but he's never far, usually in the courtyard or on the roof above us. And he's no longer restless during his sleep, as he was when he first returned to us. I believe that's a good sign."

"Well, we shall have to be grateful for small progresses, then."

"Yes, Mistress Mizi."

CHAPTER 6 Transferring Ilena to Castle Nijou

Three weeks after Ilena had been publicly declared dead, Doctor Bonner, who'd visited regularly, did a full check on Ilena's hip in the early morning. All of her bruising was gone, which was a good sign. She also didn't have as much pain except for the odd moments. He gave her the approval to travel, with the requirement she still wasn't to sit upright or put any unnecessary pressure on the hip for another two weeks. With that approval of the surgeon, they all got ready to depart for Castle Nijou.

It was well known that Ore had a penchant (and requirement) for showing up places without warning at random times, so having him show up at Osterly wouldn't be too suspicious, but having Mizi with him would be, since she was supposed to be at the castle. Mizi was given a long, hooded white cloak of the soldiers to wear as her disguise. She would sit in the wagon with Ilena to appear to be the on–board guard while Ore would drive the wagon.

The guard detail assigned to be with the wagon was small. Behind the wagon about ten to fifteen minutes, the captain would send out a general patrol to follow it. Coming from the other direction would be Rei and another patrol. Once the wagon passed Rei's patrol, the patrol from Osterly Garrison would turn around and return, and Rei's patrol would turn around and catch up with the wagon to bring it on in.

The first part of the trip was certainly uneventful. All three of them were greatly enjoying breathing the fresh spring air and being out of the cramped walls of the garrison. After they left the town, there weren't many other travelers on the road. Mizi climbed out of the back of the wagon and sat next to Ore for company, keeping her hood up to conceal her hair.

Ilena had fallen asleep, as she still did frequently. Even though the wagon bed had been filled with straw and a sheet covered it so that she had padding, it was still somewhat painful to travel long, bouncing and jostling over the road. Sleeping was a way to reduce the pain.

As they neared the half–way point, Ilena opened her eyes suddenly. "Mistress! Please come back here with me." Mizi looked back at her, and Ilena nodded. "It's them."

Mizi looked at Ore who also nodded. "If she says so, then go. She knows what they feel like." Mizi nodded back and carefully climbed into the bed of the wagon to sit next to Ilena.

"It will be okay, Mistress Mizi," Ilena told her with a smile. "Ore and Rei know what to do." Ilena looked up at Ore, who'd turned to look at her, seeing him upside down from her position. "Rei's close enough that a run should get us to him fine. If we can make the ambushers yell after us in frustration, he should hear it and come running."

Ore nodded and turned back to face the road, letting the squad of soldiers know an ambush was imminent. He reviewed in his mind what Ilena had said to him and Mizi the evening before.

She'd prevented him from leaving after dinner, saying she wanted to talk to them about the trip to the castle. Ore had been a little surprised that she'd automatically included Mizi in the conversation, since as a group it wasn't normally done, but as he thought about it, if they'd done that before Mizi wouldn't have been so upset with them.

"As I said to Prince Rei, Earl Shicchi is very predictable. Any ambush his men may carry out will also follow and expect predictable patterns. Will you please hear my suggestions on how we may pass them?" She'd been specifically asking Ore if he would patiently hear her out, he could tell. Remembering her interview with Rei and knowing that everything that would help them escape any attack could be critical, he'd nodded curtly.

"They'll wait until we're in the middle of the trip," she'd sighed. "I would have attacked just outside the village, before any following soldiers were being sent out, mainly for logistical reasons, but that is neither here nor there. I'll know when we're near. Having lived with their kind on my guard so long, it's like I can sense them on the stillest air from a far distance. I'll give you warning.

"Mistress Mizi, it would be best if you came and lay down with me then so that if Ore needs to protect our rear he may do so without injuring you." Mizi had nodded. "Ore, they'll expect you to stop the cart and parlay, surrounding us at that time so we can't escape. Of course, if we do what they expect, that will be the outcome. I personally find that rather unacceptable.

"Instead, what I would do is have the majority of the guards rush the ambushers in the front and push them to either side of the road. I would only leave one or two guards at the back of the wagon to dissuade the ambushers closing in from the sides and rear. They would find that confusing. In being confused they'll be slower to react.

"The point, however, is that you won't stop the wagon. You may slow down the wagon as needed while the front guards open a hole, but as soon as they've opened a hole large enough for the horse — the horse mind, not the wagon — whip the horse into a full run. Don't mind me. Just get the wagon moving as fast as possible.

"The horses on the road will move out of the way of the wagon, so you don't need to mind them either. ...It may help to put blinders on the wagon horse, though, so as it passes through the fighting, it doesn't rear or shy from it's course." She'd frowned, thinking about it.

"The riders behind the wagon should follow it through, staying as close as possible, and protect the rear. Then the guards who've opened a space for us to pass can either remain and have fun keeping the ambushers occupied until the patrol catches up, or follow after us, as if 'running away' so that they can continue to protect us. Our goal is to remain unharmed, not to win a battle. The patrol coming after us can take up the fight with the ambushers trailing behind us.

"As long as we in the wagon don't stop until after we've passed Prince Rei's patrol, we'll very likely receive little to no damage, although it's possible you'll have to knock one or two extra passengers off if they can recover quickly enough."

Ilena had looked at Ore with slightly narrowed eyes to see if he would accept her words. "That's what I would do, knowing how these men work. I would also have a plan in place for if there were suddenly two ambushes, the one I've described, and then another that came after we'd passed Rei's patrol and before it caught back up with us, although I don't know if one will actually be thought of. I'll let you decide what you'll do, of course."

She'd turned back to Mizi without comment at Ore's calmly closed face. "You should remember while we're going through it that you aren't a delicate wallflower waiting to be plucked. If that's what you are we should use you as trade for us to get away freely. You are someone that Rei relies on with intelligence and strength of your own. Use them freely. If someone climbs in the back of the wagon with us, what will you do? Decide now."

Mizi had looked at Ilena with wide eyes, then shook her head. "I've had to deal with such things before."

"But not for a long time, I think. You've become very over–protected and are forgetting your strengths. Tell me otherwise." Ilena's challenge was absolute.

Mizi had gotten her firm look in her eyes. "I would slide down and kick him in the jaw to knock him loose from the back of the wagon."

"And if it only rocked his head back?"

Mizi looked at the scene in her head. "Um...I would stomp on his hands so he let go of the wagon."

"And then if he looked at you threateningly, so as to scare you?"

"Ah... eh...."

"You've only used one of your tools, that of your body, which is your weakest tool. You also have the tool of your voice, and the tool of your companions. You must use your voice only when needed, but never forget to use it. If you've knocked him loose enough, call Ore so that he can throw a dagger at him, finishing the work. Ore's dagger alone will also not likely be enough to completely deter him, but working together you will both save us all from injury."

Mizi mused, "...The tool of the voice...can I also use that to call to Rei? If he were close enough and we made noise he would likely hear."

Ilena's eyes had lit up in approval. "Very good, Mistress Mizi. That idea also uses the tool of companions. You should wait until we've left enough of the ambushers behind and we're close enough for him to actually hear you. Wasting your voice early isn't helpful. If we were to be closed in and not able to escape, calling to the patrol behind us would be a good weapon also." Mizi had nodded her understanding, looking like she all of a sudden had more pluck and less fear.

"Mistress Mizi, also, while you can call a name, there is no weapon more formidable in a woman's arsenal than her scream. The louder and more terrified it is, the better. These men delight in hearing such a thing and it will goad them into over–reaching their capabilities. The guards will react by fighting harder to protect you.

"Ore will cry — or laugh in delight if he knows you're using it as a weapon — and the patrols coming from either direction will spur their horses on all the faster to reach you as soon as possible. Rei will die, of course, and be angry at you later when he discovers you aren't actually injured, but that's a small price for having been spared capture, I think.

"I, personally, would prefer that I not have to use my own voice. It would be better for them to continue to think I'm dead. However, if it's necessary, I will." She'd smiled at Mizi, encouragingly, and Mizi had looked very determined.

Ore had excused himself and gone to make plans with the captain and the squad that would be assigned to the wagon. In the main he'd gone with Ilena's plan. They were even now falling into those formations. As he scanned the trees around them, he could begin to sense now that they were indeed coming up on the ambush and his senses heightened all the more. Ilena's distance was pretty good when it came to sensing these men, but, as she intimated, they weren't bright.

Ore had time to remember when he'd gone back to their room. For once, he hadn't been late, excusing it because they'd have an early morning, but also because he had a question for Ilena. "Why did you tell Mistress those things and include her in the discussion?" It wasn't an accusatory question. He wanted to know.

Ilena had smiled. "Ore, a person who doesn't understand a thing can only fear it. A person who doesn't understand what their weapons are and how to use them is powerless. A person who feels powerless only knows fear.

"Why should Mistress Mizi be left by us to be weakened by fear when we can give her the strength to stand and do what needs to be done? Shouldn't a person who knows a thing be willing to give understanding if it's asked for or needed?" That made sense to Ore.

"Also, if I desire to follow a mistress, isn't it my duty to ensure she has those qualities I'll be obedient to? The mistress I choose to follow needs to have the power and strength of understanding, and of knowing what her weapons are and how to use them. ... Ah, though, it's also your duty to see I don't stray too far from the qualities that Rei desires to see, so I'll be obedient to your guidance if you see anything amiss in what I teach her."

"Why are you always so thorough in your answers?" he'd asked a bit grumpy as he'd been reminded he was her leash and she was his. Then quickly he'd followed it up with, "Never mind, don't answer that," as he saw her mouth open. He'd climbed into bed and ended the conversation. But he'd thought about it, glad she'd aided Mizi to be strong.

He'd wondered if he was afraid of Ilena because he didn't understand her. By what she'd said, did that mean she'd be willing to help him understand her if he chose to ask her? He couldn't do that yet, but maybe by watching her, he'd still be able to come to understand her. Likely she was already trying, considering how desperate she was to have Kase. He'd rolled his eyes, sighed, and rolled over to face the wall, falling asleep soon after.

A movement in the trees told him it was time. "Mistress Mizi, please lie down now," Ilena whispered behind him and he heard Mizi shuffle on the straw. Just before they engaged, he had the sudden thought, *"A person who feels powerless knows fear. A person who doesn't understand what their weapons are and how to use them is powerless."*

Do I feel the fear of being powerless regarding my brother because I don't understand what my weapons against him are and how to use them? Was that what she was trying to tell me? ...Is she trying to help me understand that she's my weapon? He had to leave the wonder of that thought for later. The ambushers were on the road ahead and beginning to move out onto the road behind them.

Ore slowed the wagon slightly as if he was confused or worried, and several of the mounted guards moved up ahead of him, using bluffing words as they went. "Hey, hey. Get off the road. Castle business coming through."

"No, we're here —"

The guards cut them off. "Come on, come on, we don't have all day." "Got a deadline to meet."

"*Pfft!*" Ilena had already understood what he'd told the guards to do and couldn't help the laugh. Ore smiled his predatory grin.

"Here, we're not lettin' you th—"

The first set of guards had their horses in the faces of the ambushers. "Come along, you, out of the way!"

Ore increased the speed of the wagon just a touch, the guards around him keeping pace. Then, there it was! *Snap!* the reins came down hard on the back of the wagon's horse and they shot forward. Ilena was right. The horses in front moved out of the way on their own accord.

"Hey! Come back 'ere!" came from beside, then behind them.

"Next time, get out of the way, like we tell you!" yelled the front guards, who were now the rear guards as they slapped the rumps of the horses of the men they'd moved out of the way, making them jump. That made the ambushers have to pay attention to their horses instead of their escaping quarry, and tangled that group up enough that the rest of the band of thugs couldn't get through for over a minute.

Ilena couldn't help it. She began to laugh. "*Ah hahaha! Ahh! Hahaha!* Oh, Ore, that was wonderful! *Haha hee hee.*"

Ore grinned to himself. It had turned out well. All he'd had to do was remind the men of their strengths and the weapon of intimidation, then outline the plan. They were all still quite aware that the men behind them would likely take up the chase and weapons might still be brought out, but they had the advantage now.

"What happened, Ilena?" Mizi asked confused.

Punctuated by giggles, Ilena told her a play by play. Ore was impressed. She'd 'seen' it with her ears. "Ah, Ore, if you've got a whistle or some such to call Rei with, he's close enough to hear. If he gets into view quickly, the ones catching up to us will quit the chase, I think." Ilena interrupted herself.

He smiled back at Mizi. "Want to give it a go?"

Mizi looked up at him startled, then smiled. "Okay." She got up onto her knees and leaned on the back of the seat Ore was sitting on, placing her hands on either side of her mouth. Taking a deep breath, she shouted, "Rei! Rei!"

"Count to five, then do it again," ordered Ilena.

...five. "Rei! ...Rei!"

"Repeat."

The count to five. "Rei! ...Rei!" and he rode into sight, his men following him, all of them galloping as hard as they could. Ore could see them taking in the situation, then splitting to go around their little group and head straight into the fray behind them. Ore slowed the horse slightly and turned to look behind them.

The ambushers were in disarray. The ones closest to them had broken off and turned to run the other way. Mizi's shout, though surely heard less clearly, had apparently alerted the patrol behind them. They were also running up to flank the other end. Within short order, the two patrols had surrounded the ambushers and were ordering their surrender.

As Ore turned back, Ilena caught his eye. "Well?" she asked.

Ore smiled at her. "The ambushers just got ambushed, from both sides. Looks like there won't be a battle. Master will probably catch up after they've prepared the other side to go back with the garrison patrol."

"Nope. He's too impatient." she answered him.

Ore looked back up over his shoulder. Sure enough, Rei was coming after them. He slowed the wagon horse down to a quick trot so Rei could catch up. "How do you do that?" he asked Ilena.

She smiled a secret smile. "Survival instinct. You understand, I'm sure, Ore."

He nodded. He did, but her ears were still very good. "Ah, is this why the rumors you're a witch?"

She shrugged. "One of the reasons, I suppose." Her smile didn't waver, and it seemed to take on a predatory look to match his.

"Ore! Mizi!" Rei called as he caught up. They looked over at him and smiled. "Eh? Smiles?! From you too, Mizi? I thought you'd be in danger for sure when I heard you calling me."

"Well, Rei, I decided that calling you *before* I was in danger was a better choice than after. It's what you've been trying to teach me, right?" Mizi answered.

Rei had an amazed look on his face. "Ah. Yes, I guess I have, haven't I? Very good! It's certainly much better to see you two smiling when I get here than dark and worried." He smiled back at them, looking at Ore.

"Don't look at me. She did it," he pointed with his thumb to Ilena. "She's the one who explained it."

Rei rode up closer to the wagon to a place where he could look in and just see Ilena's eyes. They were sparkling with pride and excitement. "That was quite fun, Rei! Wasn't Mistress Mizi's use of her vocal weapon very timely, not to mention beautiful?" Rei nodded, trying to wrap his brain around "ambush" being equated with "fun".

"But really, Ore's use of my lesson was the best. He had the guards bully our way through, then did as I suggested and ran the horse. You were in the right place at the right time, too, so it all came together just right! Ah! I love it when plans come together like this. They really make it all worth it, don't they?"

Rei couldn't help but smile. "Thank you, all of you, for staying safe."

"Oh, we're not safe yet," Ilena contradicted him. "We've just passed a hurdle. Safe isn't until we're in the castle."

"Ah, that's why Ore's not stopping?" Rei nodded his understanding.

Mizi nodded. "Ilena said we should also plan on there being another ambush on the way from here to the castle, although she said it wasn't too likely."

Rei smiled wider. "We took care of it on our way here. They were pretending to have a wheel off their cart, so we pretended to help — a small number of us anyway. The rest of us continued on, then circled around behind the ambushers in the brush.

"If it had been really a broken cart, we would have helped them and sent them on their way, but we did actually find more men in the brush, so we arrested them all. I'm a little short handed because we left some behind to take them back to the castle." He looked at Ilena again.

She smiled back up at him. "While I warned them it might happen, I didn't bother to plan. You're the better strategist, after all." That comment got filed away as another one of her clues that she knew more than she let on. "I'm surprised they thought they could get away with letting you see them before you passed them, instead of waiting to lose their wheel after you passed."

His smile turned predatory. "They lost the wheel before they anticipated they would. It made them nervous enough to give them away when we did pass."

"Ah, tough luck," Ore said unsympathetically.

Ilena laughed again, then sighed happily, snuggling down a little further into her "bed". Then she looked up at Mizi. "Mistress Mizi, do you want to ride with Rei?" She had no idea of the shock that went through everyone's spines.

"Eh...ah...," Mizi hedged.

"Mistress Mizi," Ilena said warningly, "look at me." Mizi looked in Ilena's eyes nervously. "Are you going to choose protection, or strength?" her tone was one of impatience. Rei and Ore both shivered. They couldn't refuse or complain now, given how angry Mizi had been when they chose protection over strength for her.

"Strength," answered Mizi calmly. She turned to Ore. "Stop the wagon for a moment."

While Ore stopped the wagon, Rei took his horse over to the other side of the wagon so that Mizi could step from the wagon seat onto his horse's back. In order to help steady her, he had her sit in front of him, the way she and Andrew had traveled together in the past, then they got going again. In the end, both of them were blushing pretty hard.

Ore thought it was the most amusing thing he'd seen in quite some time. He looked over his shoulder at Ilena, who smiled up at him. "Did you do that to tease them on purpose?" he asked her.

"It was her reward," she answered simply, "but if it pleases you to see them teased, then yes." Ilena sighed. "Really, Ore. I've wondered for a long time why things aren't happening as they should between them."

"I'm beginning to learn it's because the rest of you keep preventing anything from happening, or perhaps it's a little less bad, and you're all just stumbling around in the dark. I'm afraid I'm going to be more difficult than Rei is thinking. Don't let me get too far off the mark too fast, eh?"

"You're going to be *more* difficult?" His eyes narrowed. "What are you thinking?"

"How long before he gets pushed into a marriage he doesn't want, Ore?"

He turned back to make sure the horse was pulling the cart in the right direction. "At most a year."

"Yes. There isn't much time, is there? We only have at most a half a year to turn her into the princess they want her to be. I can only hope that's enough time, but they'll have to work very, very hard." Then she muttered quietly, "And it will be even less time with me not at full capacity for many more weeks to come... *sigh*. Ore?"

"Hmm?"

"Don't let her get off his horse. Distract them until they're riding together into the castle grounds, okay?"

When Ore glanced back at Ilena, she was sleeping again. Well, maybe this Ilena was alright. One thing was certain: she was going to liven up the castle. He sighed. It was going to be his job to make sure she didn't light it on fire. Rei and Mizi had come up to the wagon again. "What was that sigh for?" Rei asked Ore.

Ore looked at them plaintively. "Are you sure it's me you want yoked with her?"

"Yes," they both said simultaneously. "Why?"

"She's likely to kill me off before I can properly get my brain wrapped around what to do with her."

"But, Ore," said Mizi, "you've already got the proper instincts."

"How's that?!" Ore was wondering if he should be offended, but he didn't really understand what she was talking about.

"You're both wild creatures, I think she's saying," Rei teased him. Ore was right, he was supposed to be offended.

"No," Mizi shook her head, disagreeing. "You already love her. That will lead you." Ore, and to some degree Rei, stared at her, disbelieving. A sudden soft coughing fit from Ilena distracted them and allowed them to move on to other topics.

Ore spent a lot of time the rest of the trip thinking about protection versus strength, what his potential weapons against his brother were and how he might use them, Ilena as a shield for Rei and a weapon — or a shield — for him, and what it meant to be and to have a partner.

-o-o-o-

Rei couldn't decide if he was feeling pleasantly comfortable or unpleasantly warm. It seemed to keep switching between the two. He was most certainly feeling *happy*, although he wasn't sure he was supposed to. The temerity of Ilena. To not only suggest to Mizi she might ride with Rei, a thing he'd only gotten to do with her once or twice before, but to seal his and Ore's mouths shut in one go so they couldn't utter one protest.

If anything told him Ilena was going to be hard to handle, it was that one act. There were, after all, reasons why he normally *didn't* get to ride with Mizi, and they were equally valid. It felt like a whisper of warning. Kind of like Mina's warning to let things unfold before making any decisions. Things weren't yet fully in play, and so he should remain wary.

All of a sudden I feel like Elder Brother Sasou. He considered that thought. *No, I feel like I'm sparring with Sasou. Having to stay on my toes and remain alert for his, or in this case her every move and comment in order to understand how the board is being played.* But...she played it differently; Rei could see that.

Ilena taught while she played the court game of test, strength, and manipulation. She didn't expect people to just pick it up or lose their advantage, like Sasou did. But then, Sasou didn't have time to be patient.

Ilena seemed to enjoy having others play well, like with her enjoyment that Ore and Mizi, and even he, had played their parts well just then. She was free with her rewards, as well — praising each of them openly. *Hmm...well we'll see further later, but, even though I don't enjoy being made to play the game, I like the way she plays better.*

Ah, but he was supposed to be the one testing her, and she seemed to always be in control of the board. Maybe that was okay, though. He played it by observing the movements of the others on the board to see what they did. When he understood it as a whole, then he made his moves.

He'd learned to be patient already with the game. He could let her play it out, then make his decision the way he always did. It might actually be fun to watch her play, as long as he had a block ready for if she went too far.

"What are you thinking about, Rei?" asked Mizi.

"Mmm...Miss Ilena. And Ore's comments. And Mina's. ...What have you learned about her now that you've had more time with her awake? Are you still okay with her next to Ore?" he asked Mizi.

"Yes. They did well together yesterday and today, in handling this trip. She was a great strength to me, too, helping me be strong for it. It was rough at the first, though, and that may not change for a while." She sounded a little dejected.

"What's wrong?" Rei asked.

"Ore's frustrated with being tied to Ilena when he still doesn't understand her. He takes it out on her by teasing her. She just calmly shoots him down and that frustrates him more. I talked to her about it, although I couldn't help much, and she promised to try something else so that they don't fight so much. It was getting hard to be between them all the time.

"Today has been much calmer and nicer. I think it helps for Ore to see examples of who she really is inside. ...Of course, the part of her that's irritating is still who she really is, too, but I think it comes from some amount of insecurity.

"And, I think she's a bit claustrophobic as well. There were times we would all be in the room together and she'd close her eyes and breathe carefully, as if to keep the walls from closing in."

Rei frowned a little. "Ah, well, that may be difficult. I'm putting her in one of the rooms in the infirmary so she can be close to you and Ryan. I'd like you both to help watch her. I'm going to have to take Ore away frequently, but I'm not sure about most of the castle help yet. Until she gives her testimony in the Lord's Court, I don't want to risk her being discovered and silenced. I've had Mina vet a nurse, though, who'll help with taking care of her daily needs."

Mizi considered Rei's plan. "Okay — although those are small rooms. Well, if she doesn't have to be in there for very long, it might be okay. She doesn't complain. I think Ryan will like her, too."

"Anything else?" Rei asked.

"Well...she's been busy as best she can. She's picked both my brain and Ore's brain for everything she can learn about the castle and its daily running and...well everything we could tell her. ...And then she memorized it all." Mizi gave a small sigh of resignation.

"Did she say why?" Rei hugged Mizi, then took her right hand in his to hold it lightly.

It took a moment before Mizi remembered Rei's question. "Ah, something about so she could be a good guest at your home since she hasn't been in a castle in a very long time and she didn't want to be impolite."

Hmm...so she's been in a castle before, but when she was too young to learn proper court etiquette? She seems pretty polite, though. Is it a deeper quest than that? "Well, she'll probably be just fine in that regard. It's good that she likes to keep herself busy." Rei squeezed Mizi's hand lightly.

"Yes, that impressed me, too." She gingerly squeezed his hand back.

"And what have you been doing to keep yourself busy? I know she surely didn't catch up to you in that." Rei smiled at the back of Mizi's head.

Sounding a little embarrassed, Mizi laughed. *"Ah, haha.* The usual. Studying herb books, talking with Ore and Ilena, and, as I said getting my brain picked, and having to step into their fights. It's been more lively than I thought at first. Being home will be nice, though. Ilena did complain about having to be more still than she's used to. I've been feeling the same. It will be good to be busy again."

"I'm jealous," Rei said. "I wonder when I'll get a vacation next?"

"I think Ilena would tell you that you have to make your vacations. You are your own boss, after all." Mizi's rare tease held her smile.

"That's an interesting thought. I wonder if I can have the rest of the day off today?" Rei wondered.

Mizi laughed, "What does your boss say?"

Rei smiled. "He says, 'You're getting it right now. Get back to work as soon as you're back at the castle'."

"Ah," Mizi smiled. "I get to spend your vacation with you. That's nice."

Rei finally gave in to the urge and buried his head in her hair, resting on her shoulder. "Yes, it is. I'm glad I'm getting to spend it with you. Especially this way." They both blushed, but Rei didn't move just yet, just lightly brushed Mizi's hand with his thumb. "You know, I really wish we could spend more time like this together," he finally admitted to her. "I really have missed you."

Mizi sat quietly for a while. He wondered if he'd made her mad again. Then he noticed that her grip on his hand had gotten tighter. He looked up and around into her face as best he could. She was fighting tears.

He wrapped his left arm around her, although he couldn't let go of the reins, and held her close. "I'm sorry, Mizi. I'm sorry I'm finding it so difficult to find the next step. I really wish I knew what to do."

She reached up and held onto his arm with her hand, the best she could do to give him a hug back, and shook her head. "I know you're trying your best. Something will come. We'll think of something." Then she dropped her head and smiled a little smile. "If worst comes to worst, I'll ask Ilena for help."

Rei's lips pressed together. "Hmm. I think I might want to find other options first. She'll fly away with it, I think."

"Well, yes..., but I think she would have our best interests at heart." Mizi still had faith in Ilena.

Rei couldn't disagree completely. "Probably she would think that. However, there are things she doesn't know, as she's even said."

"True," Mizi blushed again.

Probably thinking like me about the impropriety of what we're doing right now ...and how Miss Ilena unknowingly has turned it upside down. But we can't complain — mostly because we don't want to. Somehow the remainder of the trip turned out to be very short.

-o-o-o-

Their arrival at Castle Nijou was uneventful. Ilena was asleep when they moved her to her bed, which was probably for the best since it had been a harder trip for her than she'd thought it would be. But when she woke up, she was sad she'd missed her last bit of blue sky and open space for a while, especially when she perceived the room seemed just as small as the one she'd left. It was fairly dark in the room, and they'd been scheduled to arrive in the mid evening. Maybe it was dinner time? Or had she slept through it and it was night now?

She listened closely to the strange sounds of a new place. Still two guards on the door. *She* wasn't going anywhere. Rei must have a distrust of a few people in the castle still. She hoped she could fix that for him, to some degree, but that would depend on if he would end up trusting her or not. She sighed. Sometimes, particularly when she got lonely or claustrophobic, it was hard to be patient.

For now, as long as she fed them the information a little at a time, and as long as she remained a cooperative witness under protective custody, it was a positive symbiotic relationship. That was much better than the negative leech–like relationship she'd been in before, but this was — so far — more restrictive.

The fault of the wound of course — there was nothing to be done about that. The fact that she still had her life was a great blessing. She could hold on to that as a ray of hope that things might still turn out okay...even though it went against all the training she'd had up until now.

She couldn't help it. The tears slipped out without her permission. It was quiet here, wherever here was, at least at this time of night. If she was being guarded, it was likely it would stay fairly quiet. It was doubtful Rei wanted many people to know she was here yet. *Damn the tears.* They wouldn't quit. *Must be from having years of practice at being let out at night.*

Well, nothing for it then, but to fall asleep again. Wonder when I'll get to have a bath again. I miss being really clean. A tear dripped off her cheekbone to land with a plop on her ear. *Haa. Need to stop. Just sleep. Life will happen again tomorrow.*

... I'm just tired of being lonely. Probably more tonight because today was the first time I've laughed since...well...forever. Like... the last time I was in a castle in Ryokudo. Ah, now why'd I have to go and remember that!? Now the tears really won't.... The door opened before she could get control of her sobs.

Someone entered quietly, then gathered her head in their arms and let her cry. It was an odd thing to be both depressed and crying, *and* also be very surprised at the same time.

"Wh–who?" she finally managed to say once the sobs stopped and the tears slowed down.

"Ah!" the person jumped a little, then quickly, but carefully, let go. She grabbed a sleeve before he could disappear from her range.

"Please, don't go...just yet." He stopped moving and let her hang on. "Thank you. That was exactly what I needed."

"I...I thought it might be. ...It's what someone did for me, the first time I was away from my family and at the castle."

"Oh? That was a very nice gift that person gave you, to be able to give it to me. I thank that person too." She felt this kind stranger smile. It seemed a shy kind of smile, just like his words. She guessed he was a young man. He'd seemed rather short, although not too short, when he'd been hugging her. "Ah...I'm Ilena, and I was just feeling very lonely. May I know your name, so I won't feel quite as lonely?"

Again a shy smile? This time he moved his arm she had hold of. He took her hand and set it on the bed, then kept his hand lightly on hers, like a kindly physician might. "I'm Ryan, Head Court Healer at Castle Nijou. Prince Rei asked me to take the second watch over you. Mizi has first watch, and Ore will come for third watch. ...I thought I'd work outside so I wouldn't be a bother while you were sleeping. ...They — Ore and Mizi — told me that you might be lonely tonight, so...I was...." He petered out, embarrassed.

She flipped her hand over and grasped his wrist briefly before releasing it to allow him to escape if he wished to. "Thank you for thinking of me, Head Court Healer Ryan. I truly appreciate it, although I admit to some surprise that Ore and Mistress Mizi would think to say such a thing. That makes me feel somewhat better also." *Ah, good, he didn't move his hand. I guessed right.*

"Eh...is there...anything you need?" he asked. *He's trying so hard. He's come a long way, but this is still a flustering situation to be in, isn't it?*

"I guess I am thirsty and a little hungry. I take it I've missed dinner," Ilena admitted.

"Yes," his voice was professional now, though young, "but food was brought for you. ...I'm sorry, I've already eaten mine."

"That's alright. If you'd like to join me again, I'm sure there's more brought than I can eat myself. They usually do that, after all." She put a smile into her voice.

"Well, I'll need to feed you, so I'll be keeping you company that way."

"Well, but this is an embarrassing situation for me to be meeting you in, Mister Ryan," she admitted to him.

"Why?" he sounded genuinely surprised. He'd moved, maybe towards a desk and candle.

The light flickered to life as she answered, the sparkling light dancing in her smiling eyes, "Because I respect your work and your research. I've read several of your treatises, although my favorites are your untranslated works."

He stared at her in amazement, his dark almost black eyes open as wide as they could go. His chopped black hair stood up on end, likely from being frequently rubbed without thought. He was chubby and indeed short. It looked like he might be almost as tall as Mizi now, although it was hard to tell from Ilena's horizontal position.

His cream shirt was under a bright blue jacket and tucked into pants to match. Over them all was a doctor's coat of cream color, the symbol of the Regent's court on the breast pocket. It looked rather creased and slept in. There was a faint smudge of ink on his forehead where he'd likely brushed his hand to move a stray set of hairs. "My...my *untranslated* works?"

"Yes. The ones you wrote at your parent's home. I take it you felt they weren't worthy of publication because they were rough? I found them extremely useful for my own work."

"You...you've used them?"

"Yes. In particular I needed the one on salysilic phosphoresis, but I found the others nearly as useful."

"You're a researcher?"

"Well, ...I assisted a researcher, specifically a surgery researcher, and dabbled in practical applications of herbs, drugs, and medicines since he was a little thin in that area."

"...." Ryan blinked several times, trying to process it all. "How did you read them? And, how did you get ahold of them?"

Ilena smiled, hoping she wouldn't scare him off with the answers to those questions. "I understand multiple languages. It took a bit of effort the first paper to understand the more technical terms, although you weren't quite sophisticated enough yet to completely lose me at the time you wrote them. I might have to be coached to read your current untranslated works, though as I said I prefer to read them that way. It's easier to follow the flow of the progression of your thoughts."

"Yes, I think so too," he said faintly.

She laughed lightly. "I should think so, Mister Ryan."

He blinked, then smiled as he realized his joke. He blushed slightly. "You're a lot like Ore," he said.

Ilena's mouth fell open. She blinked. "I am?"

He blushed a little more and turned towards the door again to fetch Ilena's meal. "You're easy to talk to." She smiled at his back. He was fun to talk to.

Ilena was actually surprised that Ryan had been assigned to watch over her. He was a busy young man, being the youngest healer in the history of Ryokudo, and the youngest to ever be made a Head Court Healer. He'd been trained at the main castle after being scouted by the Head Court Healer there. It must have been her who'd comforted him that first night there. He'd been a Court Healer by the time he was eleven, *or was it nine?*

He'd been given this position just around a year ago by King Sasou after his research with Mizi on the plant that flowered in the winter snow of Suiran, *Holegn Hanatake*. That was still her project and why she'd been out of the castle when she'd rescued Ilena.

Ryan was very shy, but his time at Kouzanshi — two years, if Ilena remembered correctly — had certainly helped him open up enough to talk to patients better. He was even more open with other researchers. His lack of height, that made him seem even younger than he was, had somewhat to do with that.

Well, he would never be very tall, sadly, but any height he gained was a triumph, she was sure. What was he now, in his middle upper teens? He probably had four more years of good growth, or so, to go — now that it had started.

While she had a moment, Ilena looked around her newest room. It was very small. Her bed was centered on the room so that she could be attended to by her healers as needed. There was a desk in the far back corner over her right shoulder that held the lit candle. There was a chair that likely sat by the desk normally, but at the moment was near to hand by the bed.

Mizi liked to sit where she could see Ilena to talk to her, even if she was sleeping. Ilena had woken many times in Osterly to see the red head bent over the books that seemed ever–present in Mizi's hands. Ilena had enjoyed listening to her read when they didn't have anything better to talk about.

There were no windows in the walls of this room, making it feel even more depressing, but Ilena couldn't fault Rei for not wanting any extra entrances. She did find it a bit concerning that he thought his own castle was this dangerous, though.

She could look towards her toes and see the top of the open door, but she had to contort a bit to actually see out the door. Ryan was returning into the room just then, and she could just catch glimpses of the clothing of the guards to either side of the door. It looked the same as the guards she'd had at Osterly.

He returned with a small cart of food, mostly the easy to digest things she'd been eating at the garrison for several weeks now. She sighed at it. Ryan looked worried. "Ah!" she said before he could get any more worried, "I'm sorry. It isn't your fault. It's just, I'm already at three weeks of healing and it would be nice to be graduating to some real foods sometime soon."

Ryan shook his head. "It isn't that you couldn't eat them, it's that you can't sit up to eat them. The concern is that you'll accidentally choke on the foods that take more chewing. In two weeks, when you can sit up properly, then you can have them." He pulled the chair closer to her bed and sat in it, preparing to feed her.

Ilena sighed. "You wouldn't happen to have a tincture or a poultice that would make two weeks go by in, say, ...three hours, would you?"

Ryan looked at her seriously for a moment, then stopped, looked at her again, and smiled. "You are like Ore. You like to tease, also."

"Well...I wouldn't say I was teasing so much as having fun while complaining, though. I know you have no such thing, after all." She let him feed her her first bite of food, chewed it thoroughly, then swallowed carefully, looking at him all the while very carefully. He'd indeed watched her do it, and with some small concern. When he looked up at her with the next spoonful ready, she smiled at him. "That was teasing, Ryan."

"What?" his eyes opened wide and she smiled wider.

"Look at the food, Ryan. Does it really require that much of my attention to all the detailed parts of eating it?" He looked at the fairly thin porridge, and shook his head. "Come, now. I'm not teasing you now." He lifted his head, surprised.

"I'm explaining what it was that I did that was teasing, so that you might understand the difference... although it's perhaps very indistinct... hmmm... well, regardless, —" he stuck the spoon in her mouth, then laughed a giggle at her surprised expression.

She smiled back after swallowing the mouthful. "Touché. You win. I will admit you already understand teasing, based on the solid evidence presented to me just now."

He smiled back. "You sound a lot like a professor, even before now."

"Well, yes I guess I often do. Somehow the lecture format is comfortable for me." She ate the next bite while thinking about it. "Maybe it's because I've had to teach so many people so many things over the years, even from the time I was very young."

"What do you do?" he asked as he offered her the next bite.

"Mmm...right now, I'm bored out of my mind while the hip heals. I'm still waiting for Prince Rei to decide what I'm going to do next." He waited. She could tell he wanted the rest of the answer but couldn't decide how to ask for it. Gently, she asked him, "Ryan, how much have you been told about me?"

"Umm...not very much yet, I guess." *Well, that was it, then, wasn't it.*

"Ryan, I think they're trying to protect you. Is that how you see it?"

"Well, I guess they might be thinking that. I was thinking they were just not telling me things again."

"Hmm...I noticed they do that to Mistress Mizi, too. It seems to be that they just don't think of it?" He nodded. He didn't seem too offended, but he did seem sad. "Well, give me another bite or two and I'll think about what I might be allowed to say." He obliged and she thought.

After a few bites, she asked him, "Ryan, have you ever thought to ask? When they start talking about something you don't have the background to understand, or the early pieces to fit into the picture, do you ask for them?"

He continued to feed her while he thought about it. "I guess I don't, not usually. I just wait to see if they'll tell me...but they usually don't."

Ilena nodded. "Well, then, you could solve a lot of it by yourself, just by remembering you're an investigator."

"Investigator?"

"Yes. Researchers have a question, then go and look to see if anyone else has answered the question, and if not, they probe, experiment, etc., until they have the answer to the question. Investigator is the same, but is the first part. What's already known and who knows it? What still needs to be understood? Because you're a researcher, you're already an investigator."

"Ohhh," he spent time mulling that over, absently continuing to feed her.

When he seemed to come back, she continued. "If you don't ask the questions, do you get any answers?" He shook his head. "If you want people to become used to doing something what do you have to do?"

"Train them," he answered promptly.

"Exactly. If you want the people around you to become used to telling you things, you need to train them to tell you those things."

"...By asking them questions?"

Ilena nodded. "The more they get used to answering your questions, the more they'll begin to anticipate your questions and answer them before you ask them. If they answer the wrong one, you can ask the correct one and still get the answer you need. Eventually, they'll just naturally include you, or in other words, naturally supply you with the missing data without you having to ask for it. ...Of course it may take a year or two, humans don't learn all that fast after all, but consistent effort always bears out."

She eyed him a moment as he digested what she'd said. Then she casually said, "You could even practice on your patients. They are who you already ask investigative questions to, right?"

Ryan nodded. "To find out what the problem is and how it was caused so we can find the appropriate solution."

"Right. But you could practice asking for more prior information. Why did they do what they did that caused the problem? How did they feel about that? Sometimes the answers to these kinds of questions can help you understand a deeper problem that needs to be addressed. Like...if a person keeps stubbing their toe.

"Is it because they can't see? Or do they need new shoes? Is it really because they keep getting angry and kicking the chair, forgetting that it hurts every time, and so they need to learn to manage their anger, or maybe need proper training to remember that kicking a chair hurts every time? Or...." She stopped. She'd managed to get him to giggle.

"I understand," he said when he recovered. "If I want to know about you, first I need to ask Prince Rei, or maybe Mizi or Ore, so I know what they're willing to let me know. Then you'll know what you can talk about because I can talk about it first."

"Yeah, you are a genius," she smiled at him, "but also, it's so you don't feel lonely and left out. If I tell you any old thing, whether I should or not, it isn't going to help your relationships, is it?"

Ryan stopped. He put the spoon down in the bowl and lowered the bowl to his lap. "It helps relationships?" he asked wonderingly.

Ah, he's so lonely. It's sad. "Yes, Ryan. Do you know why?" He shook his head. "Because relationships are built on communication. If we don't talk with one another, we can't know who the other person is, their dreams, desires, dislikes, likes, their personality.

"It can be scary to tell those things to another person, and it can sometimes be scary to hear them from another person. But if relationships are better than loneliness, then the scary is easier to bear. Especially if you can remember that the other person participating in the conversation is just as lonely, scared, and hopeful as you are."

His eyes looked up into hers, wide, and she nodded. "Yes, I am. Remember what I was like when you first entered the room." He did and nodded. "In order to ease my loneliness, and fear, I used the hope to talk to you, to try to bridge them by communicating with you."

She smiled at him. "If it's easy to talk to me, or to Ore, it's because you're a person who's easy to talk to." He looked to be in denial. "It's true, Ryan. It's just you who needs to believe it. If you can believe it, it will become true for you. Please, let me urge you again, practice it with your patients. Treat it as an experiment: the 'Ryan is easy to talk to' experiment.

"All you have to do is ask questions and listen and when it's right, take the chance to talk about yourself, to let them know about who you are, too. ...And, with your friends, always remember you're an investigator first. They know it. You won't offend them."

Ryan leaned back in his chair and tilted his head at her, looking at her with his usual very serious expression. "You're a very good teacher. ...Mizi was right. She said you were very nice and that I would like you."

"Thank you, Ryan. You are also very nice, and I like you, too." His eyes got big. "But, Ryan," she tried very hard to be gentle, "that like and the like you're looking for are two different things." He turned very red. "Please, consider me a friend only. One thing I can tell you is that Rei won't give me to you, I'm sorry. It's the same as he won't give you Mizi."

She sighed. "I'm sorry, Ryan. This is part of the pain of communication and understanding each other's dreams and desires. Please don't run from it. ...You don't run from Mizi. It's the same."

He took a breath and nodded. "But still... it is, as you say..., something I'm finding I'm looking for. ...It's becoming a distraction."

Ilena smiled. "That's to be expected. For all you're a genius researcher, you're also a male of the human species. ...May I be of further service to you in this area?"

His eyes lit up, "You can be?"

"Yes, somewhat. You'll have to do the work of communicating by yourself, of course, but I suspect you're looking for someone specific. Like someone who is a researcher or understands researchers; someone who is easy to talk to, preferably; ...obviously a female...." She smiled as he blushed again.

"You're teasing again."

"Very good, you've passed your exam," she winked at him and he smiled shyly back. "Have you taken the opportunity to leave this place and go into town yet?" He shook his head. "That's the first step. You're limited here by who comes to see you, although you could choose to spend some time just wandering around the castle and see who you run into. That's often very educational and sometimes productive.

"But for you, I suggest in the main, that you become a regular at the Scholar's Tavern. Ore can take you there the first time or two since I'm sure he already knows where every tavern and bar are." Ryan nodded in agreement.

"The owners are friends of mine. They've specifically set it up for researchers and scholars to go to for a quiet environment in which to rest their minds, to give them a different environment in which to get a different perspective. It's also a place where different kinds of researchers can synergistically come to solutions to problems that one is having difficulty with."

"Like Kouzanshi?" Ryan perked up.

"Like Kouzanshi," Ilena nodded. "The owners are originally from Kouzanshi and wanted to have a place here that would provide that same kind of atmosphere for the Kouzanshi transplants, although of course others have found their way there as well. If you can go regularly, I believe you may be provided with opportunities to meet others who can help you widen your circle of acquaintances.

"When it's wide enough, the woman you're destined to meet will enter that circle and you'll be able to finally find what it is you're looking for. Though don't hate me if she comes through some other means. It's just a better opportunity than staying here in your offices will provide."

Ryan understood. "Thank you, Ilena," he said.

"You're very welcome, Ryan. I wish you the most happiness. ...Now if you wouldn't mind, I'd love a drink of water."

-o-o-o-

Shortly after getting food and water, and a nice visit by a new friend, Ilena felt much better and started to drift into sleep. She apologized, and Ryan left to continue his work outside the room.

She was awakened by Ore coming in later. "Ore?"

"Yes." He sounded tired but content. That was good.

"I met Ryan. He's very nice."

"Yes, he is. He said the same about you."

"I'm glad. It was hard to not scare him," Ilena admitted.

Ore laughed a bit, "I know, right? It must have been particularly hard for you."

"Um–hm. I did have to work hard," Ilena answered sleepily.

Ore gave a rather thunderstruck pause, then walked over and touched her forehead for a temperature reading. "Are you feeling okay?"

"I am now," Ilena sighed.

"What?" he was confused for a moment, then he jerked his hand away. "Are you teasing *me* now?"

"No. I'm not."

"Okay, what's going on, Miss Ilena?" She was sure he'd put his hands on his hips, but in the dark she wasn't sure.

"I'm lonely. I missed you, although Ryan was kind to comfort me and keep me company."

Ore was silent, then he moved to the right side of the room from her and leaned against the wall, which really wasn't all that far away. They could probably reach their arms out and just barely be able to interlock their fingertips. "Yeah. He said that, too. ...I'll be here until after breakfast, but I won't be able to be here every night. Those nights Master will have a night nurse here for you."

Kindness? Amazing. "I'm glad you're here tonight. I'll try not to miss you too much the nights you're gone." He snorted. Because they hadn't been having a very good relationship until now, it was likely hard for him to believe she'd really miss him all that much. "And I guess you'll be gone after tonight for a while."

"Why's that?" He was sharp as always whenever she made educated guesses or leaked information he thought she shouldn't have.

"I owe Rei the first list. He'll probably be sending you off right away to collect them, won't he?"

"...Yeah, probably." Ore didn't sound thrilled by the idea.

"You'd rather stay and babysit me?" Ilena asked in surprise.

"No, not really. I'm ready to be let out to run some," he admitted.

"...It's that, isn't it?" He didn't answer. "Ore —"

"I don't want to hear it," he rejected her yet again. "I'll do what I'm ordered to do by Master. It's enough."

"...very well," but she was very sad about it. "...Do you remember what to say?"

"Mother has sent me for you."

"Good. ...Be gentle with them. They're willing to help, but most are very afraid." She wished she could go with him and see them herself, to know they were all okay.

"...I will be," he said it very gently.

"Thank you, Ore." She was fading again. "Good night."

"...Good night."

The next morning Ore woke Ilena up for breakfast. She wasn't quite ready for it. Even with Ore there, she hadn't slept well. "I'm sorry to not be able to let you sleep in this morning, but the only time Master has to come visit is on his way to his office this morning."

"Eh? Okay." She rubbed her eyes, then stretched as much as she could. It was getting very hard to stay in this one position all the time and she could feel every muscle atrophy daily. Maybe today would be the day she started to work on muscle strength and tone, even if it had to be from this position. If she didn't do something she was going to start getting testy with people, and that wouldn't be a good thing just yet.

"You doing okay?" he asked as she wiggled and writhed.

"Just laugh," she said tiredly, "it might make me feel better. Can I get you to take my muscles along with you? They've turned into jelly, almost. It's embarrassing, this place I'm forced into. A good soaking bath is really the thing I'm most looking forward to, though.

"Ah, don't say it! It's bad enough I'm thinking it." She wrinkled her nose at herself to prove the point. Ore had to turn away to not let her see his smile. He really did want to laugh. "I said to, didn't I?" she answered his unspoken thought.

"Ah," he sighed. "I'm sorry. I'm sure it won't help you feel better. But here, breakfast might. They've added oranges today."

"Oh, that's wonderful! Finally some flavor! Can that come first and last then? And everywhere in between?" She opened her mouth for the first one, then closed it at his look. She held her hand up. "Give it here. I can feed that to myself."

"No, really, I can help," he said with a smile he couldn't keep down.

"No, really. I don't need that kind of help," she refused. He relented and handed her the orange piece. It had been cut cross grain so it was a thin circle, easy to suck on and get just a little meat from. "Ah, that is wonderful. I wonder if Ryan lodged my complaint from last night."

"Did you complain?" Ore was somewhat surprised.

"Yes. I asked for real food. He told me I couldn't because they don't want me to choke on hard–to–chew foods. Maybe he decided other things could be done."

"Why did you complain to the little Mister and not us?"

Ilena assumed by "us" he meant Mizi and Ore. "It broke the ice, one does not complain to one's mistress, and complaining to you wouldn't get me anywhere."

"Hey, that hurts."

She stopped and looked at him, with her piercing, "was that a lie?" look. He was surprised she used it. "Sorry." It was perfunctory but sincere and she went back to her orange.

He sighed. "You're still weird this morning, too."

She raised her eyebrow but continued to focus on her orange. She could just manage to eat it herself. The biggest problem, of course, was that she either had to eat without lifting her head at all, or just ever so slightly. That meant that food had a tendency to just fall down to the back of her throat if she wasn't very careful. If someone else lifted her head, it worked better. If it required a utensil, she couldn't manage at all. The angles were just all wrong.

Ilena had been pondering Ore's comment, though. "I think...I'm just cross. Next comes testy. Then somewhere along the line, I give up and start throwing tantrums. ...It's actually amazing I can remember that. It's been so forever ago I've been in a place I could do all that. Being locked up in a small room for so long doesn't leave me much else to do but fall back into that, I suppose."

"That's some serious self–analysis, there."

Ilena jumped and stared at Ore. Somehow he'd ended up at her elbow without her knowing, and his voice had been louder than she'd anticipated. "H–how did you do that?"

"Do what?" he was confused. "I just walked over here."

*Ha...hah...*it was hard to get her heart to stop beating so fast. "Just a minute...." She closed her eyes. Behind her eyelids, she could see a young man. *It was like that, wasn't it?* She really was reverting.

Ore's hand was on her forehead again, and when she opened her eyes, he was frowning, but he didn't say anything about it. "Would you like some porridge? It looks like they seasoned it with cinnamon, another concession to real food, I suppose?"

"Okay," she said meekly. He looked at her blandly, then started feeding her, keeping his comments to himself.

-o-o-o-

Rei arrived shortly after they'd cleaned up breakfast and cleaned up Ilena. It was a shared job by Mizi and Ore since they had to carefully roll her a few times to get everything taken care of. They were quite experienced at it now, so it didn't take as long as it used to.

Rei and Mizi happily greeted each other, and Mizi just as happily greeted Andrew and Mina. Rei had brought them along to introduce them officially to Ilena, since they hadn't been able to the time before. Ilena cordially welcomed them, but didn't really know what to say to them, although she watched the interplay between them and Mizi closely. They were formal retainers that morning and took up quiet positions in the background.

Ilena watched them until they settled, then she looked at Rei. He couldn't help it. She looked just like a falcon that had just had it's hood removed and was trying to figure out it's surroundings. He paused, thinking about where to start.

Ilena spoke first, calmly. "Regent Rei, I have your word they'll be kept in a safe location until after their enemies are no longer a threat to them? That they'll be treated kindly and well? That they won't be incorrectly assumed to be enemies of yourself or the country in the way they are handled and questioned? That if they have immediate family members, they'll also be taken along and be protected and treated the same?"

Rei nodded. "You have my word."

"Ore, please prepare to write." They all waited until he was ready. Then, still just as calmly, she listed off ten names with their locations, listing them at the pace she could hear Ore writing.

"Ore, if you'll ask after them by name, you'll find them. If anyone asks you why you seek them or what evidence you give that you have a right to find them, that one is an enemy. Speak no further to that one. Remember that your face is your key. You need no other proof. Only give the keywords to the one who says to you, when you ask them if they are that person, 'I am waiting to hear the words of Father.' ...Repeat to me these instructions."

Ore stood and carefully said, "I'm to seek after them by name in the locations given. My face is sufficient to be directed to them. If anyone asks me for proof or a reason, that person who asks is an enemy to be avoided. When I'm in front of the person who is said to be the one I'm looking for, I'm to ask if that's who they are. If they are, they'll answer, 'I'm waiting to hear the words of Father'. Then I'm to respond, 'Mother has sent me for you'."

"That's correct. To aid you further, there's one more thing I can tell you, if you wish it." She hadn't taken her eyes off Rei this whole time.

Rei instinctively understood that she was going to ask for payment if the aid was accepted. He held up his hand. "Is what you've already said sufficient to the task?"

"Yes."

"Then it's not necessary at this time."

"Very well." She was neither pleased nor displeased with the decision.

"Is there anything else at this time?" Rei asked Ilena.

She paused. "...Yes. May I make an unreasonable request?"

Rei thought about that. Did that mean it was a request that she wouldn't be able to pay for? "I'll hear it." He was careful to promise nothing but that.

Ilena blinked. "If an elderly man asks at a lesser gate to speak to 'the Missus', may he be allowed in to speak with me?"

Rei agreed with her. At this point it was unreasonable. That seemed unlike her...which meant it was very important to her. "I'll consider it."

"Thank you."

Rei thanked her for the list, then excused himself, taking everyone with him except Mizi, who was now on duty with Ilena.

CHAPTER 7 The First Set of Witnesses

Ore was quite busy the following six days. He had a lot of people to collect. At least most of them were centrally located in Suiran, and thankfully, four were actually in the town by the castle. He decided to work from the farthest reaches back towards Nijoushi.

He arrived first at a baronial manor halfway between the Earldom under investigation and Kouzanshi. He figured the person he wanted wasn't going to be very high in the order of things, so he knocked on the kitchen door. The cook shouldn't be too surprised to see a messenger. "Hello," Ore said in a friendly voice. "I'm looking for Peter of Fentress. Can you please direct me?"

The cook, a thin man who looked rather ragged today, looked at him sourly, then called over his shoulder, "Hey, boy! Someone to see you!" The cook looked back at Ore. "Don't keep him long. He's not yet finished chopping the onions. He keeps crying so hard he can't see to cut them."

Ore blinked. That was rather easy, quick, and fortuitous. It made him suspicious. The cook left to go back to his pots and a thinner boy, who looked like he hadn't eaten well in several years even though the clothing hadn't kept up with him regardless, took his place. His dusty light brown hair might actually be blonde if the kitchen soot were washed out of it. When he saw Ore, he froze, then more tears started trickling down his face from his grey eyes. Ore gently asked, "Peter of Fentress?"

He jumped a little, wiped his eyes, muttering, "Onions...." Then he said, "Ah...umm. I'm waiting to hear the words from my Father."

Ore figured it was close enough. "Mother has sent me for you."

Peter shifted his feet. "He...he'll get mad, the cook, but can I come now?"

Ore tilted his head. "I can't give you an excuse. Can you think of one that would get you out right now?"

Peter thought about it, then turned around and called to the cook, "Cook, he says my Grandpa's asking for me. Can I go?"

"Is it that urgent?"

"He sent someone, didn't he?"

"Fine, fine. Stupid old fart, just needs to kick off already." The last was more muttered, as if the cook had stuck his head into a cupboard while saying it. Peter turned back to Ore. "I'll wash up at the pump on the way out," and he shyly led the way.

When he was done washing, he turned to look at Ore expectantly. Ore asked, "Do you have anything to collect?" Peter shook his head. "Alright, then. Can you ride?" Peter shook his head again. "Can you hold on?" This time Peter nodded. "Then let's go."

He led Peter to Fenrier and boosted him on, then climbed up in front of him. Looking over his shoulder, he warned, "This will be an uncomfortable day and night for you. Eventually we'll have enough...Children to get a wagon."

Peter nodded. "It's okay. ...Am I the first?"

Ore smiled as he got Fenrier going. "Yes, so I'm quite new at this. I feel fortunate that my first was so easy to find. It would be nice if the rest could be the same. Master wouldn't pay...Mother's price to let me know how to make it easy to find anyone. I only know I have to ask around everywhere I go."

Peter was quiet for a while, trying to find his balance. Ore had decided to go at a fast canter. Since the boy didn't know how to ride anyway, he may as well learn to keep his seat at a pace Ore wanted to go, although he was sorry to make it a little more difficult. After a while, Peter did figure out how to ride with the horse instead of fight against the motion. Then he was finally able to relax a bit.

Ore wondered if he'd answer questions. "Do you know any of the other Children? Ah, and not just the ones I'm collecting now, just any others?"

Peter shook his head. "I've only been at the Barony. Mother put me there about ten years ago, after she saved me from my first House. I've been doing what she said to do, and waiting for you, ever since."

"You've only met Mother once?" Ore was very surprised.

"Yes," Peter's voice was soft and worshipful.

"You're a very loyal son," Ore praised him.

The arms around him tightened and he could feel Peter's body begin to shake. Ore quietly respected Peter's tears. After some time, Peter started talking. "It was when I was seven. I'd been sent out to the fields and told not to come back until I'd filled the basket with potatoes. I'm pretty slow for working, and it had already gotten dark, but it wasn't full yet. I was getting hungry so I was even slower, when I noticed a glow coming from the main house.

"I stood up to get a better look and it was burning, the whole of it. Ma was there, down sick, and my little sister was taking care of her. All I could think about was them. I ran towards the house when all of a sudden someone popped up in front of me and grabbed me, holding my head so I couldn't see.

"I called and called for Ma and my sister, but she didn't let go. She put her mouth down to my ear and said, 'They're already dead. They all are. You're all that's left. You need to be quiet now, or you will be, too, and I don't want that. I need you to live.' I stopped yelling, but I couldn't stop crying.

"She just held me for a while, then she said, 'I'm going to take you away from here to another place. It might not be as nice as here, but it won't be as bad as my place. Until we get there, you only talk when talked to. Do what you're told. When they ask you where you came from, you say, 'The Missus found me', and nothing but that. Can you do that?' I nodded and she let me go.

"When I could finally look up at her, she was the most beautiful girl I'd ever seen, glowing in the gold light of the fire." Ore guessed the boy's memory had modified that some since that time. Ilena was regal and not bad in the looks department but "beautiful" probably wasn't the best descriptive word.

"She told me to never forget what had happened that night, and if I could, to never forget anything that the Houses had done for the last couple of years before that, especially anything the Masters had ordered done. When she brought me to the Barony, she said the same: to pay attention and never forget the evil deeds that men can do. She told me, 'But don't you do any of it. You keep doing the best you can to be the son your mother would be proud of.'

"I asked her if I'd ever see her again. She smiled at me and said, 'Most likely some day, but it may be years.' Then she told me that now she'd adopted me, I was part of a big family, and she told me how to recognize another family member, saying I might get a visit every now and then from them.

"The last one came by a half a year ago and taught me how to recognize you and what to say." Peter started shaking again. "I'm glad you came today. ...I was cutting those onions and thinking of using the knife on me instead, almost wishing Mother'd let me die with my Ma and my sister."

"Well, that wouldn't do, for such a faithful son to give up. Especially right when he's needed most," Ore scolded kindly.

"Needed? Most?" It sounded like Peter believed he wasn't needed by anyone.

Ore nodded. "Do you know why Mother sent me?" Peter shook his head. "It's time to avenge the deaths of your Ma and sister, and to talk about all the evil doings of men that she told you to remember." He looked back over his shoulder at Peter to see his surprised reaction.

"I'm taking you to a safe place with others of Mother's Children. There, you'll get to visit with those of your adopted family whom we're collecting. And you'll be fed, although you'll have to help with the house chores." Peter definitely liked the word food and was already used to helping with chores. "In exchange, there'll be some people come who'll ask you to talk about those things you saw, heard, and can remember. Answer their questions honestly, okay?"

"Okay. That's easy enough. ...Will Mother come? I really want to see her again." Peter dropped his head.

Ore was quiet for a while. "I'm sorry, I don't have an answer for you." It was all he could say.

Peter nodded his head. Ore could feel it moving against his back. Then he was quiet for a long time.

The whole northern two–thirds of Suiran was forest in the main. The roads of the region cut through the trees. In most places they were maintained by the lords well enough to have the forest cut back from the roads, but in some places the forest edged right up to the road.

Ore took note of where so he could add those locations to his report when he returned. In particular these main roads were supposed to be maintained with funds from the castle coffers. In those places where it wasn't, the lords were likely pocketing those funds for themselves instead.

Most of the trees were bare, with the tips of the branches showing signs of color and life: reds, yellows, yellow–greens. Here and there were stands of conifers, their dark green needles standing out in the early spring woodland.

Here and there were also open areas of land, dark brown earth that was loamy, fed by the leaves from the trees. Those were the areas that would soon see men and older boys walking behind horses pulling plows. Others would follow the plows to plant the seeds that would bring the grain and other food for the region to survive on.

Ore breathed the fresh spring air as Fenrier ran with the two men on his back. It was nice to be able to be outside in the cool air. It was finally warm enough that the heavy winter coats, hats, and gloves could be left behind. The thick wool cloaks were enough. It had been nice to be here in the north and finally be warm this past three winters. When he was young and on his own, one thin blanket and a begged hat had been all that warmed him then. ...And his memories.

Ore frowned slightly. Memories weren't enough to help him face the reality of now. He wondered just what had happened to Ilena during that same time? She'd obviously used her memories of him to help her through, like he had, but he'd changed and so had she. The glimpse Peter had just given him made him even more curious. Why would Ilena have been at Peter's household when it was being burned to the ground? Had the earl taken her with him when he'd destroyed an early ally? Why?

What had Ilena really seen, done, and become from the time Ore had left Tokumade and now? Ore spent the rest of that ride trying to imagine it based on what little he'd already been told. He found himself wondering what more he might hear from the other people on his list to pick up.

-o-o-o-

It was late at night when they arrived at the next destination. It was a hunting lodge for a noble lord, set in a clearing filled with the lodge, a stable, and a few outbuildings. The woods barely managed to stand back enough to give those buildings room. The main building looked quiet and dark. Ore figured that was probably a good thing.

He dismounted, then helped Peter down. Even though they'd had a couple of stops, it was still very difficult for Peter to walk for a few moments. Fenrier snorted and shook his head. Carrying two at a fast pace for most of the day had worn him out and he wanted a good rest in the stable. Ore stroked Fenrier's nose and spoke to quiet him, loosely tying the reins to the outside pin of the stable.

"Oh! I say!" Peter said in surprise. Ore looked over at him. Peter was looking down at a young child that had attached itself to his leg. Himself, upon closer inspection.

Ore squatted down to be closer to eye level with the boy and asked after the next person on the list. The child looked over at one of the smaller outbuildings. "Well, then, let's go see shall we? That's Peter you have hold of, by the way."

The child looked up at Peter and said, "Bro."

Ore smiled. "Works for me. How about you, Peter?"

Peter smiled shyly at the child and nodded. He detached the child from his leg and took his hand. "Do you have a name?" he asked the small boy as they walked towards the servants' quarters. The little boy shook his head. Peter looked worried.

Ore smiled, "It's okay Peter, he's got one. He's just a bit young, is all."

Just as they reached the house, a young woman came running around it from the side of the house and nearly ran into them. Ore grabbed her elbow before she could topple over. "Oh, I'm so sorry!" she gasped. "Ah! Thom! Where have you been?"

The lad pointed at Ore's horse and said, "Horse." Then he pointed at Peter and said, "Bro."

"Come here at once!" She reached for Thom and he scuttled behind Peter.

"It's okay, Miss," Peter said shyly. "I don't mind."

"I'm sorry." She curtsied. "What may I do for you gentlemen tonight? We don't often get visitors here."

"Well, I was hoping we might be able to beg to stay the night tonight. It's gotten late and my horse is rather tired," Ore requested. "Anything is fine. We aren't fancy people, just travelers." The young woman looked unsure, but she also didn't want to refuse when it would obviously be difficult for them. "If it's too much trouble, we can just go on down the road a bit," Ore said, "though if I could water my horse before we go...."

The child, Thom, all of a sudden let go of Peter's hand and went running off, "Da!"

The young woman sighed. "Well, if he's back, it'll probably be okay if you stay."

Thom came back pulling a large man after him, babbling about the "horse" and "Bro".

"Whoa, whoa!" The man laughed, then scooped up the small boy. "You're all excited tonight, Mister Thom. We have guests do we?"

The man walked up to the house, smiling and tickling the boy until he giggled so much he couldn't breathe. The small light from the house window wasn't really enough to make out detailed features on any of them, but the man was quite tall and broad in the shoulder, and his teeth shone frequently from his smile.

"Foster, these gentlemen have asked if they might stay the night and stable their horse," the young woman said.

Foster wrapped his arm around the young woman and kissed the top of her head, then turned to them, "You're welcome to stay. You can have the floor in front of the fire, if you'd like to be warm. If you'd rather be comfortable, you can have the hayloft. I'm sorry that's all Sallie and I can offer, besides a bit to eat."

Peter shivered. "I'm used to the floor, if that's alright." With his skin and bone, it looked like he didn't stay warm on his own well.

"If you don't mind, I'll take the hayloft," Ore said. He was still feeling closed in from all the babysitting of Ilena. "Do you mind if I take care of my horse first?"

"Let me fetch a lantern and I'll help you," Foster said. He turned towards the house and opened the door, allowing more light to spill out. Sallie gasped. She was staring at Ore.

Ore winked at her, held his finger up to his mouth, and turned away from the light to head towards the stable. He heard her hiss at Peter as he walked away, "Is that...?" He knew Peter was probably nodding, but he hoped he'd seen the warning to keep it quiet for now. He'd wait until they were settled in the house.

He had the saddle off Fenrier by the time Foster made it out with the lantern. Ore was careful to move so that the light never fell fully on his face, but he'd had to do that before, so it was almost second nature anyway. Foster made up a pail of grain and told Ore where the pitchfork was so he could give Fenrier some hay while the forester fetched water.

When Fenrier was watered and fed, they walked companionably to the house. Foster told Ore that he was the caretaker for the hunting grounds and the young woman was his wife, Sallie. Thom was their son.

Foster headed through the door first and went to put the lantern on the table. Thom was attached to Peter again. It made Ore smile to see it. He walked up to stand next to Peter. When Foster turned around, Ore faced him and asked, "Foster of Wexford?"

Foster stared at him in shock. Sallie had her hands to her lips, and was looking very worried. Foster's mouth worked up and down a few times, nothing coming out. He shook his head, and then teared up. He looked down at his hands, then back up at Ore resolutely. "I am waiting to hear the words of Father."

"Mother has sent me for you," Ore gave the response.

Foster fumbled for a chair behind him and sat with a thump. Sallie went up to stand behind him, and wrapped her arms around his neck. After a moment he reached up and touched her arm, and she let go, leaving her hands on his shoulders. "The master this past fall hunting season took my oldest son with him when he went back to the manor. We don't want to leave him behind."

"Who is your master?" Ore asked.

"Viscount Delay."

Ore thought through his list and the locations of the various lords. "What's your son's name?"

"Thayne of Wexford."

Ore smiled reassuringly, "He's on my list." Foster slumped in relief and Sallie cried out slightly in happiness, then hugged Foster. Ore clarified, "But I expect you to help me find him."

Foster nodded. "I can get you to the place, but if I'm seen it'll be very bad for all of us."

"That's good enough," Ore answered.

Sallie happily began putting a simple meal on the table. Foster started packing the few things they thought they would need with them for the trip so they could leave first thing in the morning.

Ore leaned against the side of the fireplace. "I assume the Viscount only comes during the fall hunting season?" Foster nodded. "If we could get you back here before the season, such that he wouldn't know you were gone, would you want to return?"

Foster paused, considering, then looked over to Sallie. The look said, *I want to protect you...what do you want to do?* Her mouth set into a thin line. Foster went back to his work. "Nope," he said shortly.

Ore nodded, then crouched down next to Thom and Peter. "Does Peter remind you of your big brother?" Thom nodded. "Do you miss him?"

"Bro gone 'way," Thom answered, looking sad.

"Shall we go fetch him?" When Thom looked confused, Ore tried again, "Do you want to see Thayne again?" Thom nodded very seriously. "Alright. We'll go tomorrow morning, okay?" Thom's eyes got big, and he nodded again. Then he turned and climbed into Peter's lap. Ore smiled. "It looks like Thom has a very good big brother in Thayne. Are you okay with being a substitute for now, Peter?" Ore looked up into Peter's face.

Peter smiled. "Of course. I always thought it'd be nice to have a little brother."

"Well, I suspect Thom might just make Thayne share him," Sallie said, coming over to collect Thom and get him washed up for dinner. "You're welcome to join us, Peter."

"Thank you, ma'am," Peter said, his face turning red.

"Onions," whispered Ore to Peter, catching him just in time for Peter to laugh instead of cry.

"Well, then, come sit up," said Sallie. "It's not much, but we're glad to share our table."

"Thank you very much," the men said, and they enjoyed a quiet meal together.

-o-o-o-

The following morning it turned out that transportation was going to be a problem. Foster's family had nothing but their feet to walk on and Ore only had Fenrier yet. After talking to Foster about where Viscount Delay's manor was, and considering the various options, it was agreed that Foster would take his little family and start walking to the next village down the road.

Viscount Delay's manor was actually a bit off of the main road, although still on down it a ways. Ore would take Peter and go collect Thayne, then meet the rest of Foster's family. Whomever made it to the village first would see about acquiring faster transportation for the growing group.

The two groups headed to the main road together, then Ore picked up the pace and left Foster's little family behind. Just as they were getting to the place where he was to turn off the road and head for the viscount's manor, they came upon a small group coming down that road. Ore and Peter stopped and waited while the group turned and went in the same direction Ore had been traveling, likely going towards the village.

Ore noticed it was all riders. Near the head was a well dressed man. As the tail of the group turned the corner and passed him, Ore noticed one young man saw him, and then stared, almost stopping his horse until a companion complained at him. He kept riding but looked back once.

"What do you think, Peter? You think that's him?" Ore asked casually.

"That's what I'd have done if it was me," Peter said.

"If that's the Viscount, gone to the village, it won't be safe for Foster to show his face there. Hop down and head back to Foster. Tell him the Viscount's in the village and so's his son, like as not. Keep coming down this way. After I get Thayne, we'll get transportation and come back and get all of you.

"If you make it to the village before I get out of there, come round to the far side very carefully so he's not seen, then you leave them there and come into the village to get me."

"Okay." Ore helped Peter slip off Fenrier. Peter walked a bit to straighten out his legs, then headed at a country lad's lope back down the road they'd just come on.

Ore urged his horse after the group that was receding into the distance. As he watched, a single horseman with wavy hair that was brown with varying shades of blonde streaked through it and that looked like a comb and brush together wouldn't get it to be anything but slightly unruly for a brief half–hour detached from the group and stopped ahead.

As Ore got closer, he could see the rider dismount and start checking the straps of his saddle. It looked like the young man who'd recognized him had found some sort of excuse for waiting for him. He rode up beside the young man and stopped. "Everything okay?" he asked as if trying to be helpful.

"Well, that depends," the young man said looking at him very seriously, hope and worry playing over his face.

"You seem to recognize me," Ore said. The young man nodded. Ore looked after the group the young man had split off from. "Is that Viscount Delay and his men?" The young man nodded again. "Are you Thayne of Wexford?"

Joy lit his face, making his grey–blue eyes sparkle. "I am waiting to hear the words of Father."

"Mother has sent me for you." Thayne's smile split his face. "You have your father's smile," Ore remarked.

"You've seen my Da?" Thayne asked anxiously.

Ore nodded. "They're coming behind as we don't have enough transportation right at the moment. Climb up on your horse. Let's get moving before the rest of the Viscount's men get suspicious."

"Oh, right," Thayne clambered up onto his horse. "Where are we going?" he asked when Ore continued towards the village.

"If you leave right now, the Viscount will coming looking for you. We don't need that now, do we?"

Thayne's face fell a little, "No, I suppose not."

"What kind of man is the Viscount?"

"Sly, cruel, proud." Thayne's answer was cold.

"*Hah.* The hardest to reason with, then. Hmm. Is there any reason he'd let you go? Without killing you?"

Thayne thought for a moment, then shook his head. "Can't think of one, sorry."

"That's okay. We'll see what happens when it happens, then." Ore knew that most of the time things like this couldn't be preplanned.

They caught up to Viscount Delay and his men just after they'd arrived at the village. The viscount was speaking with the village head, who had two young men behind him. "Those are the head's son and nephew," Thayne said quietly to Ore. "They're old enough to conscript."

"The Viscount conscripts? Why?" Conscripting wasn't unheard of, but it was uncommon in times of peace. Thayne shifted uncomfortably. Ore looked at him out of the corner of his eye. "Deeds nefarious and treacherous, I take it?" Thayne gave a short nod, flushing with anger. "How many does he have in total now?" Ore asked him.

"Mmm...I'd say about two hundred fifty?" That was enough for him to bring them to a war and more, several times over what his allotment would be. How was he paying for them all?

"Stay put," Ore told Thayne, then rode close enough to hear what was being said. Glancing at all the villagers who were listening, he could see that there were no young men among them, only in the group on horseback behind the viscount. Looking closer, he could see several of the young men were sneaking looks at villagers, and vice versa.

The village head was arguing — politely of course — with the viscount, trying to refuse to let the boys go with him. The problem was, the viscount had the right to take them if he saw fit to do so. "We need them to help with this year's planting, my lord, or we won't be able to provide the annual taxes to your house that's required," the village head was saying.

"And I'm saying I need them now," answered Viscount Delay impatiently.

"But my lord, they are the last two with the strength to plow the rocky land. Please, come for them after the planting's been completed."

"That sounds reasonable to me," Ore said mildly. "I think such a compromise would be good...although if it's only this two it may take a while. Maybe you could spare a few others of those behind you to help? Then you'd get these two sooner."

The viscount turned to him, anger on his face at being interrupted by a stranger. "Who might you be?"

"Messenger of the Regent of Suiran." He dared the viscount with his eyes, but his face stayed conciliatory. "Just thought I'd try to mediate the disagreement since I was passing through." The viscount's face couldn't decide whether to be red or pale. "As a matter of fact, I'm glad I ran into you here, Viscount Delay. It means I don't have to detour to your manor.

"The Regent wanted me to stop by on my way through and see why you were short last year on your duty to the castle." The viscount's face picked pale. *Good. I guessed right.* Not that it wasn't that hard to deduce. "If it's just a matter of being short on strong backs...?" Ore looked at the village head, who nodded fiercely, glad to have an ally show up out of nowhere just when he needed one.

"Well, then, that's easily solved." Ore raised his voice, while looking at the lads behind the viscount. "Can we get some volunteers who'll stay here in the village and help with the spring planting until it's done?"

For a second, the men behind Viscount Delay looked at each other in confusion, then Thayne rode up. "I will." Ore nodded at him.

"Any others? Three will take a long time. If we could get, say six more of you or so?" He looked at the village elder. "That would get it done in about, what — three weeks?" The elder nodded, his eyes getting misty.

Ore looked back at the viscount. "Once the planting's done, you won't have to worry about being behind this year, the same as last, and then they can rejoin you. Three weeks isn't really all that long. Sounds like that's a benefit all the way around." Several of the other young men behind the viscount were starting to quietly move up to join Thayne.

Viscount Delay scowled, his brain finally beginning to catch up to the suddenness of Ore's decisions. "What proof do you have you're a messenger of the Regent?"

Ore reached into his jacket and pulled out a large round amulet. It had the arms of the Regent of Suiran engraved on it as well as other things that marked him as a messenger. "Ah, sorry, I forgot. Here it is." He held it out for the viscount — and incidentally everyone else — to see. He tucked it back into his jacket and waited, keeping his face mild.

Viscount Delay went for one more try. "These are my men and I say I need them now!"

"More than you need to be able to pay the Regent and Crown your yearly due?" Ore let his face harden a little.

"I need them for the protection of my manor!" Delay insisted.

"Against what?" Ore kept his tone lightly questioning.

"...Ah. ...It was a hard winter...the – the wild animals from the mountains have come down farther than normal...."

"You need two hundred fifty men to protect you from wild animals?" Ore asked, steel in his voice.

The viscount froze, and so did every member of his mounted group. "Ah...ah! That's just a rumor!"

"Oh, is it?" The steel was still in Ore's voice. "Well, that would be good. After all, those kinds of numbers are usually questioned in times of *peace*. Well, then, if you're sure you can't spare ten young men to help you meet your yearly quota, and the wild animals are that bad, you won't mind me coming to your manor and checking, would you? Just to be sure, of course. The Regent would like to know if you're needing his assistance, after all. That's what I'm here for — to help him ascertain what your needs are."

Viscount Delay caved. "No, no. You're right. Just ten men for three weeks won't be too big a burden. We can manage the wild animals for that long. They'll probably leave my lands in that time, anyway, now that the spring thaws are beginning to reach the mountains."

Ore let the steel leave his voice, but it stayed firm. "Very well, if you're sure the Regent can't help with anything else...?"

The viscount shook his head. "No, no. I can manage. Thank you very much."

Ore looked at the mounted men, "Any more volunteers?"

In the end, there were ten volunteers, plus the two whom Ore had saved from conscription temporarily, and Thayne. Ore made an excuse to stay at the village a while longer, and the viscount made an excuse to escape back to his manor.

As Ore turned back to talk to the village head, most of the mounted volunteers were getting off their horses and greeting family members, many with tears. The village head bowed to Ore. "Thank you, Sir Messenger, for your assistance in our behalf."

Ore looked at him with sharp eyes. "I'll take this to the Regent myself, Head. ...May I ask for a few things to aid me in my other tasks?"

"Of course, if we may be of help."

"I would like to take...," Ore made a show of turning and looking at the remaining mounted men, and pointed to Thayne, "this one with me." Turning back to the village head, he added, "and I've recently found myself in need of a wagon and horse to pull it. It only needs to be serviceable. I can have the closest garrison return it in a few days."

"Certainly, Sir. If you could give us some time to prepare them, we can have them ready for you shortly."

Ore nodded, and the head had his son and nephew run off and get them ready. Thane moved to sit next to Ore. Ore looked at the remaining men of the viscount, who hadn't already moved off with family. "Do you have someplace these fine volunteers may stay while they help with the spring plantings?"

While the village head was distracted finding homes to put the volunteers up at, Ore said quietly to Thayne, "When they bring the wagon, tie your horse up to the back of it and drive it. We'll go back the way we came."

"Okay," Thayne said.

After about fifteen minutes, the village head's son came up, driving a wagon. As he hopped off, he smiled at Ore. "Thank you, Sir Messenger. We — my cousin and I — really wanted to help Father this year. We were the only ones left to harvest last year and we lost over half of it because we couldn't get it all in before frost. The Viscount took most of it, so the village suffered. We didn't want that to happen again this year."

"You're good lads," Ore said approvingly. "I'll let the Regent know what you've told me. I'm sure he'll do something about it soon. Thank you for the wagon. It should be returned to you within the week."

The young man bowed, then ran over to his father. Ore followed him while Thayne switched from riding his horse to driving the wagon. "If you have any further need, and the Viscount continues to be difficult, send a message to the local garrison directed to the Regent."

"Yes, Sir Messenger," the head said. "Thank you again."

"Thank you for the use of the wagon and driver," Ore said and they parted.

-o-o-o-

Ore led Thayne out of the village and back up on the road. Once they were away from the village, Thayne said, "That was wonderful, Father! I've never seen the Viscount given such comeuppance before. I wanted to crow." He laughed now.

Then he grew sober. "He's really cruel at the manor, refusing to let any of the lads go home, me included. Mostly so we don't rat on him, I suppose. He has captains of twenty that are allowed to use the lash if they feel they need to, to keep us in line so there isn't much disorder, but there are plenty who don't like what's going on. The Regent really does need to know about it all."

Ore nodded. "You'll get your chance to say. I'll tell him what I learned myself."

Thayne was quiet for a while, then asked, "We're going to pick up Da and my stepmom?"

"Yes. It surprises me Sallie's not your wife." They looked to be close to the same age.

"No. Da married her about four years ago. Mom died when I was thirteen. Sallie's pretty young for Da, in my opinion, but she's sweet and he's been happier since then, so it's alright." He grinned, "...and Thom's great, even though he's a handful."

Ore smiled, remembering the night before. "He found us first last night. Ah, the young man with me before is Peter. We'd just gotten off the horse when Thom attached himself to Peter's leg. I hope you're not the sort to get jealous, but they've taken a liking to each other. Though really it's because Thom's been missing you."

"Nah, it's okay. There's enough of Thom to go around. Another set of eyes and hands on him's a good thing," Thayne genially waved it off.

"That's good, because I think Thom will be good for Peter. He lost his family when he was seven and hasn't had anyone since then, except Mother and the Family, and even then it's been very little contact." He looked at Thayne out of the corner of his eye. It looked like he was openly sympathetic. "One tip that might help you deal with Peter...if it looks like he's about to cry, say 'onion'. That should help clear it up."

"Onion?"

"When I arrived at his place to get him, he was in the middle of cutting onions, and using it as an excuse to be depressed. When he saw me, he started to cry again, then claimed it was the onions. So now I use it to tease him out of his depression,"

Ore gave an innocent smile to Thayne, who laughed, "All right, I'll remember."

When they passed the road to the manor, they didn't see any remnants of the viscount or his men. Ore was relieved. He started looking sharply for signs that Foster might have taken his family off the road. Then they saw four figures on the road ahead of them and Thayne asked, "Is that them?"

When Ore nodded, Thayne whipped the wagon horse into a fast canter. Ore kept up with him, a faint smile on his face. As they came level with the family and Peter, Thayne reined in the horse, then jumped down and ran to his father and grabbed him in a happy embrace, nearly disappearing in his huge father's great hug.

When his father finally let him go, Thayne hugged Sallie gently, then grabbed up Thom, who grabbed the hair on either side of his head and hugged him, crying and calling "Bro! Bro!" Then, holding Thom in one arm, Thayne stuck his hand out to Peter, a broad grin on his face. "Thayne. Nice to meet you."

Peter shyly took his hand. "Peter. Nice to meet you, too."

Foster took the reins of the wagon horse and turned the wagon around, then helped Sallie climb in. Thayne tried to put Thom in with her, but Thom held onto his hair tight and wouldn't let go. Thayne laughed. "Hey, Peter, you get in first. We'll see if Thom will go to you."

Peter looked pleased to be asked to help and climbed in, then held his hands out to Thom, "Thom. Come to me."

Thom thought about it for a minute, then released Thayne and went to Peter. Thayne looked up at Ore. "Is it okay if I ride with them for a bit?"

Ore considered it, then answered, "After we're out of the danger zone."

Foster touched Ore's boot to get his attention. Softly he said, "Thank you, Father, for getting Thayne out and back to us."

Ore smiled back, but his words were more serious. "I don't know if the Viscount left men to watch the road or not. Until we're past the village, you aren't in the clear. It would be safest if you, Sallie, and Thom could lie down in the bottom of the wagon and cover yourselves until we reach that point. I legitimately have Thayne as the driver for the wagon, and if they remember Peter, it was that he was already with me.

"I understand it may be difficult for Thom, now that he has his two brothers with him, but if you could help him understand, that would be very helpful. Once we're past the village would be the better time for a family reunion. I don't anticipate any difficulties, but I'd like to be safe, rather than sorry later."

Foster nodded his understanding and climbed up into the wagon. Somehow they managed to convince Thom to play hide and seek with Ma and Da, and Thayne took up the reins again and got the wagon going.

"I'd like to pick up the pace a bit," Ore said. "I'm sorry if it makes the ride uncomfortable, but we need to be at the next place by evening, I think." Thayne nodded. Ore set the pace back to the fast canter he'd used with Peter, and Thayne kept up, although the horse pulling the wagon was a bit lazy and had to be encouraged.

They made it past the village without mishap, and Ore couldn't sense any watchers from the trees and scrub at the point the road went up to the viscount's manor. He hoped that was a good enough escape for Foster and his family. After they passed the village and turned east towards the castle, still several days away, he let Foster know and the little family came out of hiding.

Foster traded places with Thayne so that Thom could have his brother sandwich. Ore noticed Sallie had a bit of a tear in her eye, looking at all three boys together. It looked like Peter would be alright. Thayne told the "exciting" story of how 'Father' had bested the viscount. Sallie looked at Ore with misty eyes. "I'm sure the families of those other boys are as happy to have them back as we are. Thank you for that, also."

Foster nodded. "And thanks for helping the village. There was more than one poacher from there I ended up turning a blind eye to by the end of the winter. They were starting to get as scrawny as Bean Pole, here," he jerked his thumb at Peter. "I figured since the Viscount was starving them of grain, he could feed them meat."

Ore nodded. What had happened there was sad, and needed fixing. He did wish, though, that these "Children of Mother" would stop crying over everything, happy or sad, that happened.

While the family caught up, and learned about Peter, Ore thought about what was next. It was likely to be difficult, the one after this. This one, they would be able to find a place to sleep again, and could stay together. But the next one.... He'd just have to send them in the wagon on to the garrison and meet up with them there.

He looked in speculation at Thayne. "Thayne," Ore slowed to be level with him, "what kind of training were you getting at the Viscount's?"

"Eh? Oh, well, simple arms, sneak hit and runs, that kind of thing."

"Good."

"Heh?" But Ore had already moved back up into his position ahead of the wagon, just behind the level of the wagon's horse to goad it on.

-o-o-o-

They arrived at a roadside inn at early evening. Ore wanted to get there early enough that they could already have rooms before it got crowded with that night's main travelers. It looked like they'd made it in time. While Foster and Thayne handled getting the horses and wagon put up in the inn stable, Ore went in and paid for two rooms.

When he came back out, he gathered everyone where they wouldn't be overly noticed. "I'm really sorry to have to break up the family group so horribly tonight, but I'd like us to not be memorable so much. This is a public place so we're likely to be noticed if we all stay together, and if any such semblance of the Foster family is seen and remembered, the Viscount will be able to track us. So, for tonight, I'd like for Sallie, Thom, and Peter to sit at one table to eat, and be in one room." He handed Sallie a key.

"Foster, Thayne, and I'll sit at the other. Because of Foster's size, he'll be remembered. The Viscount might think twice about continuing to find you if he thinks I was pumping you for further information about his deeds that need to be reported. If you're with your family, he may think he can find you and use them against you." Everyone nodded. "We'll be across the hall from each other, so if something happens, call out, or come knock," he looked at Sallie, then Peter. They nodded.

Ore looked around the still quiet grounds of the inn. It looked like they had more time. "Tomorrow, I want Peter, Sallie, and Thom to start walking east as soon as you're done eating breakfast. Eat as early as you can, to be among the first to leave. Foster, Thayne, and I will come down a little later and be leisurely.

"Foster, you'll pick up the wagon after the bulk of travelers have left and head out. Make sure you're as clear of as many as possible by the time you pick up the rest of the family that's walking. Then head on straight for the garrison. Don't stop until you get there, as you'll already be getting there pretty late. If you can get that lazy nag to move, move her." Foster nodded.

"Tell them you're 'part of the circle' and that you've been told to wait for the messenger. They should give you quarters, and stable the horse. Then wait until Thayne and I get there."

"What are we going to do?" Thayne asked.

"We'll leave here in the morning as some of the last travelers, then ride hard to where we need to be." Ore looked at Sallie and Foster, "One of you will have an additional member to your group by morning, but I don't know who yet. If someone shows up and goes with you, just go with the flow." They nodded.

He sent Sallie and her group in first as Thom was getting too hungry to wait around any more, then he made sure his group was obvious in the courtyard between the stable and inn for a while before going in to get their supper. Once they were sitting down, Thayne asked Ore, "So what are we really going to do?"

"Sneak hit and run," Ore said seriously. "We've got two to get out of a high place. I'm not expecting it to be simple for that one."

Foster frowned. "Are you sure you don't want me to come along?"

Ore smiled at him. "Thanks for offering your strength. I'd use it if I needed it. But for a sneak thief job, you're a bit big. Plus I think your strength would be better used to protect the others, if it should be needed." Foster nodded. He could appreciate that.

"Hey, handsome!" a woman's voice came from Ore's right as a plate was set down in front of him. He looked up into a grinning face that would be considered appealing by most men. "I like this table!" she put a plate down in front of Thayne and carelessly ran a finger up his arm, making him blush. "But you're really a piece of work," she put Foster's plate down in front of him, then put her hands on her hips as she looked at him. "You really stand out, don't you?"

Foster looked at her disinterestedly. "I suppose, but it can't be helped." He dug into his food.

The woman looked back at Ore. "But you interest me most. Are you looking for anyone to talk to tonight?" Just the right amount of flirtatiousness. Sometimes he'd liked this kind of person, at least to flirt with.

He put his chin in his hand, like he was thinking about it. "Well, actually, I was. You wouldn't happen to know Elandra of Kouzanshi, would you?"

"Well, actually, I might," her eyes lit up and a real smile actually curled her lips.

"Then, later, when it's getting to after hours, I'll come looking for her. You'll let her know for me, will you?"

"Sure thing, handsome." She waved a little wave back at them as she walked off to bring out the next order.

Thayne looked at Ore with big round eyes. "Is that it?"

Ore shrugged as he shoveled food into his mouth. "Just about." Even though it was his first time to be collecting people like this, it somehow all felt very familiar. *Ah, just like the work I used to do, all rolled up into one big job.* But somehow it felt a lot better. ...Which surprisingly was making it feel like fun. It was stuff he was good at, and he didn't have to feel bad while doing it. Maybe he'd thank Ilena when he got back, if he survived the next night, but even that kind of excitement was fun, in it's own way.

But...now that he'd thought of Ilena again, he was having troubles not thinking about her. He wondered if she would have had just as much fun as he was. Peter's story had given him a clue that she didn't just always stay around the manor and be just a steward. She'd been on jobs, too. "Foster, how'd you meet Mother, if you can say in this place?" Ore asked.

"The Viscount is one of the Earl's allies," Foster said shortly. "She came with when they would meet at the lodge for meetings mixed with hunting.

She's an excellent shot, by the way, at least back then. ...I didn't think much of her back then." His face got dark. "Then one of the Earl's higher–ups decided he liked my wife — that is, my first wife. When I found her ravaged and dead, I howled in grief. ...Mother heard it and found me." He stopped.

Ore was horrified, although he tried not to show it too much. "I take it she was her usual self at her best, then," he said softly. "Mother through and through."

Both Foster and Thayne nodded. "She had me lift my wife up and got us into the house — the main house. I didn't even know until her cold, angry voice cut through my grief. We were standing in front of the Earl and she cut into him with that cold, steel voice until he was near to weeping himself. Then she demanded payment in kind and the Earl coolly turned and in one blow sliced the head off the man who'd done it. He followed it up with an apology to the Viscount, and then to me, although I barely heard it, then went right back to eating." Foster shook his head at the callousness.

"She led me back out and to my house, gathering up a few of the maids. She cleaned up my wife with her own hands and put her favorite dress on her, while one maid held Thayne and one held my hand. Then, while we said our farewells, she marched several other of the men out to dig a burial grave right then. She came back in and said she wouldn't make me put her in the ground yet, but a man shouldn't have to beg the earth to open up, just ask it to be a soft bed and blanket." A tear dripped down Foster's face. "I'll ever be grateful she said and did that."

He wiped the tear off his face. "The next time she came, I found an opportunity to thank her. She looked at me, her face stone as ever it was, and said if I really wanted to thank her, I'd stay where I was and remember every last thing the Viscount and Earl were doing. And when she called for me, I'd come. If I'd come, then my revenge could be complete, if I wanted it. If I didn't, her revenge would be. That was enough for me."

Foster shrugged. "I told Thayne about that little talk, and before I married Sallie, I told her, too. Course Sallie would have come anyway. She was one of the junior maids there. She saw the burial of my first wife. And then...," he couldn't say it. Anger and grief were mixed in his face. He waved at Thayne, who gently touched his dad's arm, then took over the story.

"Thom isn't Da's son, least not his body's son. They were getting sweet on each other, although I wasn't liking that much. Then one night, when the Viscount and his men were at the lodge, Sallie came to the door really late at night. She'd been raped by one of the Viscount's men.

"When she found out she was pregnant for sure, Da married her right then. I didn't complain. We all promised we'd raise the child as part of our family. He hadn't done nothing wrong, neither had Sallie. He's a handful, but we love him as our own."

Ore shook his head. No wonder they all kept crying. Ilena did always seem to pick the hardest hit folks. Any kindness, any caring was like water to a man dying of thirst. She provided it both naturally and with precision, and without reserve. It was looking like not only had she not changed at all, but she'd become stronger so she could be herself to an even fuller extent.

There was an element of manipulation in it. Probably because she'd had to learn to manipulate Earl Shicchi...but her manipulation of these witnesses, it was only ever made as an offer. Not coerced or forced. An offer for payment. A reward for effort if effort was made. It couldn't really be called bad.

"I'm sorry to make you remember past pains, but thank you for telling me," Ore said. As a pair, they shrugged. *Like father, like son*, Ore couldn't help but think.

"You of all people ought'ta know," Foster said. Ore wondered why he said it, but he nodded anyway. *Because I've lived through it too, or because they want me to understand who she is now?*

They wrapped up dinner and headed to the bedroom. Ore ordered them to bed. "I'll be back in a bit," he said as he went out the window. "It's time to collect the next Child." The other two nodded.

CHAPTER 8 Ore Pays a Price

Ore went up to the roof and scouted around both there and at the ground on all sides of the inn. While he was looking, a light came from the back of the inn briefly. The kitchen door had been opened, then closed. He sat on the roof and waited. After a bit, he heard quiet scrabbling, then soft footsteps. He smiled when he saw the waitress from dinner. "Elandra of Kouzanshi?"

She smiled back, flirtatiously twirling a curl of brown hair around her finger. "I am waiting to hear the words of Father."

He answered back, "Mother has sent me for you."

She dropped to her knees in front of him. "Took you long enough."

"How many times have you been up here looking for me?"

"Only eight," she said with exasperation.

"Liar."

"Okay, this is the second."

"Sorry I'm late. I had business to take care of." He wasn't late and she was his business.

Elandra pouted, then gave up and sighed. She rolled off her knees to sit, pulling her knees up to her ample chest. Looking up to the sky, she breathed in a deep breath, then let it out. "It's nice to be out where there's space." Ore agreed. He'd been missing it too, even though he'd gone up on the Osterly garrison roof plenty. Somehow that had still seemed closed in.

Here, they were surrounded by woods and scrub. It felt comfortingly open with the mountains in the backdrop to the north and the stars in the sky, hidden by small intermittent clouds as they passed overhead. "Is there space where I'm going?" she asked, her eyes closed, her face still upturned to the sky.

Ore leaned back on his hands and thought about that. Would he like to be there? "The house roof is harder to get up on, but if you go on the stable roof, that's about right."

She nodded. "That's alright then."

"Can you just walk away?" he wanted to know how to add her to the plans.

"Mmm, yeah. I've been training another waitress for a few months now, getting ready. I should let them know tonight I'm leaving, though. I'd like to get paid, after all," she grinned at him.

He grinned back. "I'd like you to leave first thing in the morning, then. Can you handle that?"

"I don't get to sleep in? Aww." She turned away from him. "Well, really, I've been ready to go. That's alright with me."

"The young woman, really skinny kid, and the little boy. You remember them?"

"Um–hm."

"Wait until they've left for the road. Follow after them and catch up. She's the wife of the big guy that was sitting with me, stepmom of the third one at the table. The big guy, Foster, will be coming after you with the wagon later. Thayne and I will catch up with you all tomorrow night."

He paused and looked at her, then leaned over and grabbed a strand of curly brunette hair, pulling her head back until she was looking at him in the eye. "And if you betray me, or any of us, I will fillet you alive."

She flipped over so fast, Ore almost didn't see it. She ended up five feet away, in a cat pose. Her eyes glittered. *I thought so.* "What's a nightwalker doing as a Child of Mother?" he asked her in his usual way of just wanting to know.

He hadn't moved much, but he was now completely balanced, ready for anything. Elandra rushed him. He dodged and deflected her attack, then made a sweep at her legs. She lept over his legs and directly at him.

Ore snatched her arm out of the air as she went past his dodge, twisted it and slammed her into the roof, holding her other shoulder with his other hand and putting a knee on her hip. He couldn't afford to just play this trip. If she really was a plant, she had to go.

She was about to move again when she felt the tip of his throwing knife against her throat. She froze, breathing hard. Ore's eyes glittered, the pupils having gone into slits.

"If you'll fight this seriously to protect *them*, will you fight this hard to protect me?" she demanded to know.

"If you're really one of Mother's Children," his voice was as sharp as his eyes, though quiet.

"She picked me up out of the gutter after I was thrown out like an extra kitten no one wants. I'd been promised position and prominence because I had a pretty face, then was promptly tossed when something better came along. ...But I wasn't just tossed out, I was tossed to the wolves while the bastard watched and laughed. I assume you know what that means for one like me." Ore did.

"I was nearly dead when she found me. She carried me into an abandoned house, washed me, bandaged me, then held me while I cried the last tears I've ever cried. She gave me strength, what I needed to know to become what I am today. She's never judged me, not for my face or my anger, but she has asked for my loyalty. ...She has it. I'm ready to go, if she says it's time."

Ore couldn't fully trust Elandra. Such a thing didn't exist between nightwalkers, but they could declare a truce until it was broken by one party or the other. He slowly moved off of her, backing up to four feet away. She didn't move until he was set, then she carefully sat up, her hands resting loosely on her knees, a position of defenselessness. That set the truce agreement. She'd behave or she'd die. It was the unspoken rule of the darkness.

He slipped his throwing knife back into its place and very slightly relaxed, but he didn't take his eyes off of her. He nearly considered taking her as back up to the next place, then decided against it. She was just a bit too flashy, and having a second as back–up to Foster wouldn't be a bad thing. Especially since she'd be with the defenseless group before Foster could get to them.

"You know what to do then," he stated.

She nodded, "Follow, then join up with the mom, kid, and toddler. Wait at the next stop."

Ore stood, still looking at her. "Off you go."

She carefully stood, then ran lightly to the edge of the roof and dropped off. He waited until the light from the kitchen door being opened and closed disappeared. Then he made sure there wasn't anyone else on the roof. When his senses declared it was safe, he dropped into a crouch.

Mother was insane. That's all there was to it. She'd taken a red light district girl and turned her into a man–eating machine. They were the worst sort to run into of all the female nightwalkers. There was no doubt Ilena had known exactly what she was doing when she did it.

Why? Why did she need such a person on her payroll? Here...out in the middle of nowhere...flirtatious in the dining room, deadly in the bedroom. Why here? Why had Ilena been in Kouzanshi to even be able to find Elandra to pick her up, heal her, and add her as a Child?

He raised his own face to the sky, not seeing it. *Ilena, you crazy woman, why do I have to keep liking you more and more? Would you run with me, if you could? How crazy it must be making you, to not have your legs.* He thought about how she'd loved the race through the ambush and how she'd been acting the night before he left. *Yeah, you wanted to come, too, didn't you?*

He dropped his face back down to look at his hands. His right hand curled, remembering the warmth of her forehead when he touched it to see if she was fevered. *"Are you feeling okay?" "I am now."* He gently closed his right hand. *"I'll get them back to you."* Somehow he couldn't quite bring himself to say the words, *I'll come back to you.* Not yet.

After a while, he stood and took himself back to his window and let himself back in. He dropped into his bed, and he was suddenly back in those early years, when he put himself to sleep by remembering her small, thin but strong arms wrapped around his head and shoulders. His heart ached, but then it always had when he was on the run, that wasn't anything new. He fell asleep the same now as he did then, slowly drifting into her warmth.

-o-o-o-

"Hey, there, little fella'!"

Sallie jumped a little at a strange voice so close to them, and she quickly looked back behind her. "Thom!" she scolded.

"It's okay, ma'am," the curls in the chestnut brown hair of the woman behind her immediately made Sallie jealous. She couldn't keep her plain hair looking nice, no matter what she did to it. "He's just being rambunctious."

"Ra–buctus?" Thom looked up at the new woman puzzled.

131

"It's another word for 'little boy'," the woman explained to him with a smile.

Thom started to skip around all three of the larger people as they continued walking, chanting: "Ra–buctus, 'buctus, 'buctus!"

Even Sallie had to smile. "Isn't that the truth."

"Do you mind if I travel with you guys for a bit?" the new woman asked lightly.

Peter was eyeing her like he might eye a dangerous, or creepy, creature. Sallie could tell he wanted to shake his head "no" at her...as in "no, don't do it!" But Sallie remembered Father's instructions from the evening before. "As long as Father said it's okay."

"Ah," the buxom woman put her hands behind her head, and looked away over the mountains, "...he did, but I had to pass his test first."

Sallie raised an eyebrow. The man she knew as 'Father' hadn't tested any of the rest of them, as far as she knew. But then, she would have tested this woman, too. Come to think of it, hadn't she been working the room last night? ...Yes, she had. She was the one that had taken food to Foster's table and flirted with them, although Foster'd been good and ignored her.

Ah. She'd been letting Father know who she was. They must have met up some time after that for the formal introduction. "I'm Sallie, the 'rabuctus' over there is Thom, and this is Peter. I've decided to adopt him because he needs more family." Peter shyly ducked his head at the woman, but wouldn't look at her.

The woman smiled at him, then looked back at Sallie. "Hi Sallie, I'm Elandra. It's nice to make your acquaintance. Hey, Thom Rabuctus, can you say 'E–landra'?"

He looked up at her with innocent eyes, "E–lad–wa."

"That's close, try again, 'E–land–ra'," she encouraged him.

"E–land–wa."

"Great say it again: Elandra."

"Elandwa."

"Awesome. That's me," she pointed at her chest. "Elandra."

Thom pointed at her and said, "Elandwa," very seriously.

Elandra smiled, then turned to Peter, "Now it's your turn. You say it too." He blushed bright red, but wouldn't look up. "Oh, no! You can't let a three year old best you! Come on, you can say it: E–land—"

Thom grabbed her hand. "Elandwa, Peto cwy. Don't."

Elandra looked at him in surprise. "Don't make Peter cry?" Then her face softened. "I'm sorry, Thom. I didn't mean to. You must really care for Peter, huh?"

Thom nodded. "Bro–Bro." Peter's eyes widened.

"Bro–Bro, Thom? Are you sure?" Sallie asked him.

Thom nodded emphatically. "Bro–Bro." He let go of Elandra's hand and skipped over to Peter and took his hand. He looked up into Peter's face and said it again, "Bro–Bro." Peter looked at him softly, a smile on his face.

"Haah. That's the way it is, is it?" Elandra sighed.

Sallie tried to explain what Thom meant by the newest nickname the way adults must. Peter smiled at her. "It's okay with me." He looked away before they could see the tears in his eyes again.

-o-o-o-

Elandra was paying attention to Peter out of the corner of her eye. He was pretty fragile. She'd have to tone it down for him. Ah well, that would be nice for a change, right?

She kept up light chatter while they walked, getting Sallie to talk girl talk with her until she finally opened up and relaxed. It was painfully obvious Sallie hadn't had another woman to talk to for quite some time. Peter still would at best watch Thom, answer Sallie's direct questions, or throw frightened glances at Elandra, but that was okay.

After a while, when Thom was riding up on Peter's shoulders, his little legs finally having given out, they heard a horse and wheels coming up behind them. Sallie turned around to look, then stopped, smiling. The others stopped and turned around also. Foster pulled up next to them, halting the horse. He smiled at Sallie and Thom, nodded at Peter, then looked at Elandra and sighed. "Of course."

Elandra raised an eyebrow. "Should I be offended that you're disappointed?"

Sallie said, "Foster, this is Elandra. She says Father tested her before letting her come along."

Foster gave Elandra another appraising look. "Well, okay, then. ...Hop in, everyone. We're supposed to travel fast today."

Once they were in and going, Elandra looked at Thom. "Your Dad wasn't kidding was he? I feel like we're riding a grasshopper. Bounce, bounce, bounce!"

Thom laughed. "Gwasshoppeu! Bounce, bounce, bounce!" He added his own bouncing to the bouncing of the wagon. Elandra and Sallie laughed and even Peter smiled at Thom's antics, then grabbed him when he got a little too close to the side of the wagon.

"Don't bounce out, grasshopper rider," he said tenderly.

Thom laughed and patted Peter, but settled in his lap saying softly, "Bounce, bounce, bounce."

Elandra looked at the two boys a moment, then turned her head and looked north towards the mountains passing on their left. They were still covered with snow. Here and there where shadows were deep, snowbanks could still be seen only feet from the road. Every now and then her eyes glanced back behind them.

After about a half–hour, the sound of galloping hooves could be heard coming up behind them. She'd been watching them for a while now, waiting for them. As they got close enough for their features to be made out, Elandra sighed. Why did Father have to be Mother's?

She'd liked the face when she first saw it, and she knew how he moved instinctively, but last night.... That'd been something else. He'd put her down faster than she'd ever been put down. The tempo of her heartbeat from her fear...it had been over an hour before she'd calmed down enough to sleep.

She knew he wouldn't ever be hers, and not because Mother said so. His body and his words had said so. He was Mother's through and through. The same as she was, but even deeper.

The riders slowed a little as they came up on the wagon until they were matching speed. Father smiled at them. "Are you guys getting along okay? I'm glad to see you met up."

Elandra gave him one of her flirtatious smiles. "We're doing great. Wish you could stay, too."

He shook his head, a worried look flitting across his face, then gone. "You guys need to get on to the garrison. We'll see you later tonight."

"Bro! Bro!" Thom was waving his hands at Thayne.

"Hey, Mister Thom!" Thayne grinned at him. "Are you keeping Peter company?"

"Yup!" Thom said proudly.

"Good job," Thayne said. "Don't let him fall out, Peter." Peter shook his head and clutched Thom a little tighter, although he stayed gentle.

Father had moved up to talk to Foster. He called back to Thayne, "Let's go."

Thane said, "See ya!" and took off after Father. Elandra watched them leave and sighed as she rested her chin on her fist, her elbow propped up on the side of the wagon. *See ya.*

-o-o-o-

Ore was buried in the trees by the side of the road, changing his clothes. He'd come prepared for this one. When Ilena had listed off the names, he'd recognized one of the two for this place. It was going to be his hardest 'theft'. He frowned, still not sure his plan would work, but hoping it would.

It helped that Thayne had some training, even if it was for less than a year. Ore restraightened everything one more time, hoping it looked alright. It was the best he could do without a mirror. Maybe it could be excused by the fact they were riding, and that tended to muss things up generally.

He walked out of the woods to where Thayne was walking the labored horses to cool them. Thayne whistled as Ore walked up to stow his riding clothes. "That's some fancy get up."

Ore grimaced at him. "They're my official formals." He pulled out another packet of clothing and handed it to Thayne. "Your turn." He nodded his head at the woods, and Thayne trotted off to get changed into Ore's more casual black uniform. They were about the same height, but Thayne's larger girth would strain the seams just a bit. Ore didn't care much. It would only fit more comfortably that way, and it was only for a few hours.

Ore had watered the horses and fed them a bit of grain (not enough to cause stomach troubles) by the time Thayne walked back out. Ore eyed him appraisingly, then straightened a few details. "That'll do." *If you can act cool, strict, and stand up straight for a long time...and keep a straight closed face at all times, well...never mind.* "Do your best."

He stowed Thayne's clothes, then hung the bag containing their clothes up in a tree that he marked with his own special mark. Their things were going to be searched. "Now you look like a royal guard for a high and mighty messenger. Let's get going." They mounted, but took it at a slower canter now that they were this close and dressed up.

Thayne grinned at Ore. "You're going as yourself, eh? I hear that's always the best disguise."

Ore shook his head. "No, I'm going as a pain in the arse bribeable messenger. I'm not bribeable, but I need an excuse to talk to both the high and the low at this place. You remember the plan. When I send you to the stables, get the horses ready immediately. Knock out stable hands if you need to. Getting the horses back is the weakest link and we have to have them to run fast enough to get away." Ore stopped, Ilena's teachings coming to mind, along with a back up plan.

They rode up to yet another mansion. Ore sighed internally, then relaxed into his role. "Call the house steward out," he ordered Thayne. "When he gets here, tell him Lord Oxley, Messenger of the Regent, is here to pay a call to the Earl Malkin."

Thayne nodded, then pulled in a deep breath and called loudly for the house steward. It took a while for him to appear, probably because they weren't expecting guests, so Ore played the impatient lord and made Thayne call for him again. He could feel eyes on him from windows and around corners. He'd already pasted a thin sneer of impatience on his face when they rode up.

When the steward finally showed up, panting slightly from hurrying to the door, Thayne played the serious but slightly bored guard, who just bordered on impatient from having to deal with a slime bag of a lord and introduced 'Lord Oxley' easily. Ore was impressed. They probably had half a chance.

He produced his messenger's token in a bored fashion for the steward, slipping his little finger over the part that identified him specifically, then put it away after the steward nodded satisfied. The steward bowed and sent off the paige that was behind him to inform Earl Malkin of his unexpected guest.

"If you would please come this way, Lord Oxley," the steward invited them in. Both men slipped off their horses as a middle–aged stable hand stepped up by the heads of the horses. They handed him their reins and followed the steward into the house.

The steward showed them into a receiving room, properly apportioned. Ore noted that it was simply decorated, but what was there was quite valuable. Earl Malkin prized value over opulence — and was using his money for something other than trinkets, although that was just what this public room said.

He sat in the room's head chair, keeping to his half–bored, half–proud face. Thayne took up a position behind and to the side of him. Good boy. He'd been paying attention at the viscounty Ore had stolen him from.

The steward offered Ore a glass of wine. He accepted it half–heartedly, as merely his due, but as if it was just tolerable, then sipped it. Ah, a reward for the hard work he was going to do: the wine was the same as the trinkets in the room. He allowed his surprised appreciation to leak through just a bit and relaxed into a more accepting pose.

The steward bowed himself out of the room. Ore looked around, bored. It happened a lot when he had to deal with nobility. For right now it was wait until their things had been brought into the house and searched.

Earl Malkin walked into the room when Ore was about two–thirds done with his glass of wine — and he'd sipped it slow. He allowed his displeasure to show, a cross scowl that hid nothing of his disdain for this Earl. "Really, Earl Malkin, surely there is nothing so important to be doing in such an out of the way place as this as to have you keep me waiting so long?"

"I apologize, Lord Oxley." The earl said in a smooth bass voice. He was a seasoned veteran, likely in his late fifties, or early sixties, and his bulk was honed muscle, Ore was sure. "What may I do for you so late in the day and far away from the castle?" Here was an opponent worthy of Ore.

"I'm sorry to have to impose on you tonight," he didn't sound sorry, "but when I learned that the only places to rest on this stretch of the road were the garrison and the rowdy inn," he allowed himself a slight shudder. "Well, of course the only place to come was to visit Earl Malkin." The earl gave a tight smile and his eyes slit just a bit.

Ore swirled the wine and looked at it appreciatively, completely ignoring the fact that the earl was justifiably upset that he hadn't bothered to send notice ahead of time that he was coming. But that oversight could be a benefit as well. It meant it wasn't an official visit. "I was pleasantly surprised to find that the rurality of your location has not affected your ability to appreciate the refined." He sipped the wine again.

He could feel Earl Malkin about to take him down a notch, and looked over the edge of the glass with cold, hard eyes. The earl stopped short, surprised. That wasn't the look of someone who was just a hopeless sop. He recalculated. Ore could see it in his eyes.

"I haven't had the opportunity to make your acquaintance before, Lord Oxley." Earl Malkin smoothly sat down in the second most important seat in the room and the steward, who had followed the earl in, poured him a glass of the wine.

Ore held his out for a refill, ignoring the steward. When he'd been topped off, he let it slip to dangle from his hand. Now it was time for the back and forth under–the–surface testing. He took a mental breath and let his eyes narrow to half lidded annoyance. "I was recently called up to Suiran from Ichijou. Regent Rei apparently is having troubles getting the lesser lords of Suiran to bow to his assignment and sent the request for assistance to his home castle."

He looked up at Earl Malkin without moving anything but his eyeballs, gauging his reaction. The earl was good. Nothing showed of what he thought...yet. "But, I'm sure that isn't the case with Earl Malkin, of course," Ore added smoothly, as if he didn't care if it was or not.

The earl sipped at his wine thoughtfully, a look of false concern on his face. "The wilds of Ryokudo's north are certainly a difficulty for someone used to the refined culture of the capital. Is the Fountain of Oren still as beautiful as it was?" The earl addressed the emotion behind Ore's look rather then the words, and tested to see if Ore had actually come from the capital. Since Ore had, it wasn't that hard.

"It is even more beautiful, now that the reconstruction is complete and the new gardens around it are beginning to bloom." He pouted. "I was looking forward to seeing more than just the early spring crocus, but my new assignment pulled me away before the full glory of the spring flowers appeared." Ore was beginning to have a tired tongue. Lords always had to talk too much.

Earl Malkin murmured sympathetically, and Ore took another sip of the wine. It was time to lay down a careful lure. "But even more beautiful are the gardens of Flower Row." He looked away as if into memory...that wasn't hard either, although it was now a more distant memory. "...Such beautiful flowers. I have yet to see anything of their like in the harsh north of Suiran, however." He frowned regretfully into his drink, then decided not to taste it yet.

He looked up suddenly, as if thinking a sudden thought and caught the look in the earl's eyes before it was smoothed over. He'd caught the lure. He thought he knew now, how to reel in Lord Oxley.

"Well, I hope you're able to at least find a comfortable rest tonight." The earl said comfortingly. "I'll have rooms prepared for you." The steward bowed slightly and stepped out of the room to give the order. "Dinner will be ready shortly. Is there anything I can do to help you in the meantime?"

Ore drank a sip of the wine, then downed the rest of it and set his cup on the table in front of him. "It's been a long ride in the saddle today. It would be nice if I could stretch my legs a bit before eating."

The earl slowly finished his wine, looking sideways over the brim at Ore, then stood and set his cup down deliberately. "I would be happy to have one of my children show you about the manor, if you like. I have things to do in the meantime, myself."

Ore stood also. "Thank you for your hospitality." This time, he didn't sound the sop. Rather it was the conclusion of a business transaction.

"This way please." The earl led him out of the receiving room and back into the large entry hall, with Thayne following silently. He stopped a household member and asked where Dane was, then sent that servant off to fetch him. "Dane is my second son," Earl Malkin explained. "My eldest, Tairn, is at Castle Nijou in training. My daughter is married to the Marquis duLuke."

"Ah, I see," Ore allowed a slight look of regret to pass quickly across his face, as if he'd hoped the daughter would be coming to escort him. "I have no children of my own." *Yet somehow, I can all of a sudden claim just how many? I should ask Ilena when I get back. ...On second thought, that might be too big a blow. I'm not really that old yet.* Ore entertained himself on the inside while the outside was as bored as ever.

Presently, a man about Ore's age came quickly around the corner, "Yes, Father?" he said automatically, then stopped short when he saw Ore.

"Dane, this is Lord Oxley, messenger for Regent Rei. He's recently come to Suiran from Ichijou and is affording himself of our hospitality for the night." It was said neutrally enough, but it let Ore know he was still a little ticked at being used. Not that Ore cared.

Ore nodded in a sop–ish sort of way at Dane. "Pleased to meet you, I'm sure," he said a little coolly.

Dane recovered a little slow and his father looked at him reproachfully. "Ah, ah yes, Lord Oxley. Pleased to meet you, likewise."

"Dane, please take Lord Oxley on a tour of the manor to pass the time before the evening meal. I'm sure you can be of help in allowing him to feel our hospitality." The earl was not fond of this child, from the sound of it. *The fifth wheel?* Ore felt a little bad for the son.

"Yes, Father," Dane bowed again to his father, his attitude one of cool obedience. Earl Malkin looked after them, calculatingly, until they turned the corner, then went his own way.

-o-o-o-

The tour inside was just as boring as any tour would be, but Ore carefully memorized the layout of the manor. He also would interrupt Dane any time it looked like he was about to say the words he wasn't supposed to, since he hadn't been acknowledged yet. And he stayed in character. Finally Dane asked, nearly in tears of frustration and desperation, "Is there anything else you could care to see, Lord Oxley?"

Ore looked at him, his eyes saying *finally!*, "A bit of fresh air would be nice. Do you have any gardens? Or is it still too cool here in the north for them to have bloomed as of yet?"

Dane's face took on a more happy look and his eyes said, *Oh! Sorry, of course. People are around.* "I'm sorry, Lord Oxley, only the early spring blossoms have appeared, but I would be happy to show them to you, if you would like."

Ore waved his hand, "I guess it will have to do. That was all I was able to see in Ichijoutsu before I came as well. How much longer before the spring

138

blooms appear here in Suiran?" He asked this question as they were exiting the manor out the back door.

"I believe it should be within a month or less," Dane said leading them around to where there was a small but pleasant garden.

Ore took a deep breath of the outside air, glad to be there for even a moment. He looked around the grounds of the manor, placing the family rooms and the guest rooms on the inside with where the windows exited to the outside. He turned towards the mountains rising with their rocky peaks into the evening sky, the snow reflecting oranges and reds, although the sun was no longer in the sky where they stood.

"The majesty of these mountains is certainly a thing the south doesn't have," he commented appreciatively. "But the north doesn't have the sea, which in its own way is just as grand."

Dane deprecated. "I haven't seen the sea, so I can't say."

So the father had left the son here when he'd been to Ichijoutsu. "Does your mother tend to the garden?" he asked Dane.

Dane shook his head. "Mother was from the south and her constitution was never quite suited to the north. She passed when I was eight."

"Oh, I'm sorry to hear that." Dane was surprised by the genuineness of Ore's comment. Everything else had been coated with the oil of disingenuity. They'd moved through the garden far enough that Ore could now see the placement of the stables in relation to the manor. He crouched down and looked down at a flower at his feet. "Oh! Is this the *Holegn Hanatake* I've been hearing about?" Ore knew all about it. It was the research Mizi had been working on for nearly three years now.

Dane nodded proudly. "Yes, I was finally able to obtain some seeds from Kouzanshi last fall after hearing about it. It's been doing well. I'm looking forward to seeing the blossoms...." He trailed off. Ore looked up at him sympathetically, putting his real face on for a brief time. Dane looked at him with serious consideration for a moment, then determination.

Softly Ore said, "Are you Dane Malkin?"

Dane took a breath and a much greater leap of faith than all the rest and said, "I am waiting to hear the words of Father."

"Mother has sent me for you," Ore said with great respect. Then, while Dane collected himself, Ore stood up and brushed himself off fastidiously, allowing his outward actions to continue to be the sop for the benefit of the servants who were likely watching them.

Thayne, who was trying to hide his surprise, had been following behind them silently. Ore turned to him now and said casually, a disinterested look on his face, "Do you have the distance measured and the path calculated?"

Thayne nodded a curt bow. "Yes, Father."

Ore began to lead them around the garden again, pointing now and again at a flower, or looking off into the distance. His words were very different, however. "Dane, this is Thayne. — Ah! You rhyme! — Can you get to the stables at night without being seen? Can you saddle your own horse? And what is the best time for us to leave tonight?"

Dane did his best to imitate Ore. "Yes, I can do both. Father retires at eleven to his room and his bed at midnight. It's best to wait until an hour later, when the rest of the staff have also retired."

"Will he sit up later or set an additional watch because a stranger has come?" That was already late enough, he really hoped it wouldn't be much more.

Dane pondered that. "If he must sit up to entertain you, he may, but if he's found a distraction for you he won't."

Ore smiled not a very nice smile. "I've already requested the distraction."

Dane looked at him, his eyes wide. "A–are you really sure?"

"You have a 'Sister' here that needs to come with us as well. It was a convenient way to assure she could be brought out easily. Please, will you assist me with that?"

"Who are you looking for?"

"Freida of Nakaba." Dane went pale. "Is there a problem?" Ore was concerned. Last minute problems were not his thing for already difficult jobs.

"Ah...ah...well, perhaps. ...Father knows I favor her, and has been being harsh with her. If you pick her, Father will not likely hesitate to let you have her if it looks like it will be hard on me...it's just.... Well, you seem to know what you're doing. I'll play along appropriately, and help if I can."

"Really, Dane, if it's something that could endanger us all I need to know to plan how to get us through it."

Dane went as red as he had been pale. "I'm afraid...the last time Father was away from the house...I was rather indiscreet. ...Freida is pregnant," he said the last in a rush. "I've refused to admit it to Father, that it was me, because that would only cause more problems for Freida," Ore closed his eyes, *Give me patience for young lords and their indiscretions, and help the servants of the same.* "...but Father suspects all the same."

"Have you ever considered that he's being hard on her *because* you won't acknowledge her? That if you would just do it, he wouldn't have to keep testing to see how far he has to take it before you break? That her life would be easier if you'd just own up to it?"

Dane looked at him like he was crazy. "You don't know my father."

"Yeah, that's what they all say. Every last lordling that gets a servant girl pregnant that he likes." Ore put his hand over his eyes. "So, tell me, Dane, why are you one of Mother's Children? Why are you worth risking my life and Thayne's life?"

He looked back at Dane, who was looking very crestfallen and punished. Ore really hadn't seen or heard anything yet to explain why there were problems at this place, or why these people needed to come out. Dane was almost too young to have been a participant in those early antics of the Earl.

Dane finally went even redder. He clenched his fist. Then looking into Ore's eyes defiantly, he said, "Freida was my nurse when I was a child, and was the one Father sought comfort with when mother died. He liked her first, as far as needing a replacement woman went. But she was mine from the beginning!"

Ore held up his hand, his eyes very hard. "You're digging your grave even deeper, Dane." Dane stood there with his mouth open in shock. "If you cannot answer appropriately for yourself, I will speak with Freida after dinner tonight and then decide if I'll take you away from here or not."

The youthfulness of Dane's face left him and his eyes became as hard as Ore's. "Did you think I would leave with you, with someone who would play with a woman, who would stoop to being self–important?"

Ore stopped and considered. It was true, that when looked at from Dane's perspective, Ore would have had to be tested, and tested hard, given the persona he'd picked. Just because he'd been told Ore was 'Father' and 'Mother' trusted him, didn't mean squat when it came time to actually act on it.

"No," Ore admitted. "That was wrong of me. I've picked a part to play, not knowing what I was walking into, but it wasn't a fair part to play in front of you."

"You really don't know what's going on here?" Dane asked.

Ore shook his head. "All I received was a list of names, where to pick them up from, and the instructions of what to hear and what to say. That was it."

Dane looked at him, just a little flummoxed. "Well...that just isn't fair, is it?" he finally said. "That could get you into quite a lot of trouble."

"You think?" Ore asked sarcastically, though not angrily. "This is the first difficult one for me, and only my fifth to pick up."

"I'm only the fifth?" Ore nodded. "Well. Well, well." Dane seemed pleased by that for some reason.

"If at all possible, I'd like to move along as soon as we can. After you two, there are still four more to go...this round."

"How many more rounds after this one?" Dane asked.

"Two."

Dane shrugged as he answered, "Well, next time, just walk in as you every time. It will make your life easier."

Ore was a little puzzled. "I knew I'd have to face your father."

Dane looked confused for a minute. "The steward would have gotten you in just fine. You didn't have to face the Earl at all, if you hadn't wanted to."

"Eh?!"

"Ah, right. You don't know. Mother has more than one, or two in our case, Children in each place. We network across all of Suiran, and farther. It's just a select few of us who've been told to go with Father. Just knock on the door.

Everyone in the Family will recognize you as part of the Family, even if they don't recognize you as Father, or if they aren't supposed to go with you."

Ore sank down to the ground in a crouch and put his hands over his face. He couldn't decide if he was going to kill Ilena or Rei first.

"Yeah, it's true *most* of the time," Thayne corrected Dane, "But in my case he needed to use strategy to get me out of my Viscount's House, and we've just come from that. We were just lucky to run into each other on the road, or it would have been as difficult as he was expecting it to be here."

"Hmm...well I suppose that could be the case," Dane understood. "But you could just go twice then. Once as just you to see if you can get in, then go back as someone else if you can't. Most often, it will just be that easy. On the rare cases it's not, then do it the hard way."

Thayne nodded. "That would work. It's not like it supposed to be hard, after all." They both grinned down at him. Ore changed his mind, he'd kill these two first.

"So, smart alecks, how do I get out of this one?" He crossed his arms over his knees.

"Hmm," Dane considered. "You want to get all of us out of here as soon as possible, right?" Ore nodded. "If you didn't care about the two of you, you could just spend the night and leave in the morning, just as you've already told Father you would, although you'd have to keep playing sop." His eyes glittered, saying it would be a price Dane thought he should have to pay. "But if you want to leave sooner, just find an excuse and leave whenever. Now that we know you've come, we'll just meet up with you wherever you want us to."

Ore stood up and shook his head. "No can do. First off, Freida's not official yet, and second, it's my duty to see you're all protected. I'm not comfortable with having my eyes off you too long."

"What about the rest? They aren't with you right now." Dane was dubious.

"It's not that. Until I've seen with my own eyes and felt it for myself, that the Children are safely away, I can't let it go."

Dane looked at him closely, then glanced at Thayne, who smiled back his big smile and asked, "Father's just like Mother, no?"

Dane nodded slowly. "It looks like it might be so. ...Well, then, if that's the case, eat dinner with Father, or not, whichever you want. I'll ask the steward to say a message came recalling you to the castle immediately. That gives you the excuse to leave. I'll have Freida meet you on the way back in now.

"Circle back around behind the stables and wait for us to come out, or wait on the road just out of eyesight of the house. I'll get us out of the house — just after dinner is easiest. We've been setting that up for ages now. No one will think anything of it."

Ore sighed. Dinner would be good, most likely. But he'd have to play the sop...or he could fess up to the Earl, too. "What's your father like?"

"Exactly what he looks like. Mother doesn't want me because of what's going on around here."

"Is he loyal?"

"He plays the game, but he's loyal for the most part."

"Right. Dinner then so we don't have to leave hungry and eat garrison leftovers." Both other men grinned. "And, you don't have to have the steward lie for me."

Dane raised an eyebrow and nodded. "Freida's this way." They walked to the laundry part of the back of the house. The laundry maids were collecting the clothes that had been hung to dry during the day. They called greetings to Dane and looked at the strangers curiously, but were courteous.

Dane walked up to a little patio just near the door and to an old woman in a chair. "Freida, there's someone here who would like to say hello." He said it kindly but loudly. Ore took that to mean she was going deaf. He felt his heart freeze. His little play really would have gone very badly. The Earl would have laughed his head off if Ore had asked to have this venerable lady for the night.

Freida looked around. Ore walked up close to her, in case she was also going blind. "Are you Freida of Nakaba?" he tried to be about as loud as Dane had been.

She looked up at him, "What a good looking young man. Have I seen you before?"

Dane touched her shoulder, "Yes, you have Freida. Do you remember what you're supposed to tell him?"

"Oh, you're that young man! Ah, yes...it was...I am waiting to hear the words of Father." Good she wasn't so forgetful yet, but they might be picking her up just barely in time, it looked like.

Ore bowed to her, his right fingers lightly touching his chest over his heart. "Mother has sent me for you. If you're still willing to come, we'll leave after dinner. I'm sorry to make you ride into the night."

"That's all right, deary. We do it every evening, don't we Dane?"

"Yes, Freida, indeed we do. I'll ask June to help you get ready this time, though, since we won't be coming back for a long time."

"Okay." She reached up and squeezed his hand. "It's nice to meet you again," she said to Ore.

"Likewise," Ore said bowing again slightly.

Dane led them into the house, stopping in the first room to speak briefly with a younger woman about getting Freida prepared for the trip. In the hall, Ore stopped Dane. "Okay, you seem willing to tell me things I need to know. How is it that all of you recognize me? Even Freida says she was happy to 'see me again', when I don't ever recall seeing her before."

"Mother didn't tell you that yet either?" Ore glared at them. Dane and Thayne looked at each other. They both shook their heads. "Nope. It isn't our place to say."

"And was I going to be told about how to find all of you, really? Or was the messenger just giving me a hard time?"

"Ah, that.... Well I can't say. Was she going to?"

"For a price. Master wouldn't pay it."

"Well...that would be his fault then, wouldn't it? Mother's price is always worth paying."

Ore thought about that. It was possible that Ilena was testing Rei, and that he'd failed it, or at least was going to learn the lesson, because he, Ore, was going to tell him off for it. "Well, would it be best to come clean to your father now, or as we go into dinner?"

"As we go into dinner. Interrupting his work will make him less willing to listen, but they're about the same time anyway. I was taking us to the dining hall," Dane answered.

"Okay," Ore ran through what his apology was going to be. He hoped to be forgiven. He was getting hungry and the really nice wine from earlier was a hopeful expectation of what was to come.

-o-o-o-

Earl Malkin walked up to Ore and Dane, who were waiting outside the dining room. Thayne was still standing guard nearby. Ore had told him they'd not go too far from what they'd already started, so to stick to guard duty.

"Did you enjoy the tour of Nakaba's house and grounds?" Earl Malkin asked Ore politely.

"I did, thank you very much," Ore answered sincerely. He'd dropped the facade of a spoiled sop. Earl Malkin looked at him directly, wondering what was going on, most likely. "Your son, Dane, is a very fine man."

"Thank you. I like to think so," Earl Malkin had just a little crinkle at the edges of his eyes.

I wonder how much of the conversation in the garden he was watching? Ore wondered. He took a breath. "Earl Malkin, I am not Lord Oxley; however, I'd appreciate it if you'd continue to use that name for me at this time. I am a Messenger of the Regent, as I've said, however, and will produce my token if you desire to see it for yourself. I'm also a Knight to the First Prince." He bowed. "I apologize for testing you today and arriving without prior warning."

"Hooh? It seems a bit early to be giving up on the testing, if that's what it was?" the Earl didn't choose to become angry, at least not yet.

"Your son has been very convincing in your stead. It isn't necessary to continue to do so at this time. Nor is it necessary for me to impose upon your hospitality for the night."

"Mmm...and what is it you wish to do, then?" Earl Malkin wasn't buying that it was a hit and run testing visit.

"I'll be imposing on you for the persons of your son, Dane, and your householder Freida. I've been sent to fetch them on behalf of Regent Rei." Both Dane and Thayne reacted to him just saying it outright.

"Hmm...and just when would you like to be taking them away?" Earl Malkin narrowed his eyes.

"I'm sure it's an imposition, but no later than directly after dinner this night." Ore didn't flinch, although he did feel somewhat bad. He'd had to be like this for Rei before.

"*Haah*," Earl Malkin turned to Dane. "Is this okay?"

Dane bowed slightly, "Yes, Father." He looked at his father with a little smile playing on his face.

"Are you prepared?" Dane nodded. Earl Malkin turned back to Ore. "Very well. They'll go with you after the dinner meal. You may join us if you like."

Ore bowed politely, "Thank you very much. In truth, I should very much like to have a meal at your table rather than yet another one at a barracks."

Earl Malkin smiled. "Indeed. They should really only be stomached when they must be. Your man here may eat in the kitchen with the other servants, if you wish."

"Thank you very much," Ore said for him and Thayne bowed in thanks.

"If you would please," the Earl motioned for the younger men to go before him into the dining hall and they all entered.

After they were seated and had begun to eat what was indeed a delicious meal, but not so grand as to be wasteful, Earl Malkin casually said to Ore, "Miss Ilena has always been a welcome guest here. Is she well?"

Ore's fork paused on its way to his mouth very briefly, then continued. Ore used the chewing time to figure out what to say. "You are aware that at last news, she'd been caught in a landslide that killed Earl Shicchi's Lady wife and all her attendants?" He looked at both men, wondering just what it was they did know if they knew Ilena directly.

They glanced at each other, then Earl Malkin said carefully, "Yes, we had heard that. Very sad news indeed."

Ore left it at that for a moment while he ate another bite of his meal. Dane fidgeted briefly and the Earl looked at him forcefully from the corner of his eye. "You're also aware that if she is alive at this time, her life is in danger?"

Dane looked depressed, but Earl Malkin responded smoothly. "It would certainly be an imposition to press further, then. Perhaps later you may be able to tell us more about what has happened in the case."

"Perhaps. It might be possible to understand it yourself should you be able to come to the castle again. After all, the Regent must present any evidence of foul play to the House of Lords, if there's any to be had."

"Mmm, indeed," Earl Malkin agreed, eating another bite from his plate, seemingly satisfied. It looked like Dane decided to trust his father. He ate another bite as well, and the conversation turned to sundry light topics for the remainder of the meal.

After the meal, Earl Malkin, followed by the steward, led Ore, Dane, and Thayne out to the front courtyard where the servants had their horses saddled and readied. There was also a carriage. Freida was waiting beside it with the maid. They said their goodbyes to Earl Malkin, Freida thanking him for taking care of her, and entered the carriage. Ore and Thayne thanked him for the meal and Ore apologized again for the short notice, and they mounted their horses.

Dane said his farewells to his father and climbed up into the driver's seat of the carriage. He smiled down at Ore's surprised expression. "This is just what Freida and I've been doing each night for quite some time. This time we'll be going a little farther, is all."

Ore nodded. "Farewell, Earl Malkin. Until we meet again." The Earl lifted his hand in farewell and the little group left the Earldom of Nakaba, stopping to pick up the bag of clothes on the way.

Having to go at the carriage's speed, although Dane did take it as fast as he dared for the older woman's bones, it was well after dark when they reached the barracks. While that was late, it was earlier than Ore had hoped of ever reaching it under his original plan. The late–comers were given rooms and quickly went to bed. Ore lay awake until he had the outline of a plan for continuing on, then he slipped into sleep.

-o-o-o-

In the morning, they all gathered to breakfast at one of the tables in the barrack's dining hall. Everyone introduced themselves all around again, except Ore, who preferred to let everyone pretend he was just "Father".

He was thinking about Ilena's comment to him the night before he left. *"Be gentle with them. Most of them are very afraid."* Well, he hadn't come across anyone who was afraid. Willing to be cautious, but not afraid. They had to cross north of Earl Shicchi's lands next. He needed to know how they felt about that. He always felt *his* nerves tighten up for that stretch. It had been the only thing about coming north he'd disliked — other than winter's cold.

They could stop at Osterly garrison at a reasonable hour in the evening and continue on the next day, or continue into the night and make it to Nijoushi in one long, late night stretch again. He'd decided to put it to a vote. He didn't really need to push them all hard, and he'd felt bad about pushing Freida hard last night, although she'd fallen asleep in the carriage. He just personally felt some inner push to get everyone 'home' safely.

After he'd explained this to everyone following breakfast, they thought about it some, then voiced their opinions. Dane was first. "While it's kind of you to think of Freida, she'll sleep in the carriage whenever she feels like sleeping. As long as I can stay awake to drive it we could continue all the way on to the southern coast and she wouldn't mind. I can do either plan."

Elandra smiled at Ore invitingly. "The longer we can make it the better for me, but that's because I want to keep trying to get you for myself."

"Next," Ore said. Elandra pouted. Ore ignored the pout.

Foster said, "I personally don't care either way, but Thom may be hard to handle if it's a full day and most of a night again. He was in pretty bad shape when we got here in the late evening yesterday." Sallie nodded agreement. Ore looked at Peter. He shrugged. He'd go with Foster and Sallie.

Thayne smiled. "I'll ride with you wherever and whenever you want to go."

Ore nodded a thanks at the underlying sentiment. "*Haah*. You guys aren't making this easy, are you?" He thought about it for a moment, then suddenly came to a strange realization. Even if his brother had seen any of these people before, he wouldn't remember them, except maybe the tall forester.

Perhaps the more pressing problem would be if they all went to the garrison, like he'd originally been planning. That would be stranger than if they all met up again at the small inn at the village. He probably shouldn't be seen with them, though, since the Earl's men knew he'd been with Ilena. *Haah, what a problem. Well, one thing at a time then.*

"Dane, get you, Freida, and June on the road as soon as you can. You're the slowest. When you go to the castle, who do you usually stay with in Osterly?"

"If it's a formal visit, the village head, but that's rare. Usually it's the inn," Dane answered immediately.

"Go there, then, and stay the night. The next morning get started towards Nijoushi. I'll tell you where we're going after we catch up to you that morning. I'll settle with the inn when I get to Osterly."

"Okay, Father," Dane winked.

"Foster, you'll take the same group as yesterday and do the same. Stay over in Osterly at the inn. I'll let you know where you'll end up when I meet up with you." Foster nodded and Sallie looked relieved that Thom would have a little bit of a reprieve. Elandra pouted again.

"Elandra, you're rearguard for Foster. Pay attention to the road, especially that section of narrow road Mother was ambushed at. If you think there's an ambush being prepared there again, go take out whomever is putting it together." Elandra lit up. Work! That was more like it.

Ore looked at Thayne. He wanted to take him with.... "Dane, I'm going to assign an honor guard for you and the carriage. It's unlikely you'll actually need it, but having a deterrent in place will make me feel better." Dane nodded. "Thayne, you'll come with me, if you think you can ride as long as I can?"

Thayne crossed his arms and grinned, "Shall we make it a bet or a race?"

Ore laughed. "Neither, now that you've offered. Oh, Dane, you've been to Nijoushi before, haven't you?" Dane nodded. "Then where do I go to most easily acquire the rest of the Children?"

Dane grinned. "You're learning. There are about five inns and taverns you can go to and any of them will get them for you."

"The closest to North Road."

"That would be the Black Cat. ...I hear it was named after you."

"You're teasing me," Ore accused.

Dane's eyes were smiling. "Maybe, maybe not."

Ore decided to not follow that thread. "Does the inn at Osterly have one of Mother's Children in residence?"

"Yes," this time it was Elandra who answered. "Ask for Misty."

"Thank you, Elandra."

"Glad to be of help!" she said cheerfully.

"Any questions or concerns?" There were none. "Then, if you make it to the Black Cat before I see you again, stop there, okay?" Foster and Dane nodded. "Get yourselves going, then. Be safe and protect yourselves. I don't wish to be badly scolded for leaving you on your own. Ah, but just to be sure, by a show of hands, who's just putting on a front and is actually really terrified inside but refusing to let me know? Because that would make me upset."

Everyone looked at each other, then Peter stood up hesitantly. He bowed to Ore. "Father, I think we wish you to understand that because of the strength of Mother, we've all been able to find our own strengths. Even though I'm the weakest here, besides the very young and very old, even I've found strengths I didn't know I had because Mother helped me see them, and every day that I remember her, I find more strength.

"Also, we discussed it earlier...in your own way you also give us strength. You're providing for us, although I can only imagine it, what a good father would provide. We'll surely be fine. You may do what you need to do."

"Besides," Elandra leaned on her elbows, "we can all tell that you're really just in a hurry to get back to Mother. That's fine by us, too." She grinned a wicked teasing grin.

"But," interjected Dane quickly, "it would really help us if you'd let us know what her status is. We may not be afraid to travel, but we are very worried about her."

Ore looked at them all. He really wanted to tell them, because for some reason they were starting to feel like family, and family would definitely want to know. "Master won't let it me say it yet. When we arrive at the place prepared for you that will be your home and your place of protective custody until the matter is settled, then I may tell you." They had to be content with that.

CHAPTER 9 The Black Cat Inn

Ore led Thayne to the garrison captain's office. There, he requisitioned an honor guard of four guards to go to the Osterly garrison with Dane and the carriage, warning them of the place that was perfect for ambushes. He also wrote a requisition for the same from the Osterly garrison so the guards from this garrison could give that to them and be substituted out and return rather than continue on to Nijoushi. Then he requested that the horse and wagon he'd borrowed be returned and requisitioned a horse and wagon from the garrison for Foster's group.

He took the time to pen a note to Rei. He asked that it be sent by bird, if possible. It was like most of his notes: it took forever to figure out what to say, and then said it too briefly. It went something like, *I almost lost two witnesses for not understanding the easiness of my job.* It was meant to carry the weight of a lot of frustration and be very scolding.

Once those chores were done, Ore and Thayne got on the road. They made it to Osterly shortly after lunch. Ore decided to eat at the inn, that way he could get everything done at once, even though it would take additional time. They were seated, and a young woman brought them the midday meal. "Would Misty be available for a minute?" Ore asked pleasantly, as his plate was set down in front of him.

The waitress winked. "That'd be me. You've got me for thirty seconds."

"Two groups of Children are arriving here tonight. I need to cover their costs for the night: dinner, beds, breakfast. I don't want my money covering the wrong people, but you I'd trust to get it right. One room with two beds, two rooms with three beds each. How much do I leave with you?"

She named a price and Ore fished it out plus their lunch fee. While waiting, she asked, "How do I recognize them?"

Ore raised an eyebrow. Thayne smoothly cut in, "Roses and a thorn. The hare and the tree."

Misty nodded, took Ore's money and moved on to the next customer. As the men dug into their food, Ore said, "That was cryptic."

"Mmm," agreed Thayne around his mouthful, but he wouldn't elaborate.

Ore sighed. "Am I going to have to take you everywhere with me in order to translate?"

Thayne looked thoughtful. "Yup."

"Whhyyy?"

Thayne tried to put it into words that would be understandable but not offensive. "What is Mother to you at this point?" That was still a dangerous question for Ore and these folks, as far as Ore was concerned. When he couldn't answer right away, Thayne said, "That's why. It'll come with time we figure. When the time's right, you'll learn it all. In the meantime you need a translator."

Ore was quiet, then nodded. It did make sense. As much trust as he was willing to give was what he was going to get. Everyone seemed to know pretty well what their boundaries were — what they could say and what they couldn't.

Compared with the nightwalker organizations he was acquainted with, this one was pretty sophisticated and well ordered, what little he'd brushed against anyway. It didn't have the dark overtones, though. More like light overtones instead. Except Elandra.

-o-o-o-

As soon as they were done with lunch, they were on the road again. They made it to Nijoushi just an hour or so after sunset. Ore did his best to find the Black Cat. They asked what folks were on the road and got pointed to the right area, but then they had to hunt. He finally picked one that looked right by the sign and they went in.

Thayne immediately said, "This isn't right."

"Oh?" Ore couldn't tell, of course, but there were some unsavory characters in the place that made his senses go on alert as soon as they walked in. "Mind if I experiment?"

Thayne shook his head. "Do we get to let off steam if I'm right?"

Ore shook his head. "We're on business." Thayne shrugged. Ore walked up to the closest barmaid. "I'm looking for some people."

"Who ain't honey?" she said disinterestedly.

"Could you perhaps tell me if you know them?"

She glanced up at him, irritated with the interruption of her work. "Who wants to know and why should I?"

"Well, thanks for your time anyway," Ore said, and turned to walk out.

A man that had been leaning against the wall near the door stood and addressed Ore as he neared the door. "No, really, we want to know." His voice was soft and almost sibilant.

Ore raised his hands and smiled disarmingly. "It really is nothing. I've been looking for my sister and brother–in–law, but I can't remember which establishment they said to meet them in. I'll just keep looking on down the road. ...If you could let us pass?"

The man looked at him a little longer, then moved out of his way and returned to the wall. "Good luck," he sneered as they walked out.

"Well, that went better than I thought," Thayne said. "You really are very good. That's why I wanted to come. You're a lot of fun to watch."

Ore reciprocated, "You're not bad yourself. You handled yourself much better at Dane's than I expected."

Thayne smiled and said, "Thanks!", but Ore felt it covered something more significant. At the same level as the cryptic way they had of recognizing each other.

A young lad, making Ore think of a castle paige, came running up to them. "Mister, mister! You missed it. It's over there!" He turned and pointed at a larger establishment that was well lit several buildings back.

"Thanks!" said Thayne to the lad and he ran off again.

Ore watched after him. "Another one?" Thayne nodded once. "Why do I get the feeling I'm going to be seeing a lot more of them more often?"

Thayne grinned. "Because Mother's finally taken your blinders off?" Ore wasn't sure whether to be surprised or irritated. Thayne slapped him on the back. "Cheer up. You've just been told where you want to go."

Ore looked at it as they walked up. "Did we miss it because I wasn't looking for a two–story family place?"

"Yup. You still see with eyes of darkness, so you still seek that first." Ore filed that comment away for further study later. They entered and Ore could feel the difference. If knowing what kind of an establishment one of Ilena's Children was running was based on feel, it would be obvious to Ore now. This one felt inviting and comfortable. It was still noisy, and crowded, but there was laughter and life here.

Barely before he had time to scan the room, a young girl ran up and grabbed his hand. "Hey! Welcome! Come in, come in. We've got a place for you two right over here!" She pulled him over to a table centered on the fireplace, but not so close it was hot. He noticed she didn't pull hard enough to put him off balance, just enough to direct him. As she seated him, he nodded his thanks. "Dinner?"

"Sure, and drinks for the two of us."

"Okay!" and she was off.

Ore looked around. Thayne was having a hard time not laughing. Pretty quick Ore could tell why. He caught the eyes of several other young people looking at him. "She beat them to it, eh?"

Thayne grinned, "Yup."

"I also notice she seated us at the throne table."

"Is that what you'd call it?" Thayne asked innocently. Ore glared at him through slitted eyes. Thayne laughed again. "But not everyone here recognizes you."

"No, but I'd bet everyone knows about me."

Thayne looked around. "No. There are lots of other good people who like to come to establishments like this. It's my first time here in Nijoushi, but I've been to Kouzanshi and there are several there, too. You've probably been in them."

Ore thought about it. He probably had. This was the kind of place he looked for to take Mizi to. *Ah!* That felt like an important clue to understanding Ilena. Ilena's Children liked to create spaces for others that even Mizi would thrive in.

So, could Ilena make a space for Mizi to thrive in? Is that what she was trying to do? Like with teaching her how to be strong in a scary situation, just like what Peter had said. They'd been frightened until Mother had taught them to be strong. He'd seen that very thing in practice himself by the person herself.

Ore had a very strange feeling in his stomach. Like something tight was trying to unravel. Like the light of this place was trying to reach through the darkness that surrounded him. ...Hadn't he dreamed about something like that recently?

His thoughts were interrupted by a mug and plate being set down in front of him. Another one went in front of Thayne. "There you are! Enjoy! Is there anything else I can do for you?"

"Yes," said Ore absently. Their waitress waited but he was still trying to return to the room from the thoughts in his head so it took a bit for him to continue. "Ah... paiges. Runners. Got a couple in the room?" If he was going to be set on the throne by them, he'd act the part for now.

"Marcus! Henry! You're needed over here!" she called out, then said, "Let me know if you need anything else. The name's Mary."

"Thanks, Mary," Ore said. He eyed the two young men up and down as they arrived and waited in front of him. They were the eager types, but for some reason, they looked a little...grey? Like not quite as much light. "Marcus?"

The sturdy youth with wild blond hair and hazel eyes raised his hand. "That's me!"

Ore looked at the other youth, taller with serious eyes but a youthful smile, straight brown hair and light brown eyes. "Then you'd be Henry."

"Yup."

He listed off the four remaining names. "Go get them. Have them here by the time I'm done eating, if you can. Let them know they're going on a trip and to say their goodbyes before they come."

Four eyes went round. "Yes, Sir!" They looked at each other significantly, then were off.

"Not going to go find them yourself?" Thayne asked.

"Why? It's always faster to let runners do it. City or castle. Plus they speak both my dialect and yours so they're just as good at translating as you. Besides," Ore looked at him curiously, resting on one arm, "aren't you tired of running? We've been on the road all day. I'm perfectly content to sit and enjoy my mug. ...Even if I have to be on display while I do it."

Thayne's eyes smiled at Ore as he took a drink. "Absolutely a natural, aren't you?" he teased as he set his mug down.

Ore blushed just faintly. "No. Hate to be the center of attention, but I've been around Master too long. He's rubbed off."

"Well, that's alright then," Thayne said approvingly. "We like him, too."

Well, really. What interesting things I'm learning tonight. "Will you call Mary back over, please?"

"What? She'd love it if you did it."

"I'm thinking."

Sigh. "All right. Can't think and talk at the same time," Thayne muttered. Ore ignored him. "Mary!" Thayne called and waved her over.

She came as soon as she got freed up. "Yes?"

"Rooms?" Ore asked.

"Yup, upstairs. How many?"

"Three two beds. One night, breakfast early. How much?"

She named a price. "Payable when you leave."

That surprised Ore. "When we leave?"

"Yup. Just for you, of course."

"No it's not, Mary. Speak truths." An older woman had walked up behind her. "I'm Cathy. My husband and I run this place. He's head cook, so he can't come greet you just yet. Mind if I sit for a moment?" Mary ran off to another table that was calling for her and Ore waved Cathy to take a seat. "You'll take them tonight and have them sleep here rather than at their homes?" Cathy came straight to the point of her concern.

"I'd take them straight from here when they get here if I could." Ore answered. "As it is, I want to leave as early as possible in the morning. If I have to have them all collected then, it will run us late."

"He takes his responsibilities very seriously," Thayne explained to Cathy. "We're okay with it."

"We're? You too?" she looked at him curiously as he nodded.

"I'm his translator," Thayne said with a smile.

"And companion," Ore said absently, his mind still working on other things.

He missed the look of surprise they gave him. Thayne smiled gently. "He's like that, huh?" Cathy said quietly to Thayne.

He turned the same smile on her. "Yes," he said just as softly. "I think it's going to be just fine."

She searched his face, then smiled. "That's good, then." She stood up, "Well, enjoy your evening, then, good sirs."

"Thanks!" they both said.

After a bit, Ore returned to full alertness again. He looked at Thayne without moving his head. "What's going to be 'just fine'?"

"Ah, you heard that did you?" Thayne smiled a private smile.

Ore sighed. He knew a sidestep when he heard one. He let it drop. "Speak truths, huh?"

"What?"

"Nothing."

"You're doing heavy thinking tonight. Does it usually follow heavy drinking?" Thayne asked in teasing accusation.

Ore defended himself. "I haven't had any more than you, and I don't get drunk."

"Really?"

"Really. I've tried. I can get sick after a while, but that's because the stomach can only hold so much liquid. You know, like eating too much dinner kind of sick."

"Now you're boasting," Thayne declared.

"You're the one that said it." After a pregnant pause, Ore grinned. "I really do like having you around. After you're let out, come find me. We'll do this again."

"I'd like that, Father," Thayne said respectfully. He turned his head away and looked towards the door, which opened right at that moment. "Father," he said urgently but very quietly, "look at that man."

Ore looked up and into the tawny eyes of the man who'd just walked in. Black hair like his own but long like Ilena's, a slightly dark complexion, like he could also be a distant relative. As tall as Sasou, and well muscled, with a small, kind smile he was now turning on several of the young folk who'd come running up to greet him.

The eyes for just that instant had measured Ore, then had carefully disengaged to feign disinterest and distraction. It almost felt to Ore as if he'd looked into the face of a prince. For some reason, Ore felt electric. "Remember his face," Thayne said. "You'll see it again."

Ore's thoughts were interrupted as the door opened once again and an older middle aged man walked in. He looked around the room, saw Ore, and immediately strode towards them. Ore quickly glanced around for the first man and saw he'd been seated where he could surreptitiously watch. Ore also noticed he was just close enough to overhear what was said at the table if it wasn't whispered. Whoever he was, he wanted to know what 'Father' was going to do about collecting people tonight. And maybe who. The list was important.

Ore all of a sudden regretted having them come here. It made it too obvious which list he was on. Then he shrugged. Thayne had recognized the man and not said "run". No one else in the room felt off. He suspected true outsiders were uncomfortable here, and if they tried to stay were made unwelcome. It was okay with him if the Family knew what was happening, if it was in bits and pieces.

The older rotund man had reached his table and was standing in front of him, holding a hat in his hands, showing the partial balding on the top of his head. Ore looked up at him and welcomed him, "Thank you for coming straight away."

The man nodded. "I'm Robert of Pence."

"Robert of Pence?"

"I am waiting to hear the words of Father."

Ore smiled gently at him. "Mother has sent me for you. Please have a seat," He indicated the seat on the other side of him from Thayne. "Do you have family?" The man shook his head. "Have you had dinner?"

"Ah, yes...."

Ore eyed him. "Mary!"

"Coming!" In a few minutes, Mary showed up with another plate and mug and set them down in front of Robert. "Here you go!" Then she was off again.

"Eey!" Ore called at her back. "I need a refill!"

"I'll get it!" she called over her shoulder.

But another mug was thunked down in front of him before she'd finished with the table she was on. "I got it, Mary," another young voice called out from behind Ore.

He looked behind him. "Thanks!"

"No problem." The youngster was already heading away.

That had given Robert enough time to get started on his dinner. He ate as if he hadn't really eaten. Ore leaned his chin on his hand and said to him, "It's hard for us bachelors to get decent meals, isn't it? I mean, who has the time to work, market, make it, then finally eat it just to clean it up? It's more of a hassle. I usually just grab a quick snack from the market and call it good, which of course isn't good for one's health, really."

Robert looked up at him, startled, then shyly nodded. "Yeah. I guess that couldn't really be called dinner, eh?"

"Well, it's certainly not as good a dinner as this one," Ore agreed.

"I'll let the chef know you said that," said Mary as she dropped three more mugs on the table and whooshed away again.

"No competing!" called out Thayne.

A chorus of "Awww!'s" rang out.

"Thanks," said Ore quietly. He agreed. It was fun, but that would get out of hand. "Are you ready to go?" Ore asked Robert.

The eating man nodded. "Been ready a while."

"Good. When you're ready to call it a night, get a key. You'll be joined in the room by one more tonight, so be expecting that. We leave at daybreak. Eat breakfast before that. Do you have transportation?" Robert shook his head. Ore had been expecting that. It was one of the things he'd been pondering earlier.

It wasn't likely that any of the town Children had long–distance transportation of their own. They should be used to walking. If he could get them out of here early enough, they should be able to meet up with the wagon at about the right place. If anyone needed to, they could share the carriage, too. It wasn't that Ore, or Rei for that matter, was stingy. It was just Ore's way to be as practical with the finances and creative with the solutions as possible.

The door opened again. This time it looked like a husband–wife pair. They were greying, but still had youth and strength in them. She was carrying a sewing basket, and he had a full knapsack on his back. Ore smiled at them as they came towards him. Somehow they seemed like the kind of people grown kids would love coming home to. They reached the table. "I'm Roy of Nijoushi," the man said.

"I'm Betty of Nijoushi," the woman said. Ore knew instinctively they'd been given aliases. That was a first.

"Roy of Nijoushi?"

"I am waiting to hear the words of Father," he said quietly.

"Mother has sent me for you. Betty of Nijoushi?"

"I am waiting to hear the words of Father," she said, also quietly, a slight quaver in her voice.

"Mother has sent me for you." Ore still couldn't help but make his voice gentle when he said those words. They somehow felt like they were an embrace from her to them, and they seemed to receive them the same way...all of them. Betty wiped her eyes. "Please sit."

Roy pulled out the last chair for Betty, moving it slightly around. She sat with the sewing box in her lap. Roy borrowed a chair from the next table over that had one available, then removed his knapsack and sat, placing it between his feet. "Are you ready?" Ore asked them. They both nodded. "Have you eaten dinner."

"Yes," Roy said looking gratefully at Betty.

Ore smiled. "You're a lucky man, then. We were just bemoaning the fate of bachelors who must fend for themselves at meal time."

"Yes, I am," Roy said as Betty blushed.

The door opened again. This time it was Henry and Marcus, each carrying a bag. They were shepherding a middle aged woman and three children who looked to be in the age range of eleven or twelve down to five or six. The woman said something to Henry and Marcus and they led the children to a corner table and sat with them. Cathy walked up to the woman and spoke with her a moment. The new woman took a deep breath and ran her hand through her bobbed hair. Then she relaxed and responded.

Both women came to Ore's now full table. "I see why you were concerned now, Cathy, but please remember for next time that I like to be made aware of such things as soon as possible so that I can decide on the best course of action to take earlier." Ore's rebuke was gentle.

She flushed a bit. "I'm sorry. I'll remember it."

"But it isn't really your fault either," he said kindly. "I was only given one name and one city to look in. I'll complain to the person who gave me the information. Perhaps next time they'll be willing to expound so I can be more prepared, if it's possible."

He looked at the last Child he was there to retrieve. "I apologize for the difficulty this is for you and your children at this time of night." She waved her hand, her cheeks rosy. "Rose of Lilith?"

She took a deep breath, looking like she was steeling herself. "I am waiting to hear the words of Father."

"Mother has sent me for you." He looked at her trying to see deeply into her the way Ilena would. There was something holding her back. "What is it that's keeping you here?" She startled. "It's okay. I'm not here to drag anyone away by force. If there's a thing I may help with I would like to know."

"Ah...it isn't a thing keeping me *here*, per se. More of a ...concern about where we're going."

Ore smiled. "Would it help if I told you it's a place in the countryside with plenty of room for children to run in? That there's already a four year old and two seventeen year olds, all boys, in our group?"

Thayne coughed and muttered under his breath, "One nineteen, one twenty–five."

"Sorry," Ore said without looking away from Rose. "As he said. And also a pair here who look like the best grandparents in the world, and a great–grandmother." Roy and Betty flushed in pleasure of his praise. "I don't think you'll need to feel like a parent alone, caged in a small place in that place."

Rose couldn't help the tears dripping down her cheeks. Cathy put her arm around her and hugged her from the side. After a bit, Rose recovered and wiped her face with a handkerchief. Ore guessed she had a lot of them tucked all over the place. Her two youngest were boys, the oldest was a girl.

If anything the girl would be the most left out where they were going, but the older women would be able to help her, and they were only the first group. Who knew but other children, including girls, would come.

Rose took a stabilizing breath then said, "We're ready."

"Very well. Have you and the children eaten?"

"Yes."

"Cathy, if you could please rearrange the rooms? Robert can room with Thayne and I if you have any three–bed rooms. Keep a two–bed room for Roy and Betty. And change the other room to a four–bed room."

Cathy bowed slightly. "Certainly. Rose, do you want me to have the boys take the kids up there now?" Rose looked a little uncertain.

Ore asked, "Miss Rose, can you have them up and breakfasted by first light in the morning? I would like for us to set out then."

She nodded. "I can do my best."

"That will do. You may retire with them now, if you wish."

"Thank you." Rose left with Cathy and they went to gather up the children, the runners going with them to take the bags.

Ore watched them go. "Thayne, we'll take one bag each on the horses tomorrow."

"Yes, Father."

He turned to the other couple and Robert. "You'll be walking for the first part of the day, but we'll be joining up with a wagon and carriage for the remainder of the journey. Do any of you have any difficulties with walking, or with that arrangement?" They all shook their heads. "Mister Roy, Miss Betty, do you understand the morning's schedule?" They nodded. "Then you may retire when you're ready."

Roy looked at Betty, then at Ore. "We would like to do that now, then." When Ore nodded consent, Roy rose and pulled out Betty's chair for her. They retrieved their things, bowed, and followed the direction Cathy had gone with Rose and her group, Roy returning the extra chair to the table it had been sitting at originally on his way.

Robert drained his mug and set it above his empty plate. "Do I need to pay for dinner?" he asked. Ore shook his head 'no', in the middle of a drink himself. "Then I think I'll take myself off to bed also," he rose.

"Tell one of the runners — one of the boys that helped Miss Rose's family upstairs — which room it is we should come to and leave the door unlocked for us, please," Ore requested.

"Of course," Robert touched the brim of his hat he'd put back on, then followed after the older couple.

Mary swept up and collected the empty plates and mugs. "Do you want any more to drink?"

"I'd like one more, please," Ore said.

"I'm good," Thayne smiled at her. She smiled back and swept off to the kitchen.

"*Hah.*" Ore put his chin on his hands. He wanted to put his head down on the table. He closed his eyes, then felt the princely man stand from his chair. Ore looked over at him tiredly. It had been a long day. The man was walking away from his table towards the door. He looked briefly over to Ore and saw Ore looking at him. He gave Ore a small, satisfied smile. Ore nodded a brief nod of acknowledgment, then the man was out the door and into the night.

Thayne looked at Ore through lidded eyes. "Looks like you passed the test."

"What test? Wasn't it you lot that told me to just be myself?" He just couldn't keep in a yawn any more and let it out.

Thayne chuckled. "I think it's time I helped this doddering old man to bed."

"What doddering?" Ore said in mock offense. "And I see no 'old' here, unless it's in your beard."

Thayne, who was clean shaven and thus why he looked younger than his years, stood, "Come on, old man."

Ore looked up at him. He didn't know it was with fondness again. "Actually, go on ahead. I'd like to just sit and be quiet for a bit before coming up." It was getting quiet in the dining room as most people had already returned to their houses to prepare for the next day, and that was what Ore needed: quiet. It had been very noisy these last several days.

"All right, but come up before you're sleeping on the table."

"I will, or Mary will pick me up and put me in the sink, thinking I'm a dirty dish to wash."

"Or in the bin, thinking you're a dirty cloth, more likely," Mary retorted as she set down his last mug.

"Whatever," Ore was too tired to banter any more. She smiled at him and left him alone, and Thayne went to find the room.

-o-o-o-

Ore sat thinking about how close the castle was to where he was, and who was in it. It wasn't an unusual pastime. He often thought about Rei and Mizi when it was late and he was tired like this. Andrew and Mina, too. This time, there was a new person he thought of as well. Ilena was in that castle now.

Next to the four bright lights he saw there often in his mind, it seemed like her light was beginning to glow, too. If he'd been able to express that thought to those who'd seen him tonight, they would have explained that his light was also glowing brightly, a sixth as bright as any of the others.

Ore was interrupted by the arrival of the runners. "Sorry, sir, for disturbing you, but you're falling asleep and we've got to go home."

"Ah, I am aren't I?" Ore answered.

"You're in room eight." They turned to leave the building.

"Wait a bit." They turned back. "I've been learning to see the light tonight, instead of just darkness. But...I noticed you two look like your light is dimmer than most that were here. Can you tell me why?"

They looked at each other trying to figure out what he meant. Then Henry of the serious eyes said, "It's that, isn't it, Marcus?" his face falling from pleasant to sad.

"Probably," Marcus answered, going from playful to serious. He looked back at Ore. "You're the only one who'd be able to answer to it, though."

"Oh?" Ore raised an eyebrow.

"It's Mother," Henry said, and Ore suddenly realized it was the same dimming of the light he'd seen but not recognized until now in Dane.

"I see. ...Those of you who feel particularly close to Mother are concerned about her. Because she's your source of light, and you don't know where to turn to find her, or if you even may, your own light is dimmed."

"Ah, yeah. That's an interesting way to put it, but it sounds about right." Henry agreed.

Ore rose, feeling heavy. "I appreciate your help today. I hope to see you again." He put four coins on the table and pushed them slightly towards them and looked them in the eyes sadly. "I'm sorry I can't enlighten you today. Master has sealed my lips. ...Good night." He turned and headed towards the door to the stairs. He could feel the runners looking after him, then they turned and left out the front door.

Ore fell into bed and slept soundly for the first half of his night. He dreamed he felt Ilena's young arms around him. She was comforting him again. The warmth from her caring heart filled him again. He pushed her away. She looked at him, hurt. Then she faded away and there was darkness around him.

He cried out for her, but all that came to him was dark shadows and he was running with them up over a wall, into the yard of an enclosed manor. Fighting was erupting around him. Then a slashing pain in his chest. He looked down and there was blood on his hand and on his chest. He looked up and it was cold darkness around him.

He looked down again, his hand feeling warm upon his chest. His chest was bandaged, his hand clean. *How? How had that happened?* Then a hand was upon his chin, gently lifting it to make him look up. The eyes were brilliant blue. Rei's eyes. The hair was fire red with orange gold highlights. Mizi's hair. The smile...warm...it leaned towards him and kissed him...warm...Ilena's warm.

He wrapped his arms around the warm person, this person who represented all the ones he loved, and held on, feeling the begging feeling of wanting to be held in return. *Ore.* It echoed and he searched for the one who said it. *Ore. Love me. ...Love my Children.*

Ore faded awake from the dream. He lay there pondering it, replaying it. This Ilena. The early Ilena. His ache for his master that drove him to return again and again to Rei's side. The joy of being with his mistress and the desire to touch her like one would touch a rose just to feel its softness. What feeling was it for Ilena?

He remembered the kiss, the warmth of the body he hugged in the dream, the desire to be hugged in return. That ache. The ache of wanting to be held by Ilena again. It had been so long. Ever so long. Always in his memory, his dreams, but withheld in reality. Could he be held again? Would it be allowed? He couldn't wish it, but the ache cried out for it.

Not like the ache he felt for Rei, but similar. It was what he'd felt sitting by himself before coming to bed. That ache of wanting to be close to her, to be touching her. To be within reach of Rei. To be within eyesight of Mizi. To follow after them both closely.

To stand next to Ilena, close, touching hands the way they had as children: hands back to back, only middle fingers wrapped around each other, so that the household wouldn't know. Wouldn't know that Ore was grieving his Grandfather. That Ilena was grieving also, alone in the world except for her nurse and Kase.

Ore shivered. That name made him feel so cold, but she'd said it. She'd said *Ore* when he'd asked her about her present feelings. Could he accept that? His ache cried out, but his mind remained firmly fixed, except for that growing light that was putting pressure on the darkness. Requesting, insisting that the darkness give in, that it be recognized.

Maybe he couldn't accept her feelings, but he could accept the light. He'd always been drawn to light. Her light back then. Rei's light. Mizi's light. If Ilena's light now could be given full birth...he would accept that as well. With that thought, he relaxed and fell back into dreamless sleep.

-o-o-o-

"...er. Oi! Father!" Ore was being shaken awake. He moaned. "Are you always this hard to wake up? You're the one who wanted everyone up early." It was Thayne. Ore stretched and Thayne moved away. "How do you usually wake up?" Thayne asked him, watching him sit up on the bed and scratch an itch.

Ore yawned and began his morning routine. "Miss Mina threatens to slowly slip a knife through my ribs." He pulled on his boots. "Mister Andrew drops books on my head." He walked to the water and splashed his face and rubbed some through his hair. "Mistress threatens to come in," muffled through the towel. He paused, holding the towel. "On the bad days, she opens the door. That gives me a fright. Master would kill me."

He set the towel down, shrugged on his jacket, and buckled on his short sword Rei had given him when he'd been made Rei's personal knight. He looked at it for a moment, then led the way out the door. "But Master never wakes me up the way I keep hoping."

"And how's that," Thayne looked at him, curious.

"With kisses," Ore said, "...but I've woken him up with threats of kisses before. Once I almost made it, but he lept out of bed so fast I couldn't. He was unkind and had his hand on his hilt, too." He put on a sad face.

Thayne shook his head. "You are a strange man."

"Oh?" Ore smiled at him. "Would you like to be woken with kisses next time?"

Thayne looked at him horrified. "No!"

"Haaa. Just like Master," Ore deflated.

They walked into the dining room. Everyone else was sitting at tables, finishing up breakfast. The kids were still sleepy, too. "Morning," he said to everyone and walked up to the table with the kids. He yawned as he sat, then said to them, "Can I join you? If we put our heads down on the table like this —" he demonstrated, "we can sleep just a little longer, no?"

Thayne hit him on the head. "Oi! I said, this is your fault in the first place."

The littlest boy giggled and then covered his mouth with his hand. Ore winked at him and smiled ruefully, rubbing his head and sitting up. "All right, all right. I'm up, Dad." The oldest girl finally smiled. A plate was set down in front of him.

"Hey, that's your job, not mine," Thayne protested.

"But every Father's got to have a dad," Ore pointed out around his first mouthful. Breakfast was good. It helped him wake up. "What are your names?" he asked the kids, still blinking sleepily.

"Boy!" piped up the youngest.

The oldest girl snorted at him. "It's not! You just get called that all the time." She had just the perfect 'boss' for an oldest girl who had to be mom all the time — because she chose to be, Ore guessed. "That's Micky. He's Mat," she pointed to the middle son. "I'm Millie."

"Millie. Mat. Micky." Ore nodded to each of them. "Nice to meet you. Are you ready for adventuring today?" Millie shrugged. Mat shook his head "no". Micky said brightly, "Yeah!" and kicked his feet under the table to accentuate his readiness. Ore looked at Mat and said conspiratorially in a loud whisper, "Tomorrow morning, let's hide under the bed so we can sleep longer."

Mat looked at him like he was strange. "That won't work you know," he finally said.

"Oh? Have you tried it?" Mat blushed and his mother had to hide a smile. Ore sighed sadly. "That's too bad. I was going to try it next time, too." Mat smirked. Then Ore perked up, "But I have just recently found a good hiding spot for naps that Miss Mina doesn't know about...yet." He sighed. "She's gotten really good at finding me, though. So I don't know how long it will get to be my secret." Mat nodded sympathetically.

"I can find Mat really good now, too," Millie said proudly. Mat scowled at her. Ore was about to lean over to Mat when both Rose and Thayne moved to interrupt him.

"I don't think Mat needs help," came from Rose.

Thayne grabbed Ore's collar. "Eat. The sun's up."

Ore looked sadly at Mat, and obediently finished eating. When he was done he pushed away from the table and stood up, looking around at the group. The other adults had been quietly chatting, nursing warm drinks. "Let me pay, and then we'll be on our way," he announced. They started to rise and collect things.

A short heavy–set man came out of the kitchen, wiping his hands on his apron. He walked up to Ore and held out a hand. Ore took it. "I'm Fred, Cathy's husband. Thank you for staying here this past night. I hope you had a pleasant stay."

"I did, thank you, and thank you for hosting us. How much do I owe?" Fred eyed him, thinking. "Don't cheat yourself. The castle's paying, not me. ...And don't cheat the castle. I'm paying." Ore winked, but his face was serious. Ore was pretty sure Fred wanted to say it was on the house, but that wouldn't do. He was running a business. Fred nodded, understanding. He named a fair price and Ore handed it over. "Breakfast was very good, and dinner was delicious," Ore said to him.

"I'm glad you enjoyed them," Fred smiled. "Please feel free to come by anytime. Oh, I've given Rose a packet of food for lunch for everyone."

"Thanks!" Ore said, pleased, as the owner–chef headed back to the kitchen.

Ore looked back at everyone. They were standing, waiting for him. As he walked over to join them by the door, Thayne handed him one of Rose's bags, keeping the other. Ore hefted the bag over his shoulder. Rose was carrying a large basket that likely had the lunch in it.

Right then," Ore said opening the door, motioning for Thayne to lead off. "Ready for adventure?" he smiled down at Mat and Micky as they passed in front of him following their mother.

This time they both smiled and nodded. "Yup!"

"You're pretty good with kids," commented Betty as she passed Ore last. He followed her out.

"I like them," he said simply.

Thayne looked back and said over his shoulder as he led the the group towards the outer wall of the city and the stable that held their horses, "That's because he still is one."

Ore laughed. "So are you, squirt! You just keep forgetting it."

Thayne rolled his eyes at him. "I would guess that's because I have to babysit you."

Ore looked over at Betty and Roy, including Robert in the glance, and shrugged. "There's just no helping him."

They smiled as Thayne sighed. "Get up here old man, and lead the way."

Ore put his free hand behind his head. "Nah. You're doing a great job. ...I'll have to lead later anyway. You can take your turn now."

Thayne shook his head and looked at Rose and the kids. "There's just no helping him," he said sadly. Everyone laughed, although Micky didn't quite get it. Thayne looked back into Ore's eyes and they shared a satisfied smile.

-o-o-o-

Everyone waited near the city gate while the two fetched their horses. Rose's bags were tied behind the saddles. Ore ran his hands down Fenrier's legs, checking them for swelling. They'd been riding hard the last few days. He was pleased when they seemed okay. He checked Thayne's horse as well. Not too bad.

He rubbed Fenrier's neck as they walked back to the group. "You'll get a rest this morning. That'll be nice, no?" Fenrier nodded his head. Ore was quite certain horses were as intelligent as humans, even more so than some.

Millie's eyes were wide with awe as she watched the horses. "You like horses, Millie?" Thayne asked. She nodded enthusiastically. "Would you like to come ride? You just hold on. I'll lead him."

Her eyes lit up, "Can I, Ma? Please?" she begged Rose.

Rose looked at Ore. He nodded approval as the kids wouldn't be able to keep up with the adults all morning with their shorter legs. "All right," she allowed.

Thayne helped Millie up into the saddle, then adjusted the stirrups so she could put her feet in them. They were still just a little long. "Keep your feet in them anyway," Thayne instructed her. "That way if you lose your balance, your feet have something to grab onto to keep you in the saddle." She nodded, clutching the pommel. She was excited, but it was a bit frightening to be up so high on such a large animal. "We'll walk it slow until you get your balance, okay?"

"Okay," she said.

The boys were looking a bit disappointed. They weren't as excited about horses as Millie, but they didn't want to be left out either. Ore looked from them to their mother. She asked the question with her eyes and he nodded. "Come on," she shepherded them over to Ore. "Father says you can ride his horse." Their eyes got big.

"Come on up here first, Mat," he waved him over, then put his hands around the boy's waist. "Up we go," he boosted him until his stomach was on the side of the saddle. "Grab the pommel — the round thing on the left — then boost yourself up and swing your right leg around, like you're going to sit on a fence rail."

The boy was obedient and was soon sitting up. His eyes were wide. "It's high."

Ore nodded. "Like being in my favorite tree," he agreed. Mat got the connection of trees and height and relaxed a bit. "But a horse moves, so you'll have to learn the balance. That's a bit like walking the fence. You have to move your body with the horse."

Ore looked down at Micky. "Mat, shift back a bit in the saddle until you're just sitting on the part that rises in the back. That's good. You can hold onto the back of the saddle to keep your balance while I put Micky on."

Roy walked to the other side of Ore's horse and put his hand on Mat's knee. "I'll help keep you balanced. You're doing a great job."

Ore picked up Micky, then tossed him into the air and caught him, grinning into the boy's surprised, scared face. "Oh, sorry. You can't fly? ...Or do you want to try flying again? I didn't give you a head start that time."

Micky thought about it, then grinned. "Fly"

Ore threw him up in the air again and Micky laughed. Ore faked disappointment. "It didn't work, Micky. I guess you'll have to ride, then." He put him up in the saddle in front of Mat. Having already been up in the air, he wasn't so nervous of being up on top of a high horse.

Roy put his other hand on Micky's leg and steadied both boys until they were settled. Micky held onto the pommel and Mat put his hands on his brother's hips. Fenrier shifted to rebalance himself and the boys startled.

Roy smiled at them. "I'll stay beside you until you get used to it." They looked at him gratefully. Rose decided, to calm to own heart, to walk on the other side so they wouldn't slip off the other way.

-o-o-o-

They left Nijoushi, going slowly at first until the kids were balanced, then at a fast walk for the adults. That of course was still fairly slow for the horses, but they found a compromise speed that seemed to work. They did let the kids down to run before they got too tired from riding. It was a lot of work to stay balanced on the back of a horse if you weren't used to it.

Ore led them back the way he and Thayne had come from. The kids were the first to start getting hungry for lunch and started whining and teasing each other. Rose was exasperated early with them as she didn't want them to act up in company.

Roy and Betty each took a boy by the hand and distracted them with conversation. Millie took her mother's hand and walked quietly with her. Rose relaxed, then asked Millie if she'd be willing to help carry the basket by taking one side of the handle while she took the other. Ore figured it was probably getting heavy by now.

When the boys couldn't be distracted any longer, Ore looked back at Rose. "Did Mister Fred put anything like fruit in that we could munch on while we walk? I'd like to hold lunch until we're at the meeting spot." She looked in it and pulled out some apples and oranges.

"Here, let me have an apple," Robert said. He pulled out a knife and cut it in half and gave a half to each of the boys. He did the same with the rest of the apples, passing out halves until they were all munching.

"You can give the horses the cores," Thayne said to the boys when they got down to them. "Just hold your hands open with the core resting in the palm. Then hold it in front of their noses."

The boys gingerly did as they were instructed, giggling when the air from the horses sniffing the apple cores tickled their palms. "Soft," Mat said when Fenrier grabbed up the core with his lip. Ore nodded.

"Can I try?" Millie asked, her core ready. Thayne nodded and watched as she carefully held it in place then steeled herself to not drop it as the large teeth got close to her hand. The horse picked up the core with its large lips and munched happily. Millie smiled brightly.

Ore handed his core to Mat. "Give another one to Fenrier so he's not jealous." Mat nodded and complied. After that, all the cores had to be fed to the horses, with the kids taking turns. Ore patted Fenrier's forehead. "That's a happy thing, to have a rest and get apple treats, huh? Makes all that running worth it."

He hoped he'd get a treat when he got back to the castle. He was doing a lot of running this time, too, but it was more of a rest to be doing this than to be locked in the castle. Poor Ilena might be lying down, but it wasn't any more restful for her to be locked in the castle either. Ore wrapped his arm around his horse's neck and hugged him. He was glad he was allowed to hug something warm, even if it was a big creature trying to step on his heels.

Shortly before the noon hour they reached a fork in the road, where one of the roads that went south towards the capital of Ichijoutsu met the main North

Road they were on. Ore had them pull off the road and set up lunch in the southwest corner field near the intersection.

He told them that they would likely have several hours still to wait, so everyone ate slow, rested, and meandered. He lay down for a short cat nap, putting on his alert ears to listen for oncoming travelers.

His internal timer went off about the same time he realized he'd actually fallen asleep. Early mornings always seemed to do that to him — made him really take naps. He sat up and looked around. Betty had some hand sewing out and was showing Millie how to do some stitch or other. Roy was squatting with the boys, looking at something they seemed very interested in. Probably some insect or other, Ore guessed. Rose was passed out, but seemed like she'd wake up soon.

Thayne was sprawled, leaning against a rock and looking towards the direction his family would be coming from, his hands behind his head. He looked over as Ore moved. Ore looked at him questioningly and he shook his head. Ore's timer said that it should be soon. He thought for a minute, looking around at everyone briefly. Robert had seen him move and was on his way over to talk to him it looked like.

Ore really wanted two defenders per group, but he also wanted to know how far away the other travelers were. He decided to be patient for now, at least until he'd seen what Robert wanted. That would distract him for a little bit. He crossed his legs and smiled at Robert who crouched down next to him.

"Father...," Robert was hesitant. Ore waited patiently. "...May I know how long we'll be at the safe house?"

Ore tilted his head and partially closed his eyes thoughtfully. "I don't know.... You're the first group going, so it will be the longest wait, I'm afraid. But I do know that Master is moving at the best pace he can. I would have to guess."

"Well, that would be okay."

"Mmm...well, about...two, three months?" Ore answered

"Ah. Months. Well." Robert frowned and shifted uncomfortably.

"Is it work? Your employment?"

"Eh, ah, no. I've left that with the others to do. It's more that...I don't seem to fit in well. It seems like that's a long time to be with strangers."

Ore's alarms went off, but he didn't let on. "Strangers?"

Robert stuttered a little, trying to explain. "Well, I, um, I'm a loner, a hermit. It's difficult for me be around people for long periods of time."

"Well, Robert, I can tell you that you'll get your own room, so you'll have your own space inside the house. Everyone will need to help take care of the house and the chores — there isn't much support staff in order to keep everyone safe — so you'll have your own work to do. And there's plenty of space, although there is a boundary we ask you not to cross. After all, we can't keep you safe if you're not close enough to be kept safe."

He looked at Robert, assessing. "There are also going to be just enough people that you may find someone to talk to when you do want to just talk. This is just a small part of them." Ore thought Robert might get along well with Peter, actually. Robert nodded, still a little doubtful. Ore shifted to lift one knee and rest his elbow on it, leaning against his arm. "Robert, will you tell me your story? Why do you follow Mother?"

Robert shook his head, turning red. Ore waited. Robert took his hat off and started turning it around in his hands, then he shifted to sit, still clutching the brim of his hat. He refused to lift his eyes from the ground.

Finally he started talking haltingly. "I'm a stonesmith. She scouted me out, showing up out of the blue behind me one day. She'd been watching me work for a while before she came to talk to me, I guess. She praised my sense of balance and understanding of how the rocks talk to each other, which ones will stay with others and in what way. Which places to ask them to divide to get the results I need.

"I remember looking at her and thinking, *if human beauty could be stone's beauty, it would be this*. Not a speck of her was out of place. Her face could have been chiseled by a stone sculptor's hand, but at the same time it moved and flowed with life. Not the over–animated life of people like those children or their mother," he glanced at them, "but completely controlled life. Like she knew exactly what she wanted already, and how to get it.

"Every motion, from her words and the decisions she made to the minutest movement of the muscles in her face seemed to move exactly to her will. I couldn't stop looking at her. I was looking at what I see all the time in the rocks, but come to life, in constant motion."

Robert paused thinking. "It wasn't like she was perfect. She isn't, I know that. No one is. I could see the imperfections — where if I struck with my little hammer just right, a piece might crumble off — but all the stone I work with is like that. It just made it all the more real to me. ...I think she could see that I was looking at her too much. I couldn't hear her.

"She reached out and gently turned me around so I was looking at the stone I'd been working on again. That pulled me back. Then she put her hand across my eyes and spoke in my ear very quietly. She said that she needed someone like me, that knew rock intimately. That she would have several very important jobs over the years for me, but when I wasn't working on them I could do whatever jobs I wanted. Would I be interested, and would I be willing to train others to do what I can do?"

He blushed again, looking very embarrassed. "The perfect living stone had said she wanted me for my talents, and only my talents, and would give me everything I'd ever thought I might want. I couldn't say no. I desperately wanted to say yes. It was like being tempted by the seductress. But I also couldn't say yes. I knew I had to say no. It hurt so bad I trembled. She could feel it, she was so close.

"Then she said, 'I don't want you to feel that I'm buying you from your owner. I want you to come to me freely, so that you may work with your whole heart. Your work is exceptional, but it isn't what it could be because you can't give it your whole heart and being. I won't buy you, but your freedom. When you're content with that as the price, when you love being able to give your whole heart to your talent, I hope that you will give your talent to me.' Then she left, her warmth slowly leaving me. I loved her already."

Robert stopped suddenly, looking up at Ore in shock, "I don't mean it that way...I mean like I love the stone."

Ore held up his hand. "I know Mother," he said softly.

Robert stopped, then nodded. Picking back up his story, he said, "Two, three days later, in the evening, my work was interrupted by noises coming from nearby, and getting closer. I looked around in confusion, and a very fast, darkly wrapped person was coming for me. The noises weren't near me yet, and this person was very quiet. But as soon as she touched me, I knew who it was. Every muscle perfect. Every motion exact.

"With one hand she grabbed my tools, with the other she grabbed me. We didn't stop until we were up on the hill, about three–quarters of the way up. Then she turned me around to face the destruction below us. Again she spoke to me in my ear softly from behind. 'Remember this. Remember what was done here, before this and now. Someday I'll send for you, and you must recall all of this for me.' I nodded.

"She said, as she placed my tool kit in my hand, 'And when you're ready to give me yourself, your talent, call me and I'll come.' She was pulling away, and I managed to somehow ask what I should call her. Whispered back on the wind was the word, 'Mother', and she was gone." Robert shivered.

"I stayed hidden until the middle of the next day and it was still. Then I made my way to a place where I would be safe, found employment and started working. When I was able to give my whole heart to my work, I started wondering how to find her. Then one of my regulars, who purchased small works every few months, touched a piece I'd done with Mother in mind. I wanted to find her so badly, I'd put it into that stone.

"He looked up at me and said, 'Mother will love this. Will you please hold it for me, so I may bring her to see it?' I didn't want to part with it, but he planted a small seed of hope in me with his words, so I agreed. Two weeks later, I was working in the back. Someone had come into the shop. The help was out there, so I didn't move.

"Then, just as I paused in my work to inspect it, a hand went in front of my eyes. 'You've finally called me, Robert. It's beautiful. It makes me want to have it, but I want to have you more. Are you ready?' I couldn't help it...," he was embarrassed again. "I felt like I was five again. I spun around and held her, sobbing. She held my head against her shoulder, letting me let it all go.

"When I was done, she let me go and let me look at her perfection one more time. Even her smile...." Robert looked away. "...Then she said, 'I'll contact you again. I look forward to what you can show me.' And she was gone. I haven't seen her since then, but that memory is enough.

"That regular customer was my one contact with her. Sometimes he would just come to purchase, always one of my best small works, so that I soon started making special ones just for Mother for him to buy. Other times he would give me work to do for her.

"And then he started bringing me apprentices. Excellent ones that had eyes to see, hands to do the work. One here, one there. I know how hard it is to find people with the talent, and each of them is different, but she's done her best to find the best possible talent. And every one of them loves her, too. They know why I'm here. It's not the work I'm worried about." His speaking stopped and he sat in memory.

Ore reached out to get Robert to look up at him. When he had Robert's eyes, he said, "And everyone you're going to be at the house with is the same. You don't need to be worried about being *there*, either. I'll help you understand so that you can know you're not surrounded by strangers, but truly by Mother's Family."

Robert drank in the soft look on Ore's face. "Thank you, Father. ...You are also a living stone, ...when you're thinking of Mother." Then, his face red, he got up and walked away to recover. Ore watched after him thoughtfully for a moment, then put his head down on his knee, his arm relaxing over his head, letting the emotions Robert's story had evoked wash over him. He stayed that way for a while, the others respecting his need for space.

The sound of hooves and wheels came from a distance off, his sharp ears catching them early, and he looked up to Thayne. He'd stood up and was shading his eyes to see. "Go get 'em!" Ore called to him. Thayne looked at him with a big grin and grabbed up his horse's reins. In just a few seconds he was on the horse and galloping away.

Ore stood up. "They're about here. Time to get packed up," he called loudly enough for everyone to hear. There was the usual bustling motion as people got ready to go.

"Hey," asked Roy, "how do you know it's them? Plenty of other wagons and people have passed us in this time."

Ore shrugged. "Practice? Timing? The way the horses step? Dane's carriage horse walks like a dainty woman that doesn't want to get her shoes wet. Even when she's going fast. The previous wagon horse was lazy and dragged it's feet. The wheels sounded different, too."

Roy shook his head. "Amazing."

There was general mayhem when the wagon reached the group. The carriage was surprisingly not far behind. Foster saw Ore's expression and jerked his thumb back at the carriage. "He left before sunrise, so we'd get to where we thought you might be nearly together." Then he grinned a somewhat regretful smile. "Of course, I'm afraid I couldn't help it and made the nag step quickly, so we managed to overtake him. But not by much."

Ore grinned back. "Works for me. Glad you're finally here. Everything go okay?"

Foster nodded. "No problems."

Ore relaxed. "Good."

Dane pulled up to a stop behind Foster. "Hey, Father! Told you we'd be all right, didn't I?"

Ore walked over to stand at the side of the carriage and look up at him. "Yes, you did. Good job."

Dane looked at him a moment. "You've got more light in you. Was it a good night?"

"Yes. I learned how to see the darkness and the light. ...And Robert just told me his story."

"Ah," understanding came to Dane's eyes. "You just got a good dose of it, then." Ore nodded then turned and looked around at everyone. It was a good feeling. The women folk were quickly becoming friends, and Thom was completely excited to be meeting three more siblings. Even Millie, who was feeling a little left out, had to smile at his antics.

Thayne was smiling big. Thom would run off to greet someone new, then run back to him to grab him and babble excitedly, then repeat the process. Peter and Robert were shyly looking at each other, recognizing kindred spirits.

Ore walked over to the carriage door and opened it. "How are you Dame Freida?" he asked politely and nodded at the maid, June.

"Just fine, dear," Freida answered as brightly as ever.

"We've got everyone now. Would you like to come be introduced?" he held out his hand for her.

Once he and June had Freida outside the carriage, Ore looked significantly at Thayne, who grabbed up Thom. Then he looked at Foster. "Listen up," Foster called out over the mayhem, and everyone quieted down.

"Congratulations, everyone," Ore said, "although it might be a little early, on being the first. I hope you'll all be able to get along. The tone you set now will be the tone for the rest when they come."

"Which, of course is the tone Mother set a long time ago," Dane couldn't resist.

Ore ignored him. "We've still got a ways to go, and I'd really like to do it in one stretch, as always. We'll stop at an inn for dinner, but not stay to sleep. My hope is the little ones will fall asleep after eating a good meal and sleep as we go for the rest of the trip." The moms nodded, relieved.

"When we get there, crash wherever you want. You can rearrange rooms tomorrow." He turned to Freida. "I'd like to ask if Roy and Betty may ride with you and June in the carriage. Would that be okay with you, Dame Freida?"

"Certainly," her eyes crinkled up with her smile. "We'd be glad for more company, wouldn't we June. I sleep so much she's become quite bored, I'm afraid." June deprecated, but Ore was sure it was true. He smiled at her. "Any time you want to switch out, now that we have more of us to sit with her, let Dane know. That would be fine." June nodded her thanks. "The rest of you, hop up into the wagon. Let's get going." There was a mad scramble to settle in.

Ore rode Fenrier over to the four soldiers that were the day's honor guard. "Thank you for helping out today. We've got enough swords between us now, we'll be okay. You may return...unless the Captain gave you furlough long enough to go into town?"

The soldier in charge shook his head regretfully. "We're to go back."

"Ah, well. Safe travels." They turned and headed back to the garrison at a much faster pace than they'd come out. Ore rode to the front of the group, leading them south on Castle Road, "Let's get this adventure on the road again!" he called. The kids all cheered, glad to be moving again with new companions.

-o-o-o-

The trip to the safe house was long but uneventful. Ore was grateful, and so was everyone else, truth be told. Exciting trips were usually dangerous trips. In reality, though, Ore had taken them on a circuitous route in order to confuse as many of them, and any followers, as he could. He figured Foster would figure it out eventually, but it should be sufficient for most. They weren't really that far from the castle, a little more than an hour southeast of it by fast horse, down in a little bowl.

It was a small two–story manor house, only thirty–one rooms. The land also boasted a servants quarters, a good sized stable, a deep well, chickens and a couple of cows, and a good sized garden. There was grassy field around it, sufficient for all the horses being collected and the two cows, but as the bowl rose it turned rocky. Once you got up on top of the bowl — a good distance from the house — scrub, then trees, grew. You could see the mountains from there, but the distance wasn't determinable.

The one thing you couldn't see was the castle, so there was no frame of reference to leaving, other than the road leading to the house at the southwest end of the bowl. There was also no reference for coming except by the road, since it all sat down below the level of the rest of the area, so you didn't actually see the house and it's land until you were up on the rim of the bowl. It was the perfect safe house.

The squad that was assigned to protect the witnesses bunked in the servant's quarters and patrolled the rim regularly, as well as the road. They had a station built along the road far enough out that the house couldn't be seen from it. That way they could turn random travelers away and not be discovered. Ore's face had been necessary there, too. The guards wouldn't have let the group pass if he hadn't been with them.

For servant staff, there were a cook, a housekeeper, and their young teenage daughter who helped with the animals and garden. (Millie was excited when they met the first day.) Rei had decided to keep it simple at first since he didn't know what skills the people coming would bring with them.

He expected folks who could take care of themselves for the most part. It was very unlikely that Ilena's witnesses would all be nobles, after all. But he didn't want it to be too much like a prison, so he'd wanted some kind of personal touch. He figured a small family that had the basic skill set would fit in well with what he envisioned Ilena would pull in. He wasn't too off the mark.

He'd also very carefully selected the guard squad. They were all genial sorts who had mothers and sisters of their own, so to speak. They'd be fierce protectors, firm with keeping everyone there, yet kind to their faces. Since the head of the guards would be collecting the reports to send in, they were headed by the most personable soldier Rei knew.

Ore introduced Colonel Garen and the three staff members at the breakfast table the next morning and had them tell a little about their background as an icebreaker. He'd instructed for a late breakfast so everyone could catch up from the short sleep they'd all been getting. Once the basic introductions were done, and the little children were finished eating — because of course they finished first — he had Alice, the teenage daughter of the cook, take them outside to explore.

The tables were set up in a square, but the people present only filled up two sides of it, it was such a big dining room. Ore finished his meal, then stood up and went inside the square where he could be seen and heard by everyone.

"Welcome to Falcon's Hollow," Ore said, getting their attention. "We anticipate this will be home for you for the next two to three months. Hopefully no more than that. We should be getting the rest of the witnesses little by little over the next three weeks or so. Colonel Garen will be getting your testimonies of what Mother has asked you to remember. He's a nice guy, I promise." Ore smiled encouragingly at them. "Master can read his handwriting, too, unlike mine." He got a few chuckles.

"The main reason for the long stay isn't the fact that you have things to say we need to hear. It's because Regent Rei wants to have time to review what you've all said, put it all together into a proper case against the criminals in question, make the proper arrests, and have time to announce and hold the Lord's Court. He's hoping that can all be done within two months. We're hedging with another possible month for unforeseen difficulties...you know, such things always show up in bureaucracies." There were nods of understanding around the table.

"Let's see. House rules. Don't leave the bowl. The guards promise to be sweet and nice up until that point. Only people I bring in come in. The same for going out. Mother may know your names and faces, and I've come to love you all too, but we'd like to prevent any suspicious behaviors that make it look like a spy is trying to get out and leak where you are. It's just general security protocol. If the little kids forget and get out, send the soldiers. Then there won't have to be any doubts or worries, okay?" He got nods. Good. No disappointed looks either. That was also good.

"Everyone helps with the chores. Bill will be head chef, but he'll need help. Lilly knows where everything in the house is already, but everyone needs to help keep it clean. And Alice will help babysit if you'll help with the garden and animals. Lilly and Bill will set up rotations, but you're welcome to have your input.

"I'm sure it will take a few days to work it all out, but we do want to keep it all family while you're here. If you fight, make up. If you can't make up, take it to Lilly or Bill. If they can't resolve it, it goes to the Colonel. If it needs addressing by me, I'll come spank you."

Ore paused, looking at them all again, his eyes sharp. He wanted to see their reactions to the next few things he was going to tell them. "...And heaven help us all if I have to call in Mother." He definitely had their full attention.

"I promised I'd tell you once we got here. She's alive. She's safe, but her hip was crushed in the landslide. She's recovering, but at the moment it's looking like she won't ever have use of her leg again. A tendon was torn that our surgeons can't fix. Master is still looking for one who might be able to help, however, so it isn't a given just yet.

"I won't be staying — I have to go fetch the rest, of course — but I'll bring what news I can each time I come." The typical reactions had gone around: relief, sorrow, worry, understanding.

"I expect she's going to want to see you." They all wanted it, he could see. "If you're willing to stick around long enough, you may get to. Master will be willing to let you go home before he's able to let her out of her protective custody, is the current plan. That may change as your testimonies arrive and are added to the evidence we already have, though."

He wasn't telling them everything. He couldn't. But he suspected they already knew. It was the same as at the Black Cat. He wasn't going to be told everything about the Family she'd built yet because of the same reason. It went both ways. Trust would continue to be built up little by little. He looked at Garen. "Have I left anything else out?"

The colonel stood. "We'll be holding regular 'family councils' like this for people to air out concerns and complaints. We'd like to keep the rules as simple as have been stated. 'If it's not yours, don't take it' kind of rules need to be just common sense, please. We'll also use the meetings for passing on of news from the outside and other such things." He sat down.

Ore continued. "I'll be leaving shortly, but I want to make one recommendation. I've greatly appreciated hearing your individual stories about how you met Mother. Although I haven't heard everyone's yet, it's helped me get to know you better, and her. I'd like it, as Father, if you'd all take the opportunity to tell each other your stories, so you'll understand better why it is you're all here, and how you can best support each other, and her.

"Bill and Lilly, if you'd like to take over for the housekeeping side of things." He looked at them all one more time, fondly, looking a little longer at Thayne. "Be well." He nodded at Garen and the two left the dining room.

He gave his final orders to the colonel on the walk to the stables where Fenrier was still waiting for him in a stall, the others having been released to the field. "Sit in on the times they talk about Mother. I want a record of all their stories. Send them directly to me. The testimonies can go to Mister Andrew. He'll review them first. Daily reports, but you can send them every two to three days. They come to me, too." He sighed. He was giving himself a lot of work. "They're a good bunch of Kids."

Garen looked at him a little strangely. "Will do. But...why are you 'Father'... and even acting the part?"

Ore climbed up on his horse and looked down at Garen. "Ask them. They won't tell me the why. They probably won't tell you either. I'm acting it because I feel like it." He smiled. "Good luck!"

He turned onto the road and left them behind. Once out of sight of the house, and past the guard station, he kicked Fenrier into a gallop and headed on the direct route for the castle. It was time to answer the ache to see his master.

CHAPTER 10 The Burden That is Ilena

Rei finished reviewing a report, put it down, and sighed. He leaned back in his high-backed royal blue padded chair and looked up at the white ceiling. It was about lunch time and he felt like he'd already done a day's worth of work. He looked back down at his desk and counted. Compared to two and three years ago, he had.

He took a clearing breath and just looked around the room. His office, the Rose office, was on the second floor in the center of the general Region office building. It perhaps wasn't the largest one, but it had been the most opulent one when he'd arrived.

Personally he'd found that very distracting, so for four days shortly after he'd arrived the room had been full of painters and construction workers removing ornate dark wooden brick–a–brac from the ceiling and walls, sanding them smooth, and then painting them a calming white that wouldn't distract him.

Once that base coat of paint had gone in, he'd allowed one fine painter with a delicate hand to come and paint blue roses with gold leaves along the top of the walls as a border piece. They'd wanted to paint another thinner border at about one third up the wall as well, but that was at the point he gazed when thinking and he'd refused, thinking it would also be too distracting.

The one thing he'd allowed them to leave was the dark wood mantle over the small fireplace that kept the room warm in the winters. If it weren't for the winters, he would have gotten rid of the fireplace as well. However, it was also shared by the next office over — the Lotus office — and he felt bad about taking the heat away from whomever would be using it. Right now both offices to either side of his were empty. He still hadn't decided just who to put in them or what he needed to have that close to him.

He let his eyes look around the room, just to let them relax a bit. His sturdy mahogany desk was centered on the exterior wall, with his back to the four nearly–floor–to–ceiling windows that were curtained with brilliant blue curtains that kept out the cold in the winter.

He kept the curtains pulled back when it wasn't severely cold, believing that natural lighting was best. Plus it let him know when night was falling to keep his body in some sort of natural rhythm, even if he did work late nights. In the center of the windows were two glass doors that opened onto a balcony that stretched the width of the Rose office. They were open at the moment to let fresh air into the office.

In front of Rei's desk on his left were set two desks in a row, the front one being Andrew's and the one behind it being Ore's — when he could be tied to it. On Rei's right was Mina's desk and behind it a free one she used as her work table.

Of course there were plenty of other tables in the room. One was to the left of Andrew's desk, set lengthwise and he used it as his extra table, although he kept it very neat most of the time since it was also often used as the map table.

Right of Mina's desk were tables set lengthwise, two of them. They were in use by the new office staff Rei had been trying to train, two people per table.

There were three book shelves on either side wall, although in the corner farthest from him on his left was the small fireplace and in the corner closest to him on the right was the map cabinet. Directly in front of him in the inner far wall were the double doors that opened into the hallway, guarded by two guards. There was a bench set in the hallway directly across from those doors. Sitting on that were the three paiges directly assigned to his office.

He did often wish he could declutter the desks and people in the room as easily as the workers had decluttered the walls. It was just a few too many people for the space. As soon as he could have the additional staff trained to his satisfaction he would be moving them out to the larger sub–office across the hallway: the Rosebud office.

"Rei," Mina's voice came from behind her own stacks of work, "Ore's back."

"Already? Isn't that two days earlier than we planned?" Andrew's distracted voice came from behind yet more stacks.

"It's okay with me" Mina answered. "He can have half my stacks."

"No, I don't think that's possible, Miss Mina," Ore answered from behind Rei through the open balcony doors. "I just assigned myself two more stacks this morning."

Andrew and Mina both looked up at him with raised eyebrows. "You assigned work to yourself? That is a surprise."

Rei turned himself around. Ore was in his usual position when he was in the office, at least if he wasn't chained to a desk like everyone else. He was perched up on the banister of the balcony outside the office, looking in through the open double doors, his arms resting on his knees. He had arrived via rooftop as usual — which was why Rei had gotten used to having the doors open to begin with. "I also assigned another stack to Mister Andrew."

Andrew asked mildly, "Which one?"

"The eye witness accounts," Ore answered. "Since Master will get all three stacks, I thought it would help if you sorted those first." Andrew nodded and went back to his work.

Rei put his head in his hand. "Well, I know I need to read them, but I really don't need three more stacks."

"It's okay, Master. You don't have to read them all. I'll mark the important parts," Ore tried to reassure him.

"So...how'd it go?" Rei knew it would be easier to get Ore's report while he was still outside. Ore usually had to work up the courage to shut himself back up inside. Rei stood up, went out onto the balcony, and leaned on the banister next to Ore. He may as well get a change of view himself.

"Interesting. Ah, did you get my message?"

Rei looked at him darkly, "Yeees, but I'm quite sure I didn't understand it." He was never fond of Ore's short messages.

Ore pursed his lips. "Because Master wouldn't pay Miss Ilena's price for Ore to understand how to collect Children, Ore made a grave mistake and almost lost the trust of two who weren't going to come." He said it very clipped, a sharpness Rei wasn't sure he'd ever heard before.

Rei stood up straight and listened properly when he heard it. It was very rare for Ore to scold him. "I was told very clearly by word, and experience, by one of those two that Miss Ilena's price is 'always worth paying'." Ore came down off the banister and stood upright in front of Rei. "Even if Master doesn't like the thought of bribes, Miss Ilena is not worthy of that thought."

Rei puzzled that one over. "To Miss Ilena it isn't a bribe? Then what is it to her?"

"I've listened to several stories on the way. To them, and to her, it's sometimes a reward, sometimes an equal exchange." Ore paused, then added. "I believe, at that time, she was testing Master...." Now he really paused. He had something to say he didn't want to say.

"You may say it, Ore," Rei gave permission, and steeled himself somewhat.

"...I'm sorry, Master, but I believe you failed that test, even though the response was a natural one for you. I was only able to recover because the little lord was wise and scolded me before I could fail in my task. He was also forgiving enough to then teach me what you didn't allow Miss Ilena to teach me. His father, Earl Malkin, was also willing to forgive and allow me to take the two witnesses, one of whom is his own second son. I was very fortunate."

Andrew and Mina had stopped working. It was obvious because there was no noise from their pens. Even they were shocked at the severe scolding Ore had just given Rei. "I'm sorry to have caused you trouble and difficulty." Rei apologized properly. "I'll try to be sure next time that I don't miss an opportunity to understand."

"One thing I heard also: Miss Ilena teaches her Children to 'speak truth'."

Rei added that to his mental list, then asked, for clarification, "So Miss Ilena may withhold information, but she will always speak the truth?"

Ore nodded. "I believe so. I haven't seen it yet be otherwise. If her Children are teaching their children this, it can almost be assured."

Rei nodded. He'd had less experience with her than Ore, but it still coincided. "How many did you end up with?"

"Six men, six women, two sets of them are couples, four children. The oldest is very old, the youngest is three. One I like very much. One is from the world I came from. I don't understand why Miss Ilena wants her, but she will be obedient."

"If you can find out, that would be good."

Ore shrugged. "It will be in her report." Of course. The other one....

"Ore, you found a girlfriend?" Andrew teased blandly.

Ore held up his hand in a rude gesture to Andrew, although he looked only at Rei. "The one I like, his name is Thayne of Wexford. In the world of Miss Ilena's Family he was my 'translator' and my guide during the journey. He was also with me during the time at Nakaba and was very obedient then."

"He let you make the mistake?"

"...When I retrieved him, strategy was necessary. He didn't know I didn't know at that time. It wasn't until my scolding that I told them I didn't know what I needed to know. Then he was willing to assist me when necessary. ...But, Miss Ilena will also receive a scolding, so Master doesn't need to feel lonely."

"Because she didn't tell you anyway?"

"No. Because I was given ten names and there were sixteen people who were retrieved."

"Ah," Rei nodded. That would have been frustrating to have people show up you didn't expect and hadn't planned on. Like the children and the very old. Not that they weren't welcome, just that they required different plans. "Is there anything else I need to know now about the trip?" Ore would include everything in his written report, but Rei wanted the important highlights now.

"Miss Ilena is very loved. Those who are at the safe house will stay to greet her."

"No matter how long it takes?"

"No matter," Ore agreed. "Also, Miss Ilena collects talent. Both talent that already exists and talent that she shapes herself for her own purposes."

"What are the examples so far?" This was a list Rei really wanted.

"Surgery researcher, forester, master stonemason. These are talents that already existed. The one she created is the assassin."

"She *created* an assassin?"

"As I said, I don't understand that one," Ore frowned. "I understood her story, but I'll need to also see her testimony to understand fully, I think."

Rei was still for a while. "Do you think it's possible she didn't understand...?"

But Ore was shaking his head. "The master stonemason said it, Miss Ilena lives a 'completely controlled life'. She knows exactly what she wants already, and how to get it. 'Every motion, from her words and the decisions she makes to the minutest movement of the muscles in her face seem to move exactly to her will'.

"He admitted she isn't as perfect as that description makes it seem — even I can attest to her imperfections — but there's no way she didn't understand what she was doing with that woman. Every person she deals with, it's for a specific reason. She could have saved any stonemason. Why that one? Someday we may understand, but the knowing won't come easy, I think."

"You think it's for one of the deeper things she keeps hidden away?"

Ore nodded. He paused to think. "I think Miss Ilena loves Master as Prince. Her Children said they 'love him too'. ...But I still don't understand her motives."

Rei nodded. "Well, even I think it is too early for that to be clear yet. ...I have received a clue that's important. I need to verify it or rule it out. When you speak to her next, ask her this question, 'How did you come to be living at the Earldom?' I need the answer, the sooner the better, I think."

Ore nodded. "I'll bring it to you tomorrow."

Rei turned to go back into the office. Over his shoulder he said, "Good work Ore. Your desk needs you now. It's about to collapse from the work you weren't able to do while you were gone."

Ore sighed. "And I have a *very* long report to write." He obediently followed the master that he loved into the cage that was the castle.

-o-o-o-

Ore was tired. He was glad he'd been able to sleep in that morning. His strength had all been taken away by having to sit at his desk until just recently, and he still wasn't done. He was already looking forward to the next list of witnesses to collect. That was a lot more fun, even if he didn't get any more sleep.

He'd just sent Ryan off to bed. Now he gestured to the guards to let him into Ilena's room. He very quietly slipped into the room, the smell of a sick room hitting him harder now that he'd been away and outdoors for seven day, but it wasn't so bad as to make him concerned. They'd been properly taking care of Ilena, Mizi and the nurse. That was good.

He walked soundlessly to his spot on the wall to the left of her bed, specifically level with her head so they could talk quietly. He'd rather gotten into the habit of staying on her right side to be out of the way of the work done to her left side.

He always appreciated Ryan's consideration in putting away the chair when he was done feeding Ilena her dinner. It meant Ore didn't have to stumble over it in the dark, since the candle was put out by Ryan as well so Ilena could sleep. Ore didn't mind since he was used to walking around rooms in the dark, he knew Ryan always put the chair where it belonged at the desk, and her bed didn't move.

While Ilena was sleeping, Ore slept the nightwalker's sleep: deep enough to rest, light enough to awaken at any distressing or unusual sound. She always woke up when he came in, though, even if for only briefly. Last time, she'd woken up while he was still crossing the room.

This time she waited until he was in his position, but he could tell she was already awake. Had she heard him outside in the hall? She was more than capable of it. Or had she just been unable to sleep? That wouldn't surprise him either. He quietly let out a long breath, relaxing into his position, and leaned his head against the wall.

"Are the Children safe?"

"Mmm." Ore was tired enough to not really want to put too much energy into talking, but he kept the unvoiced affirmative pleasant.

"...Are you well?"

Me? ... "Yes. Just tired from office work today. You?"

"...Mistress Mizi and Ryan have been doing their best to keep me entertained. I've enjoyed our conversations. ...They asked me if I wanted to become an apprentice healer." He could hear Ilena's smile and hear in her voice the pleasure of being asked. "Of course, I refused, although they insisted I already had enough knowledge to become one."

"You refused? It's easiest to follow Mistress as one, though."

"No. It might be for right now, but that's not her real goal, is it? ...And it's not my goal."

"What is your goal?" Ore rather automatically went to an investigative question.

"...To be completely indispensable to Rei."

So, she wasn't going to tell him at this time, but he already had an inkling. Her own people had done that. A person with that large a goal and a region wide network of people.... There weren't many positions that matched those requirements and needs.

It was quiet for a while, but the atmosphere was becoming heavy. Ore sighed. "Please, just ask me. I'll answer if I can. Have I not said so before?"

"Ore, ...I know that I'm still a prisoner under interrogation, even though it's a mutually beneficial relationship at the moment. It isn't my place to ask for such a thing, but...please, will you speak with the man at the lesser gate who asks after me, for 'the Missus'? He's...my right–hand for the running of the Family.

"I don't know if you can choose to believe me, but my Children won't betray me. I don't wish to cause them any more pain and worry for my sake. Even if you must swear him to secrecy, at least he needs to know so he may do the tasks he must do. ...One of those tasks is to aid you in recovering the witnesses."

"*Heehhh.* If Master had allowed for it to be done before?"

"You wouldn't have gone blind, and they would have been prepared to receive you."

"Mmm. ...If Master says I may do it, I'll do it."

"...It's sufficient." Ilena wasn't excited by that answer, but she only gave a humble reply.

The air lifted, and with just those words Ore no longer needed to scold her. She'd already understood.

He let the silence go on for a while, then he asked, "Miss Ilena, how did you come to be living at Tokumade?" The silence was long enough he almost wondered if she were sleeping.

"We lived in Selicia, the country to the north–west of Ryokudo, on the other side of the mountains from Kouzanshi and the northwestern parts of Suiran. Kouzanshi was always the coldest, harshest area we traveled through. Selicia is warmer, a small country nestled in a large valley and surrounded on all sides by mountains that retain the heat and moisture of the ground.

"The mountains get progressively lower as you go north until there are gaps between them at the north border. That's where most of the military defenses are stationed, to protect the land from the desert kings and nomads.

"There was peace between Selicia and Ryokudo, in the main, and at the first time we came to visit, a daughter of Ryokudo had even been wed to a son of Selicia, in an attempt to forge a deeper bond between the nations. But within Selicia, there was no peace."

Ilena paused and took a calming breath. "Tarc, the country to the east, that is north beyond where we are now on the other side of the mountains from both Selicia and Ryokudo, is highland. Barren but for grasses and wind, it is home to a nomadic people, horsemen. Because they are tribal, and seem to have no political purpose, Selicia leaders in the main paid Tarc no mind. It was their undoing."

He heard her swallow. "I was seven at the time of the coup. Using stratagem, with no concern for how long it took to canker the country, Tarc had undermined the political power of the ruling house of Selicia, until they were overthrown and a puppet house set up that even today moves to the will of the head of Tarc.

"My parents supported the original ruling house of Selicia. The fight was bloody, mainly to weaken the people, and many such supporters were dragged out of their homes and killed. We were fortunate enough to escape the city, but it wasn't together. I saw my parents leave, but had to leave by another way with my nurse. ...I haven't seen my parents since...."

Ilena took another breath as if she were now answering the question on the way down into sleep. "It took my nurse and I more than a year to make it through the hard mountain terrain to the Earldom of Tokumade, looking in every village and hovel we passed along the way for sign of my parents, stopping occasionally for my nurse to find employment so we might afford to continue onward. Of course we couldn't travel south through the mountains during the frozen time.

"My family was known by the Shicchi's, partially by distant relation, so my nurse felt it was the place we would most likely be taken in, and perhaps my parents would have fled there as well. While we agreed it was not the best place to go, it was the only place we could agree to go. It was far away from the coup and probable death. I...wanted to return to Kase.

"I was glad to be with you — Kase, even though it was a short time. But it was painful to me, your life at the manor. I was glad you were able to escape to live. I wished you well always, praying for your safety. I was happy you were free. If you'd come back, you would have been killed. He still wants to do that.

"That's the only reason Pakyo left me alive so long — thinking that you would come back for me, and then he would have you. I think often that he's only still alive because of you, the same as me. Though, I'm kept alive thinking you're alive, where he's kept alive by the dream of your death."

Another long breath–filled pause. "Even if you had come back in the next night, it would have been too late. After he discovered you gone from your bed, he immediately came to our rooms and sought you out in my bed, although I didn't understand why at the time. And perhaps I still don't. Picking me up from my bed roughly, he demanded I produce you. How was I to do that?

"After he punished me, with no satisfaction, he placed me under house arrest, naming me the cheese that would call the little mouse back. I prayed you'd stay away, and let me come find you when it was safe, like we'd done for so many times already. ...And you did, ...and I have." Ilena's breathing finally become the breath of sleep.

Ore dropped his head. She'd answered Rei's question, she'd answered some of his own, and in the same manner, she'd confirmed the Little Death dream that she'd relived at the time of her second surgery. She didn't lie. She'd chosen to find gratitude in her pain, relief in her loneliness, to love when she should have only known anger and hate. Why didn't she hate him? And why...*how* had she found him?

She hadn't even known she would find him, not right at the time when she lay on the verge of death. He remembered her first words to him and Rei when he'd confessed to Rei his own pain. "Dead. I...must be...dead." It had been unexpected. "...I...am...home." She'd found him; for some reason she'd likewise "found" Rei. With the two of them was "home". Why? Eventually, Ore sank into fitful sleep, his heart full of his own conflicting emotions.

-o-o-o-

Ore gave his report the following morning, then requested a reprieve for half a day to rest. Rei allowed it. Ore looked terrible. When he'd arrived from being outside the castle, he'd looked almost refreshed, and strong. One night with Ilena and he was washed out.

Rei wanted to be able to tell Ore to just accept Ilena as Kase and be done with it, but he couldn't. It was something Ore had to work out for himself. Ilena was buried too deeply in Ore for it to be simple for him. Even Ilena seemed to understand that. But, there was another reason why Rei couldn't tell him: Ilena's answer to his question.

After Ore left, Rei stood looking out over the balcony banister for a while at the manicured lawn below him and the tree that was Ore's climbing and thinking tree — and sometimes napping tree. It was taller than the two story wing he was in by about another story. Ore often sat in the branches at about the same height as the balcony itself. At the moment it was bare branches, with just a haze of color at the tips of the branches signalling leaf buds would be arriving soon.

When Rei was ready, he called Andrew to him. "Send a messenger to my mother. We're going to pay a visit. Tell her I require a private audience."

Andrew looked at Rei in surprise. In all the months they'd been here, he'd only seen his Queen Mother at the time she came to greet him and turn the Regency over to him. He appeared more timid of her than he was of King Sasou. "When shall I say you'll arrive?"

Rei was quiet a moment longer. It wouldn't do to appear to be in a panic. "In the hour after lunch is past."

"Yes, Rei," Andrew bowed and went to do his Liege's bidding.

Rei spent the time in between reviewing the facts and comparing them to the story that Ilena had told Ore. When he was reasonably sure he understood it well, he set it aside and continued to work on his daily work until his aides said it was time to go.

He took Andrew and Mina as usual, but when they arrived at the Dowager Queen Mother's receiving room, he left them outside the door, and removed from within any other than himself and her. It was true, he was very nervous to be in her presence, but he was here as Regent and she was a subject today. And...the topic was of utmost importance for all of Ryokudo.

"What may I do for you, Rei?" Kata asked both kindly and curiously. She had passed on her beauty and curls to her sons and always dressed impeccably to her station, even if with a slightly casual air. None of her was actually casual, though. She used that air to get the people around her to relax too much, while inside she herself was quite focused. He wasn't fooling her. She was also wondering what had brought her second son to face her. She played the game better than Sasou, and she was a worse tease. That was why he hated facing her.

Rei stood ramrod straight, but relaxed. "Mother, if a person should come before me claiming to be a cousin, how should I test that person to know if they're telling the truth?"

Even though she played the game consummately, even this question gave her pause. When she was asked things that shook her, she became dangerous, like a snake waiting to strike. Her answer was cold. "None live." Underneath the words were: *How dare you bring up the dead in my presence.* Since his father had died she hadn't ever been able to face death. She'd been left alone in the world, only two young sons and an entire kingdom to carry. She'd broken under that burden and Sasou had carried it from the time he was a fourteen year old prince.

Nonetheless, this matter must be faced, and I must have the answer. "But how should I know it, if it was claimed?"

"Mmm," Kata's eyes narrowed. *Very well. I'll tell you. Then go, and leave me to mourn in peace.* "Rei, what is the most striking characteristic of the family of Touka?"

"Pale gold hair and blue eyes."

"Yes. If a 'cousin' should come to you and have these characteristics, believe them not."

Rei raised an eyebrow. *Really?* She looked fierce. *Doubt me not!* He nodded. *Yes, ma'am.*

She continued, "Rei, a birthmark can be claimed, but the birthmarks of infants fade with time, and distort if they remain so that they can't be compared by description. Believe no birthmark claim. ...However, a mark carved with dye into the skin of an infant always remains. Not as the original, for as the child grows larger, it distorts to become nearly unrecognizable, only in form."

Rei's eyes widened. By his right hip, on his back, there was a strange mark. It was mostly unrecognizable, but appeared as stretched and fuzzy lines. He'd been taught to call it a birthmark when asked about it. "Ah. Is there any part of it that remains recognizable at all?"

"If you had a living cousin, it would be similar to what you bear, but at the bottom would be three vertical lines, rather than two. ...However, even this wouldn't be sufficient. Upon any cousin *you* would have there would be a second proof. And, this person would be able to tell you the story of how that person's father commanded that to be."

Like mine, three vertical lines below rather than two, and a second carved mark with a story that can only be said by the right person, the clue being that the father required it. Rei repeated it to himself so he'd remember it.

Kata paused and looked at him in the calculating Touka way that told him he was being tested. "What would you do with such a one?"

"... Whatever I chose to do." He didn't look away from her piercing look.

She finally said, "The original mark was an eagle, carrying a scroll." *Have it your way. I'll see what you will do and judge then.*

"And mine?"

"An eagle, carrying a sheaf of grain."

"...And brother's?"

"...A crowned eagle, carrying a sword."

Rei repeated each mark to himself so that he would remember them, then bowed slightly. "Thank you, Mother. I'll see myself out."

When he reached the door, she finally put living words to the silent words underneath. "Rei, such words bring painful memories."

He stopped and answered without looking at her. "There may come a day where it will be impossible for you to not face it." He let himself out, closing the door behind him. He left with his aides, giving silent permission for Kata's ladies and aides to return to her side.

Mizi should still be with Miss Ilena. This is a good time. Rei walked directly and with purpose to Ilena's guarded room.

-o-o-o-

At his back, Andrew and Mina looked at each other. *What could Rei have needed to talk to his mother about? And now he goes directly to the two women at the top of his anxiety list. Which one did he discuss with her? Was it the answer to the question he set Ore to that has set this off?*

Mina had done the research and written the report. Rei had told her, "Ore says there's a family connection between him and Miss Ilena. Find all the possibilities." Since she'd done the research to find out who Ore was, she already had the beginnings of where to search.

In the end there were several women Ilena could be, but there was one possibility that would have definitely been a worry to Rei, and so he would likely act quickly to rule it out. *Wait and see what Rei does. He's still in research mode.*

They arrived at Ilena's room. "Please call Lady Mizi out," Rei ordered the guards. The guards knocked and announced the Regent. Mizi came to the door, a look of surprised curiosity mixed with a little concern on her face. "I'm sorry for my sudden arrival and brevity, Mizi." She waved it off. "Mizi, Andrew, Mina, please wait out here. I must speak with Miss Ilena in private."

Andrew and Mina looked at each other. Rei was going to test to see who Ilena was. Kata held the key to the answer and the answer wasn't a thing he could tell them if Ilena passed the test, or he would have taken them in. He entered alone, closing the door behind him.

-o-o-o-

Rei, in full regal demeanor, walked up to the side of Ilena's bed and looked down at her. She looked back up at him, her face serene, a hint of a sad smile about her eyes. She already met the initial criteria. She looked nothing like a Touka. Long black hair, golden brown eyes, lightly darkened skin rather than fair. "Who are you?"

"What is it you wish to know, Rei?" Again the informal. He didn't mind it from close friends, but she wasn't that. She was going to answer for it now.

"What is your real name? Who were your parents?"

"Do you already have the proof in hand? Even if I say it, will you be able to say you know for a surety?"

"Yes."

Her eyebrow raised. "Very well. Then listen, and I'll tell you a story — a memory — and we'll see if they coincide. My birth name was Thailena Touka Polov. My father was Third Prince Raoul Polov of Selicia, my mother was Second Princess Tatiana Touka of Ryokudo, your mother's younger sister."

Rei's world rocked. He'd only learned of his mother's sister when he'd read Mina's research. His mother and brother had never talked of it before, nor had anyone, likely due to his mother's inability to face death in any way. To have another person confirm it.... He tried to steady himself by listening closely to Ilena's words. He had to see if she passed *all* the tests.

"Shortly after I was born, I was marked with an eagle carrying a sheaf of wheat, under which were placed two vertical marks. This mark was made on my back near my right hip. It was done when my mother's mother came to visit Selicia, bringing with her the only person trusted to know what the mark looked like and had the art to make it, and it was done in secret. For five years

I was the second heir to Ryokudo. Then you were born, Rei, and I was glad, for I had no desire to rule Ryokudo.

"My parents and I came for your birth celebration at the capital. During that time, the three of us children were brought together. There were only us and our parents, no servants, save the one Grandmother had brought to our home in Selicia when I was born who was there to give you your mark.

"I was taken first to a side room and made to lie on a bed and told to hold very still. The pain wouldn't last long, they said. Then they remade the mark to be an eagle carrying a scroll, and added a vertical mark. I was very glad to have that third mark when it was done, as if I'd been released.

"Because I'd been still and quiet, my father hadn't remarked anything happening. Then they took you, still yet a young infant into that room, and placed the mark on you they'd removed from me. ... It's very painful, and an infant can only cry when exposed to pain." Ilena's face was pained at the memory.

"My father demanded to know what they were doing and it couldn't be hidden from him. They showed him what had been done to me, and he demanded that if I were to be marked by the house of Touka as a child of Ryokudo, then I must also be marked as a child of Selicia with his mark. He drew it out for them, simply, and when your turn was done, I was sent back in a second time. That took longer and the pain was hard to bear.

"The second mark was placed on my back near the left hip and is a lioness rampant, three roses placed before her vertically, because he was the third son and I was his heir. When it was completed, it was beautiful. When in the palace at Selicia, I often would admire them both in private after bathing. I was sad when they were no longer recognizable, although I only saw that once since that chance opportunity occurred when I was already at Tokumade.

"When the marking time was done and I was allowed to return to be with you my cousins, you'd been cajoled and were no longer crying. In order to distract me from my pain, they allowed me to hold you and see your mark." Ilena smiled, remembering.

"You looked at me and smiled. I looked just as much at you but most of all, I vividly remember your lively blue eyes. I felt that you, who'd allowed me freedom from the weight of Ryokudo, were one I wanted to love and would be willing to give all my support to, even as I knew you would wish to give your support and love to your brother.

"I held you close to me and promised that I would always be your support and shield, to protect you in your position," Ilena paused and looked at Rei, a smile in her eyes, determination also. "When you were taken away from me, I looked to your brother. In his eyes he revealed for me, another child, his jealousy that you'd been able to free me but he would never be free.

"Understanding his burden, I went to him and wrapped my arms around him and whispered in his ear, 'It's okay to be jealous, Sasou, for you are a boy as well as a prince and it's a heavy burden to bear, but it's one only you can carry. When you are king, remember that it's okay at times to just be a man. Then, when you've rested a bit, you can pick up the burden again. Rei and I will always be with you, to support you, when you need to be just a boy or a man, and always as you are prince and king.'

"He stood there stunned for a moment. Then slowly he put his arms around me and held me in return. When he let go, his eyes were clear and I was glad. I hope that he has learned to pause and set the burden of the crown down long enough to breathe. I hope he has found a few people who allow him to rest because they understand that a prince and king is still a man and don't condemn him for it, even as you've found such people."

"And you know that I've found such people?" Rei continued to test Ilena, that being the requirement, and the only way to hold the import of what he was learning at bay for the moment.

"Yes. Ore and Mizi, and even Ryan. And they speak of the others, Miss Mina and Mister Andrew. They all love you very much, and take delight in allowing you to be yourself. I'm glad you've found such a place to be." Her smile was genuine.

Rei paused for a moment, then asked, "Miss Ilena, you say you were only a little older than five. How is it you could have said such a thing to Sasou at that age?"

Ilena blinked, "Well, I was often being told I was old for one so young, but it was because I had many cousins in Selicia older than I. There was one in particular who would come to me and speak with me. I learned such a thing from him." *Cousins, the children of the then–King of Selicia, including the heir.*

"Do you know of the mark on Sasou?"

"...I do...but you must promise to never tell your mother."

"My mother? Why?" It seemed a very odd requirement.

"I wasn't supposed to know. Later that night, after dinner, Sasou pulled me away and we snuck to a quiet place, just the two of us, and he showed it to me. Already it was losing it's shape, so he had to tell me what it was so I could make it out."

Rei stared at her for a moment. *Pfft!* "Sasou did such a thing as to get in trouble?"

Ilena grinned, "Yes. With me, he was finally able to have someone to relax with. We got into trouble several times before my family left. He'd been so serious and stuffy before that, but after, he became the friend I'd wished for, and I hope he felt the same. At least, he seemed to. ...His mark is a crowned eagle carrying a sword."

"... As a final proof, Miss Ilena, may I see your marks?"

"Of course, Rei, but you'll have to do the work to see them as I can't move myself yet. But, before that, I should say: you should let Sasou know you've seen the proof. He's been watching over me, and perhaps several other possibilities, for many years now. I know because I recognize the man he sends. He'll wish to know you've seen confirmation."

Rei was still. That would complicate matters, that his brother already knew this one could be who she was saying she was. But if Sasou already thought that it was very likely as well, it would drive a wedge between them if he didn't say as soon as he found out. He would have to carefully word his report, if he didn't wish to lose Ilena to Sasou's board.

Then he remembered his mother, and he was glad he'd warned her she might not get her wish. Yet, she would be content to not know until she was required to know. He could wait to tell her. If Ilena was to be recognized as who she was, all of the family of Touka would have to acknowledge it together. Rei nodded his understanding.

"Rei, let me tell you a thing." He nodded again. "I haven't told you who I am until now not because I don't wish to be recognized as a princess. I am and always have been one and acted as best I could in that way. ...For all that I also love him dearly, and desire to be a support to him, it's because I didn't want Sasou to know."

Rei frowned. "...Why not?" She'd just told him to remain an ally to the King. Now she was saying she didn't want to be the ally of the King herself?

"Because I am a far more significant piece on his board than a pawn or even a knight. I am the First Princess of Ryokudo. As First Prince, you understand." Rei did, with frightening depth. That was why he wanted to word his report to his brother carefully.

With great care in what she said, Ilena continued, "I've worked very hard for many years to create a space for myself. A space that, when it was time for me to be placed upon the boards of Touka, would be one that would require me to be placed upon the board of my choosing, in the place of my choosing. Yet, I understand that even though I've done this, if my efforts can't — or won't — be recognized, I'll be placed in a space not of my choosing, but of the choosing of the King.

"I'll fight to remain in the place of my choosing, but in the end, I will submit to the will of the King. I've also promised to support him, as a man and as a king." She waited for Rei to understand, then continued. "I am the heir to the throne of Selicia, unless another one should be found to still be living. ...I am a princess to two kingdoms. If I'm recognized by Touka, Selicia will come."

Rei felt the blood leave his body. She was right. Even if the new government wouldn't recognize her as a true heir, they could demand that she be used on their board. For example, requiring a forced marriage to the son and heir of the current king in order to prove their claim. Or any of the opposition to the current regime could use her living existence to begin revolution in Selicia again 'on her behalf', even if she didn't instigate it.

Ilena continued, "I believe this is why Sasou has only watched me, to see what I would do. To have claimed me too early would have likely removed me from either of your boards, leaving no possibilities for me to be of use to Ryokudo."

She lifted her chin and almost glared at Rei. Again he was reminded of a falcon who wouldn't submit. "I've spent every moment of my life since you were born proving to Sasou that I will stand where I will stand and I will make my own space. I can no longer do that alone, because you've picked me up. You now must decide where you'll place me. And from that place, I will do all I can, until the board shifts again."

She'd had her say. He'd received all the proof but the final visual proof, and it hardly seemed necessary. He'd reached a level of overload he'd never had before in his life. Ilena looked at him with the sad smile that he'd seen in her eyes when he walked in. She held out her hand to him, "Will you come here, Rei?" He stared at the hand and it beckoned again. He took a breath, then took the hand.

She pulled him to her, then reached up and gently took the back of his head and pulled him down to her shoulder. "You, Rei, are a prince. You've spent all of your effort through all of your life to be the prince you want to be. Even a prince needs to lay his burdens down, either all at once for a very brief time, or one here, a little there, until it can be taken back up.

"In this moment, just for a breath of time, there will be no judgment. There is only Rei, and only his cousin to say: I love you, Rei. I've always loved you. You're a wonderful person who loves well, and who is well loved. I'm very proud of you. You've worked hard and grown so well."

Rei's knees buckled, and he went down onto them beside the bed, his head on Ilena's shoulder, her arm holding him, comforting him. Her warmth flowed into him, and the spaces that he'd kept strong for too long melted. Rei's body shuddered, regular tremors that went through him from toe to head. He didn't shed tears; he wasn't grieving. He was releasing the great burdens that had been upon him for nearly nineteen years, and the equally great burden that had just been explained to him.

The tremors finally slowed and he was able to breathe deeper breaths and release the remainder in that manner. When he was ready he resisted Ilena and she gently released his head, caressing it lightly as her hand slipped past it on his rising. He remained on his knees, his hands going to rest on them. He took one last cleansing breath, and they looked at each other.

-o-o-o-

Ilena studied Rei's face. He had gone from cool confrontational to a peaceful calm. His previously tense shoulders were relaxed now, but he sat on his knees with strength — a good resolution. Ilena herself was perhaps rather the opposite, but she was refusing to look at herself as of yet. Now it was important to help Rei with what he'd decided he wanted to know.

Ilena knew from long before what kind of burden she was to whomever knew it. She'd had to carry herself for so long now, after all. Perhaps she might be relieved to have the people here help carry her, but that wasn't yet nor for a while. She couldn't afford to relax yet in this place. Still...to have told

Rei, to have even passed on the burden just this little bit, it made it difficult to withhold.

She took a deep internal breath and refocused on Rei so she stayed strong. "That's good. You're eyes are clearer, your face calmer," Ilena smiled. "Carry that peace with you. Claim it as your right to maintain. It will shield you. A thing that comes to you to disturb that peace should be given to someone else to deal with. It's not in it's rightful place. A thing that you must deal with will enter that peace and not disturb it, but will show itself to you as a thing that you can deal with. In this way you'll learn the proper balance.

"If it's a thing you don't know where to place, reach for your supports and ask. If it still resonates in a way you don't understand, ask the question, 'who must deal with this?' Then you'll know. Sometimes you'll take up a thing simply because you wish to. Beware of those and don't take up more than one, or at most two, at a time."

She let him ponder, merely keeping him company with his thoughts. When he was ready, he rose to his feet, dusting off his pant legs. "I'll get Mizi to come and help."

Ilena nodded and Rei went to the door and opened it. "Mizi, please come in."

When Mizi entered, he closed the door behind them again. "Mizi, there's a thing I need to see. Will you please help me lift Ilena so I may see her back? If you could stay in front of her, to protect her modesty, I'll stay behind her."

Mizi was mystified, but agreed to help. She climbed carefully up on the bed, straddled Ilena, and reached under her arms and around her. Ilena smiled gently at Mizi then wrapped her arms around her as Rei lifted Ilena's shoulders from behind. In the end, Mizi and Ilena were hugging, and Ilena didn't mind at all, needing the comfort herself. To have admitted her heritage in this place to this particular person was a sobering, even frightening thing. She'd been her own person for so long, even if her path eventually had to lead here.

Ilena was wearing a wrapped top that tied on the left side so that her wounds could be easily seen and cleaned. Rei carefully untied the ties, then pulled the top away from her back. When Mizi became uncomfortable, Ilena tightened her hug slightly. "It's okay," she whispered in Mizi's ear. "It's a thing the King needs to know, and only Rei can do it." Mizi hugged her and buried her face in Ilena's shoulder so she wouldn't have to see Rei's face.

Ilena was just as glad, for Rei decided at that moment that he needed to touch the marks to verify them with his hands, not just his eyes. She shuddered and almost swooned, biting off the moan that threatened to escape. It felt like deep grief mixed with deep desire, and she could feel the tears trying to rise up from her heart and through her throat to reach her eyes.

With this, she was caught. As bound tightly as if she were a newly caught falcon, trussed with tight bonds so that it couldn't wound itself fighting for freedom, being placed in the cage and readied for transport to the mews. Ilena shuddered again.

Rei, noticing, relaced the ties of her top. Then he knelt on the bed behind her and wrapped his arms carefully around both Ilena and Mizi, holding them both close to him, sandwiching Ilena. Ilena's sobs finally broke through.

Because Rei was behind Ilena to support her, Mizi moved her hand to hold Ilena's head close to her, unknowingly imitating the very hold that Ilena used to comfort all those whom she'd ever comforted, thus winning for herself the heart of Ilena.

-o-o-o-

Rei leaned his head forward and touched Mizi's forehead with his own, feeling more sorrow than he'd felt in a long time to have heard Ilena's story and to finally understand the depth of her loneliness and losses. She'd lost all of her family and not been able to even reach out to him or his brother to fill that loss. He kissed Mizi and gently brushed her beautiful blazing hair back from her face. Her green eyes searched his face for understanding.

"I can't tell you yet, nor any of the others, until my brother and I speak and I know what I may do. I'm sorry. I will tell you that Ilena's been marked. Because I know it, she is no longer free. As long as she lives from here on, she will either be mine or my brother's — unless we cast her off, and we won't do that. She is too precious. ...I want her to be mine, and she has told me that is also the desire of her heart."

He could see Mizi start to panic. He put his hand on her cheek and shook his head. "She claims Ore. That is, she's given her heart to Ore. I also wish to give that desire to her, but Ore must come to accept it." At Rei's words, Ilena shuddered again and a keening noise came from her.

Mizi answered, "At the garrison, I said that I desired Ilena to stand with Ore by my side. Have you finished testing her? Do you have an answer?"

Rei thought on that a moment, absently playing with a strand of Mizi's hair lightly. Then he looked her in the eye. "She'll stand there until Sasou has made his decision. Thereafter, what we've done up until then will decide whether she may stay or if he'll take her for himself."

"What *we've* done?" Mizi sucked in a breath of surprise, her eyes round.

Rei nodded. "All of us who wish to have her remain in that place must help her remain, in the same way we work to make it possible for you to stand next to me."

Mizi understood. "I'll do my part."

Rei smiled at her. "Thank you."

"Kiss her again, idiot, or I'll do it for you," came Ilena's muffled, irritated order. They both startled in surprise. "No, seriously." It seemed a rather Ore–like thing for her to say, actually, but with less play and more serious threat to it.

Mizi blushed red, but Rei reached across to take her head in his hand and kissed her gently and long. "Thank you, Mizi," he said to her, putting their foreheads together again. "Please be patient with me in this. There may be many things you can't understand because I can't tell them to you. I'll tell them to you as soon as I can."

"I know, Rei. I'll wait," Mizi reassured him faithfully.

He gently released her, then slid back and together they helped Ilena lie back down. She had her eyes closed and tears still occasionally slipped out from under her eyelids. Rei softly put his hand on her head, then took Mizi's hand in his. "How goes the recovery?" he asked her.

Mizi bit her lower lip. "It's as you just saw. She can sit up if someone else helps her up. The bone shouldn't have that done often just yet. She still has three or four more days before it can regularly bear weight, and it will have to be slowly worked. There's no function in the muscle. As of now, she won't walk again."

Rei wasn't happy with the news. Wheeled chairs were not unknown, and he could have one made for her, but it would be much better if she could walk again. "Isn't there anything we can do?"

"There's only one possibility I know of," Ilena answered. They turned to look at her. She slowly turned her head and opened her reddened eyes to look at them. "Go to the old man at the gate who asks for 'the Missus'. Tell him to send for the surgical researcher, Doctor Elliot. He has the knowledge and the skill to find a way.

"If there's anything that will let me walk again so I may stand in the place I wish, I'll do it. Even if it means I must do this all over again." Rei looked at her seriously for a moment, then nodded.

Ilena closed her eyes again. "Rei, when you're ready to plan your strategy to capture the Earl, please bring your maps and come speak to me. He'll run to one of his holes and you need to know where they are. ...Ore's returned from gathering the first set of witnesses. If you're ready for them, I'll give you the names for the next set, although I hope you'll wait a sufficient time before sending him away again."

Rei wanted to refuse her given her current state, then he remembered Ore had said for her it was a reward, or an equal exchange. She had comforted him. They had comforted her. She had given up her freedom. He...they...had promised to do what they could to give her her dreams.

Those had been the same, but she had given first, and they had chosen how they would respond on their own. He had said he would send for the surgeon. ...She was offering more information right now, even though it was a difficult time for her. He gave up his pride.

Rei stepped to the desk and got out paper and a pen. "I'm ready." He wrote as she listed eight names and their corresponding locations, again two for each of the cases. He put the pen down and put the paper inside his jacket. He stopped by the side of her bed again and briefly put his hand on her head one more time. "Thank you, Ilena. Please rest now." She gave a small nod.

Rei took Mizi's hand and walked with her to the door. There he turned to her and took her into an embrace. He didn't know what he wanted to say. The burden he carried now was still more than he could face fully at the moment.

Mizi held him in return. "I'll look after her."

After a time, he said, "Thank you." He needed Mizi to take that part of the burden: to see that Ilena was watched over and that she healed properly.

He released Mizi, his hand lingering on hers, then he turned and left the room, putting his public face back on before opening the door.

-o-o-o-

Rei led Andrew and Mina away from Ilena's room, headed towards his office. He stopped suddenly, considering. Even though he was now carrying the burden of knowing there was another royal of Ryokudo, and a royal of Selicia in hiding, the release of his other burdens was now allowing him to view his needs and requirements in a new way. He changed direction and headed for the library where the majority of the young lords and heirs spent most of their days.

This is still an interesting trip, Andrew's look told Mina.

When they arrived, Rei strode purposely through the library to the central atrium and up the stairs to the second floor landing. Turning to face the room in general, he looked around. All of his behavior was calculated to get the attention of the persons in the room, and he had it. After all, this kind of entrance by the master of the palace had only one reason: someone was being called up.

"I'm looking for the eldest son of Earl Malkin. Is he present?" Rei asked in a carrying voice.

A murmur went through the room as the word was spread to the more distant parts of it. People looked around to see if the person in question would appear. Soon enough, footsteps could be heard coming from a distant part of the upper level. People went back to work, but continued to pay attention.

A well portioned young man with slightly wavy brown hair and carrying a folder appeared from behind a set of shelves, looked around, then came towards Rei. He bowed. "I am Earl Malkin's eldest son, Tairn. How may I serve?"

Rei looked at him. He looked to be in his upper twenties, near Andrew's age, and had clear, brown honest eyes. "Who are you studying under?"

"Count Wexley, Ministry of the Interior."

"Please inform Lord Wexley that you've been reassigned to Miss Mina, in my office. You may have time to complete your current task, or to pass it on to another in your department. Please come to my office as soon as you're able, but no later than the day after tomorrow."

Tairn bowed again, "Yes, your Highness." He left immediately to carry out his new orders.

Rei turned towards his aides and pondered some more. Mina, a little cautiously, asked, "You'll pick another landed heir?" She was concerned that

Rei would have to go through what he was going through with her all over again.

Rei shook his head. "You'll train him, and when his younger brother is able to join us, you'll have Tairn train him under your supervision. Then, when you're not here, there will be the two who are necessary to fill the strength of one Mina. You'll train the younger to be able to do the work of two so that when Tairn must also return, he's able to stand in the position of Mina."

Mina blinked. It was a well considered plan. "Then what shall be left for me to do? Shall I consider myself no longer needed?"

"No, of course not." Rei wasn't going to let her go that easily.

"I have two stacks on my desk I'd be happy to pass on to Mina," Andrew said dryly.

Rei nodded, "Indeed." He considered a little longer, then came to a decision. He turned, walked down the stairs and led them back to his office. On the way, he stopped in at the office of the châtelaine, keeper of the keys for the castle, and made a brief request. "Please open the office across the hall from my office, for immediate use." As soon as the order was acknowledged, he was gone.

When they arrived at his office, he went directly to Andrew's desk. Placing a hand on a stack, he asked, "Each stack is ordered by subject?" Andrew nodded.

Rei proceeded to pick up the top report of each stack, skim it, then replace it. One tall stack, one medium stack, and one short stack were pushed to the side. He turned to Andrew again, placing his hand on top of the tallest selected stack. "Take these to Lord Nedlow. Show him an example of the sort of summary I require, see that he understands, and return."

Andrew was in shock. Lord Nedlow was one of the previous regent's aides, having served in her office. He'd retired to a lesser office when Rei had come, as was typical with a change of leadership. "You'll bring him out of retirement?"

Rei nodded. "I can no longer afford to waste trained talent. Please also inform him he'll be working in the Rosebud office beginning tomorrow."

Andrew bowed. "Yes, Rei." He left immediately to carry out the order.

Rei moved across to Mina's desk, asking as he went, "What's your organization?"

She paused. In her case she would be training someone to think as she thought. "You may consider it the same." The top file would be sufficient.

Rei also went through her stacks and pulled out three medium level stacks. "Have Tairn assist you with these to begin with."

Mina nodded, and turned to clear space for him on the desk behind hers, moving the extra overflowing stacks to the end of the table near Andrew's desk. While she did that, Rei gave orders for his four lesser aides in the office to prepare themselves for moving to the Rosebud office.

"Do I get to lose some of my stacks, too, Master?" Ore sounded hopeful.

Rei turned around, surprised that Ore had been in the room, he having been hidden by his own stacks. "No, I don't think so."

Ore had walked up behind Rei to come talk to him, but when Rei turned around to face him, Ore suddenly stopped and stared at him. His hand started to rise slowly, as if to reach out and touch Rei. Then he caught himself and put the back of his hand to his mouth instead in embarrassment.

His eyes wide, Ore said in wonder, "Master has been touched by Miss Ilena!"

"How would you know such a thing?" Rei asked him.

"Those who've been held by Mother become hers and are filled with her light. Master's own light is very bright, but her light is on you now, also." Rei smiled slightly. "...But, Master carries the shadow, too. Master's also sad for Miss Ilena."

"What do you do to remove the shadow, Ore? Do you know?" Rei asked, the sorrow in his heart pricked by Ore's words.

"You tell them she is alive," Ore said with surety, looking directly at Rei.

Rei thought about Ore's words. *Ilena is alive.* She'd survived the massacre of her parents and her father's family and had walked with only one servant from Selicia to Ryokudo. She'd chosen exile, risen to the highest level she could in her adopted home, under the very oppressive Earl, constantly under the threat of death herself, yet still had survived. She'd even lived through the rockslide.

Through it all, Ilena had lived, and lived with strength and purpose. *She is still alive. As long as Ilena is alive, she will live with strength and purpose, regardless of what may come.* Rei did feel better, as if he himself had been calmed and strengthened by thinking of Ilena's strength. He looked back up at Ore.

Ore smiled at him. "See? It even worked for Master."

Rei considered for a moment. "If I allowed you to tell one of her people she was alive, would they betray her?"

Ore shook his head. "None would. She's protected each and all of them. They'll do the same for her. Do we not fiercely protect the things we love?"

Rei understood. He was ready now to give Ore his orders. "You've learned which lesser gate the old man Ilena has asked after comes to?"

"The Pelican Gate."

How appropriate. "Go and speak to him. Give him this message: 'Mother, with the permission of the Regent, sends for the surgery researcher, Doctor Elliot.' I want him here as soon as he can get here. ...And, I won't be angry if you choose to remove the shadow."

As Ore headed out the double doors in the windows and lept down from the balcony, Rei turned to his own desk, putting his hand on the corner stack. There were many things that only he could do, approvals and signatures among them. There were things he wanted to do, like read reports his other aides had already read so that he would understand the workings of the region. There were things that others asked him to do.

He needed to sit down and sort everything on his desk into stacks of level of importance and confirm which ones he really needed to touch versus things he could either get summaries of or really should be handled by others. His real goal was to raise everyone up one notch in power, giving his closest aides the full power to act in the name of the Regent and directly handle those things that didn't actually require his own complete attention.

He'd brought Lord Nedlow out of retirement not just because he needed another pair of hands. He'd done it so the practiced aide could complete the training of the new office aides that he'd brought in. "Mina, send a messenger to Lord Nedlow. When he and Andrew are done, and he's prepared to move, I would like to speak with him directly."

Rei moved to the balcony and looked out over the castle grounds and out over the city, the craggy Northern mountains rising in the near distance a little to his right. But he wasn't looking at them. He was crafting a very important letter in his mind. He wished he could use Andrew for this, the same as he did for the majority of his correspondence, but this would have to come from his own hand. This was something only he could do, something he must do, and must do today.

-o-o-o-

When Andrew arrived back at the Rose Office, Rei was working on his fifth draft of his message to Sasou, his forehead creased in frustration and concentration. Andrew recognized the problem, if not the cause. Rei always looked that way when he was trying to write his own correspondence.

Andrew raised an eyebrow at Mina. *What's going on? Should I offer to help?* He probably shouldn't since Rei hadn't looked up in relief when he came in, as he usually would.

Mina said, quietly, "Andrew, will you come look at this for me?" Rei still didn't look up at the mention of his aide's name. Andrew's other eyebrow went up to join the first. He walked over to Mina's desk and leaned down, 'looking' at the document Mina had in front of her.

She spoke to him very quietly. They'd gotten good at talking quiet enough privately if Rei was so tightly distracted, but he would hear if his distraction ended. "Ore said Rei's been 'touched' by Miss Ilena, that he 'carries' both his own 'light' and now her 'light'. Rei didn't deny it."

They both had seen in Rei's back they watched so carefully and knew so well, that he'd left burdens behind when he'd come out of Ilena's room. They'd expected that only if she wasn't the missing princess. But his actions after that said that something else had happened in that room in addition to proving who she was. He was acting with increased strength.

Ore's words were the clue to that, they were sure. Ilena had done something in that private meeting to support Rei in a very positive way. Andrew gave Mina a puzzled look. *But does that mean she is or isn't the missing princess?*
196

Mina shrugged. "Ore was sent to tell Miss Ilena's man to fetch the surgeon. And...Rei said it was okay for him to let them know she's alive."

In one fell swoop, in one private meeting, Rei trusted her, and all her people with her. He believed her. She'd told him the truth about her past, and he'd received the witness he needed to completely believe her, and her motives, whatever they were.

While it didn't prove whether or not she was the princess, if she'd had the definite proof to say she was, that would be far more convincing for such a sudden change in Rei. *Then it's time for me, for us, to test her,* Andrew's set expression said.

"Since that time, Rei's thought very hard about the message he's trying to write. Even still," Mina told Andrew. Which meant it was both a very important message and to a very important person. He was trying to word it right to get the best outcome for what he wanted. ...But he wouldn't, or couldn't ask for assistance.

The only thing he wouldn't talk to them about right now was the matter he took to his mother, the matter he discussed with Ilena herself. It therefore must be a letter about Ilena and what he'd learned from the proof he'd gained and what she'd admitted herself.

If she weren't the princess, it wouldn't be important to send a letter to anyone about it. If she were the princess, Rei would be constrained to inform the King immediately. If he merely wished to inform the King about her existence, the letter would have required no more effort that his usual dictation took. He was working very hard to keep something he wanted.

Andrew and Mina looked at each other. *The only conclusion is that Miss Ilena is the missing princess, she supports Rei, and Rei wants to keep her by his side.*

Andrew sighed. *Another burden for Rei to worry about. And he can't ask us for support, because he can't let us know until he hears from King Sasou. So we'll have to support him as best we can without requiring him to tell us.* He nodded. "I think I need to talk with Mizi." *We'll all need to support him. And I want to know what went on in that room after she was called in.*

Mina nodded, "And Ore." *I'll talk to him. There are things he may know.*

Andrew straightened up from leaning over Mina's desk. Brilliant blue eyes under unruly pale blond hair looked back at him. The look was so familiar even though the face was finally aging from youth to young adult. "Andrew, you're back? What do you guys want to talk to Mizi and Ore about?" Rei had finished his letter the best he could. He always heard Mizi's name when it was mentioned, though.

"Your birthday present," Mina said. Andrew was proud of her. She always had the best immediate answers to distract Rei from what they were actually talking about. She could get away with it because of her straight face.

His tactic was to completely turn the conversation around to what Rei was supposed to be doing instead. "Lord Nedlow says that he'll be able to come meet with you within another hour." Andrew moved away from Mina's desk. "You were working very hard when I came in."

"It's a letter to my brother. I always have to work hard on them." Rei stretched. "We'll go to the aviary now, then, if Lord Nedlow will be here at that time." *The who is as we guessed, and it's important enough he needs to get it sent without delay.*

"Do you need both of us?" Andrew asked. He and Mina needed to be caught up to Rei quickly.

"No," answered Rei. "Do you have something to do?"

"Yes," answered Andrew. For once he answered a straight answer like Mina. "I have to go pick out your birthday present." *We'll give you what you need. You don't have to ask us.* Mina and Rei both raised eyebrows at him, but he was as serious as ever, not showing the open face he would have shown at a lie.

"Very well," answered a mystified Rei, and Mina rose to follow Rei out the door.

-o-o-o-

Andrew went to the castle medical wing, looking for Mizi. She had a patient in the outer office and was in the laboratory working on making up a tincture. "Mizi? Do you have a moment? I don't want to interrupt. We can talk while you're working if you like, or I can wait."

"Andrew! I can be with you in five minutes." Mizi was her usual cheerful, if slightly distracted self. He nodded his thanks and went to take his turn in line. Mizi came out and finished with her current patient, then invited Andrew into her office, looking up at him curiously.

"Mizi, since this morning Rei's been acting strange. Will you tell me what happened in Miss Ilena's room this afternoon?" It wasn't the first time he'd asked such a thing of her, so it shouldn't be a strange question to her. She understood that Andrew took his responsibility of being Rei's guardian very seriously.

"Mmm. When he called me in, he asked me to hold Ilena sitting up so he could look at her back. I don't know what he was looking for, but he told me after he'd seen it...," she was starting to blush. Andrew found that interesting, but she blushed at a lot of things. Did it mean she was feeling a bit jealous that Rei had looked at the bare back of another woman in her presence? She should be, or should have. "...that he couldn't tell me or any of us about it. Only that Ilena's been marked, and he was required to see the mark himself for King Sasou's sake."

She looked concerned. "He said that because Ilena's marked she's 'no longer free', that as long as she lives she must be either his or his brothers and that she's too precious to be cast off. That makes him very sad.

"I don't understand why, but he loves her. He wants to keep her by his side, and she also wants to stand at his side. But her heart is Ore's, and he would give her to him if Ore would decide to accept it." Mizi looked like she was trying to puzzle out what Rei had said. "...He's promised that he'll explain it to all of us, after he's talked to King Sasou and he knows what he may do."

Mizi shifted. Andrew felt bad for her, although he kept it off his face for her sake. She would stay stronger if he stayed neutral. It was good Rei had promised he would explain himself and explained when he'd be able to. He at least seemed to be getting better at communicating such things with Mizi.

"At the garrison, I asked for her to be assigned as Ore's partner, knowing that she loves him. Rei said that he would test her." Andrew remembered and nodded. "I asked him if he'd completed testing her; if he had an answer for me. He said that she would stand with Ore beside me until King Sasou makes his decision. At that time, what we've done to help her remain in that place will decide whether she may stay or if King Sasou will take her for himself."

Mizi's green eyes looked into Andrew's eyes. "While there are things I don't understand, I know that Rei will tell them to me when he can. I know that his love for Ilena doesn't lessen his love for me. He was very careful to let me know it." Andrew was very relieved to know Rei had appropriately conveyed it. "I wish to support his desires. I've told him that I'll do my part to help her remain in the place Rei puts her."

Andrew had heard more than enough to confirm his and Mina's suspicions. He understood why Rei would love Ilena, but he didn't know how to help Mizi to understand also. As long as her own strength could support her, it would be okay.

"Thank you, Mizi. You've been very helpful. If Rei's decided this thing, we'll stand to support him, and we'll wait until he can tell us." Andrew both was agreeing with her and setting down the law for those who loved the Prince. He bowed and left Mizi standing there, her hand clutched at her heart.

As they walked to their quarters in the wing assigned to the Regent's personal aides and knights at the end of the day, after escorting Rei to his own guarded quarters, Andrew told Mina what he'd learned from Mizi.

"The proof was a thing Miss Ilena couldn't have done herself. Rei's seen it with his own eyes. He's decided he'll do all he can to keep her by his side, and wants us to help him do it. Until he receives permission from King Sasou, he can't himself confirm it to us."

Mina looked up into her thoughts. "This is a thing we need to understand."

Andrew knew she was saying, *We need to know Miss Ilena for ourselves, or we can't support Rei correctly.* He nodded. *My thoughts exactly.* "Have you spoken with Ore yet?"

"No. Not yet." It would happen as soon as there was an opportunity available.

"Perhaps together, then," Andrew said. Mina nodded.

CHAPTER 11 A Princess Returned

Ore stretched. He was done for the night. Not that he was caught up, but that was all he was going to get done without anyone else in the room to help him. It really wasn't fair that they got decreased loads while he was still playing catch–up. So what if he was a junior aide? Ah, well. At least he was able to do his part to help Rei.

He still had a little over an hour before it was time to sit with Ilena. He thought about going to get a drink, then remembered that he'd thought of a question brought about by Ilena's answer to Rei's question. To get the answer, he needed to visit the library. He stood, put out the remaining lights in the office, secured it, and headed to the library.

He went to the foreign affairs section and found a book that looked like it would answer his question: *Historical Summary of the Leadership and Politics of Selicia*. It was the only book he could find that would be helpful. There weren't many books there on Selicia, actually.

He flipped through it until he reached the era from right around his birth. Then he looked through it backwards until he found the answer he was looking for: how he and Ilena might be related. It was no wonder they looked similar, her being of Selicia and him having a great–ancestor, also of Selicia. He wasn't sure why they would be related through the kings of Selicia, though, since he didn't know Ilena's parentage.

He held the book for a moment, his finger still holding the place of the time around his birth and the thumb of the other hand holding the place of his ancestor. What about her story of the political upheaval she'd lived through? Was it in this book also?

He went back to the page his finger was marking at about his birth and began to read forward. Before he could even get to the section that should talk about the coup, he was brought up short. He sat up so straight in surprise he nearly stood up. *What?! Queen Mother had a sister? Who married into the royal house of Selicia?*

He quickly read the few following pages. They did indeed talk about the coup that happened nine years later. It said that the entire house of the Polov royal family was killed in that revolution. *Even Queen Mother's sister.* He read a little more, but it didn't say anything about it being caused by the neighboring country, Tarc. Nor did it hint that the current ruling family was a puppet of Tarc. How had Ilena known that? Who had the correct information? Ilena or this book?

While he puzzled on that, he flipped idly through the remaining pages. Really there wasn't much. The final words had been written only a few years ago, after all. Then he stopped. At the back of the book was a genealogy of the kings of Selicia. Mostly it was names and dates — marriages, children, their birth dates. But every so often there were pictures that had been copied from paintings hanging in the castle of Selicia. Here was the face of that

Great–Grandfather. It looked just like his own Grandfather. He touched it reverently.

That page went another generation. He flipped the page and hissed a breath through his teeth. It was a two page spread of the most recent Polov royals, and all their pictures. At the top left was the King at the time of Ore's birth, King Raould Polov. His wife, Queen Sari and their marriage date. Under them were pictures of their children, in various ages of childhood, and their birth dates: Crown Prince Matthai, First Princess Attilia, Second Prince Grail whose picture was that of an infant.

In the middle was the King's second brother, Prince Reide Polov, his wife Princess Natalia, and their marriage date, and penciled in the name of a son, Prince Liam, born less than a year before the coup, and no picture.

On the right was the King's second brother, Prince Raoul Polov, his Ryoku-dan wife Princess Tatiana Touka, and their marriage date, and their daughter, Princess Thailena Touka Polov and her birth date, the picture showing a young girl who looked just like her father. Penciled in for all of them was a death date, the same one: the date of the coup.

Ore ran his finger very gently over the picture of Princess Tatiana Touka. She stood out with her pale blond hair and blue eyes, so unlike the rest of the family. She was as beautiful as Sasou, but with long curly tresses nearly down to her hips. What a treasure for the Touka family to have given up and then lost.

He moved his finger down to the daughter. A Touka who looked like a Polov, a Selician. His finger traced over the first name. Thailena. *Ilena.* Was it? He looked at the birthdate and calculated. It fit, but he wanted more evidence. The record could only say they were all dead.

He snapped the book closed and went to find the Ryokudo history section. After a bit of searching he found the equivalent book for the Ryokudo royal family and political history summary. He opened it up and flipped to the back. It ended with the reign of Rei and Sasou's father, and his death. (Ore figured the next book was still being written.)

It, too, ended with the family genealogy, showing that Rei's grandfather had only had two daughters. His oldest, the Queen Mother Kata Touka had married Rei's father, apparently a noble, and had Sasou and Rei. His second daughter, the same Princess Tatiana, had married the same Prince Raoul Polov. And they had had a daughter, Thailena Touka Polov, born the same date. Again, the death date during the coup had been penciled in, but only for the parents. There was no death date for the daughter.

Ore flipped back into the history and read the section that talked about the birth of Sasou, the marriage of Tatiana to Raoul, the birth nearly one and a half years later of their daughter. A brief mention of the royal visit of Tatiana's mother to Selicia to celebrate the birth of her granddaughter, less than a year after her husband had died and two months after she had turned the reins of the kingdom over to her son–in–law. Then, the birth of Rei. *Oh, fifteen Springthree! That's in five weeks! Should I get him a present?*

Then he stopped again. He read the brief passage three times before remembering to breathe. The Third Prince of Selicia had come with his wife and five year old daughter to the celebration of Prince Rei's birth, returning by way of the Earldom of Tokumade to "renew and celebrate common relations across the border and to resolidify the peace between the two countries".

Ore was so stunned he had to keep reading to hold himself together. Two years later, some distance into the book since it was Ryokudo's history, was the mention of the coup in Selicia, brief and with a focus on Princess Tatiana and her family. It told that she and her husband had been found dead, murdered just inside the Ryokudo border, their heads removed but the bodies left behind. *Ah, poor Ilena,* he sighed.

"There was no sign of their daughter with them", the book went on to say. "It is unknown if she died in Selicia or went missing, although the new government of Selicia claimed she was also dead. The relationship between the two countries since that time has been strained." *No doubt!*

Ore closed the book. He leaned back, closing his eyes. In his hands were two books. In his heart were two memories. There could be no doubt. Ilena was the Princess Thailena Touka Polov.

He started to laugh softly. It explained so much about her: about her personality, her strength, why she made him think of Sasou, even why everyone who loved her was filled with light. She, also, carried the light of Touka in her, and the love for and of the people of Ryokudo. He wouldn't be at all surprised if she carried a similar love for the people of Selicia. And he hadn't lied when he'd told Mizi they were cousins, either.

He paused. Rei would also know about Ilena. He would find out, the same way he'd found out Ore was Kase Shicchi. She was a rare treasure he would want to keep. But he would have to tell Sasou. Would she be a rare enough treasure the King would claim her? ...It was possible. Did Rei already know? ...Ore would ask tomorrow. For now, he was running late.

He stood up and headed for Ilena's room, taking both books with him. He wouldn't talk to Ilena about it yet. He shouldn't if Rei didn't know yet. Besides, it was Ilena's to tell, wasn't it?

His steps slowed. A princess of two realms wanted *him*. He, Ore. She'd claimed him when she was five. Her father, a prince, had given her permission to have him, after he was grown and strong enough. It was no wonder he'd said it that way. One did not give a princess someone who couldn't protect her. But, one also did not refuse a princess, particularly a doting father of a prince, when it was in their power to give it.

Did his brother hate him, continue to chase after him, believe he would return for her, because he knew she was a princess? Had he kept her alive for the same reason? Allowed her to rule the House so she would learn to rule a nation? ...What power had he thought he could gain from his little brother marrying the First Princess of Ryokudo, the only remaining heir to the throne of Selicia?

Ore's blood ran cold and he shivered and held his arms close about himself. Pakyo didn't want him dead. He wanted him very much alive, and very much under his control.

Ore leaned against the closest wall, dropping to sit on the floor, his arms wrapped even tighter around himself. Pakyo knew Ore was Kase. He hadn't presented himself in person when Ore and Mizi were at the earldom, but that didn't mean he didn't know when they left and headed out to Osterly.

He'd told the assassin to let them pass. He'd ordered his wife and Ilena back on the same day so that Ore would have no choice but to meet her when the group was attacked and Ilena was injured. He'd known Mizi would stay to help the injured and he knew Ore followed Mizi.

Ore shivered again. Ilena had been severely injured on purpose, and Pakyo had planned it far enough in advance that he could tell Ilena three months beforehand to 'stay alive'. What was his plan? Why did he want them together, now, and not under his control?

Ilena had said she was free of the Earl. Was doing everything she could to remove the Earl and his ability to control them. What did she not know? ...She didn't know Pakyo knew she was the princess. But that wasn't enough to answer the question.

Ore couldn't see it. Ilena didn't know it. If he told Rei, would he be able to understand it? Ore didn't know. First, he had to know if Rei already knew she was the princess. And...he had to know how Ilena knew he was Kase. If he knew how she knew, and when she'd figured it out, maybe he would know when it was his brother had found out. Maybe in that story would be the clue he needed. He stood up and ran to Ilena's room.

-o-o-o-

"I'm sorry I'm late, Little Mister," Ore panted.

"That's alright. ...Are you okay?" Ryan rose to his feet with his current book in hand, then paused to inspect Ore.

Ore waved his hand. "Just wanted to get here as soon as I could," he pasted on his friendly smile.

"You look a little pale." Ryan was very good at seeing slight symptoms.

"It's just lack of sleep. I'm still trying to catch up from being gone. There are many tall stacks of work on Ore's desk."

"Well, okay. Do get enough rest. Good night." Ryan was already nearly asleep on his feet and he wove his way down the hall. Ore wondered if he'd make it back, glad it was a short distance.

Ore took a deep breath, then entered Ilena's room, his heart beating loudly. He was afraid. She was awake again. "Still not sleeping well?" he asked right away.

"No. Only when you're here." It was said with calm honesty. *Yeah, I'm not surprised.* "Desk work again?"

"Yes. I'd like to get caught up soon. Like before I have to be gone again." *Ba–dump,* his heart gave one large thump. ...Would he be safe outside the castle? *Stupid, I was this last time. I know how to be careful. And the rest of the Family will continue to watch over me.*

That was a startling self–revelation and he played with it a moment. *Ilena protects them, she protects me.* Did she tell them all to protect him, too? Is that why they knew him and what he looked like? He felt the certainty of it as deep as he felt the certainty his brother knew who he was.

He shook himself. It seemed to be a night of answers and they were all stunning. Literally. He felt like he was having rocks thrown at him.

What should be first? The Family. "Master sent me to talk to Grandfather today." The old man at the gate had told Ore to call him that. It surely meant he was as important to Ilena and the Family as she'd said he was.

"*Haahh.* That's good." She didn't sound surprised, though. Ore wondered if that was some sort of clue he was missing.

"Master said he wouldn't be angry if I told him — the Family — that you were alive so their shadow could be lifted. ...That was after I lifted Master's shadow. ...You touched Master today. I could see it." It was an accusation.

"Can you see it now, Ore?"

"Yes, Thayne taught me. The runners, Henry and Marcus, taught me what the shadow meant, but I couldn't lift it from them. Master hadn't yet allowed me to speak it, but today he allowed it, and I told Grandfather so that they may be full of light again." He paused. He really wanted to know. "Why did you touch Master today? Why did he allow it?"

Ilena sighed. "He came to me today and asked a question. The answer was hard for him to bear. So hard, I needed to take it back from him and help him learn how to carry it." *Master knows. Miss Ilena told him today. This is why he suddenly trusts her and allowed me to speak to Grandfather. I'll be able to talk to Master.* "He won't speak of it to you."

Wait, what? "Why?"

"He must speak to his brother, Sasou, before he can know if he can speak of it to anyone. It's a matter of the King." *That's true. But what I have to say is also. ... I'll take it to Master, if he can't come to me.* She continued, "I'm glad you've told them, Ore. It lifts a shadow from me as well. Thank you."

Ore had offered his side. Now he could ask from her. "Why do you believe that I'm Kase Shicchi?" His voice came out rougher than intended from all the fear and emotions he felt.

There was a long pause. Then, "Ore, will you come hold my hand while I tell the story? I'm in need of human contact, I'm afraid."

Was it that, or was she sensing his own fear? He decided it didn't matter. He could afford that price to hear the answer. He walked over, taking the chair with him. He sat, barely able to see her with the faint light coming from under the well–made door of the castle. He reached out, found her arm, then moved his hand down it until he found her hand. She shuddered slightly, but grasped his hand firmly.

Ore listened quietly as Ilena told him that over the years she'd spent a lot of time and effort to find him, learning how to listen to the underworld network, and how she put together a network of helpful people on the top–side as well. It was from the underworld side that the strongest potential matches came from, but it was hard to keep ahead of Pakyo on that side. He was looking for Kase on that network as well.

It was the job where his life nearly ended where she learned for sure. He'd been careful to not take any jobs that the House of Shicchi had put out requests for, and that one hadn't had the name on it anywhere. They'd been an observing and participating House, nonetheless.

"The plan was really his: joining in with a House he normally wouldn't have without advertising his involvement. He figured he'd get you trapped eventually if he kept narrowing down his search, weeding out each possibility as he went. He was quite certain he'd get you in that one, as was I, and he nearly did."

Ilena explained that she and the surgeon went along on that trip as medical support staff. Pakyo knew heavy drug users were involved, and he wanted his men to be able to keep up. They had instructions that if Ore was found, to let him die or kill him.

Pakyo didn't really care that there wasn't solid evidence that Ore was Kase, he'd just been the last one that could be Kase on the list and had been the hardest to entrap. Ilena had done her job, but kept careful look–out for Ore. She knew who she was looking for based on the description from the information network.

Both she and Pakyo had seen Ore on the field at the same time. Pakyo had sent in instructions for those supporting Ore to pull back just enough to let him fall. Ilena had just the right chance to get word to a couple of people obviously Ore's allies to go help him. They'd arrived barely in time to deflect the final killing blow and take out his opponent, but he'd already received the wound.

"When you went off to die, or live if fortune smiled on you, the Earl ordered you followed and watched to see if you died. By then everyone was tired and wounded. One did get up and follow you, but he was lazy. He watched you until you fainted, then counted that good and came back to report you dead. Elliot managed to make a sufficient diversion so that I could slip away and track you also.

"I found you in the hiding place you'd dragged yourself into. I assumed you hadn't been unconscious long after you fainted, but you were again when I got there. I was very glad we'd played hide and seek when we were young. I knew exactly what kind of hiding place to look for.

"I'd had enough experience working with Elliot that I knew what to do to bandage you, but not enough to do a full and proper job. It was very frustrating." Ore put his free hand to his chest. He'd been unconscious the whole time in that hiding place while she'd bandaged him. "If I could have, I would have sent him after you, but he wouldn't have found you, and the Earl would have noticed right away he was gone. I also had to work quickly, since Pakyo would know I'd gone looking for you.

"As a matter of fact, he did come looking for me, making the first tracker bring him to where you'd fainted. I came out of hiding in a different location, looking as if I was also still searching for you. It took some verbal dodging, and he never really believed that I hadn't found you. But I think unconsciously he didn't want to know, since his reason for living would disappear if you were really dead."

No, Ilena, Ore thought sadly. *He wanted me alive. He let you go to find me for sure, but also to save me because he believed if you did, it meant I was Kase. To him that was enough proof.*

"Of course, none of that really proved you were Kase. I'd had to leave you to fate as well, but you had a fighting chance as long as you weren't bleeding to death. So I kept all my information lines open waiting to hear if you'd made it. Imagine my surprise when a positive match came from southern Ryokudo.

"I was even more surprised that it came from the part of the network that overlapped Prince Sasou's network. I had someone watch you on detail for a while, learning about Prince Rei and Mistress Mizi's relationship, and how you relate to them."

Ore could tell that Ilena smiled. "That was the evidence I needed. No other Shicchi than Kase could walk into the darkness, then turn, see the light, and run towards it and grasp it with both hands. No other nightwalker would have wanted to. ...And none of the other Kase–candidates I saved did." *Wait. She saved all of 'us'? She continued to watch all of the possibilities until one acted in a way to confirm her expectations. That's why she was able to tell?*

"I don't know how it was that Rei found out who you really are, but I know he did...perhaps you told him. If it was to have been a test, no other test than the fact that he kept you would have been necessary."

She paused. "But even more telling, was that you went back to him. Not just the first time, but every time. ...You stayed away from him the first time so long that I almost caught you in my web. But you managed to slip through it, and I wasn't sad. If anything, it blew the fire of my goals back into life."

Ore remembered that: that he'd begun to feel something coming for him. His return to Rei had been a choice, but it had also been an escape from that feeling. Why had she been trying to catch him? Was it like what she'd done for the master stoneworker? Was she finally trying to ask him to be hers? He'd finally gone to find the light, so she thought he might be ready? He didn't ask.

"At the same time, because Pakyo didn't have connections to the southern network, he couldn't know you were at the castle. He's been reverting to his old volatile state, a dying ember that glows dimly when a breeze blows by it. He's already a pawn worth throwing away. I wasn't sorry to be part of this current plan, although I really could have done without the final injury."

Her understanding is indeed different from what I see. Why does she see he's weak? She sees someone is controlling him? Or is it that she thinks she's been controlling him? "Is the Earl your pawn?"

"No."

The current plan. Which plan is she referring to? "What was the plan from the beginning?"

"He only ordered me to go, and if I could, to stay alive. I had to figure out for myself what he might be planning. When he laughed, I wasn't sure if it was out of delight that he would finally be rid of several problems at once, or if it was just madness. Even if Rei doesn't kill him, he'll likely be dead by his own hand soon.

"Maybe he intends to die in the coming fight, going down fighting, rather than by a traitor's death meted out in court. That would be like him. Choosing to let the House of Shicchi go out in a blaze, taking out as many as possible with him, raging and delighting in the bloody chaos as his eyes close for the last time."

Ilena paused again. "I was glad the boulder didn't kill me. It meant I could keep walking towards my goal. However, currently I'm blocked from reaching my ultimate goal, not being able to walk or run again. I know it doesn't have to be so. I already have someone who can fix this if it's not left too long." There was determination in her voice.

Then she sighed. "Even though I'll have to put up with a second set of five weeks of flat on my back, four walls closing in on me." Her grip on his hand tightened. "I hope you'll be willing to keep me company some of that time as well. Sometimes.... Ah well. Wishful thinking isn't as useful as purposeful action and it's difficult for me at this time to be in action." She blew out a breath in frustration.

Ore could only think of the life the Touka's he knew led. "Relax and consider it a vacation. Maybe even the only vacation you'll get in your life."

"It's certainly a nice vacation when you're here, Ore. And Mistress Mizi, too. ...And Ryan is very kind. ...This is a place that makes one want to relax." She was getting tired.

He thought about her position, about the fact that Rei would likely not want to give her up. There was one more question to ask tonight. "Miss Ilena, what do you think of Master and Mistress?"

"Mmm?" Ilena asked sleepily. She thought for a moment. Then she softly said, "I love them. And, I'm glad they love Ore. ...I have always loved and supported Rei. As he has grown, my surety of that has grown with him as well. To stand at his back, and at the side of Ore — these have always been my goals.

"As for Mistress Mizi, it's been like watching a brilliant red sun rise over the horizon, ever so slowly approaching the sun that has stood in my blue sky for the longest time, and finding great joy in the approaching and in their dance in the sky.

"What will it continue to look like? ... It's like I'm a pool upon the darkened land. When I look into the sky I see the moon I love to gaze upon that is Kase brightly reflecting the light of the two suns, and I'm glad I'm able to see that light.

"I also wish I could rise up from the earth and be a moon, too. ...To dance with the moon I love within the light of the suns. ...That is my dream." Ilena's voice had been growing quieter, her words coming slower, and now her breathing turned into the soft steady breathing of the sleeping.

Ore held her hand for a long time. Then he picked it up and kissed the back of it gently. Putting it back down, he released it and moved the chair and himself to their proper places.

She'd supported Rei as Prince since he was born because she was the First Princess, and because she loved him as she loved all who she chose — including himself, who'd been chosen so many years ago. She'd begun to watch over Mizi when Rei chose her, the same as she'd watched over both Rei and Ore, and she'd come to love her as well. Those were the answers Ore needed to hear.

Still.... *How is it in your dream you are the least of the lights? Do you not know you are a sun as well? ...And if I am a moon, how can a sun dance with a moon?*

-o-o-o-

Sasou, twenty–eight–years–old King of Ryokudo, sat in his velvet evening robe in the overstuffed lounge chair in his apartment. For half his life he'd been running the kingdom of Ryokudo. For even longer he'd been watching one thin, scrappy, black–haired waif of a girl. One who had more strength and firm commitment to her goals than almost anyone else other than himself.

He rubbed his fingers over the letter he'd received that morning. It had come by messenger bird, arriving in the very early hours no doubt, marked for Sasou's eyes only and bound in the blue ribbon that identified missives from his younger brother. Typically such messages between them were somewhat important. Even if they weren't it was right to afford each other the proper respect of not letting them languish. The answers sometimes could, however.

Sasou had finished his task of that moment, then lifted the message. It was a bit long of a letter to come by messenger bird, which had piqued his curiosity. The first scan of the first paragraph had made Sasou put it down, setting it to the side.

He'd not let his face register anything, but his heart had suddenly started beating faster, and he couldn't tell if it was fear (a thing he fastidiously worked hard to not feel), or the thrill of anticipation like the sun finally bursting up out of the sea to shine brightly on it and upon all the sky around it.

He'd held on to the letter until he'd reached his apartment following dinner. He'd not stayed over–late to the meal, nor to his office afterwords, earning him an interesting look of approval mixed with supreme curiosity from his head aide, Michael Barret. Likely his guardian had also noted that Sasou hadn't faced the letter, nor written an immediate response, since the messenger bird had arrived on the office balcony. Lord Barret had found the bird there when he'd arrived that morning and retrieved the message from it.

Sasou had tucked the letter into his jacket when Lord Barret hadn't been watching. It wasn't like the man wouldn't also be thrilled with what it contained (he had a soft spot for the said waif), it was that Sasou needed to be in a place he could properly face what the letter said, and that was best done alone the first time. He'd already sent all of his servants out of the apartment once they'd been satisfied with their fussing.

Sasou took a deep breath and unfolded the letter again. The gas lamp next to him flickered slightly, but provided plenty of clear lighting to read Rei's careful lettering.

Sasou Touka, King Ryokudo,

It wasn't common for Rei to be so formal in his letters. Only when they contained very important things of note to the kingdom, or if he was trying to very carefully feel his older brother out. Sasou was already sure it was both this time, based on his initial scan of the letter.

While investigating the matter of the assassination of the Lady Tokumade
—

Sasou could easily imagine that his brother had erased and started over multiple times that singular sentence and what followed that opening phrase. It read very much like Andrew hadn't helped with the letter. Sasou knew how much Rei hated to write letters to him, and how heavily he relied on Andrew to see they were worded perfectly.

To have forgone that almost necessary assistance spoke to just how important the letter was to the kingdom, and the level of secrecy Rei had decided the message contained within it required. Sasou could forgive somewhat the minor mistakes contained in this letter. Rei had been right to keep it a secret even from his most trusted aide.

Sasou smoothed the letter on his knee again, his eyes searching for the place he'd left off, trying to not jump ahead. He really didn't want to rush this letter. He needed to face it not just as a man, but as the King as well.

— information gathered from the main witness to the event led me to look more deeply into her own past. Ilena, Steward to the Earl Tokumade, has been in protective custody since she was retrieved from the site of the assassination. I have ordered her injuries to be tended to properly here at Castle Nijou so that she can testify before the Lord's Court that will be held when this office has finished compiling the evidence against Earl Tokumade himself.

Sasou paused again, looking out of the window that looked east towards the mountain that divided Ryokudo from Brulac. It wasn't a calming direction to look, but it was a beautiful mountain.

Sasou considered the first paragraph. It was right and proper for the Regent of Suiran to take care of an important witness to an assassination, particularly if the man behind it was a lord. In this case, Sasou felt particularly vindicated. That lord was an Untouchable, and Sasou had been waiting for him to fall for many years now. His own efforts had gone into laying the foundation for that fall, as a matter of fact.

Even more than his own efforts, the efforts of that same Steward had been even greater for the same outcome to arrive. That it was finally within their grasp was something to reach out for and not let slip away. Thus why Sasou had already sent guards of his own to make sure that Miss Ilena stayed alive to testify at the upcoming Lord's Court.

My Messenger, Sir Ore, admitted to me nearly immediately upon my arrival at Osterly Garrison to confirm for myself the assassination, that he knew Miss Ilena from before, when he had also lived at Tokumade. I'm sure Your Majesty's office is already aware that Ore is the youngest son of Tokumade, and its heir. He let me know at that time that Miss Ilena was a cousin, from what he could remember.

Based on his strong attachment to her and that comment, I had my office investigate more closely who Miss Ilena might be. There were several possibilites, but one was particularly concerning and significant.

Given that she of herself hadn't made any claims to any family relationships with Sir Ore, but had been willing to trust him with answers to questions about herself and the case, I asked him last evening to specifically ask Miss Ilena how she had come to be living at Tokumade. His report this morning sufficiently coincided with the research of this office, that I chose to speak with Queen Mother Kata early this afternoon.

Sasou drew in a long calming breath. His brother had acted with proper speed to determine something so important. Even more telling was that he'd sent this letter directly as well. It spoke to Rei's continued willingness to be a servant and support to Sasou as King, which he always found relieving and held gratitude for. It also spoke to Rei understanding the strength of taking that same position. Sasou wouldn't be able to deny him any requests based on any question of his loyalty.

The mentions of Ore specifically were also calculated to prove Ore's loyalty. Sasou already knew Ore was completely loyal to Rei, but these statements had been phrased to point to that same loyalty being loyalty to the King. Sasou blinked. Those proofs were good to have in hand as well, even if they were difficult at the moment.

Upon receiving from Queen Mother Kata the proper and sufficient tests of evidence for the final understanding, I went directly to Miss Ilena's room. I confronted her alone and directly. Just as directly she answered me with the story of who she was, and what the proofs were. When I had heard sufficient,

I called Lady Mizi, who is her medic and caretaker and has been since Miss Ilena's retrieval from the assassination site, into the room.

Without letting Lady Mizi know what my purposes were, I asked her to assist me so that I could see the physical proof myself, since Lady Ilena is incapable of moving of herself as of yet. I wish to inform you that I have seen with my own eyes the proofs and have heard with my own ears the same. Miss Ilena is the missing Princess Thailena Touka Polov of Selicia and of Ryokudo.

Sasou had to stop reading. He was glad to not be holding the paper in his hand. His hand was shaking, even though it was merely resting on his knee to hold the letter in place for reading. He closed his eyes and breathed.

He'd already known it; for many years he'd known it. But to read the words, to know that Rei had seen the proofs that he himself had seen as a child, to know that his beloved cousin was truly alive and finally within the walls of the House of Touka where she belonged left him stript of his crown, as he'd known it would. Only she had ever been able to help him rest and know that as a man he was as much beloved as he was as a king.

Not really wanting to be that man just yet, he couldn't prevent it. Tears slowly slipped down his cheeks, escaping from under his closed eyelids. He'd been so afraid he'd lost her when the news of the coup came and she'd not been found — alive or dead. Only that she hadn't been found with her parents had given him any hope for years. Then when he'd seen her again, the one brief time, tied to the Untouchable House of Shicchi, he'd been stricken and furious simultaneously.

It hadn't been a sure thing until he'd researched it himself. She'd proven it to him more than once since then. How she'd greeted Lord Barret when he'd gone to prove her for himself. How she'd worked with him to bring down lords and nightwalkers alike once she'd reached her own position of strength. And then her letters to him when she'd worked up the courage to communicate with him personally.

Never had she openly stated who she was, giving him the ability to pretend so that he wouldn't have to call her up too soon. She'd done the same with Rei, it sounded like. Made him come to her first, made him force her to admit it. Likely she'd also advised Rei that he would have to let Sasou know immediately, since she knew he was watching her.

Sasou looked down at the letter again and smoothed his hand slowly over it as if he could soothe Ilena herself with the motion. She was likely both just as happy as he that they knew, and was likely frightened as well. Life would have to be different for all of them from this time on. It was difficult even for Sasou.

He loved his cousin more than he loved almost anyone else in the kingdom, yet she would never be by his side, never any closer than Suiran and Rei's side. He'd decided that long ago, also long before he'd become king. Since then, he'd only seen it had to be. The whole of the kingdom would come crashing down otherwise.

Tarc had made it even more a requirement, and Tarc was what had made her have to come back to them. Sasou wouldn't deny Rei or Ore from having her — he would only be supremely jealous for all of his life. A jealousy he would keep buried very deep because his requirement to Ryokudo and its peace and prosperity was so strict.

It would be enough to know that she was supporting him and the kingdom from where she would be placed. She would still work with him, still be where they could meet and talk. If she could pass her final tests, then being able to acknowledge her as sister and cousin would give him the rights to be with her when he would need her most, and would be sufficient.

Sasou waited until those thoughts and time helped him calm down. He sat in his chair a little longer, then rose to his feet to walk to the small desk near the fireplace. He pulled out pen, ink, and a small piece of paper. His return letter was only one sentence long. He folded it and walked to the door to his apartment and opened it.

The guards on the door glanced at him. He handed the letter to one of them. "See this is sent immediately by messenger bird to Prince Rei."

The guard took it and bowed. "Yes, Sire."

Sasou closed the door to his apartment again. He blew out the lights in the room and walked by the pale glow of the embers in his fireplace to his bed. He slipped out of his robe, to leave it lying across the foot of his bed. He climbed into his bed and lay down, his hand still holding tightly to the letter, taking it with him into sleep — his comfort finally after sixteen years. Thailena was alive.

-0-0-0-

In the morning, when Mizi arrived in Ilena's room and woke Ore up, he sleepily stumbled to his room and dropped on his bed, falling back to sleep for a few more hours. In the midst of getting himself ready to go to the Rose Office, he stopped and looked at the books he'd dropped on his nightstand.

He touched the history of Ryokudo. He wanted to show that passage to Rei. The one that made him think Earl Shicchi knew Ilena was the princess. He slipped it into his jacket, leaving the other one in his room.

Everyone in the Rose office was very busy as usual, so he got to work, but he was waiting for a break time. He set the book down on his desk so he could talk to Rei about it. He completed a stack of work on his desk and stood to move it to the table of things to be filed. As he did, he brushed against the book and it fell to the ground. Andrew stood up and picked it up for him, since his arms were full.

All of a sudden Rei was standing next to Andrew, snatching the book out of his hand. Both other men were surprised by his sudden move. "Why do you have this book?" Rei asked Ore accusingly.

"I have a question for Master about something in it," Ore answered innocently.

Rei's face closed down hard. "I won't answer it. Don't touch this book again." He took it to the bookshelf and put it on the very top shelf in the corner, where he could keep an eye on it. Then he sat back down and went back to work.

Ore blinked. Andrew and he looked at each other, stunned. Andrew shrugged. Ore shook his head, feeling very sad, and finished setting his work pile down, then returned to work. He wouldn't be able to obey Rei in this thing.

Later that afternoon, Rei had an informal tea to attend. Andrew and Mina found a way to make sure Ore was there with them to watch over Rei. The three of them stood together along one edge of the small formal garden, Ore in the middle feeling a bit like he was a prisoner being guarded again, just like when they'd made him return to Osterly garrison.

"So, what was that about, Ore?" Andrew asked him. They were all facing into the garden, but they used this way to converse on a regular basis when they didn't want Rei to overhear.

"Ah, well, if Master doesn't want it talked about...," he tried to not get into more trouble.

"Ore," Mina's voice was dangerous, and she fingered her knife.

He stood up straighter and gulped. Of course he must cave in the end, but what part should he tell them about? "It's a history of Ryokudo detailing the rule of Master's father up until his death."

"Well, that would contain sad memories...," Andrew allowed.

Ore shook his head. "It's not that. Well, it might be partly that, but that's not what I was going to ask him about. ...Do you remember my report from when I talked to Miss Ilena about how she'd come to the Earldom?" They both indicated they did.

"That book includes that history. It seems that the Queen Mother's sister was married into the royal family of Selicia. The third prince. The book says that they had a daughter, born about five years before Master. It also says that a few years after Master was born, — Did you know he was born in Springthree? Are we going to get him a present?"

"Ore," hissed Mina.

"Ah, right. — They were all killed in a revolutionary uprising in Selicia. Miss Ilena said her family had supported the outgoing rulers, and they were all being killed. She said she'd seen her parents flee the city and had to leave separately, but couldn't find them." His heart hurt thinking about it again.

"Last night, as I was thinking on it, it suddenly seemed to me that the times and ages of Miss Ilena's story matched the story of the little princess." Both Andrew and Mina were quiet. They weren't going to protest? "Well, anyway, I was going to ask Master if it was possible, but he wouldn't let me."

"She doesn't look anything like Rei or his mother," Andrew tested Ore's theory.

"Well, no, but she does look like a certain high lord of Selicia that was pictured in the one book of Selicia history we have in the library."

"Ore! Just how much research did you do on your own?" They were shocked he'd gone to the library and picked up books on his own initiative.

"I can do it occasionally, you know. It just has to be interesting enough. Also," he scowled in mock frustration, "she certainly has the Ryokudo royal family temperament, and drive. I'd even told Master himself they were very similar."

Andrew and Mina looked at each other. "Ore, we have a thing to tell you," Mina said. Ore listened closely to Mina's story of what had happened the afternoon before as they'd followed Rei to his mother's office, then to Ilena's room, and what had happened after he'd come out, up until the time he'd sent his letter to King Sasou via message bird. It did seem like odd behavior.

Then Andrew told Ore what Mizi had told him about what had happened in the room after she was called in. Ore felt like he couldn't breathe, almost. He definitely wasn't seeing well.

It wasn't that he was surprised that Rei had confirmed it for himself, that Ilena was the princess. He'd already surmised that. It was that Andrew had said that Mizi said, "because she is marked she is no longer free." And she also said, "what we have done to help her remain in that place will decide whether she may stay or if King Sasou will take her for himself."

Ore had given Rei his reins freely. Ilena had been taken forcefully, thrust into a life of forced obedience, of likely being placed into a space not of her own choosing, because Pakyo had decided to make it so. Ore ached for her, and he was furious. To Ore it felt like his brother was telling him, "If you won't come to her so I can control you both, I'll destroy her dreams and make it impossible for the two of you to ever be together."

Maybe Ilena was right and Pakyo really had finally slipped back into the madness he'd been in after the death of their father. Ore couldn't know, but if Pakyo had done it to make Ore finally stop running and turn to face him ...it had worked. He was done running. It was his turn to protect Ilena. He would start with removing the influence of the Earl altogether. Then he, too, would do his part to help her stand in the place of her choosing, so that Pakyo couldn't have the reward of having taken that from her.

Andrew and Mina looked with concern at Ore. His face was as dark as they'd ever seen it. "Ore?" Mina asked softly, her worry coloring her voice.

"I need to speak to Master. Will you help me?"

His friends looked at each other. *He has something more he knows. Something important to all of this.* They faced forward again, standing tall, and nodded. Ore was grateful for their support and their strength they lent to him.

CHAPTER 12 Understanding the Proper Board

That evening, Andrew and Mina finished up their work a little early and excused themselves, leaving Rei and Ore alone in the office. Rei wrapped up what he was working on, then looked up at Ore. "You wanted to speak to me?" His face was as closed as Ore's was hard. Rei didn't want to talk about Ilena, and Ore was determined to.

Well, Ore really wanted to talk about Earl Shicchi. If he went with that route, they might not clash too badly. Ore walked up to Rei's desk and stood at relaxed attention, his hands behind his back. "Master, there's a thing Miss Ilena doesn't know. It's about Earl Shicchi."

That got Rei's attention and he visibly switched mental tracks. "The Earl?"

Ore nodded, then went and took down the book he'd brought in earlier. He flipped to the page that discussed the visit of the Selician royals to his family home. He found the passage, marked it with his finger, and put it in front of Rei. "Read this." Rei did so quickly — it was a brief passage — then looked back up at Ore, waiting for an explanation.

"I was young enough at the time of this visit to not understand what was going on, or who came, but my eldest brother was old enough to not only understand, but to remember." He waited. The light of understanding came into Rei's eyes and he sat straight up. "I know you can't speak of it, Master. You don't have to. Mister Andrew, Miss Mina, and I already know. We'll support you."

"Wha..?" Rei was surprised, then rueful. He should know by now that he couldn't keep things from those closest to him. They definitely knew him too well. He closed his eyes briefly. "Thank you." He was very grateful. He didn't have to carry the burden of the knowledge alone, but he also didn't have to do a thing he shouldn't do. That was why he loved them.

"Master, I spoke with Miss Ilena last night about how she knows I'm Kase. What it took to convince her was more than what it took to convince my brother. For him, it was enough that she rescued me from death." He put his hand on his chest over his scar.

Rei had seen it before and understood. "She healed you?"

Ore nodded. "She said she followed after me and bandaged it as best she could, then left me to draw away my brother from my hiding place. But he wouldn't believe her, when she said she hadn't found me.

"I believe he allowed her to be the steward of the House to teach her how to lead in the way she would need to be able to lead, and I believe he desired to have me, alive, so that through her claim on me, he could have power. If not here, then in Selicia." Rei's eyes glittered dangerously. He was as angry as Ore at the Earl with that thought.

"I've been trying to understand why he's chosen to let her go at this time. It seems contrary to his being able to have that power. I believe that four months ago when he sent Miss Ilena to Osterly he already had a plan, but I can't determine that plan.

"I can only see that he knew Mistress and I would also be going to Osterly. That he knew I followed after Mistress and she would want to help the injured. He ordered his assassin to allow us to pass unharmed, then to make sure Miss Ilena was the only one to survive, but to survive injured so that she and I would meet again, and she would be brought here.

"But I don't understand why he should want that, why he should seem to give up his access to power, even his very life, knowing that she hates him and would use this as an opportunity to destroy him. She said last night that he's descending into madness again. That he's a 'pawn to be cast away'." Rei raised an eyebrow. "The only thing I can see is that he's stolen her freedom from her in front of my face. He knows I won't forgive him for it. He's forced me to turn and face him."

"Why would he give up the ability to control you and a nation merely for a confrontation?" Rei asked. "Even if he wanted you dead, if he wanted power he wouldn't have given Ilena away."

"I don't know. The only explanation I have to understand it is as she said. He's mad with the same madness that killed my second brother. He now only cares to see my face again so that he might rid himself of it."

-o-o-o-

Rei thought for a long moment. "There's some reason he believes that he can no longer control you, her, or her through you. If his opportunity's gone, then he would at least have his revenge upon you." Rei tapped the desktop and thought aloud for a moment. "Is it because you've given yourself to me?"

Ore considered then shook his head. "They've both known that for many years."

"So it's something more recent that's happened. ...Is it because I was transferred here by my brother?" For some reason Rei couldn't name, it felt right. A strategic piece on the board had been moved. The Earl had moved in response.

The board that had been played was Sasou's board. The Earl wanted Ilena to be found by Rei to force Sasou's hand. Why? It was going to take careful thought to figure out. It had always frustrated Rei that he could never quite see Sasou's board and what was happening on it.

Ilena had said Sasou knew about her and her whereabouts; had watched over her, but made no move to remove her from her place. That meant he knew what she was learning, probably even what place she was setting herself up to be in. She'd certainly not kept that a secret. He would have redirected her early if he wanted something else for her.

Sasou was very good at letting people do their best to be in the place they wanted to be, then using them precisely and to excellent effect in that place...if they passed his tests. Rei reached out and picked up the message that had come to him on the breakfast cart that morning. He read it again. *I will come to see for myself.*

The surface message was, *I want to see if it really is her. I want to see the proof myself.* But like his own message to Sasou, there were always layers to Sasou's brief words.

The next layer down was what bound Rei from telling anyone who and what she was. Sasou wanted to prove her to see if she was worthy of being claimed by the house Touka and publicly recognized as the missing princess.

The third layer was political. Whether or not Ilena was publicly recognized, they couldn't let her go because she was the third most valuable political piece on the board, after Sasou and Rei themselves. Where she ended up, what she was told to do by Sasou, was as important to Ryokudo as what Sasou did with Rei.

"Ore...tell me...how did she know you were going to be in that fight? How did they know you followed Mizi? ...What are the details of that story?"

Ore answered him completely. While he was typically terse and cryptic in his speech, when he gave reports they were detailed, as if he'd memorized them and was repeating them back. He knew that any detail could be important. When he was done, he waited patiently again.

Ilena had told him. In this story, she had finally told Rei what he had suspected already, already seen the cusp of. The research surgeon, the old man Ore said was called "Grandfather", the fact that Ilena was both "the Missus" and "Mother", were all examples.

She was the spider at the center of an information web. She separated it between the underworld, the "dark network", and those who were good people, the "light network". She understood how to deal with both sides. She could call in witnesses for him because she had, years before, known there would come a time she would need them. *He* would need them.

For years now she'd been preparing for this very time, for his sake. He'd seen it, but now he understood what the space was that she'd been making for herself. Ilena had told him herself and had followed through. She'd seen a need, both for herself to find Ore, and then also for him, because he'd neglected to see it for himself.

Or rather, he hadn't been encouraged to see it. He knew his brother had a similar network from experience, but Sasou hadn't trained him to put one into place for himself. Rei hadn't thought much of it because he'd thought Sasou's would be sufficient for the protection of Ryokudo and Sasou would let him know what he needed to know.

But it clouded Rei's board. It was what made it difficult to see all of Sasou's board. Just what would happen if he didn't have Ilena's information today? How much information did she have yet that he didn't know? ...Was she doling it out slowly not just because she did a reciprocal trade with information, but also because she was testing him?

She was a Touka. There was no way she wasn't testing him. He'd failed one test already. She wouldn't give him her network if he couldn't use it properly. ...No...she was training him. Step by careful step, protecting what she'd built at the same time. "*Haaah....*" Like he wanted more training just when he thought he'd graduated up from it.

"Master?"

Rei waved his hand. "Sorry. Still thinking." Ore relaxed.

There was that one statement that stood out. Ore said that she'd found him again, after he'd recovered from his wound, after he'd appeared at Ichijou Castle. That one of her people had been allowed by Sasou to watch over the three of them meant Sasou was aware of her network, knew she was at the center of it and was willing to work in concert with it, and had probably known for some time.

Rei considered their ages. It was possible that she'd begun to put it together long before Sasou even considered whether or not to teach Rei about it. If Sasou had decided not to teach it to Rei at all...did that mean that he already approved? What if his brother wanted to know not whether Ilena could stand in the place she'd made for herself, but if he, Rei, could learn to use her in that place? And that was why she was teaching him, little by little, being ever so careful.

If Rei wanted to keep Ilena, he'd have to learn how to use her and her networks effectively. He'd have to show he understood the value of what she offered. He'd have to refuse to let her go. That would mean training her to come to his wrist, this wild falcon he'd captured.

Rei looked up at Ore. "Ore, I believe Ilena knows much more than she's telling us. There's a piece missing from the picture still. She wants to know if I can figure out what it is. She tells me step by step a thing I'm ready to know because I've asked to know it, whether it's you who asks the question, or me. I'll think about what you've said. Within it is the next question I need to ask. ...Please continue asking her questions as well. Your assistance in this matter is very valuable." Ore nodded.

"Also, I understand what her place is, and what my brother wants to see in order for me to keep her." Ore's eyes lit up. Knowing was the greater part of the battle. "I'll say it again, Ore. I need you to stand by her side."

Ore sighed. "...Do you know what she said to me on the way to the castle, after she made Mistress ride with you?"

"No."

"She said she was going to be even more difficult than you're thinking. I'll ask you again. Are you sure it's me you want to stand beside her?"

Rei thought on it only briefly. Ilena was most certainly going to be difficult. She was of the finest breed there was. There was no question he wanted her; that the struggle would be well worth the result if he won out in the end. And there was equally no question that the only man she would listen to would be Ore. "Yes."

Rei paused, another thought coming to his mind. "Is there something that would stand in your way of doing it?" Ore had been about to move, but stopped and raised an eyebrow in question. Rei hesitated, then said, "When you first agreed to follow Mizi for me, you said that there was one in Tokumade that you would bring out, and would leave me for if that one couldn't stay. ...Was it Ilena, or someone else?"

Ore dropped his eyes, then slowly bowed a quarter bow, answering as he held it. "It was indeed Miss Ilena. I am already hers first. Where she goes, I will also go, ...although I have no desire to leave Master."

Rei sat back, steepling his fingers together. "I also have no desire to lose Ore," he answered quietly. The tips of Ore's ears went faintly pink. "However, if that's your answer then it will be fine. If it was someone else, then I would have worried. Please walk by her side so that I may continue to have both of you with me to strengthen me."

Ore bowed deeper. "Yes, Master." Then he stood up straight and grinned, "But this time, I'll call on all of you to help if I get into trouble, not just Master."

Rei answered him very seriously, "You do that."

"Hoooh? You believe me, then?"

Rei just looked at Ore. *I'd be crazy not to.*

-o-o-o-

Ore went back to work at his desk, as it wasn't time yet to go to Ilena, and Rei wasn't ready to leave yet. Rei continued to think about what he'd been told.

Even back in Osterly, Ore had expected the Earl to try both assassination and kidnapping to retrieve Ilena or to silence her so she couldn't tell Rei what she knew. The only thing in town that had been tried was that they wanted to confirm she was there and in Rei's hands.

On the way to the castle there'd been the two failed ambushes, neither of which was effectively planned to begin with. They'd been backed by incompetence, or they were for another purpose altogether. ...Such as information gathering, the same as in Osterly: to find out if she was really dead, or how important she was to Rei, or both.

Neither Ilena nor Ore believed the Earl wanted Rei, only them and what they could give him. Anyone in the underworld in Kouzanshi would have known Ore followed Mizi. Most anyone paying attention would know that Mizi stood next to Rei.

The Earl had left Ore alone for over three years, even though he'd been in plain sight, even though he should recognize him, even though he'd even been at his house the day before the accident. He hadn't wanted Ore. All the evidence pointed to someone wanting Ilena and Rei together. Why?

Someone. Someone else? Was there someone else making the decisions now? Ore said she'd called the Earl a "pawn worth throwing away" and that he wasn't her pawn. Was the Earl following the orders of someone else? Then Rei remembered a thing Ilena had said in their first meeting. "If you kill *an* 'Earl Shicchi' you are not assured of having killed *the* Earl Shicchi. ...Indeed, one of them is more terrible than Pakyo himself."

Rei lept up from his seat, his hands coming palm down on his desk, his eyes wide but only seeing the game being set up before him as he teased it out. The Earl had become the pawn of someone else, someone who could pass as his double. Rei picked up the book Ore had left on his desk. He quickly read all the passages pertaining to her and her story.

The Earl was related to the Polov's. Any Polov that had escaped the massacre would want revenge, would want to get back in power. If there weren't any living but Ilena, Pakyo Shicchi was the next closest heir to Ilena for the throne of Selicia. Rei's heart raced and he breathed a deep breath.

They were being asked if Ryokudo wanted to get revenge and put the Polov's back on the throne of Selicia. Either one — the Earl or his double if he knew — could pass as the Earl and sit that throne. Rei sat back down with a thump, stunned.

Ore said that Ilena said the Earl intended to die, to end the House of Shicchi in a blaze of glory. He would leave only Ore, whom Ilena wanted. What would make that worth it? If Ore could sit with Ilena on a throne. The double had to know of the family history as well, had to be planning to take Pakyo's place.

Rei looked up at Ore. He was leaning on his elbow, watching Rei instead of doing his work, infatuation on his face. "Really, Master. I do love to watch you work."

"Lazy bastard. Save that look for someone who wants to see it."

"Ore has been working hard! Didn't I deserve some kind of reward? ...Well I've taken it anyway. Is the smoke done coming out your ears now?"

"Just how much research did you do?" Rei touched the Ryokudo history book.

Ore raised an eyebrow. "There's another book just like it of Selicia history, but you can't have it."

Rei raised an eyebrow back at him for saying "can't" to his master, but otherwise let it pass. "Just tell me. Who else in the Selicia royal line was living at the time of the coup?"

Ore thought back to what he'd read. "The king, two brothers — Ilena's father was the youngest. Their wives. The King had two sons, one daughter in the middle. The second had one infant son. And Ilena."

"What were the ages of the King's children?"

"The crown prince was two years younger than my eldest brother. The daughter was two years older than me. The second son was a year older than Ilena...or was it a year younger?" his face creased into a frown.

"That's good enough," Rei said.

"But...," Ore continued, "there was one other."

"Oh?"

"He wasn't listed in the royal line, only in the history. The old king had a fourth son, the youngest. His father banished him and removed him from the succession."

"Oh? Why?"

"His second queen wife, who was younger, gave birth to the child after the time the king was capable of having children. He sent her away with the child, telling them to never return."

Rei stared at Ore. "Did the history say where they went?"

"No, but Ilena says to the north is desert lords and nomads and the soldiers protect that border. To the west is Tarc which Selicia ignored, and it was Tarc who made the House fall."

That was it. Ilena's youngest uncle wanted the throne he'd been denied. "Is it time for you to see Ilena yet?"

"Are you ready to ask your question?"

"Yes, and I want to hear the answer myself."

"Yes, Master." Ore stood. "We may go now. She won't sleep until I'm with her. But once I am with her there's only a brief window in which to receive answers before she does sleep."

"She doesn't sleep well?" Rei asked as they walked out the door.

"Those who grew up in the House of Shicchi don't sleep well in mansions with small rooms."

Rei looked knowingly at Ore, "Which is why you sleep in the trees or in my room, and wander the halls and roof at night." Ore nodded, once.

-o-o-o-

When they neared the medical wing, Ore said, "I usually don't light a light when I'm in the room. Even though I wish to hear answers to questions, I also wish for her to sleep."

Rei thought about it. "Let's do it as you usually do it. I'll follow you in and listen to the answer and leave when she's asleep." Ore wasn't sure that was going to work, but he nodded dutifully. "Ask her this question: Why did the Earl agree to make you his steward?"

"Why do you want that question?"

"The answer will confirm my understanding." Ore accepted that answer.

When they arrived, Ryan was outside the door as usual, working on his research. "You're early," he noted and went to greet Rei. Rei raised his finger to his mouth. Ryan obediently settled on just a simple bow.

"Yes, I was done enough for tonight. You may go if you like," Ore offered, as if Rei wasn't there with them.

Ryan collected his things and, bowing once again, left. Ore led the way into Ilena's room. From the light of the door, he could see that her eyes were closed, as usual. He allowed Rei to find a place to stand before closing the door, then went to his usual spot and settled down.

"You're early, Ore," Ilena said. "You have a question that needs answering so quickly?"

Ore smiled. She did indeed know Rei was here, but would Rei understand that yet? He'd never been a part of the darkness, so he didn't quite understand what it meant to have to know every sound, every scent, every change in order to live, ...although he was very good. Even now, he was quieting his breath as much as possible and holding very still.

"I suppose," Ore answered easily and honestly. He waited a moment before asking. It always helped to get her to relax into the answer first. "Have you been resting appropriately today?"

She answered in a tone that was both amused and frustrated, "No, Ore, of course not. I'm no longer capable of 'rest'. I'm afraid I've passed from cross to testy."

"Ah, that's good to know. I shall do my best to continue to come only at night then. But does that mean you're now testing Mistress' patience with you?"

"Not just yet. I've found an acceptable distraction she's willing to help me with. I'm afraid I snapped a little at Ryan, since he gets me as I'm getting tired in the evening."

Ore frowned so that she could hear his displeasure with her, "Did you appropriately apologize?"

"Yes, I did," Ilena answered humbly, "and I also explained to him that I'm testy and why. He'll properly scold me next time it occurs, he promised me."

"That's good. You mustn't frighten him."

"Yes, Ore." Again, her response was humble. Then she sighed. "...But that means you're still the one who has to bear it."

"You won't be properly kind to me also?" he knew he was teasing her.

"No, Ore. Isn't it our way to be unkind to each other from the beginning? Or are you done with that and I haven't noticed?"

Ore could feel Rei's disapproving look directed towards him, and he bowed his head in shame. "I'm sorry, Miss Ilena. I'm done with it."

"Just as of today?" she wanted to know if it was only because Rei was in the room.

"No. From before I left."

She was quiet for a while. "That's a long time ago, Ore." She sounded contrite but also something else...longing?

"So, will you be kind?"

Ilena sighed. "I have no desire to be unkind to Ore. ...But then, to whom shall I scream my distress?"

Ore felt Rei react to that question, so he waited. Then he felt Rei's question, and asked it. "Who's capable of receiving it?" Ilena's surprise was palatable. "Do you have someone?" Ore pressed her.

Ilena's intake of breath was more of a sob. "Yes. There are two. My nurse, whom you may remember, and a maid who became a friend. They are capable of calmly passing through my storms, although it takes both of them on my fiercest days."

Ilena is still very lonely. Ore looked over at Rei's faint shadow questioningly. Rei nodded. "I'll ask Master if I may speak with Grandfather on the matter."

The bed rustled as Ilena wiped the tears from her face. "Thank you."

Now he could ask her Rei's question. He waited for her to recover, then asked, "Why did the Earl agree to make you his steward?"

She pondered the question, puzzling over the meaning of it. Then she sighed. "This is a question that Ore can't hear the answer to alone."

"You won't tell me?"

"I won't tell you if you're alone. Ore requires another to be with him to hear the answer to this question." It was the first time she'd completely refused to answer in such a way.

"Am I sufficient, Ilena?" Rei asked, revealing himself. Ore wondered if she'd done it on purpose, although it hadn't seemed that way necessarily.

Ilena was quiet. "Ore's master is sufficient to hear with him, but you've said that you don't want others to hear some of what I must say." She must mean that she would need to reveal in some way who and what she was.

Rei considered it. "He's understood it on his own. You may speak it, but only in his presence."

"I understand." She seemed relieved. She paused a moment to find her starting point. "When I introduced the Little Death, as I've explained before, and Earl Shicchi agreed to my plan to use it, he was concerned. He wanted to know if I had any plans against him, but he also didn't want anyone else to know of his plans against them. Because I was always at his side, I knew everything, including those things he plotted against his own men.

"When I proposed the experiment, he said he would only agree if I would sleep in the nursery only accessible from the master bedroom. I asked him for how long. He said for as long as he kept me on the Little Death. I refused. There were many nights I needed to be doing other things...and I had no desire to be so close to the hand of death and a man I hated for as long as I anticipated having to take it.

"Rather, I suggested a four week trial period, saying that if I said nothing in that time to cause him concern, he'd allow me to return to my own room. With sufficient arguments he agreed, but required six weeks.

"By this time, the Earl had already found two doppelgängers. One was a weak man who knew nothing really of the Earl's plans but was good at playing the diplomat. The other was a strong and evil man who loved to stir up the Earl's men. They didn't know that each man was different.

"I'd hoped that within the time frame the Earl had selected, he would be able to remain at the house. However it was not to be. A week before the experiment was to be over, the Earl was called away. He chose to leave me at the house, afraid of what I might say in the presence of others while sleeping. He called for his double to come stay at the house.

"I begged for the weaker substitute, but the Earl wouldn't trust him with what I might say. The evil substitute knew all of the Earl's plans and what he didn't know that I might say didn't concern the Earl, thus he came to the house. The Earl explained to him what the experiment was and told him his life would be in jeopardy if he should touch me while I was sleeping. Then he left.

"The double was already used to me following him around, but this was new. The first morning after the first time he heard me sleep talk, he laughed and said he'd no idea I hated the Earl so much and asked, like you, why I wasn't dead. I told him, like to you, that the Earl already knew I hated him and yet I was incapable of acting on it.

"The double laughed again, saying his reward for putting up with my little scheme was going to be getting to hear my cries every night. While I would have loved to have escaped him, it was no different really than with the Earl anyway.

"As the Earl was becoming calm and the household as well, thus proving my use even more, the man who stood at his right hand over the fighting men became jealous, seeing that I was now favored to be by the Earl's side night and day. The right hand man, recognizing the change in the Earl to the one who delighted in bloodlust, suggested a plan.

"He said that all of the women in the household should learn what their rightful place was and should go through a teaching so that they would be obedient to the Earl and his men. He knew this kind of 'play' was the sort of thing this 'Earl' liked.

"The double didn't know that this was both unnecessary and redundant as he wasn't around to see the Earl deal out punishment. The proposal was that each woman be brought in and raped by as many of the men until she became unconscious. That in being made to submit until they succumbed, they would learn to submit in all things immediately.

"It was bad enough to consider that if the double agreed, and stayed to watch or even participated, that I would have to remain and watch as well without complaint the evil treatment of people I loved. I told the double, 'It isn't necessary. The people already fear you and are very obedient.'

"The right hand man had an answer. He challenged me, saying, 'They are very obedient to you, yet they won't obey us (that is, the Earl's men). They should also obey us. Aren't we the arm of the Earl? But perhaps, since they'll obey you, then it's only necessary to teach *you* to submit.'

"The Earl had never allowed the men to touch me in all my life, killing any who attempted it. When he proposed this, I realized he knew that this was not Pakyo but another man.

"The Earl's double was unsure. He knew the Earl kept me with him at all times, that he refused to allow even the double to touch me, and he didn't want to jeopardize his own position. I asked for permission to be able to handle the matter, and he allowed it." Ilena paused.

When she continued, her voice was cold. "I challenged him, in behalf of the household. The double granted permission and tossed me his knife. I snatched it out of the air and was at my opponent.

"He'd managed to draw his knife by the time I arrived at his side, and he brought it down on my shoulder, but before it could do more than slightly penetrate, my knife was through his neck. His falling weight caused his knife to pull down into my shoulder, but because of the Little Death I didn't feel it.

"The double, with the power of the Earl, declared that from that time on, by right of battle, I was the Earl's right hand, and they were all to be obedient to me. I warned the rest of the men against acting against the household and sent the men away to bury the man I killed.

"When the room was clear, the double told me to go with him to see Doctor Elliot. I asked why and he laughed. 'If the Earl sees you in such a state, he'll kill me, no?' and he gestured to my shoulder. I was surprised to see the blood.

"When we arrived at Doctor Elliot's office, it was necessary for me to remove my shirt so he could repair the damage. I sat with my back to the double, who waited lounging in the doorway, refusing to let me be alone. The wound was on my left shoulder, and he saw the markings on my right side first. He asked if they were scars from a previous fight. I answered they weren't.

"Then Doctor Elliot moved exposing the left side of my back so that the double could see the markings on the left. I looked over my shoulder at him and he was staring at them as if trying to decipher them. That concerned me, as I didn't know anyone who might be able to do so. When he noticed me looking at him he looked away until I turned back, but he said nothing. Then I felt cold steel against the back of my neck and he was telling the Doctor to back away.

"...Like for Ryokudo, there's a similar mark for the royal family of Selicia. It's in how I hold people's heads when I comfort them. As a very young child I frequently comforted my cousins, the King's children. When I would hold them, to remind them that they were Princes and a Princess, I would hold the mark that they'd received. It's slightly different from the mark of a child of Ryokudo in that it's raised and can be felt.

"To this day, I hold everyone that way, hoping to find if any of my cousins also escaped death, but can't tell me, the same as I can't. I believe he wasn't able to decipher my mark of Ryokudo, although perhaps he thought it was one after he was able to decipher my mark of Selicia.

"I didn't move, of course. He ran his hand through my hair, searching for the mark of Selicia. When he found it he separated the hairs and looked at it to confirm his suspicions. Then he backed away from me and allowed the Doctor to complete his work.

"When we were alone again later he told me, 'I'm your uncle, your father's youngest brother. If I'd known from the beginning I'd have treasured you as much as the Earl does, and even more.' Never in my life would I have expected that vile man to have been my uncle. I wouldn't believe it and demanded proof that he was my uncle. He said he'd allow me to see for myself.

"Before I could move, he'd snatched me by the head, grabbing my arm. He pulled me close so that I couldn't get away from him. As he placed my hand on his mark so that I'd know the truth of his statement, he said to me, close in my ear, 'Though you be my niece, if you whisper of who I am to the Earl or betray me, I shall have my way with you, and shall kill you after.' He held me a moment longer so that I understood that he was restraining himself from taking me right then, then he released me."

Ore's fists had been clenching tighter and tighter, and at that point he was ready to put knives through the eyes of this uncle if he were anywhere within reach. Rei reached out and put a firm hand on Ore's shoulder, squeezing it until Ore could calm down with a long silent breath. It was perhaps a good thing Ilena had said Ore couldn't listen to this story alone.

Ilena continued on, "With eyes that still threatened death, he told me that he would soon begin the transition from being obedient to the Earl to teaching the Earl to be obedient to him, and that I would properly play my part, neither interfering nor betraying him. I would start by agreeing with whatever plan he came up with to explain why I was now the right hand of the Earl, and I would keep silent about what had just happened, lest his own life and plans be in danger. He was just as careful to listen to my words at night after that until he left.

"His story to the Earl isn't important. It's sufficient to say that the Earl accepted that I would now be in that position. It was easiest for them to say that I was the Steward. In that position, I had the power I'd always desired so that my own plans could be more fully set in place, and they were able to have the greatest control over the words that came out of my mouth, although mine is greater."

"Your's is greater. ...You mean you can control what you say at night when you sleep talk," Rei said. Ore's ears perked up at that thought. Was that why he couldn't get her to tell him how she knew Rei during the sleep talking experiments?

"Yes, but also I can control who will hear what. My uncle threatened me with certain death for speaking what I've told you tonight. My life is now forfeit in his eyes. I locked it away so that only the one person who would need to hear and understand it could access it. If you hadn't been here, Rei, to receive that memory, it would never have been heard."

"But you knew it when Ore asked you the question?"

"No. He shed light on the lock, letting me know there was an answer to be given, and that it was safe to do so if the key was also present. There are many things in my memory that must be touched by one of you to be brought out. There are a few, such as this one, that require both of you. It's so I protect myself for the sake of Rei and Ore. And so that Rei and Ore may be protected by me."

Rei pondered a bit longer. "Ilena, the second ambush, when we were bringing you here to the castle, was that set by your uncle?"

"I don't know."

"Did you believe the Earl would have ordered it?"

"No."

"Then why did you think there might be a second ambush?"

"There are several others who've also been watching me. I don't know who among them it might have been. I'm only grateful that there wasn't an ambush for every one of them. That would have been a frustrating journey."

"Do you have many enemies?" Rei asked, somewhat surprised.

"More than I like." Ore was going to have to puzzle over that one for a while. Why would Ilena have made enemies?

Rei asked his next question. "Was it your uncle's plan to have the Earl's wife killed and you injured at just the right time for Ore and Mizi to find you?"

Ilena thought on that. "All of the plans from the last several years have come from my uncle's mouth to the Earl's ears, but have been carried out by the heart and will of the Earl."

Rei's next question was, "How do we ensure that your uncle will be present for us to remove when we go against Earl Shicchi?"

"If you can ask that question you likely already have an answer, but I'll give you one to ponder. Ask him to hand over the Earl personally as a sign of good faith. If played right, one of them will kill the other as a traitor, and you may kill the one left standing. ...You may know how to confirm who is who." It was an invitation.

Rei walked up to the side of her bed and felt for her arm. She picked up his hand, turned her head to face him, and placed his hand at the back of her head, under the strands of hair. He stood there for a moment, then moved away.

As he slipped his hand out of her hair, Ilena grabbed it, holding it firmly. "As much as I fear the Earl, I fear my uncle more. As much as I hate the Earl, I hate my uncle more. When you return from doing battle with them, bring me his head, that I may feel the mark and confirm for myself that he's dead. And bring me his left hand, that it may reside with the living right hand, leaving his body with no more means to plan nor to act." Her hatred and anger could not be constrained.

"I'll do it," Rei promised and she released his hand.

"I'll kill the Earl," Ore said from behind Rei, "for being willing to throw you away and take from you your freedom."

"Ore?" Ilena asked surprised.

Ore walked up to stand beside Rei and touched her on her head. "Because the Earl has allowed for the plan of your uncle to continue, I'll stand and face him beside Master. ...You'll no longer need to fear either."

"Thank you," she whispered.

His hand lingered slightly, then he turned to Rei. "Master, I'll take you to your room now."

"Good night, Ilena. Thank you for telling me the answers to my questions," Rei said.

"You're welcome," she replied.

-o-o-o-

Ore walked Rei to his bedroom, made sure he was secure, then returned to Ilena's room. She was resting, perhaps lightly sleeping, when he returned. He debated asking her any questions, although he had some on his lips.

As he stood in the middle of the room, undecided, he heard her quietly say, "Ore?" It sounded like a plea. He walked over to her and, finding her hand, placed the back of his hand against it and took her middle finger with his.

"What's made you sad, Ore?" she asked, coming more awake.

Sad? Did I do this because I was sad? Ahhh..., because I'm sad for her. "I read the history, of both Selicia and Ryokudo. ...The Ryokudo history included a few sentences on your family's visit to Tokumade, that first time. It was apparently supposed to be a memorial of the marriage from three generations before, and a celebration to renew the ties between the nations since another marriage had occurred in our parent's generation."

"Oh. That's what it was." She hadn't known either.

"I think Pakyo remembered you, or at least your nurse. I think he knew who you were from the beginning."

Ilena sighed. "It's possible. Perhaps that would explain why he came to find you in my bed the night you left."

"Perhaps. ...I believe it also explains why he protected you and kept you by his side."

She seemed to smile. "Yes, that would explain that properly, wouldn't it."

"Did...did he really want Kase back dead, and not alive to use for his own gain?"

Ilena lifted their interlocked hands and kissed the tips of his fingers. A warmth spread up his hand and wrist from those fingertips. "Ore. I'm sure there are times he thought that, but there were also times where his rants against you were very fierce. Even though he was able to be calmer knowing what the members of the household thought and dreamed, he never recovered from the madness. It was — is — always with him.

"He could hold on to me, hoping for you, but without my uncle he could never have fully devised, or followed through on, a plan to encompass something so grand as what you're suggesting. Not this late into his madness.

"...I haven't lied to you in saying that he's ready to die. He's lived with the madness so long that he no longer wishes to live. My uncle had no difficulty in persuading him to the parts of the plan I did hear that have led to this time.

"He has the dream that you and I will sit upon the throne, and that soothes him. But he also knows that he'll die, and he is ...happy, as much as he is ever to be such a thing. He's determined to go fiercely and grandly.

"If you'll fight him, please don't throw your life away for the sake of pride, nor even for revenge. ...Give him a grand exit, but come home." She squeezed his middle finger with her own and kissed his palm, a reminder she claimed him and expressing her need to have him with her.

Ore leaned down and kissed her forehead. "I won't leave you alone," he promised quietly.

"I'll hold you to it," she told him in a voice that told him she was already drifting into sleep.

-o-o-o-

Rei had one last thing to do that night once he'd finished putting Ilena's story and answers to his questions onto the board properly. He needed to firmly stake his claim and let his brother know he understood his requirements.

He sat to his desk in his bedroom. This time, he was direct in his own preferred way. Sasou knew when Rei was direct to his face that he'd chosen to be stubborn and wouldn't be turned from his path.

Elder Brother, I know that you have groomed Ilena to stand by me as my Minister of Intelligence. I know that this matter with Earl Tokumade is my training by her to learn to use what she brings with her. I know that Tarc will be our test.

I know these things because you yourself neglected to train me in how to have and use an intelligence network. Such a thing is required to keep even a Region of a Kingdom safe. She has admitted herself that her networks are in the main to be used in behalf of the Region. Please...watch what we will do.

Rei Touka, First Prince Ryokudo, Regent Suiran

Mid–morning the following morning, the same letter was read then set down gently next to a report being reviewed. Sasou smiled a little sadly. Yes, Rei did know, now that he'd received Ilena and the critical information that was needed to keep their beloved country safe.

Sasou hoped that for all of their sake's it wasn't already too late. By his calculations it wasn't, but they were going to be very close. He'd tried to allow Ilena her freedom for as long as he could.

CHAPTER 13 Director of Intelligence

The next morning when Ore arrived at the Rose Office, Rei and the others were very busy at work as usual; however, Andrew and Mina advanced on Ore quickly. They knew he'd stayed to talk to Rei, but they'd also noticed the book was on Rei's desk now, not on the shelf. Also, Rei had sent a request for a badge of identification down to the castle staff office.

They thought Ore had taken a very long time to get in that morning, even though it was actually earlier than he'd been arriving lately. He'd managed to sleep well, finally.

"Ah, good morning...," he said to them as they cornered him before he'd even managed to get to his desk. He glanced at Rei. Rei was choosing to ignore them. *Well, then, I guess it's okay to let them know....*

"Hi. Talk," Mina was as short and to the point as usual. Ore was a little surprised she'd even tried to be polite and greet him first.

"How'd it go last night?" Andrew was, for him, just as to the point.

Ore grinned at them. "How much will you pay me...say two bottles each?"

"Ore...," scolded Andrew reprovingly.

"Done, and Andrew will cover mine," Mina said promptly, wanting to move along and knowing Ore's teases well by now.

"Hey! Mina!" Andrew complained at her. She was always doing things like that to him.

"Okay," Ore said, accepting Mina's agreement, his eyes lighting up. They always paid him well — Andrew couldn't bring himself to buy bad wines. "It went well."

"...."

"...."

"Ore...!" Even Andrew wasn't taking the joke.

"Fine, fine," Ore relented, leaning against the wall behind his desk where they'd pushed him to. He crossed his arms and one foot in front of the other. "I told Master that we already know. He's grateful, of course, that he doesn't have to make King Brother mad. That's why he's pretending to ignore us now." Rei's ears went a little red.

"I made him read the passage in the book that talks about the visit of the Selician Prince and the Ryokudo Princess to the Earldom of Tokumade on their way back from his birth celebration, and pointed out that the current Earl was old enough to remember that visit, and a certain young princess that was with them."

Hssss! They both got it just as quick.

Ore nodded in agreement. "Then I admitted I didn't understand why he would give her up to Master and King Brother when keeping her was more beneficial to him." They both agreed that was a good question. "Then Master sat and sat and had smoke pouring out his ears. He asked Ore a few questions, then said, 'Let's go ask Miss Ilena a question'."

"What was the question?" Andrew asked.

"Why did the Earl agree to make Miss Ilena the steward?"

Andrew looked puzzled. "Wasn't it because she came up with a way to calm him down with the Little Death?"

Ore shook his head. "That was the answer to 'why are you on the Little Death?', this is a different question." They waited to hear the answer. "He made her the steward because there are more than one 'Earl'. His double let her kill the Earl's right hand man in a duel the right hand man provoked.

"The Earl wouldn't have cared, but the opponent wounded her before dying, and the Earl cared about that. So the double made her the top dog of the whole pack and the House, then took her to the Doctor to get fixed up. While there, he saw the proof of who she was...and recognized it."

He waited and was rewarded when their eyes went wide when they understood that the Earl's double had seen what Rei had seen. What Rei had had to ask his mother to know, this double recognized himself.

"Who is he?" Andrew's voice was hard.

"Miss Ilena's uncle, her father's youngest bastard brother who was exiled with his mother before Miss Ilena was born. He forced her to secrecy after proving it to her. He's behind the accident at Osterly, and everything for the last number of years, although the Earl was happy to carry them out." Ore grimaced a little sourly.

"This uncle wants Miss Ilena here at the castle, then." Mina said.

"Why?" Andrew asked.

"Because she's his gift in exchange for an army to retake Selicia," Rei answered from his desk. All three aides looked at him in surprise.

"See," Ore said with a grin, "I told you lots of smoke poured out of his ears last night. ...And that he was listening," he added as an afterthought. "Ah! That means Master owes me two bottles, too!"

"Nope, I already knew it," Rei had a quick comeback, and Ore's face fell. Rei looked at the three aides and friends before him. He rose from his chair and walked over to stand with them. "Andrew, Mina, Ore, I'm taking Ilena with me. ...I realize, Andrew and Mina, that you don't know her yet, but I won't cast her off, nor will I give her up to my brother. Mizi and Ore have already accepted. I'm sorry I'm not at liberty to wait for you."

Andrew bowed. "We'll come to know for ourselves, but already the things we've read and seen have told us she supports you, Rei. It's sufficient for now." Mina nodded her head once in agreement.

"Thank you." Again, Rei was glad for such supportive friends. "From what Ilena's said, she's already passed my brother's test for the place she desires to stand in." That news surprised even Ore. "Mina, her careful movements are because she's training me how to use her in that place." Mina pondered that thought.

"As for the Earl and her uncle...," Rei walked back to his desk and they followed him, "...we'll continue to work as we've already decided, as for now they're the same person. When we formalize our battle plan, we'll need to ensure that the uncle is at that place as well. If we can remove him early, we won't have to bring Ryokudo into war negotiations."

"Remove? Not negotiate?" Mina asked.

Rei shook his head. "There's already sufficient evidence to decide we aren't interested in negotiating with him. Selicia is content at the moment with their rulership, and he was disinherited and isn't blood relation. He doesn't have sufficient claim, particularly now that I have Ilena and he doesn't."

They were a little confused. "If...he gave up his claim in giving up Miss Ilena...then why does he believe this plan can work?" asked Andrew.

"Because he's also being manipulated by someone else." He'd lost them, but he'd expected that. "The Earl and the uncle are both part of Ilena's training. If the uncle were the test, she would have separated them and let it go to negotiations, rather than tell me now. There's another thing after that which will be the test.

"The only reason I can see for the uncle to have lost the same advantage that the Earl did when Ilena was sent here is that there is yet another force acting behind him, manipulating him to also believe it was in his best interest. I don't have enough information yet to know what it will be, but what I have so far says that it will be a dealing with Tarc, and perhaps some with Selicia since they're a puppet of Tarc — or so she says."

He looked at them, debating, then decided to say it. "I'll make her my Director of Intelligence today. If we can learn to work together, and my brother will allow her to stay, she'll become the Minister."

Hsss! Ore drew in a shocked breath.

"When will you let her know?" asked Andrew.

"This afternoon," answered Rei with firmness.

"Do you hate me, Master?" Ore cried. "She'll fly against the jesses before she's ready! You heard last night how she's already straining against her restraints."

"Ore," Rei looked at him firmly, "I want to see what she can do with less than her full strength."

"*Haaah*...But still, Master," Ore put his hand to his eyes.

"Ore, she's already admitted she had her own restraints in her own place." Ore frowned, trying to understand. "Do you remember what she said about the two she would like to have by her side? That they can weather her storms?"

Ore thought about that. He nodded. They would be able to help him somewhat. Then, "Ah! The nurse!" He nodded more enthusiastically. "She is definitely capable."

"That's good," Rei was pleased to get Ore's confirmation that they would be able to get help, especially since Ore would still be in and out collecting the rest of the witnesses.

Ore looked speculative. "Master, there's also the possibility that allowing her to see Grandfather will help."

"Do you know enough about him yet?" Andrew asked.

Ore shook his head. "But the name is sufficiently significant."

"Grandfather?" Mina asked not quite following.

Rei mused on it, then nodded. "Go see him today. Ask if he's managed to contact the surgeon. I still want to see him as soon as he arrives. Also, ask if Grandfather will come and speak to me."

"Yes, Master. Shall I go now?" Ore asked hopefully.

Andrew and Mina glared at him. "No!" they said in chorus.

Rei gave him a shrug that said that he couldn't help. "Get things done here first, then go; say early afternoon, or at lunch."

"A working lunch," Ore grumbled as he headed to his desk.

-o-o-o-

Ore stretched. He'd had a working lunch all right. They all had, because Rei had asked for a cart to be brought in. They'd gotten the packet of reports from Falcon's Hollow, and Rei had made it a priority.

It turned out the Family members believed in expediency. They'd all stayed in the dining hall that first day after Ore had left and wrote the reports themselves. It had taken another day and a half for Colonel Garen to read them all, ask questions, and annotate the reports.

So, all three aides had split the ten reports between them and summarized them. They'd just dumped the summaries and reports on Rei's desk. It was his turn, now, but it shouldn't take any longer to read the summaries than they'd taken to read the detailed reports, just four hours or so....

Ore looked at the other packets that had come directly to him, the one with the stories of the Family members, and the daily reports. Apparently they'd told all their stories to each other the second day. Colonel Garen had written in his report that he'd had his secretary record them.

When the Children learned he was writing them down, they made sure he had them right when he was done, saying, "There's more folks to come. If we just put together a book, they can read ours. This way we won't have to repeat ourselves."

Betty had a fine hand, it turned out, and she volunteered to make the copies. She'd also included a nice note to Father, thanking him for taking care of them all. Almost made him cry.... He'd far rather be out collecting more of them than sitting at his desk.

Ore picked it up and tucked it under his arm. He'd read it outside. "I'll go talk to Grandfather, next." He got silent nods from heads still bowed in effort.

Rei reached into his jacket and pulled out a piece of paper and held it up for Ore to come take, all while still reading the summaries. When Ore had it in hand, Rei said, "Next set of witnesses. Don't leave until I say."

"Okay." Ore tucked the warm paper into his own jacket, thinking happily that it had just come from being so close to his master's heart, and now was so close to his own.

He arrived at the Pelican gate, which opened to common foot traffic at the edge of the city Nijoushi where it met the west side of the outer castle wall. Ore stepped through it, nodding at the guards, then leaned against the castle wall nearby. He pulled out the "Family memory book" and started reading the first report.

He'd have to wait a bit while the lad who'd seen him come out ran off to fetch Grandfather. The stories would be a good distraction, although somehow he felt a little cheated — like he was working through what could have been a nice break from work. He must be becoming a proper aide, finally. Was that a good thing?

"Hello, Father," it was the quiet, polite voice of Grandfather some time later. "You seem very absorbed in your work."

Ore looked up. Grandfather was standing in front of him, a short and stocky man with hair a mix of dark brown and white. His stance and muscles said he was ready to fight and defend if it was necessary. It was obvious he'd not lost any of his strength of his youth. His expression was kind, but looked like it could go to stern pretty quickly. There was nothing soft about him, really, unless he chose to show it.

There was another man at his side, nervously rubbing his hands together, his hair stringy and unbrushed, spectacles balanced on his nose, and slightly hunched over indicating he either read too much by candle light, or stood over tables while experimenting, rather than sitting properly.

"Ah, sorry. It's quite fascinating, how Mother has collected her Children," Ore answered Grandfather.

"Oh? Is that what that is?" Grandfather's eyes went a little wide.

Ore shifted off the wall to stand properly, tucking the report under his arm. "Robert was unsure he would fit in with the rest, so I suggested they all tell each other their stories of how they met Mother so he could understand why he's also Family. They decided to put them together into a book so they can let the next set know, too. They were kind enough to send me a copy."

Grandfather gave him an interesting look, then turned to the man next to him. "Father, this is Doctor Elliot."

Ore brightened up. "Wonderful! It's nice to meet you, Doctor. This is a good day all around then. Doctor Elliot, Master has asked to speak to you immediately. And Grandfather, he asked if you'll also come and speak with him."

They both went a little stiff. "Eh, ah...is that okay?" Grandfather was suddenly uncertain.

Ore nodded. "No one gets in to speak to Mother without speaking to Master first. Come along." He turned and led the way back through the Pelican Gate, not really giving them any choice. He'd left them rather speechless, but they hurried to follow him.

After they were on castle grounds and away from the gate, Ore asked as they walked, "Grandfather, Mother said that if I talked to you about the collections, you'd be able to help me?"

"Yes. I can let them know you're coming and give you the details before you go," the older man offered.

"Wonderful. How much advanced notice do you need?"

"Mmm, two days?"

Ore handed him the list. "These are the next ones. Master hasn't said when I'm to go yet, but he's figured it out already so I suspect he's impatient. I'll contact you again when I know when I'm leaving."

Grandfather unclasped his hands from behind his back to take the list and read it over, then handed it back. "I'll contact them and have the information ready," he said as he reclasped his hands behind his back. His pale blue eyes went back to looking at everything they were passing as they walked, as if he were on tour of the castle grounds. Doctor Elliot fidgeted slightly and his eyes darted more nervously around him.

Ore tucked the note back into his jacket. "Thank you. Master also says Mother may have the nurse and one other to come take care of her and keep her company...the one she says is her friend?"

Grandfather looked at Ore in amazement. "Father," he said respectfully, "may I ask, what happened?"

Ore looked at him from the corner of his eye. He didn't know how much this person knew, but it wasn't likely she'd told very many people, if any at all, that she was a princess. "Maybe he'll tell you," Ore finally said.

When they arrived at the Rose Office, Ore asked the guards to announce Grandfather and Doctor Elliot, then entered with them when they were let in. He led them up to stand before Rei, who had moved to a lesser throne set in the room for the purpose of receiving guests intimately, normally kept in the corner by the windows and the map cabinet but brought out for this meeting.

Andrew was standing to Rei's right side and just in front of Rei, his formal position for intimate meetings with strangers. Mina stood in her spot behind Rei and on the other side from Andrew — Rei's left side. When Ore stood with them as a knight to the Prince, he stood behind Andrew, but today he was introducing the guests, so he stood behind the guests instead.

"Regent, this is the man known as Grandfather, and this is Doctor Elliot," he gestured to the men in order.

Rei looked at them, memorizing their faces. "Thank you for coming today." Andrew said to them.

They both bowed. "Thank you for seeing us," they responded.

"Doctor Elliot, Miss Ilena says that you're capable of repairing a tendon that has been torn from the bone. Is this true?" Andrew again was the one who spoke. He was the Voice of the Prince, as was customary in such settings, although Rei broke the rule when it suited him.

Doctor Elliot answered respectfully, "I've been researching the matter since I received Doctor Bonner's report. I've nearly completed my research but need about a week to a week and a half more. It would also be helpful if I could examine Mistress Ilena myself before then."

Somehow no one was surprised that Doctor Elliot had been in contact with the field surgeon, although Ore was itching to know why. "While we wish you to do everything in your power to restore Miss Ilena's ability to walk, you do understand that her continued safety is dependent on the strictest level of security?"

"Yes, Regent. I won't betray her existence nor her location," Doctor Elliot reassured them.

Rei looked at him with a piercing look, then nodded. "If you're willing, we'll have you escorted immediately to consult with the court surgeon who's been attending her. He can take you to see her," Andrew obediently said.

"Thank you," Doctor Elliot said, relief evident in his face and voice.

"If you'll come with me, Doctor Elliot," Mina moved forward and led the surgeon out of the office after he'd given the proper bow to Rei.

When they were gone, Andrew moved to stand at a little more relaxed position, facing both Rei and Grandfather. Ore moved up to stand next to Grandfather. "Grandfather," Rei himself said, "I'm glad to be able to meet you. Will you please tell me a little about yourself and Miss Ilena?"

Grandfather took the relaxed atmosphere in stride. "Yes, Regent. I was Earl Shicchi's grandfather's steward, as well as his father's. For the first several years, I was also his. When Mistress Ilena was made steward, I stepped down, but remained at her request in order to support her in that role.

"Several years prior to that she'd already come to me and asked if I would train her for that role. I was happy to hand it over, and she's handled it very well."

Rei leaned on his elbow lightly, one finger along his jaw: a slightly relaxed pose, but his eyes remained sharp. Ore knew Rei used the pose when he was testing people. "...So you have experience in handling Miss Ilena?"

The old man's eyebrows shot up briefly, then he looked a bit depressed. "Has she been unruly, Regent? I'm sorry. She behaves that way at infrequent times these days, but early on her nurse would have to scold her severely at times. She is very...headstrong." *I'll say*, thought Ore.

"Mmm," answered Rei, noncommittally. "Her enforced inactivity from her hip injury seems to be the problem. She said that her nurse and maid could help to temper it. Would you be in agreement?"

Grandfather laughed. It wasn't a reaction the others in the room expected. "Yes, they could, although really no one can actually deter her if she's determined." He looked speculatively at Ore, "Except maybe this one here."

Ore felt his face fall. Not again. Another person who was determined to lock them together. Even Rei grinned at that. "Well, I have figured that out. But you see, she's put so many requirements on his time already, and it isn't possible to send her with him to collect the Family members she's giving me temporarily."

"Ah, that's true," the old man nodded in agreement.

"I would rather be able to take Miss Ilena with me," Ore admitted. "At least then she would be happily occupied, such that she wouldn't find the time to be —"

"What was it she said she was at last night? Testy?" Rei asked Ore, teasing him for having had that conversation in his presence.

"Oh, my. Mistress is already to the level of testy?" Grandfather frowned in concern.

Ore nodded. "If I remember correctly she said tantrums are next. I'm hoping Master will send me away from the castle before she reaches that level." Andrew was having troubles not laughing at Ore.

"Well, truth be told, she'll have them all the sooner if you're gone. Who's attending her now?" Grandfather was willing to be of assistance.

"Mistress Mizi during the day, Ryan, the Head Court Healer, in the evening, and Ore during the night, until morning." Rei gave him direct, and somewhat sensitive, information. He was telling Grandfather that he wanted to work closely with him, and was still testing Grandfather's reactions.

"Mmm. So she's on her best behavior during the day, and trying to be nice in the evening, but not always succeeding, and she snips at poor Father at night." Grandfather turned a sympathetic look on Ore.

"Well, she does sleep for most of the time I'm there," Ore admitted, for Ilena's sake, "but in the main you have the sum of it."

Grandfather frowned a little disapprovingly at Rei. "You also have some important people using valuable time watching over her."

It wasn't the man's to question, but Rei accepted the reproof without reprisal. "Ilena is that important to me, Grandfather," he said quietly.

Grandfather looked at Rei in surprised approval, grateful that it was so. "I can have the ladies here to attend her by tomorrow morning, if you wish, or even this evening, if it would be helpful."

"Whatever won't inconvenience them too strenuously," Rei answered. "If you'll tell us their names, we'll prepare castle identification for them."

"I will, but I'm sure she intends to keep them as her personal maids, rather than have them be castle staff. Will that be okay?" Rei nodded. "They are Leah Undel and Rio." Andrew pulled out his notepad and took down the names.

Rei continued, "Ore will let the guards at the Pelican Gate know they have permission to enter until their identification badges are made. I would also like to make one for you."

The old man raised an eyebrow in question. "I believe that if she may communicate with you daily, she'll also be able to be more calm. ...And, I want to see what she'll do." Rei had his castle game face pasted on, telling nothing about what he was thinking, even though he'd just said something perhaps outrageous.

Grandfather's eyes wrinkled in a rueful smile. "I'll do my best, Your Highness." He understood. He was also being brought in to help them, and at the same time Rei was testing Ilena and the Family as a whole. Grandfather gave them his true name and Andrew added it to his notes.

"Thank you, Grandfather," said Rei, rising from his chair. "When the badges have been completed, Father will see that you get them."

Was that teasing me? wondered Ore, but he couldn't tell.

"Will you please join me?" Rei asked Grandfather. "I'm going down to visit Ilena now. You may visit with her after I'm done."

-o-o-o-

They arrived at Ilena's room just after the doctors did, the guards informed them. Rei was pleased. "Will you wait out here for now?" he asked Grandfather. "Ore will stay with you." He had the guards announce him, and he and Andrew entered the room.

The surgeons were in the process of inspecting the wound site. Rei and Andrew stayed out of the way, Andrew joining Mina against the wall. He raised an eyebrow at her. *Everything going okay?* She nodded back and raised an eyebrow. *Yes. Where's Ore?* He nodded towards the door and hallway. *Waiting out in the hall with Grandfather.*

Doctor Elliot turned to Rei when the examination was completed. "It's as I expected. The time estimate of one to one and a half weeks to be prepared doesn't change. Mistress Ilena will be my first experimental living patient, however. Multiple surgeries may be required in order to get the desired results." Rei was a little worried by that news. He didn't want Ilena to have to go through too much, especially if the outcome in the end wasn't worth it.

"Doctor Elliot," Ilena interjected, "you get two tries." He looked frightened, as if he was sure it would take more. "Three at the most. While I want to be able to walk again, I won't be able to deal with my restlessness, nor the pain, any more than that." Doctor Elliot paused, then nodded. He would just have to do his best.

When it seemed the surgeons were done with their investigation for the time, Rei requested that Ilena's court surgeon see Doctor Elliot out of the castle. They excused themselves politely and the door closed behind them, leaving Rei, Mina, and Andrew alone with Ilena.

Rei walked closer to Ilena so they could talk. "Under normal circumstances, I would take a proper amount of time to confirm you. However, after taking into consideration the time and effort you've already invested in striving to reach your goal, and what you've already built, I've decided that I may already trust you in a lesser position, expecting you to quickly prove to me that you're capable of the greater role."

He pulled her castle identification from the inside pocket of his jacket. "I would have you be my Director of Intelligence. You'll report directly to me." Ilena looked at him, her face unreadable, her eyes bright. She didn't answer him. "I think you understand that this is a provisional role, based upon your performance."

"Even so, it's too early," she finally answered him.

Rei shook his head. "I've already tested you sufficient for the position you're in. I wish to see what you'll do next."

Ilena's eyes narrowed. Any position for her in the castle shouldn't occur until after the Earl was captured, tried, and punished with the approval of the lords. Then her part could be acknowledged with an appointment. To be placed before then was perhaps foolhardy because none of the other cabinet members would acknowledge her power or responsibility. They still didn't even know of her existence.

Just to make sure he understood how she felt about the appointment coming so early, she finally answered him, "I would have thought bribery was beneath you, Regent Rei."

"It isn't bribery, Ilena. It's a restraint. I'll have you stay by my side for now." Rei was calmly firm.

She paused a little longer, then said, "Very well, ...if Master Rei wishes for me to not be taken from his side easily, I'll accept it. ...But you must place it over my head for me, as I can't correctly do it from a vertical position, I'm afraid."

Rei was angry at her words, although he still had his public castle face on. He didn't like being in the position of a master, particularly when it came to people like Ilena. He realized he had little choice because of what she was. Even so, he felt it was petty for her to make him pay for giving her the position early.

He took a steadying breath to calm down and stepped up to her, his face set. He placed the identification over her head and around her neck, settling it carefully upon her chest. Still touching it lightly and looking her in the eye, he said, "I look forward to the things you'll show me."

"Yes, Master Rei." The words were said humbly but it was a thin veneer over the pride she held within her in large amounts. Ilena would be as hard to win over as Ore had been, even with her declarations that she wished to stand behind Rei.

Rei studied her a moment longer, then turned and left, Andrew and Mina following behind. Outside her room, Rei stopped in front of Grandfather. Politely he said, "Ilena will be ready to see you in a few minutes. Have the guards announce you when you think the time is appropriate."

Grandfather looked into Rei's face, then bowed. "Thank you, Regent Rei." He, at least, could be properly grateful. As he watched Rei leave with his aides, Rei having called Ore to walk with him, he sighed. It didn't look like his mistress was starting out well.

Ore looked at his master's back. It was ramrod straight. He was angry — with Ilena, since it had been after he'd come out from talking to her. Ore looked at Andrew questioningly. It was Mina, on his other side, who answered quietly. "She made him force the appointment."

Oh, said Ore's mouth silently. Each as stubborn as the other, it seemed.

When they arrived at the Rose Office and Rei could be himself again, he let the anger go to his face, but didn't show it to his friends. Instead he walked out through the double glass doors onto his balcony and stood looking towards the city, his arms folded.

The harder part was that he was actually conflicted. He was angry at Ilena for making him force the appointment, as Mina had summed up so well, but he was also saddened by the necessity that drove it. Unlike Ore, she hadn't come to Rei of her own free will, even if she might have eventually. She'd been forced into this position, and he'd now forced her even further, likely before she was really ready, all because he knew who and what she was now.

Ore walked up next to Rei and leaned on his arms on the banister. "It's hard to tie down something that you love and wish to see free, no?"

Rei looked at Ore. It was just what he needed to hear, but, "Isn't it usually Andrew who says things like that?"

Ore turned around to lean backwards against the banister, grinning at Andrew who was behind Rei, and whom Ore had beaten to the punch. "Well, he was going to, but...."

Andrew stood against the railing on the other side of Rei and Mina stood near him, their presence strengthening and comforting Rei.

"...But?" Rei prompted Ore.

Ore looked up into the sky, pondering the answer. "...She's *my* partner, isn't she?" Andrew immediately forgave Ore, and Mina's face spoke approval. It was, indeed, Ore's responsibility to help his master forgive his partner, and also to comfort him.

Rei sighed and continued to look out over the city in the strengthening company of his friends. His back relaxed as he let his pride go and let them carry his sorrow with him.

-o-o-o-

After Rei left, Ilena reached up and touched her new identification tag. It was bittersweet. She wanted what he'd given her this day — and the more he promised — but she hadn't wanted it this way.

"Ore," she whispered, "Rei is very intelligent. He's stepped further ahead of me than I thought. He knows how to use all of the people under him to great advantage. ...Will I be able to keep up, to do my part? Ah, I'm afraid I have much to learn."

Ilena closed her eyes, glad she was able to be alone for a time. She'd convinced Mizi and Ryan to let her have some quiet time alone for the time period from an hour after lunch until a half hour before dinner was supposed to arrive. That had allowed them more time for their work, and had helped her mood because she finally had time to relax.

Rei had allowed for the schedule change during the time Ore was away. Mizi had been the one to propose it to him saying Ilena usually slept during that time, anyway, and it would allow her time to mentally rest. It wasn't like Ilena was going to go anywhere, and if something urgent came up, she could call to the guards. (Grandfather hadn't been wrong in his assessment that Ilena was having troubles staying polite around the clock.)

Today had been a different kind of stressful already, what with the sudden and surprising visit by Doctor Elliot, and now the appointment by Rei. It would be good to rest for what time was left. A knock at the door told her it was not to be.

Ilena didn't quite have to bite her tongue, but she hoped at least that it would be a short interruption. Her strength wouldn't last much longer. She kept her eyes closed to make just that point to whomever was entering this time. It wasn't like there were very many options of who would be visiting.

"Daughter," a dear voice beside her startled her eyes open.

"Grandfather?" she gaped at him. It was the most unexpected visitor of her day. She blinked a few times, then surprised herself with the realization that she was blinking tears out of her eyes. Her hand flew up to her face to wipe the tears. "Oh, my."

Grandfather smiled kindly at her. "It's been hard for you, hasn't it?" His kindness made the tears flow faster until she was bawling. He put his hand on her head, providing what comfort he could.

"I–I'm...*hic*...s–sorry," she sniffled once she could get sufficient control of herself again.

"You should be," he said gently. "You weren't very nice to Master Rei, were you?"

Ilena shook her head 'no'. "B–but...*sniff*...it...it hurts." The pain in her chest made it hard to say the words even. Things had not turned out how she had planned and hoped for at all.

"Yes, it does hurt to have to live with the consequences of other's choices. Even still, this is a place you knew you would come to. It isn't necessary to make it more difficult." He was kind but firm, as always with her.

Ilena closed her eyes in reaction to the pains in her heart. Ore's continuing rejection, Rei binding her to the Touka royals earlier than she'd expected, the lengthy enforced immobility and physical pain that went with it, as well as her even more deeply hidden fear that she really would never walk or run again and thus have her own long–term plans completely destroyed: these were all the things she'd had as her company day after night since she'd been aware enough again after the assassination.

Ilena allowed herself one more moment to really feel them all. They were truths, those feelings, but Grandfather was right. She'd known she'd come here eventually. She'd have likely still had to deal with Ore's natural suspicions. She'd have been bound as a Touka whenever she'd been discovered. She couldn't do anything about the injury, but those around her were trying their best to help her.

Ilena sighed a deep sigh, finally recovering. "No. I suppose not, but it became very difficult for me much sooner than I expected." She looked up into Grandfather's pale blue eyes and the tears, silent this time, slipped out again. "He already knows."

Grandfather was one of the few people in her Family that knew what she was. He sighed. "I wondered why the sudden changes. That would explain it."

Ilena nodded. "He's moved too quickly for me. I didn't expect to be at this point for another nearly two months. And I'm still another two months from being on my feet."

Ilena looked away from him and her hand went to hold her identification, the binding of it on her still odd, still rejected by her independent pride and her thwarted plans. Softly she said, "He's just made me his Director of Intelligence. It's odd, but apparently he uses appointments as restraints. And, he wants to see what I'll do with limited capacity. At the moment I feel like I have no capacity." She looked back at him. "But, then, I didn't expect to see you. Is that part of his plan, too?"

"I suspect so," Grandfather said. "They've asked me to bring Leah and Rio."

Ilena nodded. "He said last night I could have them." She paused a few more breaths to recover and consider what should be next. "...So...he wants to see what I'll do? Are you ready?"

Grandfather's eyes crinkled up at the corners. "Yes. Everyone is very anxious."

"Then, it may begin. Tell Marcus and Henry I want them by the time I'm set free of this room. I'll use Leah and Rio until then. That will help them learn the map. Make sure we don't step on any Uncles' toes, please. I would like the detailed loyalty report as soon as possible, and if the section on the lords could be early so I can give it to Master Rei before he goes to the Lord's Court, that would be best."

She paused to let him know he could interject if he wanted. "Father showed me the second list today, saying Master Rei is impatient but hasn't told him to go yet," he told her. "I'll be sending them notice when I return. Also, when I arrived...he was reading a document he said was a copy of the stories from each of the first set — of how they met Mother. That Robert had felt like an outsider, so Father suggested that they all tell each other their stories to help him understand."

"*Father* suggested such a thing?" Ilena couldn't believe it.

Grandfather nodded. "I suspect he was asking them to tell their stories when he was picking them up, and decided it."

"Well, yes, I expected him to ask to learn who Mother was, but for him to care about the Children so...."

"Word on the street, and in my ears, is that he's very much like Mother," Grandfather said softly, looking with pride at her. "That was my first experience to see it personally."

"*He's* seen it?" Ilena was even more surprised.

Grandfather nodded. "Father went to the Black Cat to pick up the four from town. First Son was told, so he went to confirm him for himself. He brought back an impressive report, particularly since Father hadn't been told anything from the beginning, although Thayne was with him by then to translate. They seemed to be getting along well, by the way."

"Hmm," Ilena mused. "That would be a good pairing until First Son is ready for him." Then she sighed. "Although with the way things are speeding along, it may not happen. He may just jump right to First Son, in the end."

Grandfather looked at her speculatively. "Are you going to let me retire early?"

Ilena laughed a short laugh. "If Master Rei can make me to go to work early, he can make you to retire early, no? ...Would that make you happy?"

Grandfather sighed. "I'm getting old, Mother." Then he looked at her fondly. "Would it make you sad?"

"Yes, Grandfather, it would," Ilena answered honestly. "Would you be willing to come to my house and sit with me, even if I didn't put you to work?"

"If you gave me a comfortable chair and a warm fire, I'd sit with you anywhere. I think you know that, Mother." He gave her a warm smile that Ilena drank in.

"It gives me comfort to hear it, Grandfather."

"What news can I take back with me?" he asked.

"Did Doctor Elliot come with you?" He nodded. "Then you know all of my news. But please send my love. Is there any news I need to be aware of, particularly since I've been away so long?"

"We've moved a few around as necessary, but most of your Children are well and send their love. Ah, if Master Rei is moving faster than you expected, should I step up the other plans?"

Ilena considered. "Yes, you should. He hasn't said anything yet, but based on last night's question and today's gift," she gestured to her tag, "he probably has a guess already as to what's next. He'll likely begin asking questions about it soon, and when he starts asking questions, it isn't long before he decides what to do, so we should be ready."

Grandfather could see she was thinking, trying to recalculate to be at the speed of Rei. "And the household?"

Ilena grinned at him. "I'm hoping he's putting them in the house he may give to me. Therefore they'll all be where they need to be, but get the horsemen prepared." Grandfather nodded, accepting the orders.

Ilena held out her hand to him, and he gently took it. "Grandfather, please tell everyone I'm sorry to have worried them. ...I asked on your behalf several times before it was proper to, because I didn't want to cloud anyone's eyes. Father said he was finally allowed to tell you, after Master Rei knew. That made my own heart lighter to hear."

Grandfather patted the hand he was holding. "I think everyone understood that your life was in danger, Mother. They were willing to wait until they could hear the news. It was indeed a time to quietly celebrate when we heard it.

"Doctor Elliot stopped by and visited with Doctor Bonner in Osterly. He was willing to converse on your case professionally, even though he wouldn't say it was you, of course. That was enough for us for the time."

"That's good," Ilena said tiredly. It had been an exciting afternoon, during a time she usually napped. She closed her eyes briefly, then looked at him again. "Please, tell First Son that Master Rei knows, and that I still miss him very much. I had hoped to be able to see him again by now." She frowned a pained frown.

Grandfather smoothed Ilena's hair to comfort the old pain of that long separation. "Shall I tell Grandmother, also?"

Ilena closed her eyes, unable to keep them open any longer. "Yes, please. It will help if she knows before she comes. Will you come again?"

"...Master Rei has asked that I come to visit Mother every day, if you approve," he said quietly.

"Mmm, please."

He continued to hold her hand as she fell asleep, then left quietly, telling the guards she was sleeping. He was surprised when they told him how to get out of the castle from that location and left him to his own devices. Master Rei was certainly an interesting fellow...as was Father. It looked like they would be good for Mother.

-o-o-o-

"Master, where was Mistress?" Something had been missing from Ore's day, and he'd just figured out what it was. ...Come to think of it, Mizi had been missing from quite a lot of days for him, since before he'd gone to pick up the first round of witnesses. That wasn't a good thing.

"Ah, right. That happened while you were away." Ore looked at Rei darkly. It had been Rei's fault for keeping Ore at his desk every day since he'd returned.

Rei hurried to explain, "Ilena actually reached 'testy' the day after you left. Mizi and Ryan decided that it would be helpful if she had some time to herself each day. Mizi is with her from before breakfast to just after lunch. Ryan joins Ilena for dinner. So in the afternoons, she's usual sleeping, or so they tell me."

"He wasn't going to do it, even still," Mina told on Rei dryly, "until they reminded him they are only three doors down and the guards could fetch them if she needed anything."

"Anyway," Rei pressed on to cover his embarrassment and stop Mina from saying any more, "Mizi was probably at the medical department."

"I have a thing I need to do, Master," Ore turned to walk out the balcony doors.

"Ah! Before you go...," Ore stopped and waited, although it was obvious he was impatient. He'd been kept many days already from his main responsibility, thinking she was busy with Ilena — his partner who was supposed to be watching her. Rei had been too distracted.

"I think I said it before, but I want Doctor Elliot. Find out how to get him here in the castle where I can keep my eye on him. I want his research and I want him to help us figure out how to use the lower doses of the Little Death for interrogation purposes," Rei ordered.

"Miss Ilena's Leah and Rio need a room, too," Andrew added, pushing that duty onto Ore. He also needed to let the guards know to let them in.

"Anything else?" Ore asked dangerously, looking over his shoulder at them, his hands and one foot poised on the top of the balcony banister.

"Ah, no!" "No." They waved him off. Ore took off, headed to the roof from the banister. He preferred crossing the castle grounds by rooftop when his orders allowed him to walk that path.

He stopped by the châtelaine's office — the keeper of the keys and head of the castle staff — to order a room and pick up the key. The ladies would be with the other castle staff for now. When Rei decided to give Ilena a real room, they would probably be moved in with her into a suite, like the other lords who brought staff with them to the castle. Then Ore headed for the medical department.

He dropped down into the medical wing's inner courtyard from the roof and looked up to see a startled Grandfather. "Oh! Grandfather, are you done with Miss Ilena?"

"Father! Yes. She's sleeping now. ...Ah...I've taken the liberty to scold her for her earlier behavior. I'm sorry. But she should be a little better, now, I should think."

Ore smiled at him, "Thank you. Master is also a little better, now. Were you lost?"

"Well, the guards did give me directions, but it's my first time," Grandfather probably wanted to scout the area, but Ore didn't want him getting into trouble on his first day.

"I'll walk you back, and show you the landmarks so you may come and go yourself next time," Ore offered.

"Thank you," Grandfather said.

As they walked, Ore asked, "If I wanted to visit with Doctor Elliot, where should I find him?"

"He takes dinners at the Scholar's Tavern. Would that suffice?"

"Yes. I've seen it, but not been there yet. Is it a Family House?"

Grandfather smiled at the use of the term. "Yes, it is. The couple who run it are from Kouzanshi."

"So it's like the scholarly taverns there, then?" Grandfather nodded. "Well, I may try to get Mistress to go with me, or even young Ryan, now that he's old enough to drink. They might like the memories."

Ore saw Grandfather off at the gate, introducing him to the guards. Ore made sure to tell them he would be bringing two personal maids to wait on his Missus in the near future and to let them pass, and that Grandfather himself would be coming each day, on the order of the Regent. Then Ore, glad he'd been able to get both of his other tasks done at the same time, was finally able to head to his mistress' side.

When Ore arrived back at the medical wing, he found Ryan, but not Mizi. "Little Mister! I'm back. Why were you still working nights outside Miss Ilena's room when it wasn't necessary?"

"Eh? Ah...," Ryan looked embarrassed. "It's quieter there," he turned away, looking down as he said it.

"Mmm," Ore looked at him askance. "You like her that much, then?"

Ryan traced a pattern on the table in front of him. "Eh, well, ...I've been meaning to talk to you, too, but I keep forgetting."

"Me?" Ore was surprised. But then, Ryan wouldn't have been able to except when they were passing at Ilena's door, Ore had been so busy. "I'm sorry. Master's kept me busy. What was it?"

"Well, Miss Ilena told me about a place in town I'd like to go visit, but I was hoping you could take me." The shy Ryan, who had been around him for as long as Ore had been following Mizi, was doing much better at talking to him, but it was still difficult for him to look Ore in the eyes.

Ore smiled. "Where is it?" He had a guess.

"It's called the Scholar's Tavern." Ryan blushed a furious red.

Oohhh? An ulterior motive to going? Is the little Mister finally at that age? Perhaps it should be a visit without Mistress, then. "Well, I was just looking for an excuse to go into town, and thought I might go there as I haven't been yet. When would work best for you?"

"I have a break tomorrow evening, if Mizi will take dinner with Miss Ilena." Ryan looked very hopeful.

"If you'll tell me where to find her, I'll ask for you," Ore said helpfully.

"She's in the third greenhouse. The plants have needed tending this week."

"Thank you, Little Mister. I'll come pick you up here tomorrow evening, then."

"Okay!" Ryan was very happy.

Ore smiled to himself as he left. Ilena was still being Mother, even to Ryan, setting him up like that. He hoped the teen would be able to find what he was looking for there, eventually. He really was a very likable person, if one could get through the shyness that held him back. It would be good for him to get out and practice being more social.

"I'm back, Mistress!" Ore said, appearing at the door to the greenhouse she was in.

"Oh, Ore! Welcome back!" She stood up from her planting and brushed a lock of escaping red hair out of her face, her short ponytail covered by a headcloth to keep the dirt off her head — although now it was smudged on her cheek.

That was a rather normal look for her that Ore often had difficulty not correcting. The memory of Rei's furious blue eyes always made Ore back off from wiping the smudge off the smooth cheek it covered. That had been one of Rei's super–scolds when he'd caught Ore doing just that rather without thought.

"Well...I've been back, but Master just told me now that you had the afternoons off. He's also had me chained to my desk, so I could only come now." Ore carefully put his hands into his pockets, although he made it look casual on the outside.

"Rei only told you now?" An eyebrow went up and Ore studied the garden bed behind Mizi's head instead of looking directly at her.

"Yes. I'm sorry." He didn't want another scolding for having been away from her when he shouldn't have been.

Mizi didn't seem very angry about it, though. "Well, it has been busy, even here. It was helpful to have the afternoons back, now that we're in the planting time."

"What can I do?" Ore asked. He'd been helping her with such chores since he'd first been assigned to follow her, back at Ichijou Castle, when Rei had asked him to guard her from the spies and kidnappers who were following her around, wondering if she could be used to influence Rei, those five years ago.

Ore had already disabused most of the same here in Nijou since they'd come, but he was still a little uncomfortable with leaving her with only the two hidden guards he had watching over her all the time, particularly when he couldn't be with her. Past history had taught him that wasn't sufficient.

"I'm moving these plants up to the upper level. We've decided they need more sun than they're getting here. Take them up to where you'll see a free prepared bed."

"Yes, Mistress," Ore reached down and gently picked up an arm load of plants already taken carefully out of the bed they'd been in and headed up to the place she indicated. He went ahead and started planting them when he arrived. Shortly, Mizi arrived with another armload and began to plant them, starting from the other end of the bed. "Have you been well?" he asked her.

"Yes," she said. He could tell there was still something she'd been thinking about. He waited to see if she would say it on her own. "Ore. What's Rei's day like here in this place? What does he do?"

"Mmm. He rises early, eats a breakfast in his room, and goes to the Rose office. Sometimes he needs to meet briefly with someone on the way." Ore put the next plant in the hole he'd just made for it. "Then for the morning it's mostly reading of reports ...although we read the reports now and he reads the summary so that he can get through more of them. There are many more reports now as Regent than there were as Prince at Ichijou.

"If he's fortunate, he may complete his written orders back before lunch, but often he's still writing them through lunch. The early afternoon is open for visiting with lords and others who need to bring their concerns to him directly. Or, if there isn't anyone to come to him, he'll go to them, having accepted their invitations to informal or, less frequently, formal teas. That helps him understand how the lords of the castle think. He's been spending most of his months since he came helping them understand who the Regent is.

"There's also a weekly council of the Ministers with him, and sometimes a full court meeting, or perhaps a small one with a visiting dignitary." Ore had finished planting his pile of plants during that much explanation. He rose to his feet and headed towards Mizi, consciously reminding himself (yet again) to not touch her.

Some year his hands would learn to keep to themselves instead of move on their own. It was just that same desire that made him ache to stand with Rei — that desire to touch the softness that was Mizi as if she were a rose. She had sharp thorns like one, too. He knew she would super–scold him before Rei would, so he tried very hard not to touch.

He took some of Mizi's pile of plants and began planting them, returning to answering her question. "After the visiting time, he'll go to one or another department to visit with the department heads. Then he returns to his office to write his own reports of the day and to consider where he'll be needed next. Then it's signing of documents and reading and writing correspondence until past dinner time.

"Occasionally, he must attend a formal dinner, but those aren't common, particularly as most of them are invitations to meet some daughter or other that he isn't interested in meeting." Ore looked out of the corner of his eye at Mizi. Normally she wouldn't react to such a comment, but it would eat at her. He'd mentioned it on purpose to see how she was doing.

Mizi had paused briefly, in the middle of putting another plant in the bed, then firmly set it in its hole and covered its roots. Otherwise she had no reaction. *She's thinking about how she'll stand by Master. It's hard to see he's working on it also.* "Then he takes a small stack of work to finish up to his bedroom and works until he falls asleep, the same as Mistress."

Mizi looked up at Ore in surprise and blushed a little. "You know I take work to bed with me?"

"Of course, Mistress. You can't fall asleep without it, I've seen."

"Well...it's true. It's the same for Rei?" Ore nodded. "Well, he does certainly have very full days, it sounds like."

"Especially since coming here," Ore agreed. "Even Mister Andrew, Miss Mina, and Ore have very full days helping him now. Ah, but he's opened the Rosebud office and brought back experienced help, so it's not so overwhelming now. We can focus on what's important. That's been very good. He's learned some strength.

"He also finally found someone for Miss Mina to train that will stand in her stead when she's at her home. She's extra busy with that, but says that he's very competent and soon she'll have her own load lessened somewhat."

Ore went openly sad and complained, "Ore is the only one Master hasn't found an assistant for. The Rosebud office is Mister Andrew's assistant. He has five! Surely one could help Ore?"

Mizi smiled at him, then patted his arm. "I'm sure when Ore needs one, Rei will find one." She stood up and brushed off her clothes. "Let's go get the next set."

Ore obediently followed her back down to the bed being moved. "Is it becoming hard to not be in Master's day?" he asked her, a little trepidatious. She would in the past become angry at the suggestion that she didn't want Rei to be what he needed to be, to be able to do the things he needed to do. But it had been a very long time, already.

Mizi's face set, and Ore thought she'd indeed be angry with him. "When we were bringing Ilena here, he said that he was having troubles knowing what to do next. I said that if we couldn't think of it, I'd speak with Ilena on the matter." She paused as she looked a little angrily at the plants in front of her they were removing from the old bed. "...It was she who suggested I ask what his day's schedule was so that I might understand."

"Hmm...." *Haah. Mistress is angry enough to bring Mother into it. Should I warn Master? Or will he expect me to talk to Mother about it first?* They finished collecting the remainder of the plants from the bed to take them up to their new bed.

"Ah!" Ore remembered his conversation with Ryan. "Mistress, the little Mister asked if you'd be willing to trade him tomorrow and have dinner with Miss Ilena. He said it when I came looking for you. If you're willing you should make sure he knows to have lunch with her."

Mizi nodded. "I'll speak to him."

"Also, today Master made Miss Ilena his Director of Intelligence." Ore continued to update Mizi with his news as they walked back up to the new bed with the final plants in their arms.

"Director?! Of...intelligence?" her brow furrowed in some confusion.

"And he's allowed her two maids to come take care of her, so that Mistress and the little Mister can have their time back, although you should still make sure of her. They'll likely arrive tomorrow morning, with her servant known as

Grandfather, who'll also come each day to visit with her. In this way Mistress and Ryan won't have to have Miss Ilena's testy directed at them, nor deal with her tantrums, which she says are next."

"Tantrums? Really?" Mizi's lip curled up as if she couldn't quite imagine it. Or perhaps she could imagine it all too well. Ore could.

Ore nodded. "Miss Leah and Miss Rio are used to them, it seems. But Mistress shouldn't have to bear with them."

"I would rather not," Mizi said faintly. She quietly planted a few more plants as she thought about what he'd told her. They were nearly done. "Is this because of the mark? Of what she is to Rei?"

Ore nodded as he firmed the dirt around the last of his plants. "He says even King Brother knows of the place she's aiming for, and approves. Master must work hard to show him that he can use her in that place, and we must work hard to ensure she can be tamed to Master's call." He handed Mizi the last of the plants she'd just made the hole for, then dusted the dirt off his hands.

Mizi looked a little puzzled. "Tamed?"

Ore looked at his rather innocent mistress. "Unlike Mistress, Miss Ilena isn't used to considering others, but does her own will. It would be good if she could listen to hear the words of Mistress and Master."

Mizi got the message Ore was trying to convey. Her lips pursed a little, and she nodded. Even if she asked for advice from Ilena she should consider her own ways first, and correct Ilena when necessary.

-o-o-o-

When Mizi was done with her chores in the greenhouse for the day, she led Ore back into the medical wing. There she looked for Ryan. She found him sitting over his reports at his desk in the infirmary. "Ryan, Ore says you wanted to trade me tomorrow for dinner with Ilena?"

"Yes," Ryan looked up from his careful writing, "if that would be okay with you."

"It would...but it would also be good for me if it was tonight. Would that be possible?" Mizi was always respectful of Ryan and his position, regardless of his age. (Ryan was sixteen while Mizi was eighteen, although they'd been four and a half years younger when she'd arrived at Ichijou to become Ryan's apprentice.) She was very good for him since she just quietly took care of him when he became absentminded in his focus on his research or work.

Ryan looked over at Ore questioningly. "It should be okay...?" Ore thought about it, then nodded. Rei had given him an order and this was following it. Rei owed Ore anyway. "Yes," Ryan finished.

"I'll go clean up, then, Ore," Mizi said.

"I'll walk you there when you're ready, Mistress," Ore said to her. Then, after she was out of the room, he said to Ryan, "I'll come back for you. After I take Mistress I should also leave a note for Master."

Ryan nodded. "I'll wait for you."

Ore smiled a lopsided smile. "You could change into something more comfortable first."

"Ah!" Ryan looked down at his castle uniform, then nodded. "I'll do that." He wandered off. Ore thought it was funny that he'd just gone and done it, instead of finishing his work first. He had time, after all.

When they arrived at Ilena's room, Mizi knocked to announce herself, then let herself in. Ore followed her in. "Ah!" Ilena said, surprised. "Mistress Mizi and Ore. Well, this is certainly a day of changes and surprises. To what do I owe the visit?"

Mizi answered first, "I'm trading with Ryan tonight. He has a thing he needs to do. Ah...and I hear congratulations are in order?"

Ilena's smile was slightly sad. "Yes. Thank you very much." She looked at Ore, assuming he'd been the one to tell.

Ore answered, "Good evening, Miss Ilena. I hope you're doing better."

"Yes, Ore. It was good to speak with Grandfather. Since I can't do it myself, will you please pass my gratitude, and my apology, on to Master Rei?"

Master Rei? Is it the appointment? "...I will. But Miss Ilena, you must behave from now on, yes?" Ore looked significantly at Mizi. *Whatever you're going to tell Mistress, be good.*

"Yes, Ore," Ilena said meekly.

"Then, I'll leave you two to your dinner." Having reassured himself that Ilena had properly been warned, Ore bowed himself out.

He headed up to Rei's bedroom. He didn't want to get caught up in the desk work in the office again. He got a pen and paper from Rei's desk there and wrote a quick note, leaving it with the book the Family members had put together about Mother on Rei's pillow, then headed back down to get Ryan.

When Rei arrived to his bed that night, he was nonplussed to find them there. He picked up the note and read it first:

Master, Mistress has begun talking to Miss Ilena about how to stand by Master. I'm collecting Doctor Elliot for you. Here is better bedtime reading for you. Miss Ilena says she is sorry and thank you.

The first sentence made Rei's hairs stand on end. The second was an acceptable excuse for why Ore had been gone. The third made him curious. The fourth was sufficient for now, but sounded like Ore had added it as an afterthought.

He set his other work down on the desk, settled in the middle of his bed, and opened the Family book. ...Ore was right. It definitely made for much better bedtime reading than dull reports.

-o-o-o-

Mizi had gotten Ilena ready for her dinner, and they were now enjoying the small meal together, Mizi taking turns to feed herself and Ilena. "I'm sorry, Mistress Mizi, that I must make dinner so difficult for you," Ilena said.

"It's okay. Very soon you'll be able to sit up and feed yourself." Mizi didn't mind it really.

Ilena answered slowly — a warning. "Well...no, actually. Maybe only for a few days at the most."

"What?" Mizi was surprised.

"Master Rei finally found Doctor Elliot. He was here to see me this afternoon. He says he'll be ready to attempt his surgery in eight to eleven days. After that, we'll start all over, I'm afraid."

Mizi sat still, blinking for a moment. "Well, that will be good if it works, so you'll be able to walk again. But...will you be okay?" She gave Ilena the bite that had paused on it's way, then had to wait for her answer.

"Well, no. Even though I told Master Rei I'd do anything to walk again, including this, I'll probably not be okay." Ilena looked as disappointed as Mizi was feeling. Then she brightened up, "But, you won't have to put up with me so much. Master Rei has allowed my nurse and maid to come and sit with me. They're used to it, so it shouldn't be too bad."

Mizi, having heard this news, nodded. "I'd like to meet them. They must be very strong."

Ilena laughed. "Mistress Mizi already understands Ilena. I'd like for you to meet them. I think they'll come when you're here tomorrow morning. Then you'll be free."

"Except the times I'll come to make sure you're still being properly cared for," Mizi said firmly. "You'll not be so free of me as that."

"Well, that's good, too," Ilena said happily. She hadn't really wanted Mizi to not come again. She had a lot to train her in, after all.

"...I spoke with Ore this afternoon and asked him about Rei's schedule, like you suggested," Mizi got to the point she wanted to talk about. "You were right. It's very full of paperwork and meetings. But Ore says that recently Rei's been strengthened enough to allow others to be doing more so that he can focus on what's important. He's done the same for Andrew and Mina as well."

Ilena nodded. "That's good. He'll be able to have time for you, soon, then. ...I'm sure he doesn't want to impose on your busy schedule either. Does he know it any better than you knew his?"

Mizi shook her head. "We've not discussed it before. Do you think he thinks that?"

Ilena nodded. "Master Rei respects you very much. I'm sure he wants to be as cautious about your time as you are about his. But if you wish to be by his side more, surely you must at least ask?"

"But," Mizi was doubtful, "it doesn't sound like there's anywhere to fit me into his schedule."

"That's because you've been told his current schedule, which doesn't include you yet. There are two times that are possible, from what you've told me." Mizi raised her eyebrow, listening. "There's lunch, and there's dinner. Master Rei really shouldn't be working through both. That isn't good. It helps to clear the mind and make it more rested and useful, to stop and eat well."

Mizi nodded. She'd experienced both herself, and knew it was true, and how hard it was to make oneself stop and eat.

"If you were to show up at lunch time, Master Rei would have to take the time to rest and eat. Then he could be more effective in the afternoon. And he would be strengthened because he would have seen the smile of Mistress Mizi as a reward for his hard work in the morning. Wouldn't it be the same for you?" Ilena gave an open questioning look to Mizi.

Mizi nodded, slowly. "But would it be okay?"

"Well, certainly you should speak with Master Rei to confirm it, but you *are* the Court Healer in charge of his health, are you not?" Ilena looked at her with lidded eyes. Would Mizi pick up on the challenge to find strength in her current position?

Mizi didn't disappoint her. After all, that was one of the reasons she'd worked hard to get where she was. "Yes, that's true. I wonder how to talk to Rei about it, though. As I said before, there really isn't opportunity to talk to him about things, unless he happens to come down here, or I run into him in the hallways. ...Or if I send Ore to get him. Sometimes I can pass messages to him through Andrew or Mina if I see them when we're leaving in the morning or arriving at night. This is the very problem, you see."

"Hmm...yes. Well, Ilena is very willful, Mistress Mizi. I'd take the lunch cart from the kitchen staff and walk into the office with it. And when Master Rei asked what I was doing there, I'd say that I'd been informed that he wasn't eating properly, and I was there to see that he did. Suiran can't have it's Regent fainting, after all. Then during the meal, I'd explain it to him, and see if he'd agree to it."

Ilena watched Mizi's face. She was finding it both a difficult thing to do, and yet at the same time, appealing. "But, then, as I say, I'm willful. I'm sure Mistress Mizi can find her own way." Was she going to have to push her further?

Ore had said to be good, but this was important. If they didn't ever *choose* to find time to be together, they wouldn't ever *be* together. Even Mizi now acknowledged it was important for the same reason. And...Mizi was suffering because she didn't know anything.

"I'll consider it. There is a thing I can do, it's true." Ilena nodded, content with that answer for now. Mizi was thinking now about how to use her position to get what she needed.

CHAPTER 14 Scholar's Tavern

The Scholar's Tavern was far enough from the castle that Ore opted to take Ryan in a carriage. It wasn't that Ore couldn't have walked it, it was that Ryan still had a very weak body from sitting in the medical department all day everyday since he'd been very young.

He'd learned some strength in Kouzanshi, where they'd had to walk quite a bit, but Ore was going to have to work him back up to it again already. For a first night there, it seemed a bit much to make him walk right away. Ore, himself, hated being cooped up in the small moving rooms as much as he did the small rooms of the castle, but he could put up with it for one night's short trip.

"Ore," Ryan said in his quiet voice, "what is it that Miss Ilena is here at the castle for? Is it just for the repair to her hip?"

Ore looked at him in great surprise. "No one's told you, Little Mister?"

Ryan shook his head. Ore blinked. To have watched over her for this long. "I'm sorry, Little Mister. You've been very strong." Ryan sat looking out the window of the carriage, one hand under his chin, not saying anything. He looked very lonely, to Ore. "Ah...what can I say...Miss Ilena was the household steward for Earl Shicchi of Tokumade. Like you, she rose to her position young, at the age of seventeen." Ryan looked at him sideways in surprise.

"She's well respected by the people of Tokumade, and the people of the household love her. But the Earl is a difficult man, so her ability is all the more impressive." Ore sat and thought bleakly about where Ilena had come from. He didn't notice that Ryan turned to face him in surprise, that he'd recognized in Ore an emotion that he didn't usually have.

He finally pulled his attention back to Ryan and his question, sighing a bit. "She was returning to the Earldom seat with her mistress, the lady wife of the Earl, when a landslide took the carriage and all with it, except Miss Ilena. Mistress and I had just earlier that day passed both the location of the landslide, and the carriage itself. Mistress requested to go with the rescue party to give aid.

"Because we were there, Master was able to learn about the ill works of the Earl. He's brought Miss Ilena here to protect her while she's recovering, so that she can testify before the Lord's Court against her former master." Ore looked up at Ryan and saw he was being looked at with very round eyes. "Did you receive the report about the Little Death being used in tincture form?"

Ryan nodded. "I found it fascinating. I've been able to experiment a little with it, but would like to know more."

Ore nodded. "I would think you might. That report came from Miss Ilena. She was the research assistant to a surgery researcher who discovered those properties, and the living experiment to see to it's working. Master has sent me to discover if he, Doctor Elliot, will come to the castle to continue his research there." Ore's stomach turned a little. He would still rather there was a removal of the drug from the streets than more research on it.

Ryan sat up straighter, keenly interested. "She mentioned being a research assistant. I didn't know it was for the Little Death. If Doctor Elliot will come, I'd like to work with him."

Ore smiled. "I think Master would like that, also. However, first he has another thing to do."

Ryan's face fell a bit and asked the question, then he remembered to do it himself. "What is it he's to do?"

"He's the surgeon who'll perform an experimental surgery on Miss Ilena to see if her leg can be made to work again. When he's done what he can do for that, then he'll be tasked to continue his research, if he can be convinced to come." Ryan was surprised again, and almost looked even more interested in having the surgeon come. Ryan found the most joy in research. "Do you think you'll be able to help me convince him to come, Little Mister?" Ore asked.

"I would like that, if I'm able," Ryan agreed quickly.

"Well, likely you'll get the opportunity," Ore smiled. It was perhaps a good thing he was doing two things at once again.

Ryan paused, his hands resting between his knees, then looking up at Ore he said, "I'm glad Miss Ilena encouraged me to ask questions."

Ore studied him. "Does it make you feel better to know?"

"Yes, and that you were the one to tell me." Ryan looked out the window again, pondering his deep thoughts. Ore thought he didn't look so lonely any more.

-o-o-o-

Ryan was a bit nervous, but not as bad as he would have been if he'd never been to Kouzanshi with Mizi and Ore. He was also excited. He was finally doing something for himself, for the first time ever. Ore led the way into the tavern, then paused. He wanted to see if the badge of his face worked here, too. He didn't have to wait long, although this time he wasn't grabbed by a young waitress. Rather, this woman looked like one of the owners.

"Welcome to the Scholar's Tavern, sirs." Her voice was low and smooth. "I am Ella. My husband, Rolc, and I are glad you've come tonight. We hope you'll enjoy your time here. Because it's your first time to come, please let me explain the house rules."

Ore and Ryan listened politely as she explained that the tavern was a quiet place for thinkers to come and get a different perspective on their work or to just let their minds rest for a time. Therefore, they asked for quiet conversations on the main floor. If the conversations became too heated or too many folks joined in, they were welcome to move upstairs to enclosed party rooms. They would be invited to move up to them if they forgot themselves.

"Please enjoy yourselves and relax. ...And Father," she looked at Ore sharply, "please keep your visits as discrete as possible."

Ore nodded. "Miss Ella, I also would like that very much. While my first visit to the Black Cat was fun, it was a bit overwhelming. Would it be better to give you advanced warning, or shall I attempt to sneak in?" He tried to make the question innocent and sincere.

She looked at him, trying to decide how to answer. "I suppose we could send out the word that if you come here, you're seeking peace and aren't to be disturbed."

"That would be acceptable. Then, if I'm in the mood for fun, I can visit one of the more active locations. Although if someone really needed to talk to me, I wouldn't turn them away."

Ella seemed to like that plan. "We'll see to it. Please come this way." She led them to a table, nicely laid out, and sat them down. They ordered food and drink: something light for Ryan who was still learning to hold his alcohol, a stronger drink for Ore who couldn't get drunk no matter how hard he tried.

"Do you know her?" Ryan asked Ore.

"I do now," Ore said noncommittally. Ore looked around the room, making his usual check of the area. It looked like a few people had recognized him, but most appeared to just be regular patrons, there for the atmosphere. Then he saw Doctor Elliot, finishing up his dinner. "Excuse me, Little Mister. I've found someone I need to speak with. Will you be okay for a bit?" Ryan nodded, and Ore slipped over to talk to the surgeon.

-o-o-o-

Ryan looked around at the other guests as he waited. It really was surprisingly quiet. It felt like being in Kouzanshi, in the reading library of the research campus. By decor it was obviously an eating establishment, however. The seating around the outer edge was a little different, too. The tables were booths with fixed, high–backed benches on either side rather than chairs. It looked like each bench seated two comfortably, three in a squeeze — and he could see that happening if a larger rowdy group of students should arrive.

In the center of the room were the standard tables with chairs, but the tables were round and not skimpy, so that if more than four diners wanted to sit at the table, they could. Ryan thought it intriguing that the owners had made the seating so flexible, but surely it was because of their experience in feeding students in Kouzanshi (and professors, truth be told, who could become even more heated in their discussions of their beloved research). He assumed that the upstairs conference rooms here could get as rowdy as the more lively moments he'd seen there.

The oil lamps on the tables and affixed to the walls sparkled through their glass chimneys, and the fireplace opposite the kitchen snapped and hissed a little as it warmly kept back the early spring chill that still enfolded Nijoushi, particularly at night. Ryan relaxed a little.

He was older by more than a year now since he'd been in Kouzanshi, and even finally taller. He'd probably never be much taller than Mizi, ...although if he could get to be that tall, that might be enough. It would be good if he could find some friends here to talk to, and if his friends from Kouzanshi came to visit, this would be a good place to bring them.

Ryan looked around again to see if there was anyone who was young enough to fit his personal needs when he saw Ella bringing his and Ore's food and drink. *Ah,* he looked around for Ore. Ore had seen the food come and was on his way, a nervous looking fellow in tow carrying his drink with him.

"Little Mister, this is Doctor Elliot. Doctor Elliot, Mister Ryan, Head Court Healer." Both men got sparks of intense interest in their eyes. "Is it okay if he joins us for a bit?" Ore introduced them and asked before he took his seat, waiting for Ella to put their plates of food down so he didn't get in her way.

Ryan nodded enthusiastically. He thought of all the questions he wanted to ask, trying to sort them into proper order. Then he realized that Ore had continued talking and Doctor Elliot was now answering. Ryan realized belatedly that that was probably a good idea. Talking about illicit drugs here might not be a good idea, even if it was in a place that understood researchers.

Ore glanced at Ryan encouragingly. He'd asked the surgeon to explain to Ryan what his current research was. Ryan blushed, as he hadn't heard from the beginning. "Ah, I'm sorry, it's my first time here. And...I'm a healer."

The surgeon stopped, then smiled. "I understand. Go ahead and eat. I'll start over and go a little slower." Ryan nodded his thanks and started eating, paying careful attention this time.

The surgeon explained that he'd been researching how to take a tendon with a piece of the bone it was attached to from a body that had just recently passed, cooling it quickly and deeply to keep the deterioration to a minimum, and using it to replace a tendon in a patient that had the tendon separate from the bone.

"Once a tendon has separated from the bone, it can't grow back or heal, so that limb becomes useless. But bone regrows to bone, and tendon to tendon, and muscle to muscle. I think it's harder to match muscle cells, so I've theorized that the tendon to tendon connection is better." Doctor Elliot paused to sip at his drink.

Ryan understood this concept basically and nodded while continuing to eat politely. It did seem to make sense. The surgeon further explained the basics of body matching — finding a body part from one body and putting it into another was not just as simple as that. If the bodies didn't match, the receiving body would reject the graft.

While Ryan hadn't dealt with it too much in the body, he understood it very well with plants. He commented as such to Doctor Elliot. "Many plants can be grafted, but only to specific other plants. Often it can make the final product stronger, with plants."

Doctor Elliot considered Ryan's comment and wondered with small mumblings if it was possible for human grafts to be stronger than the original. While he was off in his world, Ryan had a thought that it was very uncommon to find a place where both plant grafting and human body part grafting could be discussed casually at the same table, particularly without someone else in the room complaining.

He looked at Ore, wondering if he was okay with the topic and if he might be lost. Ore smiled back and lifted his current glass in a little toast. "It's okay, Little Mister. I'm enjoying feeling like I'm back at Kouzanshi with you and Mistress. I know how to keep up with these kinds of things, after two and a half years of practice." Ryan nodded, relieved, agreeing that the feeling was rather nostalgic.

As he watched Ore, he noticed Ore was also distracting himself a little with keeping an eye on all the other patrons. Ryan relaxed a little more. He wouldn't have to worry about people who might complain about their subject matter. If a problem did come up outside the conversation, Ore would take care of it.

The surgeon returned back to the problem at hand and Ryan gave him his attention again. "I haven't had the opportunity to actually experiment yet, and there are a few things I haven't worked out. I know how to cut the hole in the receiving bone to put the new bone into it, but I can't decide how to get it to stay still for the two to three weeks it will take for the bones to fuse. In cadavers, even the slightest shifting of the body can make the pieces slip."

He described his current vision of some kind of splint that could be attached to the receiving bone to either side of the grafted bone, but he was concerned about how to attach it, and if the receiving bone might split or splinter.

Ryan considered the problem for a moment. "How about something like a glue?"

"Eh, a glue?"

Ryan nodded. "We use knitbone to help broken bones heal faster. We also use a poultice of *arugulus minorus* to minimize the pain, and sap of willeradder, with sometimes...well, a few other things depending on the cause and need, to seal together large wounds that otherwise bandages wouldn't keep closed. I've seen it used by a field surgeon to re–attach a foot to a leg, though the bone in that case was intact.

"It's viscosity can be made variable by adding witch hazel. I think for your case, all of the things that might be used for bone healing could be added, with a pain reducer — since bone pain is pretty severe — and still be used inside the body without too much trouble."

Doctor Elliot rubbed his chin. "Hmm...that's not a bad idea. How fast does it set and will the moisture in the body cause it to dissolve or go too thin before the bone can regrow?"

Ryan paused to swallow his current bite of food as he considered the answer. "Mmm...it does need about five minutes after placement to set, but since it only thins using witch hazel, the moisture in the body shouldn't affect it too much after the set time, particularly if it was applied thickly enough. Though, would you want to have it a thin enough poultice to capillate into the bone–on–bone connection? Or do you want it to just be a surface cover?"

Doctor Elliot's brow furrowed in consideration. "Well, if it was just a surface cover, I'd want to apply it to both the front and back side of the receiving bone. My first try is on a hip, which is good because it's a wide bone with good work space. But, I would think reaching the back side of a hip on the patient might be difficult. We'd have to move too many muscles and other tendons around to get to it. If the poultice contains the knitbone I would think it would help to have it capillate into the connection, but would the other ingredients hinder the growth of bone to bone?"

Ryan took a while to think about each of the ingredients. "No, I don't think so. Maybe only the sap if it took too long to dissolve, but it's the thickest ingredient so is least likely to capillate, especially if the others fill the space first. But if you can't get to the back side of the hip, you may actually want some of the sap to enter the join so you have a more secure connection.

"I would think a longer dissolve time would be okay if you're looking at a two or more week window anyway. My longer dissolve time isn't that long, more like a few — say three to four — days at most." Ryan shrugged a little.

"Hmm...that might work then." Doctor Elliot seemed pleased that they might have a workable solution. They paused to take a swallow of their drinks, the traditional mini–celebration of reaching a positive resolution to a problem for all heavy thinkers and part–time drinkers, as well as the filler while their minds spun down and moved to a new topic.

Ore smiled to see the familiar action and followed through with a large swig of his drink, finishing it off, and waving for another to replace it. Ryan, used to this, just took note of it, but the surgeon stopped for a moment. "How many have you had of that?!"

Ore grinned. "I don't count."

The surgeon looked at him aghast. He was obviously still nursing his first just as Ryan was. He looked at Ryan. Ryan smiled shyly. "I've been at places like this with Ore a lot. He never gets drunk. It's okay."

The surgeon looked at Ore thoughtfully for a moment, his chin on his palm, elbow resting on the table. "Some day, someone's going to do research on you to find out how to patent and bottle that capability."

Ore laughed. "Then I'll have to be sure they pay me a royalty for every bottle sold. I'll be wealthy inside of a month and never have to work again in my life."

"I should say," the surgeon murmured, looking as if he wished he could be that researcher, and like he might try as his next project, if he could tie Ore down long enough.

Ryan decided to bring the conversation back. "You said you have other concerns?"

"Ah, yes." The surgeon sat back and turned his drink in his hand. "It's the tendon to tendon connection. They're very fibrous. I think they could be sewn together and they would regrow, the same as the bone would. But I personally don't have a precedent for it, or even for the muscle to muscle option, though it would be interesting if your glue method could be used there somehow."

Doctor Elliot blushed in embarrassment. "I'm afraid I've done a lot of cadaver work, but it's...you know...difficult to get ...ah, patients...live specimens, as it were. So I'm not sure how to go about thinking about it."

Ryan nodded. Surgery was certainly something most people would appreciate if it was necessary for their own health, but if it was someone else, it was often thought of as a sort of dark art, to be afraid of — not that he minded it. Many of his own patients thought he was out to poison them before healing them, as frustrating as that attitude was.

"Excuse me," a deep voice said over the table. A chair was pulled out, and a tall, muscular man sat down with them. "I might have the experience you need. Poulter's the name." He passed his thick paw around to shake hands with everyone. Ore quickly introduced everyone. "I'm a large animal veterinarian. I do a lot of work on horses, and they tear ligaments and tendons all the time."

The surgeon's eyes lit up and he turned all his attention to the new man. Poulter told them a story about a client's beloved horse that had torn a back upper tendon "...like on your hip, there, only it didn't separate from the bone, thank the gods. That I couldn't repair, as you say. I used a needle with a wide eye, cut a bit off another tendon that was long enough — one fiber's enough, really, and the other tendon doesn't miss it much.

"I was all set to go, then realized I was in a pickle." He laughed, sounding nearly like his patients. "I didn't know whether to sew it cross–wise or long–wise! But then I remembered watching the ladies sewing the straps of the kid's overalls together when they'd snapped it playing in the woods. They always did it cross–wise.

"That made sense to me you see. If it was long–wise, wouldn't the threads just pull through 'n tear the tendon up? But cross–wise should give it strength, like on the overalls. Didn't take long to have her patched up after that."

Ryan thought of his own mother's stitching that he'd watched in front of the fireplace during the winters. "Did you just do one line, or did you reinforce it with multiple lines of stitches?"

"Eh? Ah, well, when I got done with the first line, I looked at it and couldn't see it working. This was a horse after all. They've got to use a lot of strength, especially in their back legs. That looked pretty weak. So I added another row, and then kept going until it looked right for the size of the mare and the leg."

Poulter ran his hand through his hair, leaving it to slowly fall back down into place. "Heh. I suppose it was a bit much, maybe. But in the end it worked. She was up and running again four months later. And by six months the hitch in her step was gone. I've used it every time since then and had just as good results."

"Aha! That's wonderful! Thank you...Poulter," the surgeon gushed. "That shouldn't be too hard then. Hmm...though both her other two tendons on that hip were injured as well. Can they be used? They'll have had about five weeks to heal up."

Poulter scratched his head. "Well...you want to look for a strand that looks a consistent thickness. It'll break at a thinner spot, just like thread. If there aren't too many of those, you probably don't want to take one from that tendon as it's still healing up and needs all the good strands it's got. But you can take one from anywhere just so it's long enough. After all, you don't have to worry about body typing since it's the patient's own material."

"That's true. I'll remember that." Elliot nodded wisely.

-o-o-o-

Just as they were about to raise their cups to their lips, a woman's voice cut in, "Hey, ye bully boys. Just a sec b'fore ye go c'ngratulatin' yerselves." A plump woman with a height that made it look more like "ample" came up to the table, set her mug down on it and leaned on her other hand. "If yer talkin' 'bout the hip area on a woman, yeh got more things to think about."

"What's that?" asked the shocked surgeon, suddenly seeming nervous again.

"Is it a woman patient?" Two yesses and a nod of the head (from Ryan) answered her. The woman grabbed a chair from the next table over and swung it around between Ryan and Poulter. Plopping down, she faced the surgeon directly, punctuating her sentences with hand gestures as she spoke.

"Look here. I'm a surgical midwife, and one of the hardest things to get other surgeons to recognize is that a man's body and a woman's body's different." Ore snorted into his drink, pulling her gaze. "Well, yeh'd think so, wouldn't yeh? But when it comes to what's inside, they don't open up enough women, just the men.

"Well, have yeh yet?!" The sudden return of attention to the surgeon startled him and he panicked a bit. "Yeah, that's what I thought. Yeh haven't yet. Well, if'n yeh can, get yer hands on a female cadaver — at least one — *before* yeh open yer patient up. Yeh'll be glad yeh did.

"Now, see here." She pulled a piece of paper from the breast of her shirt and Ryan and the surgeon blushed and looked away. Then she pulled out a pen. Putting the pen to the paper, she drew a diagram of the hip area. Ryan was impressed, and so were the other men. It was well drawn and easily understandable.

"Here's yer hip bone and leg socket. The hip's wider and more cupped than a man's. It's got t' handle a baby, see, and birthin' it. If yeh go and put the new tendon in the wrong spot, it'll all get in the way and every birthin' will be hard to impossible and yeh get a dead mother and possibly child for yer trouble. Yeh got to know the difference there." She marked the hip area the tendon should roughly go into.

"Then there's the baby's home i'self, and the egg sack and tube." Several pairs of ears went red and Ore leaned in to see better. This was getting really interesting. She went on unfazed, like any true researcher. "While yer in there, yeh gotta check 'n see if there was any damage to either of these. If the womb is damaged and not healin', she'll keep bleedin' internally without yeh knowin' about it until her fever's too high and she's already dead."

The surgeon shook his head. "It probably wasn't considered by the surgeon who worked on her at the first, as you say, but she's already past four weeks into recovery and hasn't had symptoms of infection since..."

"...Three days in and the field surgeon took out the last of the rock fragments. That seemed to fix it," Ore inserted smoothly.

The midwife looked up at him, her eyes judging him, "*Hmph.* All right then." She looked back at the surgeon, "But remember it, a'right?" Doctor Elliot nodded.

"Then, there's this." She enclosed in a circle the diagram of a little line that extended from the womb to a small oval resting just inside the hip. "This is a tricky thing here. Small and delicate, yet essential to a woman. There's one on each side of the womb, so the other side looks the same.

"This oval, that's the egg sack. Don't get no children from a woman that doesn't have these. If only one's missin' you'll only get the opportunity to have one every other month. They alternate, once each month, sendin' an egg down the tube to the womb. Then if it's not used, it's flushed out during the woman's bleed time.

"If the tube's damaged, the egg can get stuck, but what the man supplies can get through, sometimes. Then the child starts tryin' t' grow right there in the tube." She got really serious. "I'm sure yeh can imagine that no body's built t' handle that situation." Even Ryan nodded. If the tube was really that narrow no human child would grow in it.

"I lost three mothers t' this problem. ...Actually, I became a surgeon midwife because of this problem. I dug them all back up and opened them up, and there was this tube, exploded open in the majority of the cases in this one family. It wasn't external abuse, as far as I could tell. I theorize it was a familial problem.

"It doesn't take an expert to figure out damage from an external blow would cause the same problem. And sure 'nuff. I lost another one to just that. Now, I ask all my patients before they get pregnant, or as soon after as possible, if they've ever had harsh blows to that part of the body. If'n they have, I go in and check it. If I'm in doubt, I take it out." She sighed. "Course, now I lose patients by tellin' them surgery is required if they've been damaged."

She ran her hand unconsciously through her thick curly dark hair, then continued, pointing to the thin line again. "This's a tube like the ones in a man's sexual organ. Thin and smooth and should be an even thickness 'though it flutes here at the egg sack. That should look like a beautiful fancy vase, no rips or intense folds. Just ripples." She drew a close–up of the fluted edge as she talked. "If the tube's got dents, cuts, holes, or is discolored anywhere along it, it's probably a bad'n and should come out."

She paused and looked up at Ore. "She have any kids yet? She old enough to be hav'n 'em?"

He answered immediately. "No kids yet. Perfect age to be having them."

"Know how many yeh want yet?"

"Ah, no...," Ore protested, holding a hand up, trying to say it wasn't him, but she ignored him and went back to her paper, tapping the tube with her pen.

"If yeh take out the tube, take out the egg sack too. It makes for recovery complications, but I've always felt I'd rather be safe than sorry."

"Recovery complications?" Doctor Elliot asked.

"Yeah. Ever been married, or live with your aging mother?" she raised a bit of a sceptical eyebrow at him.

"Ah, no." Doctor Elliot deflated just a little.

"Well, then yeh might not understand, but I'll give it a go anyway." She took a breath. "When a girl's becomin' a woman, she goes through emotional swings that stabilize into regular patterns by the time she gets into her twenties. Then she's the most ready to bear children.

"When a woman's body's gettin' too old, and it's endin' it's baby production time, she goes through those emotional swings again, though sometimes worse. Most women'll even have sudden sweats in the advanced stages where their bodies get too hot for no reason. There's nothin' wrong with them 'cept their bodies are shuttin' down the baby production cycle. Well, and they can be insufferable for a sane body to live with when the emotions suddenly flare up and are all over the map.

"Takin' out this," she tapped the egg sack oval, "makes 'em have those same symptoms, though more mild when only one's taken out. Take both out and it's the same as becomin' an old maid."

"Just that one small part of the body causes all that chaos?" Poulter asked, amazed.

"Yup. I've proved it plenty o' times now. So you," she pointed her pen at Ore, who tried to protest again, then gave up when he realized he actually *was* going to have to deal with it, "c'n expect to have to deal with sudden tears, depression, surprisin'ly strong anger, yellin' when nothin's brought it on, sometimes even laughin' fits from out'a nowhere that dissolve back into tears."

"Ah, how long?" ventured Ryan, looking worried. He figured he'd have to deal with it too.

"When it's both, up to ten years depending on the size and age of the woman. The bigger and older, the longer it takes. When it's one, the body stabilizes round about the three year mark, if yer lucky, but the 'off month' they'll be more moody than the 'on month', though you can't tell sometimes.

"That's until they reach the end of the baby production time. Then they get the side benefit of having that process be shorter. They've already done half the work, after all." She stopped and looked around the table.

Doctor Elliot looked like he was glad after all that he wasn't married, and maybe he'd just keep it that way. Poulter looked like a light had gone on and he could finally see. Ryan had a worry crease on his forehead as he gazed at the hand–drawn picture: his thoughtful look. He was soaking it up for future reference. Ore was morbidly resigned. He put his chin in his hand and sighed.

The midwife looked at him shrewdly. "Yeh all understand now?" Everyone nodded.

"Yes, ma'am," Ore said obediently, which earned him a smart–alec grin.

"Thank you very much, ...ah," the surgeon stopped having not received her name.

The midwife stood up, putting her pen away as she did so, and handed him the paper. "Doctor Elia, Goodwife." she winked at him. "Good luck with the graft."

"Thanks," he replied weakly as she walked off, her mug swinging from one hand, the other raised in farewell.

"Hmm," Ore said to Poulter, "even if she's your type, your wife's going to be mad if she sees you looking at another woman like that."

Poulter swung his head around to look at him, then grinned ruefully. "Yeah, well it's rare to find one your kind with that kind of head. Can't help but wish just a little bit..., but you're right." Poulter stood, "I should be getting home to the missus.

"...But I don't think I'll tell her about the fact that her emotions are controlled by one of the tiniest parts of her body. She'd throw the pitcher, the pot, and the bowl at me. I think I'd rather be warm in bed tonight with her in my arms, than cold on the floor alone. Good luck, surgeon." He waved as he walked toward the door, Doctor Elliot saying a weak "thanks" again.

The three remaining men looked at each other, then just sat and mutually wound down, silently working their drinks for a while. Ore waited patiently for the higher minds to come back to ground — his didn't take as long.

When it looked like Doctor Elliot was back to earth, Ore asked quietly, keeping the conversation limited to their table, "So, how long before you think you can be ready?"

"Mmm," the surgeon considered it a while and answered just as quietly. "Find a female cadaver. Arah! That in itself could be a month. Well, maybe a week if I get one off the black market, maybe. I've already got the potential grafts ready, so no time there, unless none of them work.

"I've only got three so I hope one of them's a good match. It might not be enough, but she said no more than three tries, and body matching is actually quite difficult. If I have to find more, it's a three week process minimum. Mister Ryan, how long would it take you to work up the glue?"

"About twenty–five minutes," Ryan answered promptly. "Ten if everything's already gathered together. But we need to use it within fifteen to twenty minutes or it will set and be no good."

"Oh. Then can I impose upon you to be present and be my assistant? I'm going to need a second set of hands. My usual assistant will be on the table this time and not able to help." He was smiling a little reminiscently.

"Okay. ...Um, maybe Mizi could help, too?" Ryan asked. Doctor Elliot nodded. He was looking a little distant.

"Is something wrong?" asked Ore.

"Ah, no," the surgeon said, "It's just...I likely won't get to have her help anymore, will I? It feels a bit...lonely, I guess."

"Yes, I suppose it would," agreed Ore, then casually added, "If it gets too lonely, maybe you could consider working at the castle as a court surgeon."

Ryan glanced at Ore out of the corner of his eye. Even he knew how to tell now when Ore was fishing. He kept his face carefully composed.

"Eh? What's that?" the surgeon was surprised out of his train of thought.

"Well, you know," Ore shrugged. "Sometimes even the palaces need new researchers with their ideas to come into the team. But I know you're probably pretty busy and all."

"Well, no, not really. Wound it all down to come out here for the Missus. I've been focused on helping her out with the hip repair, but there's not much after that right now. ...Except *you* intrigue me...," Doctor Elliot leaned forward.

Ore laughed easily, leaning away, his hands up as if to protect himself. "Well, you know, I'm in the castle at Master's beck and call. Can't say if I'd be available, but I know the little Mister has a lot of questions he wants to ask you. And the Missus will be needing you close by to monitor her recovery...."

Doctor Elliot leaned back and crossed his arms, pretending to think about it. "Well, then, alright. If the Regent will have me, I'll come. Cadavers?"

"No black–market ones, I'm afraid, but perhaps...ex–prisoners instead? And whatever you need from the normally acceptable sources," Ore negotiated.

The surgeon's eyes lit up. "Can you get me a female within this week?"

Ore smiled. Money always made acquisition easier. "I think we might be able to."

"I can be there tomorrow."

"Good. Come to the Pelican gate."

"Okay," the surgeon rubbed his hands together.

When Ryan's head was starting to droop from falling asleep having had just a little too much alcohol in his system, Ore downed the remainder of his yellow liquid then rose. "Let's head back, Little Mister, if you're ready."

"Okay, Ore." Ryan jumped up from the table then wobbled just a little. Ore gently grasped his elbow to hold him steady. When he was, Ryan turned to their companion of the evening. "It was nice to get to talk with you, Doctor Elliot. I look forward to working with you." He held out his hand, and Elliot took it in a handshake. It took a bit for them to actually make contact.

"Likewise." It looked like Elliot might be weaving his way home as well that night, although he wasn't quite as asleep on his feet as Ryan.

As they walked out the door, Ore put his hands behind his head and looked up at the night sky, then down at his companion. "That was fun, wasn't it, Little Mister?"

Ryan looked up at him, then back at the tavern. "Yes, it was." He was looking forward to his next visit.

After dropping Ryan off at his quarters in the medical wing (he slept in the infirmary following the examples of his teachers so as to be available in emergencies), Ore went up to Rei's room to report. After feeling nostalgic about Kouzanshi, he was feeling the need to see his master. Those two years he, Mizi, and Ryan had been there had been difficult in the sense that he'd become very lonely for Rei, and that had been reawoken.

Rei's room here at Nijou Castle didn't have an exterior accessway — it was considered a security risk — so Ore had to enter from the main hall. He was grateful that Rei allowed him access through the guards. He'd been made to promise that he wouldn't abuse the privilege. As Ore walked into the spacious room, Rei looked up from his reading.

"Ore," Rei greeted him.

"Can I join you on the bed?" Ore asked him.

"No. Why?" Rei was quick to answer.

Ore went and stood by the bed, rather than flopping into his usual place on the settee. Rei raised an eyebrow at the less than typical behavior. "I've just come from the Scholar's Tavern. Doctor Elliot will be here tomorrow morning. He's agreed to come to the castle. I took the little Mister with me." Ore gave the full report to Rei.

"I put in a requisition order for two female cadavers after I dropped off the little Mister. I believe that Doctor Elliot should be ready to perform the experimental surgery only a few days after he arrives, although it's a guess, of course. And the little Mister is looking forward to working with him on the Little Death experiments."

Rei was thoughtful. "What do you think of Doctor Elliot?"

Ore didn't hold back. "He's competent, intelligent, careful, indebted to Miss Ilena, capable of being easily bullied, easily bribeable if it benefits his research, a bachelor–for–life. The life of a closeted intellectual shows through."

"Eh. Then...well, for now it will do. It sounds like a reasonable plan they worked out. So, Ryan's on board? Will he be helping?"

"Yes. He wants Mistress too as well."

"Ah, well, that...," Ore could see having Mizi help with a surgery was not something Rei was comfortable with, but then not many people were comfortable with the thought of surgery. "She'll probably enjoy learning something new, though, eh?"

"That would be like her," Ore agreed.

Rei looked down at the document he was reading. "Mother — Ilena — has an interesting past, doesn't she." His voice was soft.

Ore nodded. "Watching them tell their stories is intense. If you ever get the opportunity to, you should have even one of them tell you in person. Because she rescues them from extremely difficult circumstances, they can't hold back their emotions when they remember them." Ore was remembering all the tears shed on his first trip out.

Rei looked at Ore out of the corner of his eye. "I think I've already had that opportunity, once. I seem to remember it being about that way."

Ore looked at him in mild surprise, then remembered he'd told his own story. "Heh. I suppose. But my story isn't as intense as theirs."

"No? Well, it seemed that way to me, but maybe that's because it's still being written." Ore looked at Rei with affront, but Rei refused to look at him, affecting an air of disinterest.

"Well, the stories do make it easier to understand why they support her, at least." Rei frowned. "I still feel like she's picking and choosing people very carefully. ...Although one person can only do so much. It would be like her to be careful with her capacity."

"Well, and these are the ones she reserved for the particular reason of taking down Earl Shicchi," Ore said. "I haven't yet received any stories from those she has in the general network. ...I would expect they're probably similar."

Rei nodded agreement. "If you do happen to get any of those stories, I'd like them also."

"May I have the book back when you're done reading?" Ore asked. "I expect more stories to come in as we collect other witnesses. I'd like to put them all together into one report." In reality, he wanted to be able to re–read them.

Rei looked like he knew Ore's ulterior motive. "Mmm...I'm not done, though. I'll keep it for a few days. I shouldn't stay up much longer tonight." Ore agreed that it was a bit late for Rei to be up, but he was glad that he was so they could visit. "Will you be with Ilena tonight?" Rei asked him.

Ore nodded. "I'll go there next. I sent the little Mister to bed. He's still not holding his alcohol well — and he only had one mug." He gave Rei a conspiratorial grin, which was returned.

"Well, be sure you come to the office in good time in the morning. You were gone all afternoon so your stacks are starting to increase again."

Ore groaned. "Master, how am I supposed to do all those stacks and stand with Mistress?"

"Do them at the same time?" Rei raised his eyebrows at him. "Or do them while you're with Ilena, like Ryan and Mizi?"

Ore sighed. "I do need to sleep sometimes, Master. ...Can I come sleep next to you tonight?"

"No. Why?" was the immediate response.

"Because I was made to remember Kouzanshi. I miss you all over again."

Rei stared at Ore, not quite sure what to say about that. "No."

"*Heeh.* Well, talking to you has helped. I'll sit with you until you're ready to sleep, then." He turned to go to the settee.

Rei snapped the records in front of him closed. "I'm ready now." He set it on the table beside him, on the far side away from Ore.

Ore looked at Rei dejectedly, knowing he'd been rejected. "That's harsh, Master."

"Get out. Go sleep with Mother." Rei looked at him with a firm face, but his eyes were kind.

Ore slumped his shoulders in defeat and headed for the door. "Good night, Master."

"I'll see you in the morning." Rei wanted to reinforce his requirement that Ore be in the office early.

CHAPTER 15 Mizi's Awakening

Ore wandered around the castle. In truth, he didn't want to be in that small room tonight. He was having those complicated feelings again, and they were making him restless. He wondered if Mizi was still awake, then decided he'd better not. It might make Rei upset with him if he'd been to her room this late at night. But then he looked up and found he was there anyway.

He sighed. He really needed to learn to pay attention to what he was doing better. He leaned against the wall outside her door and closed his eyes, listening. What was she doing? Was she awake and still reading, or was she sleeping?

"Ah! Ore?!"

Ore's eyes snapped open. "Mistress?" She was coming towards him, holding a book to her, still dressed in her uniform. "Are you just coming?" He wondered if he'd been asleep on his feet, to have not heard her coming.

"Mm. I had more work to get done after dinner with Ilena. What are you doing?" she stopped in front of him and looked at him questioningly, her head tilted slightly.

"I've just returned from recruiting Doctor Elliot for Master, and reporting to him," Ore explained.

"Eh, he's going to be in the castle?"

Ore nodded. "Master wants the Little Death researcher where he can keep an eye on him." Mizi nodded. She could understand that.

Ore had the sudden thought that he was going to be sent to requisition a room for him, too. Maybe he should do it on his way to the office in the morning, to just get it done early. *Hahhh.* He was getting to be too much like Andrew. "Mistress, do you want to run away from the castle for a few hours with me? I found a new place like Kouzanshi you would like." He gave her a grin.

She shook her head. "I'd like to go on my next break, but tonight isn't good."

Ore shrugged as if he'd expected that answer, and he had, but he really did want to escape. "Mistress...," he said hesitantly trying to find the words. Mizi readied herself. She'd seen this before when Ore was struggling with a thing he couldn't solve. "At this place, even Ore has become too busy." He looked at her sadly. "I can't be for Mistress what Ore needs to be. What shall I do?"

Mizi took a breath. It had hurt to hear it, although it was already becoming obvious. The fact that he'd only today been able to come to her, when he'd been back for at least a few days, had accentuated his absence in her daily life. "It's okay, Ore."

He shook his head. "It isn't okay. Mistress is too lonely."

Mizi nodded. "Yes, I am. That's why I'm doing what I can to change that. That's why I've decided to talk to Ilena. Even if I don't do things as she would, she can give me the strength to move forward to be where I want to be." Ore looked at her appraisingly. She seemed to be stronger just having said that.

"Ore, you remember I'm the one who said that you needed a partner, so that when you couldn't stand beside me, your partner could? And that when you needed strengthening, your partner would be there to strengthen you?" Ore nodded.

"*I* chose Ilena. *I* did that." Her look was very earnest. "If you can't be present for me enough at this time, rely on your partner. Even though she can't come stand with me at this time, I can go to her when I need her. She's always present at that place."

Ore did the equivalent of taking a step back, even though he was already leaning against the wall. Mizi was glowing. He stared at her, wide–eyed, then he bowed slightly, formally putting his hand to his heart. "Yes, Mistress. ...And I'll come to you when I can."

Mizi shifted her stance. "And, Ore...can I come to you?"

Ore's eyes flew wide again. He considered office and palace protocol as he placed his hands behind him to lean on them, too, so they wouldn't do things they shouldn't. After searching his brain, he nodded. "Yes. If you need Ore, then you may come to me." Mizi looked relieved. Ore smiled, trying to make a joke, "You'll almost always find me in Master's office, when I'm in the castle."

"I know," Mizi smiled, and Ore thought her expression looked very calcu-lating, for Mizi.

After leaving Mizi in her room, Ore went up on the roof again. He walked slowly towards Ilena's room, thinking. His mistress was teaching him what it was for him to have a partner to stand behind her. It did bring him comfort to know Mizi wasn't alone.

Then there was the other half. "*When you need strengthening, your partner would be there to strengthen you.*" Most of the time when he was with Ilena, she just made him confused, but when he read the stories about her, when she gave advice, when Rei had been stronger from talking to her — such things did strengthen him. Could he rely on Ilena, the way Mizi was?

He dropped down silently into the medical wing and walked up to Ilena's door. It was strangely quiet to not find Ryan there. He nodded at the guards and turned the handle on the door.

Ilena was awake, waiting for him. "Good evening," he said quietly as he walked to his place.

"Good evening," she responded quietly.

Was her being awake for him a thing she did to support him? It was almost beginning to feel like coming home. He knew his being there was a support to her. As her partner, that was also his responsibility, one he'd already come to accept.

It was his to be there to see that she was comforted of the shared feeling they had of being trapped in small rooms, so that she could rest, so that she could do her duty during the day. She did the same for him. He really could sleep better when the room had another living person in it, even when it was this small.

"Are there no questions tonight?"

"No," he responded just as gently as she'd asked.

They were quiet for a while longer, then Ilena asked, "What do you need, Ore?"

"*Haaah.* For some reason, it always catches me off guard when you're actually Mother in front of me." He could feel her smile. She waited. "For the first time since I've been back I was able to be with Mistress today. I wasn't even told she'd been given her afternoons back until after we'd been here earlier today.

"Even though I walk at the back of Mistress, Master has need of me in his office daily in this place. To be with Mistress today was what I desired, but Master has called me back already." Ore paused, not quite sure what to say next.

Hesitantly, because she wasn't sure it was her turn to talk yet, Ilena said, "I'm sorry I didn't tell you Mistress Mizi's new schedule. I should have done that first. I'll tell you first in the future, if there's a thing about Mistress Mizi." Ore hadn't been scolding her, yet she'd understood that for her to be his strength he needed to know such things.

When he didn't say anything in response, she continued. "It must be very hard to feel she's alone when you've been able to be her support for these last many years."

Ore looked up at the dark ceiling. "She said to me that she chose you to be my partner so that when I couldn't be present, I could know there was still one who was with her. She said that I should learn to rely on you. ...And she reminded me that you're always present for her at this place." He looked back down at his feet, hidden by the darkness. "It was comforting."

There was companionable silence between them for a while.

"I wish to be your support, Ore. I'll do my best from where I am. I'm glad she's willing to come to me when she has need." Ilena's full heart finally found words.

Ore paused a little longer. "...I'll leave it to you, then." It was a thing he'd heard Andrew and Mina say to each other when they'd had to carry separate burdens for a time. Now he might truly understand how difficult those times were for them.

-o-o-o-

Ore left early the next morning so he could stop by the châtelaine's office yet again, this time for Doctor Elliot. He would need both a laboratory and sleeping quarters, and regular pay. Ore received a location and keys, and a promise the castle identification would be completed by the next morning. While he was there, they handed him the identification tags for Ilena's staff, since he was the one tasked to give them.

From there Ore went to the Pelican gate, figuring Doctor Elliot would be there early. He was. "Good morning, Doctor Elliot," he said as he walked up to the gate, where the guards had asked the researcher to wait until Ore came to get him.

"Ah! Good morning!" The surgeon seemed excited to able to move forward. He had a large bag with him. The guards had already searched it, and weren't sure about letting a person with such implements into the castle grounds, thus they hadn't let him enter unescorted. Ore explained to them who and what the doctor was and that he would be on the castle staff from that day, so that he could come and go as needed.

Ore walked him first to his new residence and handed him his keys. Then they went to the laboratory, where Doctor Elliot dropped off his bag of surgical equipment. He looked around and smiled. "This will do nicely," he approved. "When can I expect my cadavers?"

"I placed the order last night when I came back. Perhaps by today?"

Doctor Elliot rubbed his hands together. "That would be marvelous. I could probably do the surgery within four days, then. I'll go back out in a bit to collect my other things, but may I first see Mistress Ilena?"

Ore nodded. "Certainly."

When they arrived at Ilena's room, she was being aided by Mizi and the castle nurse she'd been assigned. Ore felt a twinge of jealousy. That had been his job, too. There seemed to be many changes lately that didn't feel like happy ones. He stepped in and helped. While he was there with the surgeon, he may as well get in some of the time he wanted. He was already practiced at that, anyway.

When they were done, Doctor Elliot examined Ilena one more time. Ore, watching him, decided he was trying to see if he could feel what he'd learned about the evening before, not having a cadaver yet to open.

"Can you tell?" he asked over the surgeon's shoulder.

Doctor Elliot looked at him sideways. "No. It is indeed very small. I won't be able to tell until I'm inside."

"Tell what?" Ilena asked. She wanted to know what it was they were talking about. It was her body after all.

"Master Ore came and found me at the Scholar's Tavern last night. He brought Mister Ryan with him, and we had an interesting discussion with a few other patrons about your case. There was one thing in particular I was told to look for, but it's a very small thing. I can't tell by external palpitation whether there's a problem or not. I'll have to look when I perform the surgery."

At her concerned look, he added, "It isn't a thing for concern at the moment, just something that I should look at." Ilena nodded, trusting him. Ore thought it was almost funny that the surgeon didn't want to discuss the particulars with Ilena. He knew *she* wouldn't have a problem with the details.

"Master Ore's promised me cadavers for the final bits of research by sometime today," Doctor Elliot continued. "I should be ready to perform the surgery within four days, I should think, if they come that quickly."

Ilena's eyes widened a little. So did Mizi's. "That's very soon, then, isn't it?"

Doctor Elliot nodded, smiling. "The sooner we can complete it, the sooner you can be out of here, no?"

"Yes," said Ilena. It was obvious she wanted out, but that she also wasn't wanting the enforced imprisonment to continue again so soon.

Doctor Elliot turned to look at the other ladies in the room, his eyes resting on Mizi's golden tinted red hair, as was typical of most people meeting her for the first time. "Mistress, this is Doctor Elliot," Ore introduced them. "Doctor Elliot, this is Mizi, —"

He was cut off by Mizi herself. "— Ilena's mistress." She stood tall and firm.

The room was in shocked silence for just a moment. Ore quickly and smoothly recovered. "Ilena's and my mistress. This is Anna, the court nurse assigned to assist with Ilena." Anna bowed to the surgeon.

Doctor Elliot recovered. He bowed to Mizi. "It's an honor to meet my mistress's mistress. Ah...eh...when I spoke to Mister Ryan last night, it was decided that he would need to be present to help with the surgery. He suggested that you might also assist. Has he spoken to you about it?"

Mizi shook her head. "I come here first from my rooms. I won't be speaking to Ryan until after lunch today. ...However, if I can be of assistance, I'd be happy to be available."

"Thank you very much. Also, it's likely Anna could also be of assistance," he looked to her and she nodded. That was pretty much her job right now, anyway. "However, it'll be difficult to perform the surgery in this room, particularly with that many people."

He turned to Ore. "If a larger room could be found? I could do it in my lab, and we could transport her, but it would be simplest if we could perform the surgery in a room she was expected to remain in for her recovery period."

Ore nodded. "I can arrange that." Internally he sighed. It was back to the châtelaine's office for him, once again. He was going to be late to the Rose office after all, this morning. "If you're done with Ilena, I'll escort you back to the gate. Her maids should have arrived by now. I'll have to ask you to find your way back here by yourself, I'm afraid."

"I think I can manage," Doctor Elliot said. "I've been here twice now, and I can ask guards."

"Ask them for the way to the medical wing. We're still protecting Ilena's presence in the castle." Ore was just a bit harsh. Mizi looked at him strangely.

Doctor Elliot stopped with his mouth open, then closed it and nodded. "I'll do that."

They bid their farewells to the ladies and headed out to the gate again. There Ore did indeed trade Doctor Elliot for Leah and Rio, who were just being escorted through the gate by Grandfather. Ore offered to Grandfather that he didn't need to walk all that way this morning, as he could escort the maids. Ilena was with Mizi for the morning, but if he could come in the evening after the dinner hour, that would be best.

Ore was thinking that if Grandfather came after Ryan was supposed to leave, Ryan might actually go back to his office like he was supposed to. It would also occupy Ilena during the hours before he himself arrived. Grandfather agreed, accepted his castle identification, and left with Doctor Elliot.

Ore gave the maids their castle identifications while taking them to their quarters. It was always better to take people to their quarters first, then teach them the way they should go from there. "It's good for you to be here for Ilena. Here at the castle, please refer to me by my name." He looked at them quizzically. "You do know it, don't you?"

"Yes, Master Ore," the elder one, Leah answered. Rio nodded also. Ore wondered. The surgeon had refer to him as "master" as well. He was, to the Family, both "Father" to Ilena's "Mother", and "Master" to her "Mistress". He sighed. It was a reminder that she wanted him. He tried to push it aside. He was just now coming to accept "partner". The others would need to wait a little longer. "Will you tell me, in brief, your relationship to Ilena?"

Leah went first again, although she gave him a look that said, *I know you remember me and my story.* He did, but he still wasn't going to admit it — yet. "Since Mistress Ilena became the steward of Tokumade, I've been her secretary."

Rio answered next. "Mistress Ilena has been kind enough to consider me a close aide for the last four and a half years."

Ore looked at her sideways. "And Rio has been kind enough to put up with the real, very emotional, Ilena."

Rio flushed and Leah said, "Grandfather did say that she's been a bit difficult, and that's one of the reasons we've been summoned."

"Yes," Ore admitted. "She herself has done it, though. Master understood the need and approved it."

They accepted this information, it seemed with a little bit of relief. "It's good she's aware of herself, then."

Ore nodded, then thought of something. "Ah, but she may not be after this next surgery." They looked at him quizzically, a little concerned. "There may be the necessity of removing a damaged organ. The surgeon won't know until he's in surgery with her, but he learned of it last night. Apparently, if the organ is damaged, it will need to be removed.

"It isn't life threatening to remove it, but it will cause her to go through sudden emotional fluctuations that she won't be able to control." He looked with speculation at Leah. She looked old enough to understand. "The organ is one of two that, when it naturally ceases to function, causes the emotional fluctuations and hot sweats of aging women."

Leah looked at him in surprise, and he nodded. "The surgical midwife who told us this last night assured us that if the one must be removed, the emotional fluctuations shouldn't last as long, nor be as severe as if she were naturally losing the function of both. She'll also be able to have children still, as the second organ of the pair isn't likely damaged. It will just take more time and care."

Leah looked relieved. She sighed. "Well, it's good you've forewarned us. We'll take care of Mistress Ilena."

Ore nodded. They'd arrived at their quarters. He opened the door with the key. They entered and quickly put away their things. He locked the door behind them and handed them each a key to the room. "Ilena's room is in the medical wing. If, in the first few days, you need to ask for directions, ask only for the medical wing. Ilena is still being protected by Master."

They nodded their understanding, then paid close attention to the path they took to her room, as all good staff would. When they arrived at the room, Ore decided he wouldn't go in...or he might not leave. Rather, he introduced them to the guards, so they would know their faces, then said his farewells and headed back to the Rose office. He'd have Rei requisition the larger room for Ilena. It would take his signature anyway.

He walked into the office. "You're late." It was hard to tell who said it. No one lifted their heads up.

"I've been being Mister Andrew."

"Oh?" That got a head up. "What pile of mine are you taking today?"

"Orderer and deliverer of keys and tags." Ore walked towards Rei's desk.

"That's what messages and paiges are for, Ore," Andrew instructed in a calm scold.

"I *am* the Prince's Messenger," Ore pointed out.

"...True." The head went back down, and Rei's came out from behind his current summary as Ore arrived at his desk.

"Doctor Elliot arrived early this morning. I've requisitioned quarters for him with the other medical staff, and a lab, and ordered his identification. He should be receiving his cadavers by this afternoon. He says he can probably begin the surgery in four days if they come today.

"He's inspected Ilena," pens stopped scratching momentarily, then resumed, "and has left the castle grounds again to retrieve his personal effects." Ore stopped and smiled. "He arrived this morning with only his surgical kit." Rei smiled back. Surely only a researcher would think that was the most important thing to carry around, and completely forget the rest.

"Ilena's secretary and aide have arrived, as well. I took them to their room, gave them their identifications and keys, and showed them the way to Ilena's room." He could see that Rei had understood his meaning in giving their actual titles, instead of calling them generally maids. "I've forewarned them of what to expect after the surgery, as well." Rei nodded, remembering the report from the night before.

"I've asked Grandfather to visit with Ilena after the dinner hour, both to keep her occupied in the evening, and to force the little Mister to return to his office. He's been feeling too bad for her.

"Doctor Elliot would like to perform the experimental surgery in a larger room than the one Ilena is in currently, preferably one he can leave her in for the recovery period. ...It would be helpful if it were large enough to have a second bed." Ore added in his own preference to the upgrade.

Ore wasn't fooling Rei, but then Rei knew Ore didn't sleep deeply when he was on duty, for the most part. "Andrew, draw up the requisition and I'll sign it."

"Ore, write it up for one of the rooms on the other side of the medical offices, closer to the surgical section. The castle plans are in the top drawer of the map cabinet," Andrew was quick to take advantage of Ore having already started on the path of taking that task from him.

Ore sighed. "Okay."

Rei was surprised at Ore's obedience without complaint. So were the others, by the cessation of scratching for a brief moment again. Rei leaned forward on his elbow and put his chin in his hand. "Okay, Ore. What's going on?"

"What?" said Ore as he headed over to the map cabinet. "Just...my partner's handling it." He pulled out the first drawer and started flipping through the maps for the medical wing.

He missed seeing Andrew and Mina lift their heads long enough to look at each other and smile, then smile at Rei, who was grinning broadly.

-o-o-o-

Mizi was discussing with Ilena the outline of her plan to go visit Rei in his office, trying to flesh it out verbally, when there was a knock at the door. The guards admitted two women.

The older matron was fairly short and sturdy, her slightly greying hair up in the ubiquitous bun of working women who needed their hair out of their face. The other was a beautiful slender young woman roughly the age of Mizi, her dark hair plaited and coiled on her head.

"Nana! Rio!" Ilena cried out in joy, tears springing to her eyes. "Welcome! Come in...come here!" She reached out her hands for them.

Rio rushed to her and grabbed her in a careful hug, crying tears of happiness as well. Leah walked in more sedately. Mizi could tell she was just as happy to see with her own eyes that her mistress was safe. The wetness of her hazel–blue eyes gave it away.

While Ilena was occupied with Rio, Leah turned to Mizi and bowed. "Mistress Mizi, I'm Leah, Mistress Ilena's secretary and nurse "

Mizi reached out and took her hand lightly. "Welcome. I'm glad to be able to meet you. Thank you for coming to be with Ilena. She has sorely missed you."

Leah bowed, embarrassed. Then Ilena was calling for her, and she and Rio traded places, Leah comforting a bawling Ilena, Ilena's need for her comforting the nurse in return.

"Mistress Mizi, it's a pleasure to greet you," Rio was very polite, giving her a curtsy. "I'm Rio, Mistress Ilena's personal maid."

"Thank you for coming also," Mizi said. "I'm glad Ilena won't be lonely any longer."

"I wasn't that lonely, Mistress Mizi," objected Ilena. "I've had you and Ryan and Ore for company."

"Hush, Mistress Ilena," said Leah. "It's obvious by your extreme emotional display that you've been difficult enough."

Ilena pouted. "I miss everyone I love, Leah, but some more than others. You know that."

Leah relented. "Yes, I do know." She ran her hand over Ilena's hair, smoothing it, her eyes soft. Mizi could tell it was an unconscious motion from years of comforting her. Somehow it felt like what a mother would do for a loved child. She was glad to see the Ilena who could be herself with people she cared for. "And have you been able to find a place here, Mistress Ilena?" Leah asked.

Ilena looked at her soberly, then pulled out her identification. As Leah looked at it, then Rio did too, Ilena said, "Master Rei has made me to be in a lesser position until I've finished proving myself." Mizi was surprised that Ilena would say director was a lesser position than what she expected to receive. To her, a director was a pretty high office, like that of Head Healer. "But it's still more than I expected to have received by this early time. Has Grandfather said?" Leah and Rio nodded.

Ilena continued. "I *should* be very busy from then on, but I'm scheduled to have the surgery in only a few days."

Leah considered. "I don't think that Regent Rei intends for you to run overly fast at this time, Mistress Ilena. He's aware of your needs."

Mizi nodded. "Yes, he is, Ilena." The other ladies looked at her, to see what she would say. "Rei only asks for that which each is capable of, although at least that much. Even if he wants to see what you can do, he'll be angry if you don't take care of yourself the way you should."

Leah nodded and looked back at Ilena. "You see, it is so, Mistress Ilena. We'll help you, both to do your duty, and to recover properly."

Ilena looked at them both, then nodded. "Mistress Mizi and I are in the middle of a discussion. So for the morning, I would have you be my legs. Go and learn the castle. When you arrive at the library, I need reference materials on the running of a castle and it's many offices, in general and in particular. If there's a text that's specific to my title, that's also needed. I don't know what my expected duties are, only that Master Rei has said I report to him directly.

"I'll need, by tomorrow, a detailed list of those who currently fill all of the offices and what their offices are so that I may learn it." Mizi thought the last request was a bit much to be asking of two women who'd just entered the castle, but they nodded obediently, as if such a request wasn't uncommon. Then they excused themselves from the room.

"Ilena...just what is it you're to do? ...Or rather, why is it Rei has set you to be his Director of Intelligence?" Mizi's curiosity couldn't be contained any longer.

Ilena smiled. "Exactly for what I just did." Mizi was understandably confused. "I ask people to collect information for me. When I need that information, I ask them to tell it to me, or to the person who needs to hear it."

Mizi could understand that, but it wasn't really sufficient. She frowned. "But, Ilena, wouldn't it take someone with a lot of people collecting a lot of information for them to qualify for the position of a director?"

Ilena continued to smile. "Yes, Mistress." Mizi wasn't really sure she comprehended. She hadn't seen any evidence that Ilena knew that many people. Ilena didn't look away. "It also means that the *correct* information is being collected. When I began, the information I wanted to know was, *Where is Kase now?* But that wasn't the only question I was asking.

"I was also asking, *Who has the right information to prove Earl Shicchi has evil intentions towards the throne?* That's why Master Rei has brought me here to the castle and protects me. In protecting me here, he's protecting the information he needs to answer that question."

Mizi was beginning to understand, "So, Rei made you the director because you've brought that information to him?"

Ilena shook her head. "If that was all I'd done, then the position is nothing but a mere reward, or a bribe if it looked like I required it to give him the information I have."

Mizi shook her head. "That isn't Rei."

"No, it isn't," Ilena agreed, "or I would have refused the appointment more strenuously."

"You refused it?"

"Yes. It came too soon. I haven't earned it in the eyes of the other lords and cabinet members. They don't even know my name, yet. Nevertheless, there is a new Director of Intelligence for the Regent."

Mizi nodded. If Rei had told the Head of the Medical department at Ichijou to make her a Court Healer because he wanted her to be one, she would also have refused. But he'd allowed her to earn it on her own merits. "Rei isn't that way either. If he's given you the title, it's because you've earned it."

Ilena paused, then carefully said, "He believes I've earned it already in his older brother's eyes. I can neither confirm nor deny it. Basou hasn't spoken to me."

That was another thing that bugged Mizi. She may as well ask while she was asking questions. "Why do you speak so informally about the King? Even Rei, from early on?"

Ilena answered carefully and succinctly, "I can only tell you that the King and I know of each other, and I've known of Rei since he was born. I may not say any more than that."

Mizi considered the answer. She was asking for the information that even Rei couldn't tell her. It would have to be sufficient. But it spoke of a close tie between them, as she'd seen when Rei had asked her to come in and help him see the mark on Ilena. What could it be?

It ate at her, but she still must be patient, for Rei's sake. It did help to know that it was a tie between Ilena and Sasou as well, not just between Ilena and Rei. "So, ...the information you collect, ...it's things that Rei needs to know?"

Ilena nodded. "For a very long time now, Sasou and I've had an arrangement. I'll collect the information the Regent of Suiran needs to know, keeping Suiran, and therefore Ryokudo, secure for the people. In return, if Rei can learn to use me properly, Sasou will allow me to stand at Rei's side. If I can't stand at Rei's side, Sasou will use me for the same purpose, most likely, but will take me for himself. He already knows how to use someone such as myself."

"What is the place you wish to stand in?" Mizi asked.

"It's as I've said before, but I believe the position Rei is thinking of is Minister of Intelligence."

"Minister!?" Mizi's eyes got very big.

Ilena nodded soberly. "I won't be able to remain at his side if I'm anything less."

To Mizi, that was a frightening thought. How could a court healer hope to be the mistress of a court minister?

Ilena saw Mizi's panic. "Mistress Mizi," she called to Mizi. When Mizi looked at her, she kindly said. "You are thinking too less of yourself."

Mizi was confused again. "But, a Minister," she said faintly.

"Mizi." Ilena's voice was commanding and clipped, "You – are – *not* – here – to – be – a – court – healer!" Mizi's head swam. "Nor would I be willing to have you as my mistress if that's all you were here to be. I've known from the beginning what I will become."

Mizi tried to put it together. Ilena knew from the beginning she'd have to become Rei's Minister of Intelligence if she was going to stand at his back, and at Ore's side. Even knowing that, Ilena had consented to be Mizi's aide and guardian. What position did Ilena expect of her, if it wasn't the court healer she'd already attained on her own power? Her brain couldn't see it, her head and heart were so overwhelmed.

There was one thought. It came out cold. "Are you saying my efforts have been wasted? That I shouldn't strive for that which I can do to be where I want to be?" She knew it wasn't so. Ilena had already supported her in her goal to be where she wanted to be, but it *had* sounded like Ilena felt that her efforts to this point were superfluous.

Ilena's eyes narrowed. "That's for you to judge. If you'll give up halfway, I'd know it now."

That brought Mizi up short. "No. I won't give up," she said softly, her mind fixed firmly on her goal. Then she looked directly at Ilena. "If I'm not here to be a court healer, then tell me, what am I here to be?"

Ilena sighed. "Mistress Mizi, if you can't figure that out, even still, then you're already too late." She looked at Mizi sadly. "I'll give you until tomorrow to answer me that question."

Too late? Mizi's heart clenched, as did the hand she was holding over it to protect it. What had she not understood up until this point?

Ilena said quietly, "Mistress Mizi. Go, and think on the answer to that question. You can't act effectively without the answer."

Mizi nodded, floating in a sea without a boat for the first time in many years. She took her leave, going to the herb gardens where she'd be able to think while her hands kept busy.

Ilena pondered soberly for a while, then called out to the guards. When they opened the door and asked what they could do for her, she asked them to send for Ore. He needed to know. She'd promised she'd tell him the things of Mizi.

-o-o-o-

Ore arrived shortly after being sent for. He'd not once been summoned by Ilena until now. Even Rei was concerned. Ore noticed first off that she was alone, and it was still morning. "What is it, Ilena?" he walked over to a position where they could converse comfortably.

She looked back at him soberly. "It's Mistress Mizi."

Ore's heart skipped a beat and his hand involuntarily clenched. "Shall I go to her?"

"...I can't say if you're the best to go to her or not."

"What happened?"

"She's finally asked me why I'm here and what Master Rei wishes to do with me." Ore couldn't quite see. "It was necessary to answer her that I'll become a minister." Ore was starting to get it. "She was unable to conceive how a minister can stand behind a court healer."

Ore sighed and closed his eyes. "And what did you say to her?"

"That she isn't here to be a court healer." Ore felt his heart sink, but nodded that he'd heard her. Ilena continued, "She asked me what she was here to be, then?" Ore opened his eyes and looked at Ilena. "I told her that if she still couldn't answer that question, then she was already too late, and that I'd expect her answer to the question by tomorrow."

Ore held himself still by force of will. He wanted to chase after Mizi. She always took such questions very seriously and considered them deeply.

However, she was never quite able to answer them on her own, not when she continuously thought too little of herself, or needed the approval of Rei.

His second reaction was to summon Rei. In the past, that had always been the answer. Rei had been able to calm Mizi, help her to understand. But was that the right thing this time? Even Rei had been trying to help her see what position she was aiming for, but still she'd refused to open her eyes and accept it.

Ilena had pushed her very hard into this corner, to make her understand. It was a place Mizi needed to be, if she was really ever to become what she wanted to be, but Ore was still not pleased with Ilena. Rei wouldn't be either.

Ore sighed, forcing himself to relax. This was the very sort of thing Rei had put him in this place to see to. Mizi could stand to think for a while. He needed to deal with Ilena first. "Ilena, you've pushed too hard." His voice was also hard.

Ilena looked at him, not giving in, but also not retaliating. "There's a possibility I've pushed Mistress Mizi too hard. I don't know. I do know that until this time, she hasn't been pushed hard enough, but has been allowed to wander in the darkness of her own making. That is equally harmful. ...Unless Master Rei has commanded that she be led blindfolded until she's left behind?"

Ore took a deep breath. Ilena was being particularly difficult today. He was glad Rei hadn't been there to hear that comment. He narrowed his eyes at her. "Master has done no such thing. It's a thing you know for yourself. When it's a thing you know of yourself, don't speak it. Such viciousness will only bring harm to yourself."

Ilena's eyes flickered momentarily wider, as if her ears had turned back, then forward again. "I'll attempt to remember it."

Ore accepted that answer for now, but he'd watch her closely to help her learn it. "It would have been proper for you to have led Mistress to the answer, rather than force her into a corner alone."

Ilena considered that. "It's true that I became impatient with her. However, haven't the rest of you already also tried to lead her to the answer? Wouldn't my efforts have been to no point?"

Ore thought about it, then shook his head. "We've all been waiting for her to come to the understanding on her own." Ilena sighed, her disappointment in the rest of them very evident. "Ilena has a way of her own that leads others to come to an understanding and into their own strength." Ore had heard it and read it in the stories from the collected witnesses. He was well aware of her skill in the matter. "This kind of harshness isn't necessary for you to achieve your goal. Mistress is worthy of your patience."

"And has she been handled so softly from the beginning?" Ilena asked.

"Yes," Ore answered honestly.

"*Haah.* ...It's a very difficult task, then. And a very short amount of time, Ore." Ilena closed her eyes briefly. Looking at him again, she said, "I can't promise I'll always be patient with her, but I'll be more gentle."

"See to it," he answered, his eyes saying he would hold her to it, very firmly. "And, what shall we do to fix what you've done?"

Ilena thought only briefly. "Let her consider it. There'll be great strength for her if she can answer it for herself. If she calls for you, or for Master Rei, then go to her. She'll know if you can help her or not. If she comes to me tomorrow and still doesn't have the answer, I'll lead her to it. Then we'll see if she'll continue on her chosen path or not."

Ore considered her answer. The only modification he would make is that he would go to Mizi by evening to see if she needed either him or Rei. She usually wouldn't go to them on her own for these things, even if she did need them.

To Ilena, he only nodded. "I'll speak with you again tonight. I must return to Master." He turned on his heel and left her behind. He would have to have an answer for Rei on the matter that wouldn't send him flying to Mizi's side.

-o-o-o-

Rei looked up when Ore returned. "Well?" he completely stopped working and gave Ore his whole attention. Ore shivered. He stopped half–way up the room, in informal attention.

Rei narrowed his eyes. "Up here, Ore." He motioned and pointed to a position in front of his desk.

Ore twitched, then moved up obediently. This being partners was difficult. He felt a need to protect Ilena he wouldn't have felt before. He knew if he even breathed Mizi's name, Rei would find it difficult to listen. What he didn't know was that Mina and Andrew were watching him.

Ore took a breath. "I've had to properly educate Ilena today."

"Has she understood her lesson?" Rei wasn't surprised by the comment.

"Yes, Master."

"Has she agreed to properly fix her error?"

"Yes, Master."

Rei leaned back in his chair, thinking. "Is it a matter I'll be angry about if I don't act on it now?"

Ore paused, thinking. "It would be best if Master would wait to be called."

"You'll be confirming it yourself later?"

"Yes, Master."

"Very well. I'll wait to hear. You may return to your work."

Ore bowed and returned to his desk. He was very grateful his master hadn't asked him to betray his partner. This was also a new thing for him. He wanted to crawl under his desk and shiver for a while. He chose to obediently lose himself in his work instead.

Andrew and Mina looked at Ore with pity, then smiled at each other. They already knew this about Rei: he was a good master for partners to follow as well.

-o-o-o-

Mizi stood in the garden, her hand clenched in front of her heart. For the fourth time she'd stopped in the middle of her work, completely unable to put any focus into it at all. She finally just sat down on the edge of a set of herb beds. She'd worked so hard, even been away from Rei for more than two years at Kouzanshi. Had it all been a waste? Was what she'd done so pointless towards reaching her goal?

Mizi took a deep breath. She'd never been discouraged from doing what she thought she could do. Even Sasou had said he was helping her, by sending her to Kouzanshi, although she still wasn't quite sure what she'd done there that had moved her forward, other than to help all kinds of people there through the medical department so that many people knew who she was now.

After that, she'd had to go to the lords of northern Suiran and convince them to grow the winter flowering plant, *Holegn Hanatake*, so that the cure to the new, odd plague was readily available to the people of the region that were in the most danger. If there had been one thing, it had been to learn how to communicate and negotiate with the lords of Suiran, and show her face to them, so they might know her also.

While that was a step in the right direction, it wasn't sufficient, most assuredly. What was the right direction? Towards Rei. But what was it she wanted there? Her heart felt afraid when she asked that question. It always had. She loved Rei and wanted to love him for the rest of her life. He'd said he wanted the same. Even still it was hard to believe it could happen.

What would she need in order to be able to do that? Approval. That was certain. By whom? King Sasou, but he'd already said it would be okay, if they could make it happen. By the Queen Mother. That was frightening, but not in the same way. It seemed like even if Mizi didn't get total approval there, Rei still wouldn't change his mind away from her.

The soldiers loved Rei and she got along well with them. The people of Suiran, Kouzanshi, perhaps all of Ryokudo. Was that why she'd been in Kouzanshi so long? It didn't seem hard to have their approval also.

That left the lords. Her stomach clenched. She was very afraid of them, of not having their approval. She had no idea how to relate to them, or really what their expectations were. She only understood that she didn't meet those expectations, whatever they were. If the fear was a clue, it was telling her that she needed to learn how to interact with the lords. The *Holegn Hanatake* allowed her a beginning with them, but it would take more.

What else would it take to be by Rei? No, Ilena hadn't asked her to answer that question. *What am I supposed to be?* Mizi stood up and began a long pace up and down one of the aisles in the garden. Why did that question scare her so much? Was the answer at the end of that fear?

She wasn't supposed to be a court healer...at least Ilena suggested she wasn't supposed to be content with being just a court healer. *Just* a court healer. Ilena wouldn't be following after her if she was *just* that. It was supposed to be something more. Mizi felt the fear rise up again. Was it because she was afraid to be more? Or because she didn't believe she could be more? It seemed to be both.

If she was just afraid to be more, she wanted to overcome that fear. She knew it was possible. She'd done it before. It was what her determination to be beside Rei was able to combat. If it was just a matter of *becoming*, learning, acting, she could do that, if she had guidance. Instinctively she understood that Ilena had that guidance within her, was inviting her to reach out and access it. If Ilena could move her forward, she would move, no matter how afraid she was. That fear was not what was holding her back.

The other fear, then. Mizi's pace increased just a little, to match the tempo of her beating heart. She took a deep breath. She *must* face this fear. She'd faced it before. Many years before, when she'd first met him, Sasou himself had asked her: what will you be to Rei? She still hadn't answered him.

She stopped and raised her head to the sky, as if to welcome rain drops upon it, her eyes closed. She willed her heart to still, breathing in calming breaths, the scent of the herbs surrounding her many and varied, all swirling around her, comfortingly familiar. Rei had told her then it was alright to think the thought. She could see now she still hadn't believed him, not from then to now.

Who may stand next to a Prince? What must I be to stand where I want to stand? She knew the answer. She'd always known it, and it scared her. She wanted to be just Mizi. Mizi who made her own way, who lived her life as she saw fit. That was what Rei wanted also. But she needed to be that and another thing that to her was very far away. A thing she didn't believe she could attain, could not become. *How does a common girl from another country become a princess, fit to stand by a prince?*

Only a princess was fit to stand by a prince. She herself had no training in being a princess. She hadn't been born to it, born to the practice or the skill. All the noble ladies had been trained since birth, each one hoping to win out over the others for the right to stand next to a prince or other high noble. How could she ever hope to compete?

Rei had reassured her several times that it didn't matter. She didn't need to compete. She already had his heart. Sasou had indicated that if she worked hard enough, she, too, could compete, could win out against all the others born to it. There must be something innate that gave her an advantage. Even the prince of her homeland was proud to call her a friend, had worked hard to be able to be called such, and was even still working hard. His letters came regularly so that he could tell her so.

So, was it possible for her to learn it? To learn how to be the kind of princess Rei needed to stand by him? If she could learn that, would the lords accept her? She felt it was so, the same as Rei had to prove to them that he was worthy of the title of Prince, and now, Regent.

Was Ilena offering to help her learn to become a princess, then? She was saying, *Choose to be a princess and I'll help you become it. A minister can follow a prince, and a princess. But if you won't choose to become the princess* the Prince needs, then admit defeat now and move out of the way of the other competitors. Let this country have its Princess.

Mizi trembled, her hand to her heart again. Could she do it? Did she want to carry the expectations of an entire country? This is what she was most afraid of. Rei and Sasou had been born to carry those expectations. Had grown up understanding it was a necessity, that they had a duty to live out. She must choose it, if she truly wanted to stand beside Rei.

Mizi stopped thinking and just breathed again. She wanted to hear what her heart really wanted to say; what it really saw for her future. She pictured Rei up on the balcony with his mother, brother, and new sister–in–law, waving happily the day of King Sasou's wedding.

She'd been so proud of him. Yet at the same time, she'd yearned to be there next to him also; had asked why that place couldn't be hers also. Not because she wanted the populace to adore her, but because she'd wanted it to be her rightful place, there beside Rei. To show all the people that she was his support, and she supported him with her whole heart and being. Mizi paused on that thought and followed it to the depths of her heart.

What was she willing to do to support Rei to the fullest? She felt it was "anything". In fact, she'd proved that over and over. What was she willing to be to support Rei to the fullest? She all of a sudden could picture herself standing next to him on the balcony.

He relied on her so much already. He'd said he wanted to rely on her for his life, but he wouldn't be able to continue to do so the same way if he had to pick someone else as his princess. He'd have to turn to that person that way, only coming to Mizi for advice or peaceful conversation occasionally. Mizi found that unbearable. If she wanted him to turn to her and fully rely on her in all things, she must become a princess. His princess.

She wasn't qualified. She didn't feel ready. She wanted to run and hide somewhere very far away. But she wanted to be Rei's princess so badly she stayed rooted to the ground. Rei said it was okay. Sasou said it was possible. Ilena was offering to teach her how. The way was finally open to her. Could she step forward onto it? Would she? That's what Ilena was asking her. It was what she was asking herself.

Mizi thought again about what she and Ilena had been discussing the days before and early this morning. She'd told Ilena that she needed to have the opportunity to communicate with Rei whenever she needed. She felt that with every fiber of her being. She needed to be able to approach Rei freely. If she was a princess, she could do that. Even more if she was his princess.

Ilena agreed with her, and had been trying to help her do that without having the title yet. But for Ilena it was with the expectation that Mizi would one day have that title. This was just a beginning. She herself was ready to be that princess. Was impatient to be it.

That realization surprised her. She was impatient to be recognized as the right person to be standing by Rei. She was impatient with Rei. She was impatient with the lords. And, she was angry with herself that she hadn't achieved it yet. She was angry at herself for being afraid to be what she needed to be. It was the same anger she would have held against Rei if he'd acted against his role as prince.

Mizi stopped, her mouth open in surprise. Then, she turned and ran.

-o-o-o-

The door to Ilena's room burst open. Lunch had just been brought. Ilena had been thinking sadly it was likely to go cold and uneaten, although she could have just asked the guards to ask for the nurse to come and help. She looked towards the door as best she could, but it didn't matter. As soon as it was shut, Mizi was at her side, her face bright, her eyes lit with knowledge.

Hahh. I was right. She was ready to face it. Ilena kept her face neutral. First she needed to let Mizi tell it to her.

"A princess. I have to be a princess to stand next to Rei, because he's a prince. I want to be a princess — Rei's princess. Can you do it? Can you teach me?" It all came out in a breathless rush.

"Very good, Princess Mizi. You've answered the question." Mizi held herself from reacting to the new title, to Ilena's approval. "You ask if I can teach you. It's more important to know if you believe I can."

Mizi held herself tightly straight, her fists clenched by her sides. "Yes. I believe you can. I believe you're the only person I know who can do it," she said with intensity. "I want you to do it. Will you?"

Now Ilena smiled, "Yes, Princess Mizi. If you ask it of me, I'll teach you. ...But what I said about it being nearly too late was a truth. It will be very hard. I can't go easy on you. Within a year, the lords will make Prince Rei choose a bride. You must be on the list of acceptable brides within six or seven months. That isn't much time."

Mizi nodded. "I'll do it. I can work very hard, and I will. I've been impatient and angry that I'm not already there. I realized that this time."

"Very good," Ilena praised her with a smile again. "Then you should act today, even right now. See. The lunch meal has just been served."

Mizi looked at the cart. The lunch cart would have, or would soon be, delivered to Rei's office. Her heart clenched in fear. Her new–found determination fought against it and silenced it. She looked at Ilena. "What about your lunch?"

"Call for Anna." Mizi nodded. "Would you hear my one advice before you go?" Ilena asked. Mizi paused, then nodded. She wanted to hear anything Ilena could teach her. "If you've determined this is your path and you won't be swayed from it, you must do everything you do from now on as if you're *already* Rei's Princess. Carry yourself, look at others, act in the presence of all others as such. When you do, they can't deter you.

"You'll need to decide, with Prince Rei's help, what the specifics of being Rei's Princess are, but you're already capable of acting it, thinking it, and being it. You must practice it every moment of your life from now on, even in the moments you doubt yourself. No — especially then, because it's yourself you must convince in those moments.

"Accept your own errors graciously, as a princess would, learn from them, and move on. If you don't doubt your path any longer, don't doubt what you'll become, what you must be from this moment on. And always remember that when you need to lean on someone else, you may come to me, to Ore, to Rei, to Mister Andrew, and to Miss Mina. Always we've supported you in the position you've told me today you're ready to step into."

Mizi teared up. They'd all known, had been waiting for her. They all supported her in this position, already. She couldn't help it. She leaned over and grasped Ilena in a hug.

Ilena held her close, both comforting her and strengthening her. Softly she said to the young woman with the flaming red hair, "I love you, Mizi. You make a very fine princess. I'm very proud of you for facing your fears today, and becoming so much more strong. I will always be here for you."

After a moment more, Mizi was able to calm herself and she stood back up. "Thank you, Ilena. I'm glad that I was able to meet you."

"I'm grateful you were willing to come back and save my life. I'm looking forward to seeing what you'll do." Ilena smiled.

Mizi smiled back. "First, I'm going to call for Anna for you. Then I'm going to visit Rei."

"Very well, Princess. I do wish I could be there to see it."

"I'll tell you about it when I return." They grinned at each other, co–conspirators.

-o-o-o-

Rei and his aides were working through lunch again. It was just the daily pattern. If it got more work done, then that was for the better, right?

There was a knock at the door and one of the guards announced, "Lady Mizi to see the Regent."

They were all still sitting in shock when Mizi entered the room. Her eyes swept the room. "Close your mouths," she said, but her eyes sparkled. Ore was having troubles being obedient to that order.

Rei put his pen down and stood. "Mizi. What may I do for you?"

"You may eat lunch with me, Regent." She began taking food plates off the lunch cart and putting them at a clear place on the table by Andrew's desk. Rei blinked. "I've heard that you aren't properly taking care of your health, working through both lunches and dinners. I've come to see that you're at least correcting that at lunch. You may expect me to be present at every lunch from here on, unless you have urgent business elsewhere."

Rei looked at Ore. "What did Ilena do to Mizi?" he asked accusingly.

Ore wasn't sure he should answer or not. He looked at Mizi. Would he make her mad if he did?

Mizi looked up at him. "Rei has asked you a question, Ore. Answer him."

Ore blinked. He looked at Rei. Words were having a hard time coming out. "Ah, eh, well, she told me she said that Mistress wasn't here to be a court healer. Mistress asked her what she was here to be, then. Ilena said she told her," he blushed, "that if she couldn't answer that question for herself by tomorrow morning she was already too late.

"It was for saying that that I scolded Ilena. She knows how to teach people with much more gentleness and grace, as you yourself know." Rei nodded. He did, after reading all those stories about Mother. Andrew and Mina were smiling now.

"The table is set, Rei. Please come sit." Mizi sat in her seat, sitting upright, and waited for him to join her. "I'll explain it as we eat. Your time is valuable, after all, and I have much to do." She looked at the rest, still sitting at their desks. "The rest of you should also pause in your work and eat as well, so that your minds may be rested and your bodies not overtaxed."

"Yes, Mistress," Ore answered, and the three of them got up from their chairs to make plates for themselves, although they chose to sit at a different table to allow the two some semblance of privacy.

At that time, Tairn walked in from having run an errand. Unlike the others, he was in the castle blue uniform with cream colored shirt as he hadn't been made a personal knight to Rei, but had only been taken on as direct staff. He paused when he noticed the different arrangement of persons in the room and the golden–red hair of the guest seated with Rei. "Ahh, am I interrupting?"

"No, Tairn," Mina said to him. "We were just beginning lunch. Please get yourself a plate and join me. Mizi, this is Tairn, my assistant. Tairn, this is Mizi."

"It's a pleasure to meet you, Lady Mizi," Tairn bowed.

"Likewise, Tairn," Mizi answered. "I'm sure both Rei and Mina are relieved to have your assistance in the office." Tairn nodded his head in acceptance of the comment, quickly filled his plate, and joined the other aides.

Mizi took a clearing breath. "What Ore told you is true. Ilena was very firm with me and made me face my own fears with my own hands, but she wasn't wrong to ask it of me today. I was ready to do it. I merely needed the push to overcome my reluctance to face those fears." Rei smiled a small proud smile.

Mizi continued. "I'd already decided that I was going to come talk to you today." She looked up at him with determination. "If we're going to be in the place we wish to be in, then we must be able to communicate regularly, without fear, so that we may know each other's minds.

"I asked Ore what your daily schedule was. Ilena was able to help me see that if I came to eat lunch with you daily, it would both improve your health, and the health of our relationship." She managed to not blush very much at all, although she had to fish quickly for the next thing to say.

"It's also a good time for my schedule, which from this point on will, in the main, be taken up with lessons from Ilena. I intend to continue to help with the medical department as I can, but it will likely be as a rest from my other labor." She paused to eat.

"What is your other labor?" Rei asked rather nonchalantly for the topic.

"To learn what's necessary to become Rei's Princess. Ilena says I have six, at most seven months in which to learn what all the other eligible young ladies have already had a lifetime to learn. I expect to be quite busy." The listening aides were silent in shock. Even though they'd expected to hear something like this, it was still surprising to hear it come from Mizi's lips.

Pffft! Rei covered the laugh. "Ah, sorry, but it's so like you, to face such a task head on. I would think that time schedule is ambitious, but if anyone can pull it off, the two of you can."

"We'll have to do the best we can. Already I feel impatient to have been doing it." Mizi couldn't quite keep the scowl off her face that told of her frustration with herself. She never scowled at anyone else.

"But, you have been, Mizi," Rei protested. "You already have the natural qualities required, more so than most. You merely lack the court training, and in that you've been increasing steadily. I'd think it won't be too difficult for you to meet your schedule. However, Ilena likely has specific goals in mind that I haven't considered."

"Please consider them," Mizi said firmly, and Rei looked at her in surprise. "There's no point to learning a thing you don't need me to learn, nor is it acceptable for me to be lacking in a thing you need."

Rei sat back and looked at her with appraising eyes. Mizi had indeed finally understood what she wanted and what she needed to do to get there. "I'll consider it seriously, then," Rei promised.

Mizi nodded. "Is there anything I can do now that would be helpful?"

Rei considered it. He glanced over at the aides. Ore opened his mouth and Mina kicked him under the table. He looked at her, affronted, but didn't try again. "I think you've already done it, Mizi." Rei paused a moment to eat, then asked, "Are you sure you wish to come every day for lunch?"

Mizi looked like she'd expected the question. "From the first day I came to Ryokudo, I've wondered what it is that Rei does here. All of the things I've seen you do are infrequent, and not very much of what's in the palace.

"How can I truly know how to support you, if I don't know what you spend most of your time on? What are the questions in your heart? These are the things I wish to begin to learn when I come for the lunch hour." She looked up at him. "If I can't understand the things that Andrew, Mina, and Ore understand, how can I stand in front of them, at the side of Rei?"

Rei almost opened his mouth to say it wasn't necessary, then closed it again before the words escaped. If he said that to her, he'd be devaluing her determination, telling her he didn't really need her to stand by his side — that he was content to keep her at a distance. Was that what he really believed? Was he really not as willing to be as committed to their shared goal as he thought he was?

He ate silently while he pondered. He kept wanting to protect Mizi. Ilena and Mizi both had already called him to task for that ill placed desire. He wanted to protect what was precious to him, but that didn't mean he should break the strength of her to do so. Rather, he should wish to help her increase her strength, that by that strength itself she could be protected.

He could choose what she heard each lunch, of course, and thereby build up her strength little by little. If there was a thing she shouldn't know, she didn't need to be told it, but otherwise, it wouldn't hurt her to understand. "I understand," he answered her. Then he smiled, "Though I thought you said that you didn't want us to work through lunch."

Mizi smiled back. "Well, if it becomes too much of a problem, I'll come before or stay after lunch. Then I may be able to both learn what you do in this place, and we may be able to have a more healthy day."

"Then Ore will definitely request that you be his assistant," Rei commented dryly.

"If that's where I can best support you from, then I'll do it," Mizi said seriously. "But first, I must meet my goal."

CHAPTER 16 The Agreement Between Partners

Everyone headed back to their desks after Mizi left. Ore kept feeling an itch between his shoulders, but Rei didn't say anything.

"Umm," Tairn raised his hand, getting everyone's attention.

Rei looked at him, "Yes, Tairn?"

"Given what I overheard, I think I need to tell you a little more about myself." Tairn was still standing by his desk, uncertain but sure he needed to say something rather than stay quiet.

"Okay." Rei, still standing, leaned back against the front of his desk.

Tairn rather unconsciously straightened even further to have the full attention of his liege on him. "I admit that I've been wondering why you asked me to be on your staff. Because you called for me using my father's name, I thought it must be because of him for some reason. But today, having heard Miss Ilena's name, I wonder if it's because of her or my brother."

Rei nodded. "I can see where that would be somewhat of a mystery. Ore, would you please explain?"

Ore nodded, sitting half–way on the side of his desk where there was a little bit of space. "It's because of both your brother and your father. I visited at your home a bit ago, and made some grave errors. Your brother corrected my misunderstanding, and both he and your father were very gracious and forgave me for my lack of knowledge. I believe Master asked you to assist in the office based on their example?" Ore looked at Rei to see if he was correct.

Rei nodded. "Yes. While it doesn't always bear out that every child of a House has the qualities of the parents, it's usually a good indicator. Therefore, I decided we'd see if you were also of the same cloth. Your training being in the Department of Interior was helpful as well. I intend to also bring your brother in, when he becomes available. It takes two to replace Mina when she must return home."

"Ah. Well...that." The others looked at Tairn, curious as to what he had to say. "Well, what I mean to say is, isn't that a conflict of interests?"

"What do you mean?" Rei asked conversationally, but the aides had gone on alert.

"Well, he's one of Miss Ilena's agents, and...well...I'm one of King Sasou's." Tairn hedged a bit, as if not sure he should admit it.

Everyone was quiet while Rei pondered that news. "Well, no, I don't think it's a conflict of interest at all, but have I interrupted something important you were doing for my brother?"

"Mmm, I'm wrapping it up. He was...amused by my sudden change in position." Tairn gave an apologetic look.

Rei sighed. "So he said, 'go and see what happens'?"

"Yes, something like that," Tairn said apologetically.

"Is there a problem with your brother coming?" Mina wanted to know, particularly as he was the one Rei would be relying on the most.

"Well...aren't Miss Ilena's loyalties in question?"

Rei blinked. "Who do you believe Miss Ilena is loyal to, Tairn?"

The man paused, then answered slowly, "I used to believe, early on, that she was loyal to Earl Shicchi. But then, when my brother became her man, I confronted him about it. He told me that it wasn't so, but that she had her own purposes. So I could only assume she was loyal only to herself."

"Ilena is my Director of Intelligence, Tairn," Rei told him plainly. "I see no conflict of interest. If there's a thing you think my brother should know, I would hope I would tell him first, but if not, then it's good if you do. If there's a thing your brother feels Ilena needs to know from this office that she doesn't already know, I would hope he would tell her. And if there's a thing either of you feels I need to know, I need you to tell it to me without reservation." Rei watched to see if Tairn understood.

"Ah, I see," Tairn was rearranging the order of things in his mind. "But surely she wasn't before?"

"Yes, she's always been. I just wasn't in a position to be able to have her with me until now. Besides, what she was doing in the place she was in was too important to move her from. Earl Shicchi has of his own will cast her off, so it's time to bring her back to her rightful place," Rei answered with great soberness.

Ore was having a hard time preventing himself from laughing. He had to sit down in his chair and hide behind his work. Andrew was having a harder time. He could never lie, and his face was an open book. Mina took Andrew by the arm, turned him away from Tairn, and quietly pretended to ask him an important question.

"Ah, is that why the focus of the office has been on his past activities?" Tairn asked Rei.

"Yes," Rei nodded. "Ilena brought with her quite a bit of evidence against him. By the way, it's confidential information that she's here in the castle. Until Earl Shicchi is convicted and judgment passed, we believe her life will remain in danger. You'll keep that knowledge to yourself until then, yes?"

Tairn nodded, "Certainly, Pr–Rei." He was still trying to get used to not using the honorific in the office. "And...should I also keep it confidential that Lady Mizi is, with your approval, now actively seeking your hand?" Tairn was looking questioningly, but Rei could see in his eyes that he was also calculating.

Rei smiled. "Everyone in this room, and also my brother, have known for some time that she'll someday stand by my side. We've all been working towards that goal. While I think I would like for the castle to learn of it as she moves to show them, it's never been secret."

"Very well," Tairn bowed. Mina walked up to him and asked him about the errand he'd run before lunch, then she found an excuse to make him run another.

When he was gone, and likely a sufficient number of paces away, Ore had to let out his laughter. It was a bit before he recovered. "*Ah, hahaha,*" he wiped his eyes. "Thank you Miss Mina. I was about to die. *Hehe. Haaah...* Master, I'm not sure the truth is meant to be stretched quite that far. Even King Brother will see through it."

"No," Rei shook his head as he sat down at his desk again. "I'm quite sure Sasou expected this from the beginning." The aides were surprised at his words.

When he'd recovered, Andrew said, "It's interesting that he's one of King Sasou's men. Do you think Miss Ilena picked his brother to be one of her's on purpose?"

Rei was thoughtful. "When there are good men available, isn't it good to put them to the best purposes? She's already said that her network overlaps Sasou's. I wouldn't be surprised if it's often in this fashion. ...Andrew how much time do we have until the first meeting?"

Andrew looked at his pocket watch and calculated. "Ah...forty minutes."

"Then let's get work done until then, shall we?" Rei's order was mild. Everyone got back to work.

When was it Master was the one to tell us to get back to work? Ore wondered. *It was always Mister Andrew who encouraged Master before....*

-o-o-o-

Mizi was very excited and full of energy when she arrived back at Ilena's room. Ilena's staff had arrived just before her and were eating their lunch. They moved to the back corner to allow space for Mizi and Ilena to converse. Mizi explained what had been said during the luncheon, then added, "Ah, and I met Rei's new assistant, Tairn. He's helping Mina."

Ilena's eyes snapped up. "Tairn? Would that be Tairn Malkin of Nakaba?"

"Mmm...I don't know. He looks to be about Andrew's age. He's tall, of good build, brown wavy hair, bright intelligent eyes."

"Hmm...I see," Ilena said noncommittally. "Well, if it is he, please tell him I say 'hello' and that I've asked him to take good care of you. I know his younger brother well."

"Okay," Mizi said happily. "What is it that I can do for the remainder of today to meet my goal?"

"First, sit down." Mizi did. "What have you decided you want to do?"

Mizi pulled her chair up close by the side of Ilena's bed as she considered her answer. "I want you to teach me everything you think I need to know in order for the lords to accept me. And I want to learn what I need in order to represent Rei appropriately. And if I can help Rei do things, even the office work, I want to learn what I'll need to know to be effective there."

"Why do you want to learn the office work?" Ilena probed.

"I told Rei that if I can't stand before Andrew, Mina, and Ore, how can I stand next to him?" Mizi answered.

"I see. Well, it may be good to understand the workings of the royal office, even if you decide in the end there's a better place for you. However, you shouldn't consider yourself equivalent to an aide to the Prince. You should choose to do it for a different reason. Can you give me a better reason?" Ilena challenged Mizi.

Mizi thought hard for a while. "Rei's father died, leaving his mother to be the ruler of the kingdom. I don't know if she was just overwhelmed with grief, or didn't have prior experience, but King Sasou had to take over quite a lot of the leadership of the kingdom at a very young age.

"I'd like to be able to support Rei in letting him not worry that a similar thing would happen for him — that either his son would have to wear his mantle at a young age, or that I wasn't capable of standing in his place if it was necessary.

"Also, if I understand how Rei's office is run, I'll understand better how to run my own office. And, I think there are things I can learn there that I can't learn elsewhere."

Ilena gave an accepting nod. "Those are much better reasons. Remember, there's no need for the princess to duplicate the efforts of the prince. Rather, her efforts should complement his. It may be that you take some of his burden, indeed it would be good if you did, but it should be a thing only you can do. That thing is a thing you have yet to discover."

Ilena continued, "I'll consider your daily schedule and set you to it before I undergo the surgery. For now, there are basic things about this castle that you and I both need to understand. Therefore, you'll help me with my studies today and tomorrow at least.

"When we're done for today, your task will be to write a detailed list of what you'd expect to see in a princess that you'd be willing to follow. Tomorrow you'll ask Master Rei at lunch to do the same: write a detailed list of what he desires from the princess who'll stand at his side. Bring me both lists and we'll more easily be able to come up with a plan."

"Okay, Ilena," Mizi said.

"Good. Then for now, Leah and Rio have brought me the books I requested. We'll start with the most general and work our way to the more specific. You'll read them to me and we'll discuss them as we go.

"When your home is the castle, you must be able to comprehend all levels and members of it, their roles and responsibilities, how they interact, and how your own role fits within them. Thus we'll begin there, or we won't know how to act. Please select the appropriate book."

Mizi looked through the books that the maids had brought and selected one, then began reading. In the end, most of the ladies took turns reading aloud. One voice could only read for so long. They ended shortly before the dinner was to arrive, Ilena closing the book before she began, adamant that even they should reserve meals for refreshing their minds and bodies.

Mizi taught Leah and Rio what to do to take care of Ilena at the evening time and by the time the dinner was to arrive they were readied for it. Ilena thought it was coming a bit late and wondered why Ryan hadn't come yet. There was finally a knock at the door and the dinner cart was wheeled in — by Ore, followed by Rei.

"Oh. That's what it was," Ilena commented and it was Mizi's turn to be surprised by who walked into the room.

"Well, turnabout is fair play, isn't it?" Rei commented lightly. "Since Mizi joined us for lunch, I thought it was appropriate for us to join you for dinner, particularly since I knew Mizi would likely be with you for the remainder of the day."

Mizi smiled. "If it means you're getting one, too, then that's all for the better."

Leah and Rio had already begun to make plates for each of them. Ilena introduced them to Rei, who briefly welcomed them and thanked them for coming to help with Ilena.

"We've just come from the infirmary and speaking with Ryan," Rei opened the dinner conversation. "He's quite sure he wants you to help him during the surgery, Mizi. Is that okay?"

Mizi nodded. "Yes. I'm looking forward to it. I assisted the field surgeon, Doctor Bonner, with his second surgery. It was interesting how he tried to help the tendon to regrow. I look forward to seeing what Doctor Elliot has come up with."

Ore and Rei exchanged looks. Ore's said, *I told you so*, and Rei gave up. "Well, I do hope his method works. It would be good if Ilena walks again."

"I agree," Ilena said emphatically. "And I hope he can do it in one go, or an early second like last time. ...Ah, speaking of which, I wanted to ask you, Master Rei and Princess Mizi, for permission to use the Little Death again.

"I believe that the hibernative state at the beginning is the best one to be in during a surgery, and the reduction of pain is also beneficial. Doctor Elliot knows the proper dose to give me, in particular, to grant me both of those benefits while providing the least possible effect of the pain cycle in between."

While Ore looked like he was against that idea, Mizi looked thoughtful. "It was a benefit to Doctor Bonner during his surgery. While I dislike the thought of having you on such a thing and having to wean you off of it, it would be a good opportunity for Ryan to have some training in that process. I know he's expressed a keen interest in learning it.

"The only concern is the decrease of body temperature that interferes with its natural ability to fight off infection." Mizi considered it a bit more. "I'll talk with Doctor Elliot about what his recommendation would be."

"That would be good," Rei said. "If he believes he can use it to good effect with minimal negative side effects, and if you're satisfied, Mizi, then I'll accept your recommendation."

"I've put him in the third lab in the surgery department," Ore informed Mizi.

She nodded. "I'll speak with him tomorrow, then."

There was the usual end–of–topic–pause that occurs in all group conversations, particularly when people are eating, then Rei took up the next topic. "Ilena, when Ore returned to my office just before lunch, I certainly didn't expect Mizi to be coming to me in such a fashion.

"I would like you to understand that, although today's results were beneficial, the lesson he taught you should still be remembered and followed." He looked at her, his face bland but his eyes speaking volumes.

"Yes, Master Rei," she answered humbly in imitation of Ore earlier that day.

When he was satisfied with her answer, he continued. "What is it I may do to help Mizi in her goal?"

Both women were taken aback a bit by the question, not expecting it. Mizi answered, "You said that you would consider what you'd like for me to learn. Could you please give it to me in writing, so that we can be sure to include each item in our planning?"

Rei paused, a bit surprised. "In writing?"

Mizi nodded. "And if there are any particularly important items, if you'll mark them, we'll be sure to address them early."

Rei nodded slowly. While it wasn't a typical request, it was an indication of how serious Mizi was about her goal.

"Master Rei," Ilena suggested, "if you find at some point in your consideration that it's difficult, perhaps — rather than thinking of Princess Mizi specifically — you could think of what you would look for in any of the ladies that are on the candidate list at this time. Perhaps if you thought of how you would narrow those candidates down, your thoughts would flow more freely."

"I'll consider it," Rei answered her.

"Ilena, is there anything else you'd suggest Rei could do to help?" Mizi asked.

"Will you hear it, Master Rei?" Ilena asked him. Rei nodded. "Until we've completed the detailed plan, I can only tell you things in general. The most important thing you can do for Princess Mizi is to provide a place for her to stand and to welcome her into it whenever she chooses to enter it, in whatever capacity she has reached.

"Choose who will stand next to you for yourself today and let all others know you've made that choice in your visible actions. Those who watch you need to learn it and become familiar with it, even before she has reached her full capacity, even as you grow into your position.

"Your list will let you know of her progress and when she's reached the goal she intends to reach. Princess Mizi will also be writing a list of what — to her — a princess is. Together, we'll make Princess Mizi into the princess who Rei cannot turn away from, the one who the people and lords of Ryokudo cannot deny, and the one the House of Touka will welcome."

"Mmm," Rei mulled. "Always before I'd wait and see what the lords would accept before forcing the issue. But you think I should say forcefully what I want?"

"Yes, Master Rei. You're no longer a prince in training. You are the Regent, second only to the King and Queen. It's my understanding you already have the approval of the King. That's sufficient for you to act upon your own decisions." Rei was silent.

Ore ventured a comment. "Master, isn't that what you've been doing with the matter of Ilena? Even today?"

Rei looked at him, surprised, and considered the parallel. "That's true," he said slowly. "I'll think on how I may best be able to do it." Ilena and Mizi were satisfied with that.

Rei finished eating the last bite on his plate and leaned back in the chair they'd given him. Ore had decided to sit cross–legged on the floor and Mizi was kneeling between the two. Leah had propped Ilena up with extra pillows and was feeding her while Rio stood to eat in the corner of the room, being as invisible as possible.

"Ilena, I have another question," Rei said to change the topic. Ilena looked at him attentively. "Ore told me you said that 'no good thing remains' in Earl Shicchi's household. Will you please explain this to me?"

"It's true, Master Rei. I've been slowly removing the good members of Earl Shicchi's household into places where they can be freed from daily fear. Before the Lady and I were sent to Osterly, I'd already removed the last of them."

"How was the household run? And if you've done it over time, how is it that the yearly census and allotment to the Earl didn't change?" He'd already had the research done on the running of the household as part of his investigation and it had been impeccable, a testament to her capability in running the Earldom for the Earl, but her comment to Ore had opened another set of questions.

Ilena answered in her usual calm way. "It was usually the yearly census that was the cause of the need. In order for the Earl to do his evil deeds, he needed an ever increasing number of evil men who were willing to follow him. Evil men only heed the call of wealth; therefore, each year he would have me send away as many of the household as he'd taken in to increase his might.

"He was always careful to be slow to build up his strength so it wouldn't be noticed, and I was as careful to choose those whose station we could afford to lose, or those who I could nearly no longer repair. Of course, at some point the balance shifted, and the armsmen were required to step in and fill the required roles.

"At this time, only he and his men remain. The Lady and her ladies–in–waiting were the last. ...If we'd all managed to return safely to the Earl's home that day, my intent was to return them to the Lady's father's home as quickly as the Earl came to hate her again." Ilena sat quietly again, her hands clasped together, waiting for Rei's next question.

Rei was amazed. "And did you propose this plan to the Earl?"

Ilena paused before answering. "The Earl placed in my keeping the household and the running of it, including the financing. It was either suggest this plan, or make the household go hungry. To have denied the armsmen would have increased the suffering of the household. I couldn't bear it." She and her two ladies were silent as they remembered the weight of those years, and those decisions.

Rei leaned his chair back a bit on the back two legs and crossed his arms, his look challenging. "When you were the last one remaining, what would you have done?"

Ilena looked him in the eye. "I would have made a pact with the devil I had no intention of allowing him to follow through on, and made my way here. It would have been anyone's guess if I would have made it this far."

Ore sat upright in shock, his wide eyes locked onto Ilena. "You would have told him you would give me to him?"

Ilena looked at Ore, her face a mask. "Yes."

Rei was still. Mizi asked in confusion, "But...I don't understand. What does the Earl want with Ore?"

Ore said coldly, "Nothing would please him more than to see my blood upon his floor, my life taken with his own hand."

"Why?" No one answered her question. "But...but...Ilena said, didn't you say, Ilena, that you wouldn't have followed through on it?"

Ilena's gaze moved from Ore to Mizi and became compassionate. "I did say that Princess Mizi. I knew the only hope I would have is if I could somehow get word to Prince Rei that I was willing to sell my information in exchange for safety from the Earl for myself and Ore, and hope that he'd be willing to accept my word."

Ore's breath hissed. "You were willing to walk out of that House and into the whirlwind of blades of death, knowing that Master didn't know you?"

Ilena looked back at him. "I was willing to dance with those blades joyfully as I ran from that House. While it's true I didn't know if I could enter the door on this end, I didn't leave unprepared."

Rei understood first. "The household," he said.

Ilena nodded, looking at him. "They encouraged me to leave earlier, but for fear of their safety I refused. If I couldn't have received audience here, I would have continued to travel south to see if the King would hear my petition

...I carry with me the desires of the whole household, and all those wronged by the actions of Earl Shicchi."

Rei gave a satisfied nod and replied, "It's sufficient. I'm glad you didn't have to follow through, since Earl Shicchi moved first. Even though you've not come without damage, I'm glad you've come. ...I hope you understand that if you'd been required to follow that path, I would have been willing to hear your petition."

"Thank you, Master Rei," Ilena said soberly.

-o-o-o-

Ore opened the door to Ilena's room, entered, then stood with his back to the closed door, unmoving. He and Rei had walked Mizi back to her room, then he and Rei had gone back to the office.

He would have come directly back to Ilena's room, but she was visiting with Grandfather. Instead, he'd lost himself in his work, but he knew his performance had suffered. He hadn't been able to concentrate. In the end, he'd arrived early, although it was after everyone else had left her for the night and the room was dark.

"Are you angry with me, Ore?" Ilena asked quietly.

"...Yes." So angry he almost couldn't speak to her. So angry he wanted to shout, wanted to flee so he didn't do something he'd regret. It felt like the anger that had driven him away from Osterly and to Rei's side. But this time, it had drawn him to her.

"Ore, ...what are you afraid of?" she asked gently.

"Of losing you." The words were out of his mouth before he knew what they were. He was shocked by them. Had he really just said them?

But more words were tumbling out now. "You're my partner now. You must never consider acting in a way that would endanger your life. You must promise me that you'll come to me if you can't see a clear path so that we may find an acceptable solution together. And even if you do see a way, you must come to me. You are no longer an agent unto yourself." It could probably not be said who of them was more astonished at his words.

"... I promise, Ore," Ilena said when she could finally find her voice. "And...will you promise me the same?"

Ore's astonishment remained. Even when he'd given his reins to Rei, for over a year he hadn't been able to tie himself down and commit to stay. Now, within a few short weeks of being yoked to Ilena, he felt and knew that she was right to ask for it, and it was right for him to promise it. "Yes, Ilena, I promise you the same." His voice was calmer as he said it.

"Will you light the candle, Ore?" Ilena asked simply.

He walked to the desk, felt for the candle, then lit it. The small flame leaped up, giving their practiced night eyes plenty of light to see by. He took a breath, then turned to look at Ilena. She was looking at him, as he expected.

"You're no longer angry." Ilena made it a statement. Ore nodded once anyway. "That's good. What else do you have to say? I'll listen."

He stepped closer to her bed so she didn't have to turn her head quite so far to see him, their eyes remaining locked together: tawny gold reflecting tawny gold. "If I'd understood before what I understand now, I would have come for you long ago. If anything happens to you in the future, I'll come for you.

"There's a thing Master and Mistress told me: be more aware of yourself. When you're not where people expect you to be, you'll be missed. I wish you to understand this now, while you're still in a place where you can't move."

"I'll remember it," Ilena answered him. She paused, her mouth open to speak, but as if not sure. Ore nodded encouragement and she said, "It's the same for me...why I wait for you to come each night. I can't come find you, so until you're here, where I can know where you are, I can't rest.

"And it's what makes me want to say to you that I'll be very angry with you if you don't return to me. ...I think it's what was bothering me the last night and morning before you left to collect the first set of witnesses."

Ore nodded. "On more than one occasion I thought, 'Ilena wanted to come with me.' ...And I wished you were there, too." He went a little soft.

Ilena sighed and her hand plucked lightly on her blanket, then she clenched it in her hand. "*Haaah.* Yes, it was so. It *is* so. Perhaps that's my greatest impatience with my injury, that I can't be where Ore is, go where Ore goes. I'm looking forward to having that resolved."

Ore tilted his head. "You're saying you're willing to go through the experimental surgery for the sake of our partnership?"

"Yes. That's what gives me the strength to face it," Ilena answered.

Ore sat down on the side of her bed, one leg tucked under the other so that he could face her. Her tawny eyes followed his face. Ore took a moment to find the words he wanted to say. "If I can give you the strength to do what needs to be done so that you may stand and walk with me, then I'm glad."

Ilena's eyes crinkled up. "It's my goal, Ore, to be able to *run* with you. Walking isn't enough for me. I want to be able to run the roofs with you, to leap through the trees again."

He smiled back. "I'd felt that you would love to do that. I was thinking it on a roof, as a matter of fact."

Ilena sighed. "I spent my nights, when I was here alone, on that roof with you."

Ore frowned slightly. "I wouldn't think you have the experience to do it, but there were little clues in every story I heard that trip, most obviously in Robert's story. It seems that among all the other things you were doing, you were a nightwalker." She neither confirmed nor denied it.

"When we first found you, right after Doctor Bonner finished patching you up the first time, I walked in on the Captain talking to him and Lieutenant Leeds." He looked down at his hands, then back up at her.

"It was the first time I heard your name and what you'd been doing. The Captain had only good things to say about you, and evil things about Pakyo. He told of things you could do that were skills of the underworld, I thought to myself then that you must have been walking between the worlds, living a life in the twilight."

Ore paused again. His fists tightened and his tawny eyes glittered, the pupils going slightly vertical, almost almond in shape. "I want to see everything you can do."

He reached out and lifted a lock of her black hair, running it through and around his fingers. "Get better, Ilena." He looked her in the eyes, his expression unfathomable. "Learn to run again. Come run with me."

Ilena's hungry eyes matched his. "I will, Ore."

He continued to look into her eyes for a moment longer, then he stood. "It's time for you to sleep. I'll stay for the rest of the night."

"Thank you," she said quietly as he blew out the candle.

Ilena was asleep shortly after, but Ore stayed awake long, looking into the darkness, the light his heart could see shining more brightly as if the moon had gone from a faint crescent to a quarter–full or more.

Historian's Note: While perhaps most historians would begin the history of the Grand Duchy of Tarc at the Investiture of the First Grand Duke and Grand Duchess, and others on the day of the Lord's Court on 24 Spring3 545, the landslide and subsequent injury of Princess Ilena is the singular most significant event that began the creation of the Grand Duchy, being 3 Spring1 545.
— Brn. R. Tennyson, Royal Historian to T.R.E. of Tarc

LITTLE DEATH

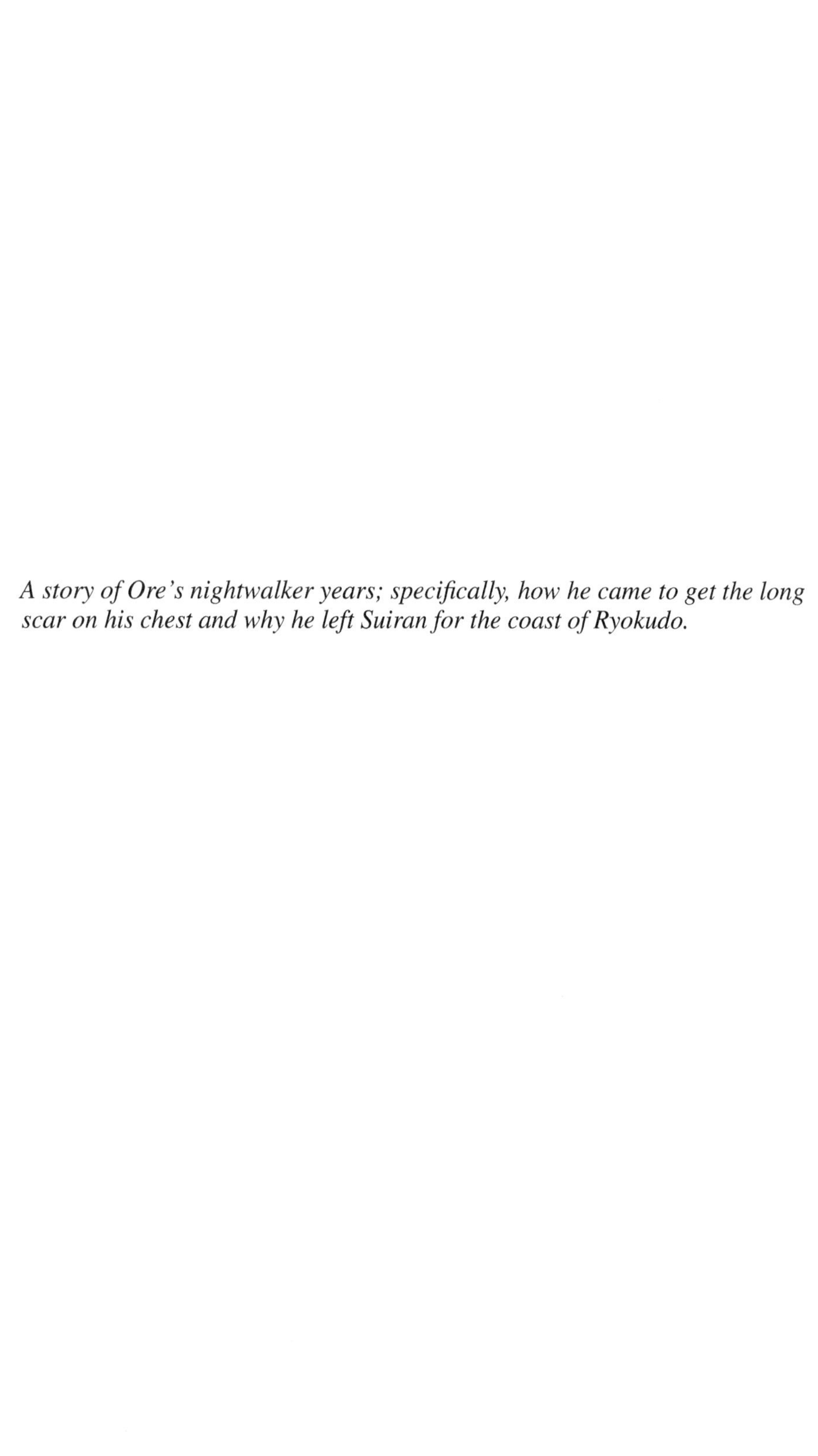

A story of Ore's nightwalker years; specifically, how he came to get the long scar on his chest and why he left Suiran for the coast of Ryokudo.

Little Death

"Hey, Mister Ore, will you spar with me again?" the fresh–faced green kid looks hopeful. He's fresh–faced, he's green, but his eyes carry the same look Ore knew his own had held when he was first on the streets, and he carries himself the same as well. Wary, tense, on–edge, desperate.

"Sure, kid."

-o-o-o-

Damn. The green ones didn't always make it. Now he's lying in the corner the alley floor and the wall of the building make, holding his stomach, his face a mask of pain...already dead. Something isn't quite right, though.

Carefully, Ore pulls the arms away from the belly of the green kid. No blood. That's what the problem is. No blood anywhere, but a look on the dead kid's face that says a knife had been used to scramble his insides — from the outside.

"Who'd you find, Ore?" One of his regular meets, or Ore would have already had a knife to his throat for coming into the alley that quiet.

"Kid who wouldn't leave me alone." A hand comes down on his shoulder as the other leans over to take a look and move him out of the way a bit for the light to shine down. "He actually had promise."

"I've seen that kind of death before."

Ore looks up in surprise. "Where?"

The look on the other's face is grim. "That's the Little Death. He either took too much, or couldn't get more."

Ore stands up, his stomach turning. The look on the other man's face looks about the same. "He didn't need it," Ore says. "He was working on his own strength." The Little Death was a crutch only used by those who hadn't the will to face each day on their own.

A shake of the head. "Don't know, man. But that's what it looks like."

-o-o-o-

Barely scraped up enough on that last job to buy a meal and all I get is swill to drink again. A light touch on his elbow and he freezes in order to not kill. There's no killing intent attached to those fingers.

" 'Scuse me?" A timid whisper. *Female? Here?*

Ore looks over and ...down... his arm. The face is full of fear, but the eyes full of determination. *...And young.* He sighs to himself. The girl is lucky. Ore's approachable by these types — he isn't going to eat them...or worse — and she's made it this far.

He raises an eyebrow at her, then quickly scans the room without looking at it. Yeah, she's already drawn the attention of too many. He scoops her up and sets her on his knee and sticks the other half of his roll in her mouth. "I won't hurt you. Sit still and do what I say, or someone else will," he whispers back.

She nods trustingly. He's surprised. "Talk."

She takes the roll in her hand, bites the bite he'd shoved in her mouth, chews, swallows, nearly chokes. He hands over his mug and she cautiously swallows just a mouthful to clear her throat. She already knows the swill isn't to be chugged. She's from the city streets, then, just not the night.

He keeps eating, waiting for her to get her words together. The room is mostly settling back down, although a few eyes say they'll wait and see what happens when the conversation is done.

"My brother...he said Mister Ore'd been helping him get stronger. That's you, right?"

She's trying hard to be brave but he can feel the shivers through the fingers he has clamped firmly on her thin shoulder, feel the fluttering heartbeat against his forearm where it crosses her small back over her heart. Her feet are crossed tightly at the ankle between his legs to keep her balanced on his one knee. Her volume has only gone up slightly, still quiet enough for just him to hear. Isn't too hard since her mouth is just below his ear height as he leans over the table.

He nods and keeps eating. One always kept eating when there was food in front of you. Never knew when you'd have to leave it suddenly to save your neck. "I haven't seen him in a month. He always comes at least once a week to bring me what he's earned and to make sure I'm still doing okay. I couldn't stand waiting any more."

Tears are threatening. Ore pushes the roll back towards her mouth. She obediently distracts herself with another bite. *She's hungry, not starving. She's getting fed, even if the brother isn't bringing money. That's good. There's a place I can take her back to.*

He shoves the last bite of food in his mouth, chugs the swill — because *he* can. "Right, then. Let's go see, shall we?" he says it loud enough to let the room know she's still his, for now. Those waiting to see what would happen next...most of them let it go.

A few eyes follow them out as Ore leads the girl by the hand out of the room. Her other hand keeps tight hold of the roll, taking another bite as soon as they're out the door. *Not starving, but has before.* It's almost an unthought addition to his analysis of this oddly brave one.

He takes a few twists and turns as they go to lose the few who'd followed them out, then asks where 'home' is.

Silence.

Ore tips his head. "I'll get you there. You tell the story on the way. They'll jump you on the way if I don't come with. You won't see me again."

Her head shakes at the last one. "I want you to find him for me."

"Okay, you'll see me again, then. Where're we going?"

Reaching up on tiptoe for his ear. He gives a little snort of humor, then bends down so she can whisper the address in his ear. He nods and gets them going: the standard street–weaving, bravadiccio, don't–follow–me traverse of the nightwalker.

It's the typical siblings–on–the–street story. Parents dead, not wealthy enough to leave much behind for them. No family to speak of. Tossed out of the house. Older brother's responsible and gets the younger sister a decent job as a housemaid, then heads to the streets to get stronger so he can take care of her. Life with parents wasn't easy, life without them isn't either. Life without the older brother: difficult.

Ore looks at her soberly. He's pretty sure he doesn't want to answer her, and that he already has it. "Describe him." She does. Yeah, he doesn't want to answer her.

He detours their feet to a small patch of city green with a tree. Hard answers are always best given in the comfort of soft green. Crouching down to her level, he holds both hands now that the second isn't holding the roll anymore because her stomach is.

"I did help him. He was doing well, getting stronger. I lost sight of him about that month ago also. Two weeks ago, I found him. I'm sorry, but he's not coming home." He's as gentle as possible in his tone, but on the street you didn't sugar–coat death. It happened too often.

But, just as when he'd found the boy, something still isn't sitting right, and it's starting to irritate him. "Did he tell you where or what he was doing next, the last time you saw him?"

She fights the tears to answer him, trying to remember. "He – he said he'd been offered a job with a house and he was going to see if it was worth it and that he'd come back as soon as he could. He thought maybe two weeks this time."

Ore looks at her, then gives a brief nod. His head is filling in a lot of details he doesn't like and she likely didn't know. ...Like that should have been "House" with a capital "H". It obviously hadn't been worth it. If he'd died trying to get to his sister....

Ore chooses to think about it later. The tears are spilling over. Ore takes her in his arms and lets her get his shoulder soaking wet. He learned to do that before he was on the street, from another girl who was like this one: strong until the world pulled the one stake of strength out from under her.

So far, Ore is still alive so that one still has her stake. At least, Ore hopes she knows she does. She's still his stake, his reason for living, like this one had been the green kid's reason for living. He probably wouldn't have died.

That's what's sitting wrong. The kid had a reason to live, had been working on his own strength, and both had been stolen from him.

Ore goes cold hard. He doesn't like taking on other people's problems; it gets him into trouble. But this is more vendetta. A House is stealing the lives of new kids on the street. As a freelancer, that just isn't right. Houses that steal the freedom of freelancers need to be taught a lesson.

-o-o-o-

"Damn it, I told you to refuse to take it if it was offered!" Ore growls at the kid shivering in his arms.

"C–couldn't. Laced the dinner drinks. No smell or flavor." The phrases come out in between wracks of pain. "It'll be worth it. If you get in. Take them down."

Ore had sent out the word quiet to all freelancers and this young one had been willing to get in and find out what was going on behind the closed doors of the House. The House isn't recruiting known faces, old faces. Ore listens carefully to all the intel this one can give him, knowing he's dying in his arms for this.

The House of the Red Lion (street name). It has plenty of strength of its own inside, but wants to move, expand, something. It's using the Little Death to make youngsters stay, already has their own addicted to it.

When they send the younger ones out on jobs, they take them off it a day first, then they have to come back or die the second day...or third day.... They aren't afraid to abuse the kids, or the drug. If necessary, they'll give everyone maximum dose if the rest of the nightwalkers come after them.

Maximum dose is certain death, but also means they don't feel pain. They can fight and fight and fight...until their heads are separated from their bodies, or enough limbs cut off they can't walk or swing a blade. Massacre is the only outcome of a maximum dose fight — on both sides.

It makes Ore's blood boil, that to survive the living hell of the streets the Little Death has become so common a way for the nightwalkers to survive the wounds they receive so regularly in their line of work. The Little Death is used to help them ignore the little deaths of wounds to body and soul that come so regularly, when they are what tell you that you still have a beating heart.

To give up to the Little Death was to admit that you couldn't stay one step ahead of death — permanent long death. To be forced to walk that path was to be stripped of one's will — an unacceptable path in Ore's way of seeing life.

He had chosen the life of a nightwalker, finding life in it compared to what he'd been not–living before. Only one thing had been left behind that he needed to be fully alive. That was his own crutch to living each day. Someday he'd return for it and fully live again.

-o-o-o-

This is the night. Lots of planning. Lots of volunteers. Freelancers going after a House is hard, only when vendetta and absolute need require it. Hardest part is getting medics to come help. Essential for this fight. A few Houses have offered their medics and blades. They have their own vendettas so are willing. That's a blessing, although often it's two–sided. One of them is actually supplying a surgeon. They might win with that much medical aid on this side. No one on this side is willing to use the Little Death at maximum. Some are already on it, wealthy enough in their skills to afford it daily, but they aren't stupid enough to waste their lives on it.

The signal is given and Ore ghosts forward along with the rest of the line. Up the wall and over. Like most fights, there isn't much thought involved. Just clear head for clear eyes to see the smallest movements and interpret everything quickly as to threat level and let the body do its job defending itself and taking out the target.

He's using a knife tonight, not just the throwing daggers. Each dagger thrown takes a life. In an eye and into the brain. Slice the artery at the neck to a spray of blood so the deaths come quick, the blade not wasted. Letting them live with a wound is the same as not having hit them at all.

When it's a vendetta against a House, the whole House is taken down. No one lives. You don't see the sex, the age, you just kill whatever comes against you. It's hard if you think about it, so you don't. You just kill. It's a job.

Normally nothing personal, but this time, it is something personal. There's an orphan girl who's still crying herself to sleep at night. There's two boys who had a lot of potential to not stay on the street, that looked up to you, who are sleeping the long death because of *this* House.

There's too much *this* House will do if left living that it shouldn't be allowed to do. And the death of *this* House will make all the rest think more than twice about following in their footsteps. It's future security, too, not just past vendetta. This is how the street keeps itself in check. The street polices itself — when it can.

Oof! That was a rough blow — backhanded. He's run out of throwing blades and is now in hand–to–hand. If they can't win against this House tonight, it will rule the night using the Little Death openly instead of in hiding. It will move up to being one of the High Houses: one of the feared Houses the freelancers and most of the rest of the nightwalker Houses can't affect. Only another High House can take it down after that.

Ore isn't sure there are enough to care if they move into this area as a High House. They have to take it down tonight, and that lends strength and power to his attacks, that determination.

Then a blow makes him mad and the Shicchi anger gets let loose and he's lost his ability to see, think, reason, and everything else except to become the blade. Everything goes down before him, even if it takes three, five, six blows. He'll remember it later. He never forgets, his reasoning mind just takes a vacation.

It isn't until he takes a thunderous blow to his chest that shakes him to the bones in his feet that he comes back. He staggers back. Just in time, two others leap under the raised blade in front of him with his long death engraved on it and the man crumples instead, two knives from two directions — one in his heart, the other having sliced the throat completely open.

Ore's being grabbed from behind and dragged away, towards the outer wall of the House's compound. He tries to shake off the hands, but they hold firm and a hoarse voice says, "You've been targeted. There's an ally who's your enemy. Get out." He's dropped outside a side door.

"Wait!" he grabs the arm before the man can get away from him. "How's the battle?"

"That was the last one. We're done. Get out." The arm is snatched away and he's gone.

Ore stumbles into the woods to slump down next to a tree. He can't believe it. His enemy, here? This was a freelancer battle. Yeah, there were Houses involved, but he'd been sure to make extra sure *that* Untouchable House wasn't involved.

He sits at the foot of the tree, going back through the fight from the beginning. What faces had been around him? Who had he fought *with* not *against*? Then the last man, just now...what little blood isn't draining out of the wound on his chest drains out of his head and goes to his feet and he's up and moving.

He'd been fighting against that last one with two others. There'd been a signal and they'd pulled back just as that blow came at him. He'd been relying on them to block it so his killing blow could get through — and they hadn't. The two who'd taken that man out hadn't been the same two who'd been helping him to begin with. They'd come running to his rescue from farther away.

"Hey, Ore, should you be moving? That looks awful. Are you okay?" It's one of the women freelancers he fought with on occasional jobs. Lack of blood keeps her name from coming to mind.

"Yeah. We defeated them, got the job done, right?" He knows his signature grin is on his lips, but it isn't in his eyes. His eyes are death still. It takes a long time for that look — the Shicchi rage — to leave his face any more, since it takes a lot to get it to come up to the surface. He's secretly proud he's finally managed to get it under his control to this extent. No other Shicchi probably had.

He hates the name — and it's coming for him, had been behind this wound, and is going to make sure it's done its job. He's gone, headed for safety, for hiding. If the Little Death had been the blade behind his current little death, Shicchi was behind the long death coming for him. That one he wants to escape at all costs, even if it means he receives the long death from this little death he's carrying on his chest. He can't afford that though...he has to live.

He stumbles, recognizes the tail he has, but not the who. He can guess, though. Maybe if they think he's received the long death already, they'll leave him alone. He goes ahead and lets the stumble turn into a fall, and holds deathly still.

The tail is breathing hard. Had been fighting hard with all the rest of them, likely. He stands there and watches a bit, then turns and walks off. Ore sighs in relief to himself, waits until the noises in the woods stop, then hunts for his usual preferred hiding place. He'll have to stay hidden.

The tail will bring back the Shicchi Ore doesn't want to see: his oldest brother who wants him dead. He'll come to take Ore's head...or fix him up just so he can beat him inches from death...over and over and over again...or just kill him later when it suits him.

It doesn't matter. Ore isn't going to ever be in the hands of, or in the family line of, Shicchi again. He wriggles painfully on his belly, his chest searing, his sight fading with the fade that says he's lost too much blood, until he's under a thicket bush.

Ore rolls and hugs his chest, lying on his back instead of his belly, hoping it will keep just enough blood in his body to stay alive. He has to stay alive. The warm arms that wrapped around him whenever he was hiding in the bushes to escape the beatings still need him, like he needs them.

How he wishes that just this once he could really feel those arms again, holding him, letting him know that he'll be okay, that he can face one more day again. He'd tell her...he'd tell her....

-o-o-o-

His chest burning brings him pain, though not awareness. He's being handled, but there's no noise, and he can't move anyway. It doesn't feel like hands of death, but there is urgency. He slips away. There isn't anything to do anyway.

Arms are around him, holding him tightly. Her warmth. Faintly, her voice, breaking with tears. "Kase. Live. Live for me. Please."

Don't cry. I'll live. I'll live for you. Always.

-o-o-o-

Birds are chirping, some small creature scuttling through leaves and undergrowth gets his attention. His breath comes in short gasps. He takes a larger breath. Pain! *Gah. Short gasps it is.* But that lets him know that the arms around him are still there. He reaches a careful slow hand up to touch his chest, but there isn't a body there, just his own.

His fingers gently brush the 'arms' holding him. It's bandaging. His chest wound is bandaged. He's sure his heart had been scratched by the blade it suddenly hurt so. Hot tears drip down his face.

It may only be a bandage, but there's only one person in the entire world who knows how to find him when he hides like this. She is still holding him. She is still protecting him from House Shicchi, while he is still leaving her behind to live there — in hell, in her own little death. The next breath is very painful.

What had he promised her? What had she asked? *"Live. Live for me,"* and he'd promised, *"I'll live for you. Always."* He groans. Why? Why did she still want him to live? He'd left her in hell. She should hate him.

...If he's going to keep his promise, he can't stay here in the north any more. His brother found him this time, knew it was him. As long as Pakyo thinks his little brother is dead here in the north, Ore can live. He'll have to go south.

Soon...soon he might have the strength and ability to go and get her... maybe.... His heart hurts again. His fear of his brother always tries to drown out his desire to save her. If she's still alive, really still alive, his brother's *keeping* her alive, isn't killing her...she'll be okay, until Ore can come and —

No. It didn't work that way. She always came for him. She'd come and wrapped her arms around him and left a bandaged wound behind, not staying with him. It wasn't time. She'll come get him, like always, and he won't go with her until he's strong enough. They both know it. It isn't time yet.

Ore listens carefully to confirm he's alone in this place, then painfully wriggles his way out of his hiding place and begins the long, slow, painful trek south. He'll go to the capital — to Ichijoutsu. That city is certainly big enough for another nightwalker to hide in, find plenty of work in.

He'd always wanted to be a cabin boy and sail the sea, too, just enough to understand how the ships work and watch the water go by from up high. By the time he makes it, he'll be healed sufficiently to work.

It will take honest work and begging to get there, but he's done plenty of that, too, in his time already. He can charm farm wives just as easily as ladies of lords. He's learned that as part of his ability to survive.

His charming smile is as automatic and learned as his ability to defend himself without realizing he's done it. It all has to be. It all has to erase how automatic the anger is. The anger is no longer the first thing that comes out...it's the last.

But as he walks, he's leaving his heart behind. He doesn't want to be this far from her. He really doesn't. He wants to run back to her, have her in his arms again. It's many days before he's willing to let the arms she left behind be changed. They're the only thing keeping him going — that bandaging — her surrogate arms.

She's his Little Death. As long as he doesn't have her, he's dead, no matter what mask he wears. It's very painful, the withdrawal of knowing she'd been with him again, even for that brief time he'd been unaware of the world. But he doesn't die. He lives. He lives for her. She'd come back to make sure he did, and he'd promised.

Author's Note

I love words. Language is beautiful. To be able to express in one word the exact concept one wishes to convey is powerful to the mind and emotions of the reader. To put them all together into a moving symphony of concepts and ideas that holds the reader enrapt is a continual journey of effort and delightful satisfaction. I'm still on that journey to the pinnacle I desire to reach. As it unfolds, I myself am joyfully stretched and strengthened (or desperately straining at the difficult times).

Because all language is beautiful, I've chosen to use multiple languages of Earth to underscore specific history or areas of the world of <u>Chronicles of Tarc</u>.

I've chosen to convey the "ancient" history of Ryokudo in the naming of places and people. At a time when the peoples that lived there were politically only clans and city–states, another sea–faring nation arrived and began to conquer them, combining them into one unified nation. The conquerors I've identified with Japanese words and names. Thus all royal names and larger place names are based on Japanese. The "common" names are still the names used by the clans that were conquered, as cultures don't go away, they merely meld.

I've chosen to loosely base the language of Selicia to the northwest of Ryokudo upon Italian. It's the same for Yamanzar to the south which is loosely based on Arabic. I've completely made up the naming convention of Tarc, but you'll recognize the people I've based it on. To continue to have fun within my work of word–crafting, I've chosen that the conceit of the nobility of Altherly is to only name themselves with names that begin with vowels. So go the sparkles of language delight I've scattered throughout my work.

To help English speakers, I wish to include a pronunciation guide for the Japanese words. Japanese has a much smaller collection of vowel sounds than English, so please don't feel you have to work so hard at understanding. Many sounds are very similar to Spanish sounds, if that helps you.

Short Vowels:

"a" as in f**a**ther, "e" as in m**e**n, "i" as in s**ee**, "o" as in b**oa**t, "u" as in f**oo**d

Multiple vowels put together are each said. So in "Rei" you should hear both the short "ĕ" and the "ee" of the i. In "Sasou" you should hear both the "o" and the "u", together making a sound similar to, "**ow**, I hurt myself".

I don't use the long vowels of Japanese much in my writing (which often merely sound like they just put two short vowels together) but there are two in my name. I've chosen to use the English pronunciation symbols instead of trying to assume an expectation anyone would understand what I mean by using double vowels or the typical Japanese–to–English long vowel symbol, which confuses many people into using the English long vowel, which is incorrect.

314

The Japanese long "u", ū, sounds like the English ü as in **ru**le. The Japanese long "a", ā, is a doubled Japanese short vowel and sounds the closest to the English ä or ȯ as in **cau**ght. Most English dictionary pronunciations would use the ȯ but because I wish the reader to *think* the appropriate "a" vowel and add in just a touch of the short "a" sound, I've chosen to use the ä in my family name.

"R"s are rolled very slightly, "j" is slightly a "jz" sound, and such go the consonants, but Anglicizing them isn't as large a matter. The "y" is soft and often swallowed and never the forceful sound of "ee". In my name, you'd barely hear it, with the longer vowel following it.

Thank you for picking up volume one of this journey I've undertaken. I hope you'll continue to enjoy it with me as it progresses.

— *Jiryü Räsen*

People and Places

Ryokudo (Jp., *wooded area; verdant area*) The country our main characters are from and royals of.

Ichijou (Jp. *ichi: one, first; –jou: castle, palace*) The main palace of Ryokudo, residence of the King and Queen, on the southern coast in the eastern corner. Placed where the conquerors first landed to begin their unification of the clans and city–states.

– King Sasou Touka (Jp. *sasou: to invite, tempt, or lure; touka: wisteria flower. The long "–ou" or –ō ending to a name means "king" or "queen".*) Age: 28. King of Ryokudo, older brother to Rei.

– Queen Aryana (Farsi, Pers., *pretty Eastern girl*) Age: 27. Queen of Ryokudo, Sasou's wife. Born in, and a noble daughter of, Kouzanshi, Ryokudo.

– Lord Michael Barret Age: 36. King Sasou's childhood guard, first aide, head nag, and Minister of Intelligence of Ryokudo.

– Parmenia (Sp. *clever, studious; of intelligence*) Age: 34. Head Court Healer of Ichjou. Mizi and Ryan's superior before they moved to Nijou.

Ichijoutsu (Jp. *ichi: one, first; –jou: castle, palace; –tsu: port city*) The bustling capital port city of Ryokudo that sits at the feet of Ichijou. Full of trade and people who smile because their kings work hard to make life simple and fulfilling for their subjects.

Region of Suiran (Jp., *suiran: the sense of being engulfed in a green, mountainous atmosphere*) The entire northern portion of Ryokudo. It's in the main dense woods with boggy soil, filling up the rolling hills that lead up to the north rocky mountains.

The people of the Region are of a more solemn and stern nature than those of the rest of Ryokudo, having banded together into two smaller nations to defend themselves before the invading conquerors reached them. Still, time and events eventually made them bow even their heads and become part of Ryokudo.

Yosai (Jp. *stronghold*) The Earldom of the House of Durand. Mina's home. Her father is the Earl and Head of the House. She is his only heir. Lies to the east of Nijou and is often on the northern front of the northeast corner battles when they occur.

Nijou (Jp. *ni: two, second; –jou: castle, palace*) The secondary castle of Ryokudo, the head seat of the Regent of Suiran. Originally it was the head seat of the smaller nation of Waldstaat (Ger. *wald: woodland; staat: country, nation, state*) before they submitted to Ryokudo's king. Set near the tri–corner border of Ryokudo, Tarc, and Brulac so they can quickly defend the regularly contested location.

– Dowager Queen Kata Touka (Jp. *kata: one of a pair, incomplete, remote*) Age: 53. Sasou and Rei's mother. She lives in isolation within Nijou, having given the rulership of Ryokudo to her oldest son when he reached a sufficient age and education to take over the throne. Her husband, previous king of Ryokudo, died young: when Sasou was twelve and Rei was three. Her sister was murdered about the same time.

Unable to properly grieve the multiple deaths because she was required to step in immediately to solidify her rule over the nobles who used the timing to take power for themselves, she eventually broke and Sasou had to step up and take the power of the throne for her in order to maintain the line of Touka as the kings of Ryokudo. As a result, he's become rather ruthless in his outward dealings with the nobility, but he's very popular with the people because of that restraint he is on the nobles.

– First Prince Rei Touka (Jp. *rei: just law, rule — as of a king, strive, the peace that comes from just laws and proper rulership*) Age: 18. Regent of Suiran, younger brother to Sasou. Our secondary male protagonist.

– Sir Andrew Marciel (Gr. *andrew: strong, manly, courageous; marciel: soldier, little warrior*) Age: 27. Rei's childhood guard, first aide and knight. Mina's partner.

– Sir Ramona "Mina" Durand (*ramona: protecting hands; durand: firm, enduring*) Age: 24. Rei's second aide and knight, Andrew's partner. Heir to Yosai Earldom.

– Mizi (Turk. *from kirmizi: red*) Age: 18. Court Healer of Nijou, assigned specifically to care for Rei's health. Rei's girlfriend and hopeful intended. Our secondary female protagonist, she's run away from her home country of Yamanzar to escape being added to that country's First Prince's harem merely because of her unique hair.

She and Rei accidentally met in Ryokudo near Ichijoutsu and quickly became friends with a shy interest in each other. Mizi has worked hard to be able to stand on her own two feet as close to Rei as she can. Although Sasou tested her as harshly as he tests anyone, and then more because of his protectiveness towards Rei, she was able to win even his trust. Enough so that he's also assigned her to Nijou to be close to Rei.

– Sir Ore (It. *from dolore: ache, as of the ache of unrequited pain.* See also Kase Shicchi.) Age: 27. Rei's third aide and knight, Mizi's guard, Messenger of the Regent. Our primary male protagonist. He has a shady background he doesn't speak about, but he's completely devoted to Rei and Mizi.

– Ryan (Ir. *descendent of the king, little king*) Age: 16. Head Court Healer of Nijou. Young genius who focuses his knowledge base on plants and their medicinal uses. He's recently been assigned by Sasou to head the medical department of Nijou. He was Mizi's senior at Ichijou when she was apprenticed there, teaching her what she needed to know to be a court healer.

Nijoushi (Jp. *ni: two, second; –jou: castle, palace; –shi: city*) The capital city of Suiran, sitting at the more–protected western edge of the castle grounds.

Tokumade (Jp. *toku: to solve or answer; to explain, advocate, preach, or persuade; shelter, shield, or hide; to prepare for; long time ago. made: until (a time), to (a place), going so far as*) The Earldom of the House of Shicchi, the House of the line of the kings of Waldstaat. Located in central northeast Suiran, west of Nijoushi.

– Earl Pakyo Shicchi (pakyo: from It. *pazzia: madness* and Jp. *hakkyo: madness*; Jp. *shicchi: lost territory*) Age: 34. Head of the House of Shicchi. He is the most insane of all the Shicchi's to date, having been broken by his involuntary murder of his father. His fits of anger and mood swings are well known and, as a consequence, most people who know him try to stay far away from him.

– Kase Shicchi (Jp. *kase: shackles, fetters, irons, restraint, or constraint; family bonds, ties, binding relationships.* See also Ore.) Age: 27. The youngest brother of Pakyo, and heir to Tokumade.

He's been missing since Pakyo went on a killing rampage that took the life of their middle brother and his wife. Pakyo is determined to find Kase and either kill him or force him to return to imprisonment at Tokumade because he's a witness to Pakyo's murder of their father. To date, no one has admitted it happened, however, so Kase is still in hiding somewhere, keeping his mouth shut.

– Ilena Age: 24. Steward of Tokumade. Pakyo called her up to that position when she was seventeen, but little is known about her, other than she came to the Earldom when she was about nine years old with one nurse and they were allowed by Pakyo's grandfather to stay. Our primary female protagonist.

Nakaba (Jp. *middle*) The Earldom of the House of Malkin. Lies in the center of the Region. An honorable House that is allied with Sasou and eventually with Rei.

Kouzanshi (Jp. *kouzan: high mountain, alpine; –shi: city*) The university city of Ryokudo, set up high in the rough mountains of the northwest corner of the country. The noble family that rules over the city comes from a line that was a younger brother to the King of Ryokudo that took over the entire area of the current Region of Suiran. He sent his youngest sibling to the farthest corner to make sure the whole of the expanded nation would obey the rule of the Touka Kings.

– Shiotsu (Jp. *second teacher, scholar*) Age: 33. Head of the Medical Department of the University of Kouzanshi. Trained Mizi and Ryan for two years at Sasou's request when they were sent for their advanced education before being sent to Nijou. A contemporary of Parmenia's.

Neighboring Nations

Altherly The nation west of Ryokudo. Rough rolling hills and a wide river divide the nations, but there is usually peace between the two nations as they're about the same size and the western border of Altherly is less defensible. It's far easier for them to have peace to their east so they can focus on their more volatile western border.

Selicia The nation to the northwest of Ryokudo, accessible only through two harsh passes through the rocky mountains. Kata's sister was married to a prince of Selicia. They were murdered in a coup in that nation about the same time Kata's husband died.

Tarc The nation to the northeast of Ryokudo, accessible through low rolling hills of trees that give way to grassland. Tarc is one wide expanse of highland grassland, populated by insular nomadic clans of horsemen.

Brulac The nation east of Ryokudo. There are tall mountains between the two nations on the south end of the border, but only tall wooded hills in the northeastern corner of Ryokudo. When they attack it is usually from that corner.

Yamanzar (Arb. *sea view*) Nation across the Inner Sea from Ryokudo. There is a small land access between the two nations: a bare roadway between a tall mountain and the sea. On the other side of that mountain is Brulac.

– First Prince Amiran (Arb. *prince*) Age: 22. The reason Mizi left Yamanzar. He was a lazy womanizing prince with a large harem from a young age. Mizi standing up to him and leaving him only her cut hair — since that's the part of her he coveted — got him started on his hunt for her.

He got more than he bargained for: eyes that judged, determination that withstood him, and firm but polite words that set him onto the straight path he should have been on to begin with. Rei's stern eyes, folded arms, and sword his fingers itched to pull backed her up and Amiran wisely relented in his quest. Since then his new quest is to learn how to have the strength of honorable royalty with the two of them his role models.